# HOLIDAY IN DEATH

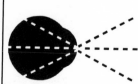 This Large Print Book carries the
Seal of Approval of N.A.V.H.

# HOLIDAY IN DEATH

## NORA ROBERTS WRITING AS
## J. D. ROBB

**THORNDIKE PRESS**

*An imprint of Thomson Gale, a part of The Thomson Corporation*

**THOMSON**

™

**GALE**

Detroit • New York • San Francisco • New Haven, Conn. • Waterville, Maine • London

THOMSON
GALE

Copyright © 1998 by Nora Roberts.
Thorndike Press, an imprint of The Gale Group.
Thomson and Star Logo and Thorndike are trademarks and Gale is a registered trademark used herein under license.

**ALL RIGHTS RESERVED**
Thorndike Press® Large Print Famous Authors.
The text of this Large Print edition is unabridged.
Other aspects of the book may vary from the original edition.
Set in 16 pt. Plantin.

**LIBRARY OF CONGRESS CATALOGING-IN-PUBLICATION DATA**

Robb, J. D., 1950–
    Holiday in death / by J.D. Robb.
       p. cm. — (Thorndike Press large print famous authors)
    ISBN-13: 978-0-7862-9888-4 (hardcover : alk. paper)
    ISBN-10: 0-7862-9888-X (hardcover : alk. paper)
    1. Dallas, Eve (Fictitious character) — Fiction. 2. Policewomen — New
York (State) — New York — Fiction. 3. Dating services — Fiction. 4. New
York (N.Y.) — Fiction. 5. Large type books. I. Title.
PS3568.O243H64 2008
813'.54—dc22
                                                      2007033686

Published in 2007 by arrangement with The Berkley Publishing Group, a member of Penguin Group (USA) Inc.

Printed in the United States of America on permanent paper
10 9 8 7 6 5 4 3 2 1

And what rough beast, its hour come
round at last,
Slouches toward Bethlehem to be born?

— Yeats

Nobody shoots at Santa Claus.

— Alfred Emanuel Smith

# CHAPTER ONE

She dreamed of death.

The dirty red light from the neon sign pulsed against the grimy window like an angry heart. Its flash turned the pools of blood glistening on the floor from dark to bright, dark to bright, slicing the filthy little room into sharp relief, then damning it to shadows.

She huddled in the corner, a bony girl with a tangle of brown hair and huge eyes the color of the whiskey he drank when he had the money for it. Pain and shock had turned those eyes glassy and blind and her skin the waxy gray of corpses. She stared, hypnotized by the blinking light, the way it blipped over the walls, over the floor. Over him.

Him, sprawled on the scarred floor, swimming in his own blood.

Small, feral sounds rumbled in her throat.

And in her hand the knife was gored to the hilt.

He was dead. She knew he was dead. She could smell the ripe, hot stink of it pouring out of him to foul the air. She was a child, only a child, but the animal inside her recognized the scent — both feared it and rejoiced over it.

Her arm was screaming where he'd snapped the bone. The place between her legs burned and wept from this last rape. Not all the blood splattered over her was his.

But he was dead. It was over. She was safe.

Then he turned his head, slowly, like a puppet on a string, and pain washed away in terror.

His eyes fixed on hers as she babbled, scrambled back deeper into the corner where she'd crawled to escape him. And the dead mouth grinned.

*You'll never be rid of me, little girl. I'm part of you. Always. Inside you. Forever. Now Daddy's going to have to punish you again.*

He pushed to his hands and knees. Blood fell in fat, noisy drops from his face, from his back, slid obscenely from the rips in his arms. When he gained his feet and began to shamble through the flow of blood toward her, she screamed.

8

And screaming, woke.

Eve covered her face with her hands, held one tight over her mouth to hold back the mindless shrieks that tore at her throat like shards of hot glass. Her breath heaved so painfully in her chest she winced with every exhale.

The fear followed her, breathed cold down her spine, but she beat it back. She wasn't a helpless child any longer, she was a grown woman, a cop who knew how to protect and defend. Even when the victim was herself.

She wasn't alone in some horrible little hotel room, but in her own house. Roarke's house. Roarke.

And concentrating on him, on just his name, she began to calm again.

She'd chosen the sleep chair in her home office because he was off planet. She'd never been able to rest in their bed unless he was with her. The dreams came rarely if at all when he slept beside her, and all too often chased her in sleep when he didn't.

She hated that area of weakness, of dependence, almost as much as she'd come to love the man.

Turning in the chair, she comforted herself by gathering up the fat gray cat who curled beside her, watching her out of narrowed, bicolored eyes. Galahad was accustomed to her nightmares, but he didn't care to be wakened by them at four in the morning.

"Sorry," she muttered as she rubbed her face against his fur. "It's so damn stupid. He's dead, and he's not coming back. The dead don't come back." She sighed and stared into the dark. "I ought to know."

She lived with death, worked with it, waded through it, day after day, night after night. In the final weeks of 2058, guns were banned, and medical science had learned how to prolong life to well beyond the century mark.

And man had yet to stop killing man.

It was her job to stand for the dead.

Rather than risk another trip into nightmares, she ordered the lights on and climbed out of the chair. Her legs were steady enough, and her pulse had leveled to nearly normal. The sick headache that tagged onto the coattails of her nightmares would fade, she reminded herself.

Hoping for an early breakfast, Galahad leaped off behind her, then ribboned through her legs as she moved into the kitchen area.

"Me first, pal." She programmed the AutoChef for coffee, then set a bowl of kibble on the floor. The cat attacked it as if it were his last meal, and left her to brood out the window.

Her view was the long sweep of lawn rather than the street, and the sky was empty of traffic. She might have been alone in the city. Privacy and quiet were gifts a man of Roarke's wealth could easily buy. But she knew beyond the beautiful grounds, over the high stone wall, life pumped. And death followed it greedily.

That was her world, she thought now as she sipped the potent coffee and worked the stiffness of a still-healing wound out of her shoulder. Petty murders, grand schemes, dirty deals, and screaming despair. She knew more of those than of the colorful swirl of money and power that surrounded her husband.

At times like this, when she was alone, when her spirits were low, she wondered how they had ever come together — the straight-arrow cop who believed unwaveringly in the lines of the law, and the slick Irishman who'd tangled with and over those lines all of his life.

Murder had brought them together, two lost souls who'd taken different escape routes to survive and, despite logic and sense, had found each other.

"Christ, I miss him. It's ridiculous." Annoyed with herself, she turned, intending to

11

shower and dress. The blinking light on her tele-link signaled a muted incoming. Without a doubt who was transmitting, she leaped at it and unblocked the silent code.

Roarke's face popped on screen. Such a face, she thought, watching as he lifted one dark eyebrow. Poetically handsome, with black hair falling long and thick to frame it. The clever, perfectly sculpted mouth, the strong bones, the shocking intensity of brilliant blue eyes.

After nearly a year, just the sight of that face could send her blood humming.

"Darling Eve." His voice was like cream over strong Irish whiskey. "Why aren't you sleeping?"

"Because I'm awake."

She knew what he'd see as he studied her. There was so little she could hide from him. He'd see the shadows of a bad night hounding her eyes, the paleness of her skin. Uncomfortable, she shrugged and pushed a hand through her short, disordered hair. "I'm going into Cop Central early. I've got paperwork to catch up on."

He saw more than she realized. When he looked at her, he saw strength, courage, pain. And a beauty — in those sharp bones, that full mouth, those steady brandy-colored eyes — she was delightfully oblivious to.

Because he also saw weariness, he changed his plans.

"I'll be home tonight."

"I thought you needed a couple of more days up there."

"I'll be home tonight," he repeated and smiled at her. "I miss you, Lieutenant."

"Yeah?" However foolish she considered the warm thrill, she grinned at him. "I guess I'll have to make some time for you when you get here."

"Do that."

"Is that why you were calling — to let me know you'd be back early?"

Actually, he'd intended to leave a message that he'd be delayed another day or two — and to try to convince her to join him for the weekend on the Olympus Resort. But he only smiled at her. "Just wanted to inform my wife of my travel plans. Go back to sleep, Eve."

"Yeah, maybe." But they both knew she wouldn't. "I'll see you tonight. Uh, Roarke?"

"Yes?"

She still had to take a bracing breath before she said it. "I miss you, too." She cut the transmission even as he smiled at her. Steadier, she took her coffee with her as she went out to prepare for the day.

■ ■ ■ ■

She didn't exactly sneak out of the house, but she was quiet about it. Maybe it was barely five in the morning, but she didn't doubt Summerset was around somewhere. She preferred, whenever possible, to avoid Roarke's sergeant-major — or whatever term you'd use for a man who knew everything, did everything, and poked his bony nose into what Eve considered her private business entirely too often.

Since her last case had shoved the two of them closer together than either was comfortable with, she suspected he'd been avoiding her as carefully as she had him for the past couple of weeks.

Reminded of it, she rubbed a hand absently just under her shoulder. It still troubled her a bit in the morning, or after a long day. Taking a full blast from her own weapon was an experience she didn't want to repeat in this or any other lifetime. Somehow worse was the way Summerset had poured meds down her throat afterward, when she'd been too weak to knock him on his ass.

She closed the door behind her, took one deep breath of the frigid December air, then cursed viciously.

She'd left her vehicle at the base of the steps mostly because it drove Summerset crazy. And he'd moved it because it pissed her off. Grumbling because she hadn't bothered to bring along the remote for the garage door or her vehicle, she trooped around the house, boots crunching on frosted grass. The tips of her ears began to sting with cold, her nose to run with it.

She bared her teeth and punched in the code with gloveless fingers, then stepped into the pristine and blissfully warm garage.

There were two gleaming levels of cars, bikes, sky-scooters, even a two-passenger minicopter. Her city-issue vehicle in pea-green looked like a mutt among sleek, glossy hounds. But it was new, she reminded herself as she slid behind the wheel. And everything worked.

It started like a dream. The engine purred. At her command, the heat began to whir softly through the vents. The cockpit glowed with lights, indicating the initial check run, then the bland voice of the recording assured her all systems were in operational order.

She'd have suffered the tortures of the damned before she would admit she missed the capriciousness and outright crankiness of her old unit.

At a smooth pace, she glided out of the garage and down the curved drive toward the iron gates. They parted smoothly, soundlessly, for her.

The streets in this exclusive neighborhood were quiet, clean. Trees on the verge of the great park were coated in a thin sheen of glittery frost like a skinsuit of diamond dust. Deep inside its shadows, chemi-heads and spine crackers might be finishing up the night's work, but here, there were only polished stone buildings, wide avenues, and the quiet dark before dawn.

She was blocks away before the first billboard loomed up, spitting garish light and motion into the night. Santa, red-cheeked and with a manic grin that made her think of an oversized elf on Zeus, rode through the sky behind his fleet of reindeer and blasted out *ho, ho, ho*s, while warning the populace of just how many shopping days they had left before Christmas.

"Yeah, yeah, I hear you. You fat son of a bitch." She scowled over as she braked for a light. She'd never had to worry about the holiday before. It had just been a matter of finding something ridiculous for Mavis, maybe something edible for Feeney.

There'd been no one else in her life to

wrap gifts for.

And what the hell did she buy for a man who not only had everything, but owned most of the plants and factories that made it? For a woman who'd prefer a blow with a blunt instrument to shopping for an afternoon, it was a serious dilemma.

Christmas, she decided, as Santa began to tout the variety of stores and selections in the Big Apple Sky Mall, was a pain in the ass.

Still, her mood lifted as she hit the predictably snared traffic on Broadway. Twenty-four hours a day, seven days a week, there was a party going on. The people glides were jammed with pedestrians, most of whom were drunk, stoned, or both. Glide-cart operators shivered in the cold while their grills smoked. If a vender had a spot on this street, he held it in a tight, ready fist.

She cracked her window a sliver, caught the scent of roasting chestnuts, soy dogs, smoke, and humanity. Someone was singing out in a strident monotone about the end of the world. A cabbie blasted his horn well over noise pollution laws as pedestrians flowed into the street on his light. Overhead the early airbuses farted cheerfully, and the first advertising blimps began to hawk the city's wares.

She watched a fistfight break out between two women. Street LCs, Eve mused. Licensed companions had to guard their turf here as fiercely as the vendors of food and drink. She considered getting out and breaking it up, but the little blonde decked the big redhead, then darted off into the crowd like a rabbit.

Good thinking, Eve thought approvingly, as the redhead was already on her feet, shaking her head clear and shouting inventive obscenities.

This, Eve thought with affection, was her New York.

With some regret, she bumped over to the relative quiet of Seventh, then headed downtown. She needed to get back into action, she thought. The weeks of disability had made her feel edgy and useless. Weak. She'd ditched the recommended last week off, had insisted on taking the required physical.

And, she knew, had passed it by the skin of her teeth.

But she'd passed, and was back on the job. Now if she could just convince her commander to get her off desk duty, she'd be a happy woman.

When her radio sounded, she tuned in

with half an ear. She wasn't even on call for another three hours.

*Any units in the vicinity, a 1222 reported at 6843 Seventh Avenue, apartment 18B. No confirmation available. See the man in apartment 2A. Any units in the vicinity . . .*

Eve clicked on before Dispatch could repeat the signal. "Dispatch, this is Dallas, Lieutenant Eve. I'm two minutes from the Seventh Avenue location. Am responding."

*Received, Dallas, Lieutenant Eve. Please report status upon arrival.*

"Affirmative. Dallas out."

She glided to the curb, flicked a glance up at the steel-gray building. A few lights glimmered through windows, but she saw only darkness on the eighteenth floor. A 1222 meant there'd been an anonymous call reporting a domestic dispute.

Eve stepped out of her vehicle, and slid an absent hand over her side where her weapon sat snug. She didn't mind starting out the day with trouble, but there wasn't a cop alive or dead who didn't dread a domestic.

There seemed to be nothing a husband, wife, or same sex spouse enjoyed more than turning on the poor bastard who tried to keep them from killing each other over the rent money.

The fact that she'd volunteered to take it

was a reflection of her dissatisfaction with her current assignments.

Eve jogged up the short flight of stairs and looked up the man in 2A.

She flashed her badge when he spoke through the security peep, shoved it into his beady little eyes when he opened the door a stingy crack. "You got trouble here?"

"I dunno. Cops called me. I'm the manager. I don't know anything."

"I can see that." He smelled of stale sheets and, inexplicably, of cheese. "You want to let me into 18B?"

"You got a master, don't you?"

"Yeah, fine." She sized him up quickly: short, skinny, smelly, and scared. "How about filling me in on the occupants before I go in?"

"Only one. Woman, single woman. Divorced or something. Keeps to herself."

"Don't they all," Eve muttered. "You got a name on her?"

"Hawley. Marianna. About thirty, thirty-five. Nice looker. Been here about six years. No trouble. Look, I didn't hear anything, I didn't see anything. I don't know anything. It's five-fucking-thirty in the morning. She's done any damage to the unit, I want to know about it. Otherwise, it's none of my never-mind."

"Fine," Eve said as the door clicked shut in her face. "Go back to your hole, you little weasel." She rolled her shoulders once, then walked across the corridor to the elevator. As she stepped inside, she pulled out her communicator. "Dallas, Lieutenant Eve. I'm at the Seventh Avenue location. Building manager is a wash. I'll report back after interviewing Hawley, Marianna, resident of 18B."

*Do you require backup?*

"Not at this time. Dallas out."

She slipped the communicator back into her pocket as she stepped out into the hallway on eighteen. A quick glimpse up showed her security cameras in place. The hall was church quiet. From the building's location and style, she pegged most of the residents as white collar, middle income. Most wouldn't stir from their beds until after seven. They'd grab their morning coffee, dash out to the airbus or subway stop. More fortunate ones would just plug into the office from their home station.

Some would have children to see off to school. Others would kiss their spouses good-bye and wait for their lovers.

Ordinary lives in an ordinary place.

It flipped through her mind to wonder if Roarke owned the damn building, but she pushed the idea aside and stepped up to 18B.

The security light was blinking green. Deactivated. Instinctively she stepped to the side of the door as she pushed the buzzer. She couldn't hear its muffled echo and decided the unit was soundproofed. Whatever went on inside, stayed inside. Vaguely annoyed, she took out her master code and bypassed the locks.

Before entering, she called out. Nothing worse, she mused, than scaring some sleeping civilian into coming at you with a homemade stunner or a kitchen knife.

"Ms. Hawley? Police. We have a report of trouble in your unit. Lights," she ordered, and the overheads in the living area flashed on.

It was pretty enough in a quiet way. Soft colors, simple lines. The view screen was programmed to an old video. Two impossibly attractive people were rolling around naked on a bed scattered with rose petals. They moaned theatrically.

There was a candy dish on the table in front of the long misty-green sofa. It was filled to brimming with sugar-dashed gumdrops. Silver and red candle pillars were grouped beside it, burned artistically down to varying heights.

The entire room smelled of cranberry and pine.

She saw where the pine scent originated. A small, perfectly formed tree lay on its side in front of a window. Its festive lights and sweet-faced angel ornaments were smashed, its boughs snapped.

At least a dozen festively wrapped boxes were crushed under it.

She reached for her weapon, drew it, and circled the room.

There was no other obvious sign of violence, not there. The couple on the view screen reached simultaneous climax with throaty, animal moans. Eve sidestepped past it. Listened, listened.

Heard music. Quiet, cheerful, monotonous. She didn't know the tune, but recognized it as one of the insidious Christmas ditties that played everywhere for weeks during the season.

She swept her weapon over a short corridor. Two doors, both open. In one she could see a sink, a toilet, the edge of a tub, all in gleaming white. Keeping her back to the wall, she slid toward the second door, where the music played on and on.

She smelled it, fresh death. Both metallic and fruity. Easing the door all the way open, she found it.

She moved into the room, swinging right, then left, eyes sharp, ears alert. But she knew she was alone with what had been Marianna Hawley. Still she checked the closet, behind the drapes, then left the room to search the rest of the apartment before she relaxed her guard.

Only then did she approach the bed.

2A had been right, she thought. The woman had been a looker. Not stunning, not an eye-popper, but a pretty woman with soft brown hair and deep green eyes. Death hadn't robbed her of that, not yet.

Her eyes were wide and startled, as the dead's often were. Against the dull pallor of her cheeks careful and subtle color had been applied. Her lashes were darkened, her lips painted a festive cherry red. An ornament had been pinned to her hair just above the right ear — a small glittery tree with a plump gilded bird on one of its silver branches.

She was naked but for that and the sparkling silver garland that had been artistically wrapped around her body. Eve wondered, as she studied the raw bruising around the neck, if that was what had been used to strangle her.

There was more bruising on the wrists, on the ankles, indicating the victim had been bound, and had likely had time to struggle.

On the entertainment unit beside the bed, the singer suggested she have herself a merry little Christmas.

Sighing, Eve pulled out her communicator. "Dispatch, this is Dallas, Lieutenant Eve. I have a homicide."

"Heck of a way to start the day." Officer Peabody stifled a yawn and studied the victim with dark cop's eyes. Despite the atrociously early hour, Peabody's uniform was crisp and pressed, her dark brown bowl-cut hair ruthlessly tamed.

The only thing that indicated she'd been rudely roused out of bed was the sleep crease lining her left cheek.

"Heck of a way to end one," Eve muttered. "Prelim on scene indicates death occurred at twenty-four hundred hours, almost to the minute." She shifted aside to let the team from the Medical Examiner's office verify her findings. "Indications are cause of death was strangulation. The lack of defensive wounds further indicate the victim didn't struggle until after she was bound."

Gently, Eve lifted the dead woman's left ankle and examined the raw skin. "Vaginal and anal bruising indicate she was sexually molested before she was killed. The unit's soundproofed. She could have screamed her lungs out."

"I didn't see any signs of forced entry, no signs of struggle in the living area except for the Christmas tree. That looked deliberate to me."

Eve nodded, slanted Peabody a look. "Good eye. See the man in 2A, Peabody, and get the security discs for this floor. Let's see who came calling."

"Right away."

"Set a couple of uniforms on the door-to-door," Eve added as she walked over to the tele-link by the side of the bed. "Somebody turn that damn music off."

"You don't sound like you're in the holiday spirit." Peabody hit the off button on the sound system with a clear sealed finger. "Sir."

"Christmas is a pain in the ass. You finished here?" she demanded of the ME's team. "Let's turn her over before she's bagged."

The blood had found its lowest level, settling in the buttocks and turning them a sickly red. Bowel and bladder had emptied, the waste of death. Through the seal coat on her hands, Eve felt the waxy-doll texture of the skin.

"This looks fresh," she murmured. "Peabody, get this on video before you go down." Eve studied the bright tattoo on the right shoulder blade as Peabody moved in to document it.

"My True Love." Peabody pursed her lips over the bright red letters that flowed in old-fashioned script over the white flesh.

"Looks like a temporary to me." Eve bent lower until her nose all but brushed the curve of shoulder, sniffed. "Recently applied. We'll check where she gets body work done."

"Partridge in a pear tree."

Eve straightened, lifted a brow at her aide. "What?"

"In her hair, the pin in her hair. On the first day of Christmas." Because Eve continued to look blank, Peabody shook her head. "It's an old Christmas song, Lieutenant. 'The Twelve Days of Christmas.' The guy gives his true love something on every day, starting with a partridge in a pear tree on the first day."

"What the hell is anybody supposed to do with a bird in a tree? Stupid gift." But a sick suspicion churned in her gut. "Let's hope this was his only true love. Get me those tapes. Bag her," she ordered, then turned once more to the bedside 'link.

While the body was being removed, she ordered all incoming and outgoing transmissions for the previous twenty-four hours.

The first came in at just past eighteen hundred hours — a cheerful conversation between the victim and her mother. As Eve listened, studied the mother's laughing face, she thought of how that same face would look when she called and told the woman her daughter was dead.

The only other transmission was an outgoing. Good-looking guy, Eve mused as she studied the image on screen. Midthirties, quick smile, soulful brown eyes. Jerry, the victim called him. Or Jer. Lots of sexual byplay, teasing. A lover then. Maybe her true love.

Eve removed the disc, sealed it, and slipped it into her bag. She located Marianna's daybook, porta-'link, and address book in the desk under the window. A quick scroll through the entries netted her one Jeremy Vandoren.

Alone now, Eve turned back to the bed. Stained sheets were tangled at the foot. The clothes that had been carefully cut off the victim and tossed to the floor were bagged for evidence. The apartment was silent.

She let him in, Eve mused. Opened the door to him. Did she come in here with him voluntarily, or did he subdue her first? The tox report would tell her if there were any illegals in the bloodstream.

Once he had her in the bedroom, he tied her. Hands and feet, likely hooking the restraints around the short stump of post at each of the four corners, spreading her out like a banquet.

Then he'd cut off her clothes. Carefully, no hurry. It hadn't been rage or fury or even a desperate kind of need. Calculated, planned, ordered. Then he'd raped her, sodomized her, because he could. He had the power.

She'd struggled, cried out, probably begged. He'd enjoyed that, fed on that. Rapists did, she thought, and took several deep, steadying breaths because her mind wanted to veer toward her father.

When he was done, he'd strangled her, watching, watching while her eyes bulged. Then he'd brushed her hair, painted her face, draped her in festive silver garland. Had he brought the hairpin with him, or had it belonged to her? Had she amused herself with the tattoo, or had he decorated her body himself?

She moved into the neighboring bathroom. White tile sparkled like ice, and there was a faint under-scent of disinfectant.

He cleaned up here when he was finished, Eve decided. Washing himself, even grooming, then wiping down and spraying the room to remove any evidence.

Well, she'd put the sweepers on it in any case. One lousy pubic hair could hang him.

She'd had a mother who loved her, Eve thought. One who'd laughed with her, making holiday plans, talking about sugar cookies.

"Sir? Lieutenant?"

Eve glanced over her shoulder, saw Peabody in the center of the hallway. "What?"

"I have the security discs. Two uniforms are initiating door-to-doors."

"Okay." Eve rubbed her hands over her face. "Let's seal the place up, take everything to Central. I have to inform the next of kin." She shouldered her bag, picked up her field kit. "You're right, Peabody. It's a heck of a way to start the day."

# CHAPTER TWO

"Did you run the 'link number on the boy-friend?"

"Yes, sir. Jeremy Vandoren, lives on Second Avenue, he's an account exec for Foster, Bride and Rumsey on Wall Street." Peabody glanced at her notebook as she relayed the rest. "Divorced, currently single, thirty-six. And a very attractive specimen of the male species. Sir."

"Hmm." Eve slipped the security disc into her desk unit. "Let's see if the very attractive specimen paid a call on his girlfriend last night."

"Can I get you some coffee, Lieutenant?"

"What?"

"Can I get you some coffee?"

Eve's eyes narrowed as she scanned the video. "If you want coffee, Peabody, just say so."

Behind Eve's back, Peabody rolled her eyes. "I want coffee."

"Then get some — and get some for me while you're at it. Victim arriving home at sixteen forty-five. Pause disc," Eve ordered and took a good look at Marianna Hawley.

Trim, pretty, young, her shining brown hair covered with a bright red beret that matched the long swirl of her coat and the slick shine of her boots.

"She'd been shopping," Peabody commented as she set the mug of coffee at Eve's elbow.

"Yeah. Bloomingdale's. Continue scan," Eve said and watched as Marianna shifted her bags, dug out her key card. Her mouth was moving, Eve noted. Talking to herself. No, she realized, Marianna was singing. Then the woman shook back her hair, shifted her bags once again, stepped inside the apartment, and shut the door.

The red lock light blinked on.

As the disc continued, Eve saw other tenants coming and going, alone, in couples. Ordinary lives, moving forward.

"She stayed in for dinner," Eve stated, looking now with her mind's eye, through the door, inside the apartment.

She could see Marianna moving around the rooms, wearing the simple navy slacks and white sweater that would later be cut from her body.

*Turn the viewing screen on for company. Hang up the bright red coat in the front closet, put the hat on the shelf, the boots on the floor. Tuck away the shopping bags.*

She was a tidy woman who liked pretty things, preparing for a quiet evening at home.

"Fixed herself some soup at about seven, according to her AutoChef." Eve drummed short, unpainted nails on the desk as she continued the scan. "Her mother called, then she called the boyfriend."

While she clicked off the time frame in her mind, she saw the elevator doors open. Her brows winged up, disappearing under the fringe of bangs on her forehead. "Well, ho ho ho, what have we here?"

"Santa Claus." Grinning, Peabody leaned over Eve's shoulder. "Bearing gifts."

The man in the red suit and snowy white beard carried a large box wrapped in silver paper and trimmed with an elaborate bow of gold and green.

"Hold it. Pause. Enlarge sector ten through fifty, thirty percent."

The screen shifted, the section Eve designated separating, then popping out. Nestled in the center of the fancy bow was a silver tree with a plump gilded bird.

"Son of a bitch. Son of a bitch, that's the

thing that was in her hair."

"But . . . that's Santa Claus."

"Get a grip on yourself, Peabody. Continue scan. He's going to her door," Eve muttered, watching as the cheerful figure carried his glossy burden to Marianna's apartment. He pressed her buzzer with a gloved finger, waited a beat, then threw back his head and laughed. Almost instantly, Marianna opened the door, her face glowing, her eyes sparkling with delight.

She scooped back her hair with one hand, then opened the door wider in invitation.

Santa tossed one quick glance over his shoulder, looked directly at the camera. Smiled, winked.

"Freeze video. The bastard. Cocky bastard. Print hard copy of image on screen," she ordered while studying the round, ruddy-cheeked face and sparkling blue eyes. "He knew we'd view the discs, see him. He's enjoying it."

"He dressed up as Santa." Peabody continued to gape at the screen. "That's disgusting. That's just . . . wrong."

"What? If he'd dressed up as Satan it would have been more appropriate?"

"Yes — no." Peabody moved her shoulders, shuffled her feet. "It's just . . . well, it's really sick."

"It's also really smart." Eyes flat, Eve waited while the image printed out. "Who's going to shut the door in Santa's face? Continue scan."

The door closed behind them, and the hallway remained empty.

The timer running along the bottom of the screen marked at twenty-one thirty-three.

So, he took his time, Eve mused, nearly two and a half hours. The rope he'd used to tie her, and anything else he might have needed, would have been in that big shiny box.

At eleven, a couple got off the elevator, laughing, a little drunk, arm in arm as they passed Marianna's door. Oblivious to what was going on inside.

Fear and pain.

Murder.

The door opened at half past midnight. The man in the red suit stepped out, still carrying his silver box, a smile wide, almost fierce, on his red-cheeked face. Once more he looked directly at the camera, and now there was madness glowing in his eyes.

He was dancing as he got on the elevator.

"Copy disc to file Hawley. Case number 25176-H. How many days of Christmas did you say there were, Peabody? In the song?"

"Twelve." Peabody soothed her dry throat with coffee. "Twelve days."

"We'd better find out if Hawley was his true love, or if he has eleven more." She rose. "Let's talk to the boyfriend."

Jeremy Vandoren worked inside a small box in a hive of small boxes. His stingy cubicle held a workstation just big enough to accommodate his computer and phone system and a three-wheeled chair. Pinned to the flimsy walls were printouts of stock reports, a theater schedule, a Christmas card showcasing a well-endowed woman wearing strategically placed snowflakes, and a photo of Marianna Hawley.

He barely glanced up when Eve stepped inside; he held up a hand to hold her off and continued to work the keyboard of his computer manually while talking rapidly into a headset.

"Comstat's at five and an eighth, Kenmart's down three and three-quarters. No, Roarke Industries just took a leap up six points. Our analysts look for it to go up another two by end of day."

Eve raised a brow and tucked her hands in the pockets of her trousers. She was standing here waiting to talk murder, and Roarke was making millions.

It was just weird.

"Done." Vandoren hit another key and had a tangle of mysterious figures and symbols swimming onto the screen. She let him fiddle another thirty seconds, then pulled her badge out of her pocket and held it in front of his face.

He blinked twice, then turned and focused on her. "I've got that. You're set. Absolutely. Thanks." With a puzzled smile — slightly nervous around the edges — Vandoren swiveled the mike of his headset to the side. "Um, Lieutenant, what can I do for you?"

"Jeremy Vandoren?"

"Yeah." His deep brown eyes slid past her, brushed over Peabody, then slid back. "Am I in trouble?"

"Have you done something illegal, Mr. Vandoren?"

"Not that I can remember." He tried a smile again, bringing a small dimple to life at the corner of his mouth. "Not unless that candy bar I stole when I was eight's come back to haunt me."

"Do you know Marianna Hawley?"

"Marianna, sure. Don't tell me Mari's nicked a candy bar." Then abruptly, like a light winking off, the smile disappeared. "What is it? Has something happened? Is she all right?"

He was out of his chair, his eyes scanning over the top of the cubicle as if he expected to see her.

"Mr. Vandoren, I'm sorry." Eve had never found a good way to relay the news, so she settled on relaying it quickly. "Ms. Hawley is dead."

"No, she's not. No," he said again, turning those dark eyes back to Eve. "She's not. That's ridiculous. I just talked to her last night. We're meeting for dinner at seven. She's fine. You've made a mistake."

"There's no mistake. I'm sorry," she repeated as he only continued to stare at her. "Marianna Hawley was murdered last night in her apartment."

"Marianna? Murdered?" He continued to shake his head slowly, as if the two words were foreign. "That's definitely wrong. That's just wrong." He whirled around, fumbled to his desk 'link. "I'll call her right now. She's at work."

"Mr. Vandoren." Eve put a firm hand on his shoulder and nudged him into his chair. There was no place for her to sit, so she eased a hip on the desk so their faces could be more on level. "She's been identified through fingerprints and DNA. If you can manage it, I'd like you to come with me and do a visual confirmation."

"A visual . . ." He sprang up again, his elbow rapping Eve's shoulder and causing the still healing wound to sing. "Yeah, I'll come with you. Damn right I will. Because it's not her. It's not Marianna."

The morgue was never a cheerful place. The fact that someone in either an optimistic or macabre frame of mind had hung red and green balls from the ceiling and draped ugly gold tinsel around the doorways only succeeded in added a kind of smirking grin over death.

Eve stood at the viewing window as she had stood too many times before. And she felt, as she had felt too many times before, the hard jerk of shock punch through the man beside her as he saw Marianna Hawley lying on the other side of the glass.

The sheet that covered her to the chin would have been hastily draped. To hide from friends, family, and loved ones the pitiful nakedness of the dead, the slices in the flesh left by the Y incision, the temporary stamp on the instep that gave that body a name and number.

"No." In a helpless gesture, Vandoren pressed both hands to the barrier. "No, no, no, this can't be right. Marianna."

Gently now, Eve laid a hand on his arm.

He was shaking badly, and the hands on the glass had balled into fists and were pounding in short, light beats. "Just nod if you can identify her as Marianna Hawley."

He nodded. Then he began to weep.

"Peabody, find us an empty office. Get him some water." Even as Eve spoke, she found herself engulfed by him, his arms coming around her, his face pressed into her shoulder. His body bowed down to her by the weight of his grief.

She let him hang on, signaling the tech behind the glass to raise the privacy shield.

"Come on, Jerry, come with me now." She kept a supporting arm around him, thinking she'd rather face a stunner on full than a grieving survivor. There was no help for those left behind. No magic, no cure. But she murmured to him as she led him down the tiled hall to the doorway where Peabody stood.

"We can use this one," Peabody said quietly. "I'll get the water."

"Let's sit down." After helping him to a chair, Eve pulled the handkerchief out of the pocket of his suit coat and pressed it into his hand. "I'm sorry for your loss," she said, as she always did. And felt the inadequacy of it, as she always did.

"Marianna. Who would hurt Marianna? Why?"

"It's my job to find out. I will find out."

Something in the way she said it had him looking over at her. His eyes were red and desolate. With an obvious effort he drew in a deep breath. "I — She was so special." He groped in his pocket and pulled out a small velvet box. "I was going to give this to her tonight. I'd planned to wait until Christmas Eve — Marianna loved Christmas — but I couldn't. I just couldn't wait."

His hands trembled as he opened the box to show Eve the bright flash of diamond on the engagement ring. "I was going to ask her to marry me tonight. She would have said yes. We loved each other. Was it . . ." Carefully he closed the box again, slipped it back in his pocket. "Was it a robbery?"

"We don't think so. How long have you known her?"

"Six months, almost seven." He stared at Peabody as she came in and held out a cup of water. "Thank you." He took it, but didn't drink. "The happiest six months of my life."

"How did you meet?"

"Through Personally Yours. It's a dating service."

"You use a dating service?" This from Peabody with more than a little surprise.

He hunched his shoulders, sighed. "It was an impulse. I spend most of my time on work and wasn't getting out much. I was divorced a couple years ago, and I guess it made me nervous with women. Anyway, none of the women I met . . . Nothing clicked. I saw an ad on screen one night, and I thought, what the hell. Couldn't hurt."

He did drink now, one small sip that had his throat working visibly as he swallowed. "Marianna was the third of the first five matches. I went out with the first two — drinks, just drinks. There was nothing there. But when I met Marianna, everything was there."

He closed his eyes, struggled for composure. "She's so . . . wonderful. So much energy, enthusiasm. She loved her job, her apartment, she got a kick out of her theater group. She does community theater sometimes."

Eve noted the way he switched back and forth, past and present tense. His mind was trying to accustom itself to what was, but it wasn't quite ready yet.

"You started dating," she prompted.

"Yes. We'd agreed to meet for drinks. Just drinks — to scope each other out. We ended up going to dinner, then going for coffee.

Talking for hours. Neither one of us saw anyone else after that night. It was just it, for both of us."

"She felt the same way?"

"Yeah. We took it slow. A few dinners, the theater. We both love the theater. We started spending Saturday afternoons together. A matinee, a museum, or just a walk. We went back to her hometown so I could meet her family. The Fourth of July. I took her to meet mine. My mother made dinner."

His eyes unfocused as he stared at something only he could see.

"She wasn't seeing anyone else during this period?"

"No. We'd made a commitment."

"Do you know if anyone was bothering her — an old boyfriend, a former lover? Her ex-husband?"

"No, I'm sure she would have told me. We talked all the time. We told each other everything." His eyes cleared, the brown hardening like crystal. "Why do you ask that? Was she — Marianna . . . Did he . . . Oh God." On his knee his hand balled into a fist. "He raped her first, didn't he? The fucking bastard raped her. I should have been with her." He heaved the cup across the room, sending water splashing as he lurched to his feet. "I should have been with her. It would never have happened if I'd been with her."

"Where were you, Jerry?"

"What?"

"Where were you last night, between nine-thirty and midnight?"

"You think I —" He stopped himself, holding up a hand, closing his eyes. Three times he inhaled, exhaled. Then he opened his eyes again, and they remained clear. "It's all right. You need to make sure it wasn't me so you can find him. It's all right. It's for her."

"That's right." And studying him Eve felt a new well of pity. "It's for her."

"I was home, my apartment. I did some work, made some calls, did a little Christmas shopping via computer. I reconfirmed the dinner reservations for tonight because I was nervous. I wanted —" He cleared his throat. "I wanted it to be perfect. Then I called my mother." He lifted his hands, rubbed them hard over his face. "I had to tell somebody. She was thrilled, excited. She was crazy about Marianna. I think that was about ten-thirty. You can check my 'link records, my computer, anything you need to do."

"Okay, Jerry."

"Have you — Her family, do they know?"

"Yes, I spoke with her parents."

"I need to call them. They'll want her to come home." His eyes filled again, and he continued to look at Eve as tears streamed down his cheeks. "I'll take her back home."

"I'll see that she's released as soon as possible. Is there someone we can call for you?"

"No. I need to go tell my parents. I need to go." He turned toward the door, and spoke without looking back. "You find who did this. You find who hurt her."

"I will. Jerry, one last thing."

He rubbed his face dry and turned back. "What is it?"

"Did Marianna have a tattoo?"

He laughed, a short, harsh sound that seemed to scrape out of his throat. "Marianna? No. She was old-fashioned, wouldn't even go for temporaries."

"You're sure of that."

"We were lovers, Lieutenant. We were in love. I knew her body, I knew her mind and her heart."

"Okay. Thank you." She waited until he'd gone out, until the door clicked quietly closed behind him. "Impressions, Peabody?"

"Guy's heart's ripped right out of his chest."

"Agreed. But people often kill the ones

45

they love. Even with 'link records, his alibi's going to be shaky."

"He doesn't look a thing like Santa Claus."

Eve smiled a little. "I guarantee the person who killed her won't either. Otherwise he wouldn't have been so happy to pose for the camera. Padding, change the eye color, makeup, beard, and wig. Any damn body can look like Santa."

But for now, she had to go with the gut. "It's not him. Let's check out where she worked, find her friends and enemies."

Friends, Eve thought later, Marianna appeared to have in volume. Enemies, she seemed to have none.

The picture that was being painted was one of a happy, outgoing woman who liked her work, was close to her family but enjoyed the pace and excitement of the city.

She had a tightly knit group of female friends, a weakness for shopping, a deep love of theater, and according to all sources had been in an exclusive and happy relationship with Jeremy Vandoren.

*She was dancing on air.*

*Everyone who knew her loved her.*

*She had an open, trusting heart.*

As she drove home, Eve let the statements

made by friends and associates play back in her mind. No one found fault with Marianna. Not once had she heard one of those sly, often self-congratulatory remarks the living made of the dead.

But there was someone who thought differently, someone who had killed her with calculation, with care, and, if the look in those eyes was any indication, with a kind of glee.

*My True Love.*

Yes, someone had loved her enough to kill her. Eve knew that kind of love existed, bred, festered. She'd been the recipient of that hot and twisted emotion. And survived it, she reminded herself and engaged her 'link.

"Got the tox report on Hawley yet, Dickie?"

The long-suffering and homely face of the chief lab tech filled the screen. "You know how things get clogged up here during the holidays. People whacking people right and left, technicians putzing around with Christmas and Hanukkah shit instead of doing their jobs."

"Yeah, my heart's bleeding for you. I want the tox report."

"I want a vacation." But muttering, he shifted and began to call something up on his computer. "She was tranq'd. Over-the-counter stuff, pretty mild. Given her weight, the dosage wouldn't have done much more than make her stupid for ten, fifteen minutes."

"Long enough," Eve murmured.

"Indications are a pressure injection, upper right arm. Likely felt like she'd just downed a half dozen Zombies. Results: dizziness, disorientation, possibly temporary loss of consciousness, and muscular weakness."

"Okay. Any semen?"

"Nope, not one little soldier. He condomized or her BC killed them. We still need to check on that. Body was sprayed with disinfectant. Traces of it in her vagina, too, which would have killed off some of the warriors. We got nothing off her. Oh — one more. The cosmetics used on her don't match what she had in her place. We're not finished with them yet, but prelim indicates they're all natural ingredients, meaning high dollar. Odds are he brought them with him."

"Get me brand names as soon as you can. It's a good lead. Nice job, Dickie."

"Yeah, yeah. Happy fucking holidays."

"Same to you, Dickhead," she muttered after she logged off. And rolling some of the tension out of her shoulders, she headed through the iron gates toward home.

She could see the lights in the windows beaming through the winter dark — tall windows, arched windows in towers and turrets — and the long sweep of the main floor.

Home, she thought. It had become hers because of the man who owned it. The man who loved her. The man who'd put his ring on her finger — as Jeremy had wanted to do with Marianna.

She turned her wedding band with her thumb as she parked her car in front of the main entrance.

She'd been everything, Jerry had said. Even a year before she wouldn't have understood that. Now she did.

She sat where she was a moment, dragged both hands through her already disordered cap of hair. The man's grief had wormed its way into her. That was a mistake; it wouldn't help and could possibly hinder the investigation. She needed to put it aside, to block out of her mind the devastation of emotion she'd felt from him when he'd all but collapsed in her arms.

Love didn't always win, she reminded herself. But justice could, if she was good enough.

She got out of her car, left it where it was,

and started up the steps to the front door. The minute she was inside, she peeled out of her leather jacket and dropped it carelessly over the elegant newel post banking the curve of stairs.

Summerset slipped out of the shadows and stood, tall, bony, eyes dark and disapproving in a pale face. "Lieutenant."

"Leave my vehicle exactly where it is," she told him and swung toward the stairs.

He sniffed, an audible sucking of air through his nose. "You have several messages."

"They can wait." She kept climbing and began to fantasize about a hot shower, a glass of wine, and a ten-minute nap.

He called after her, but she'd already stopped listening. "Bite me," she said absently, then opened the door to the bedroom.

Everything inside her that had wilted, bloomed.

Roarke stood in front of the closet, stripped to the waist, his beautiful back muscles rippling subtly as he reached in for a fresh shirt. He turned his head, and the full power of that face struck her. The poet's mouth curved, the rich blue eyes smiled as he shook back his glorious mane of thick black hair.

"Hello, Lieutenant."

"I didn't think you'd be back for a couple of hours anyway."

He laid the shirt aside. She hadn't been sleeping well, he thought. He could see the fatigue, the shadows. "I made good time."

"Yeah, you did." Then she was going to him, moving fast, almost too fast to see the quick light of surprise, the deepening of pleasure in his eyes. His arms were open for her when she got there.

She drew in his scent, deeply, ran her hands up his back, firmly, then turned her face into his hair and sighed, once.

"You did miss me," he murmured.

"Just hold on for a minute, okay?"

"As long as you like."

Her body fit with his; somehow it simply fit like one piece of a puzzle interlinking with another. She thought of the way Jeremy Vandoren had showed her the ring, the glinting promise of it.

"I love you." It was a shock to feel the raw tears in her throat, an effort to swallow them back. "I'm sorry I don't tell you often enough."

He'd heard the tears. His hand slid up to cradle the back of her neck, to rub gently at the tension he felt knotted there. "What is it, Eve?"

"Not now." Steadier, she drew back, framed his face with her hands. "I'm so glad you're here. I'm so glad you're home." Her lips curved as she leaned in and slanted them over his.

Warmth, welcome, and the underlying shimmer of passion that never seemed fully sated. And with it, sheltered in it, she could for a little while push everything outside but this.

"Were you changing clothes?" she asked against his mouth.

"I was. Ummm. A little more of that," he murmured and nipped at her bottom lip until she shivered.

"Well, I think it's a waste of time." To prove it, she slipped her hands between their bodies and unbuttoned his trousers.

"You're absolutely right." He pressed the release on her shoulder holster and shoved it aside. "I love disarming you, Lieutenant."

In a quick move that had his brow arching, she twisted and had him pressed against the closet door. "I don't need a weapon to take you, pal."

"Prove it."

He was already hard when her hand curled around him. The blue of his eyes deepened with dark, dangerous lights flickering in them.

"You haven't been wearing your gloves again."

She smiled, sliding her chilly fingers up and down the length of him. "Is that a complaint?"

"No, indeed." His breath was clogging. Of all the women he'd known she was the only one who could leave him breathless with so little effort. He skimmed his hands up to cup her breasts, rubbed his thumbs gently over the nipples before unfastening the buttons of her shirt.

He wanted her under him.

"Come to bed."

"What's wrong with here?" She lowered her head, bit his shoulder. "What's wrong with now?"

"Not a thing." This time he moved fast, hooking a foot behind hers to throw her off balance, then tumbling with her to the floor. "But I've a mind to take you instead of the other way around."

His mouth clamped on her breast, sucking hard. Words strangled in her throat, images exploded in her brain, and her hips arched to him.

He knew her, better, he often thought, than she knew herself. She needed heat, the potent flood of it, to drown out whatever was troubling her mind. Heat he could give her, and he would pleasure them both with wave after wave.

She was thin. The weight she'd lost during her recovery couldn't be spared on her slim frame and had yet to be put back in place. But he knew she didn't want gentle strokes now. So he drove her, ruthlessly, relentlessly, until her breath was ragged and her heart slammed against his seeking mouth and hands.

She writhed under him, her hands in his hair fisted tight, her breasts bared for him with the long tear-shaped diamond he'd once given her resting in the shallow valley between.

He licked his way down her torso, over ribs, along the firm, flat belly, scraping teeth against the narrow line of hip as she began to buck. He tugged her trousers lower, exposing the soft curls between her thighs.

When he swept his tongue over her, into her, the orgasm struck like a lightning bolt. Blood pumped under her skin, brought a dew of sweat to the surface. She was half in, half out of the closet, surrounded by the scent of him, trapped in it and glorying.

She felt his fingers dig into her hips, lifting her, spreading her, taking her. Her own helpless moan echoed as he urged her up again. And flying, there was nothing left inside her but the driving need to mate.

She reached for him, panting his name as her hands slid off his shoulders, around his back, as her legs lifted to hook around his waist.

He glided into her, one smooth stroke of homecoming. His body shuddered once as she tightened around him, trapped him as she was trapped. His mouth crushed down on hers, feeding there as her hips began to pump.

Fast and hard, with their eyes on each other now. Thrust, retreat, and thrust, breathing each other's air. Closer, still closer with the good, solid slap of flesh against flesh.

She watched his eyes go opaque an instant before he rammed himself home. Her body erupted, shattered beneath his. When he lowered his head, pressed his face to her throat, she once more turned hers into his hair. Once more breathed in his scent.

"It's good to be home," he murmured.

She had her shower, her glass of wine, then what she considered the ultimate in decadence: dinner in bed with her husband.

"Tell me about it." He waited until she'd relaxed, until she'd eaten. Now he poured her another glass of wine and watched the shadows come back into her eyes.

"I don't want to bring my work home."

"Why not?" He smiled, refilled his own glass. "I do."

"It's different."

"Eve." He skimmed a finger over the slight dent in her chin. "We are, both of us, very much defined by what we do for a living. You don't — you can't leave your work outside the door any more than I can. It's inside you."

She leaned back against the pillows, looked up through the sky window at the dark winter sky. And told him.

"It was cruel," she said at length. "But that's not it, really. I've seen things that were more cruel. She was innocent — there was something about her space, her walk, about her face, I don't know, but she had an innocence. I know that's not really it, either. Innocence is often destroyed. I know what it's like — not to be innocent; I don't remember being innocent. But I know what it's like to be destroyed."

She cursed under her breath and set the wine aside.

"Eve." He took her hand, waiting until she turned her gaze to his. "A rape-murder might not be the best way for you to get back into active duty."

"I might have passed on it." It shamed her to admit it, enough that she looked away again. "If I'd known, I'm not sure I would have taken the call."

"You can still pass it to someone else in your division. No one would blame you for it."

"I'd blame me. I've seen her now. I know her now." Eve closed her eyes, but only for a moment. "She's mine now. I can't turn my back on that."

Eve pushed at her hair, ordered herself to focus. "She looked so surprised and happy when she opened the door. Like a kid might. Oh boy, a present. You know?"

"Yes."

"The way the bastard looked at the camera before he went in. The big smile, the cagey little wink. And after, doing his victory dance into the elevator."

Her eyes fired up as she spoke of it; as she shoved herself straighter in the bed. Not just cop's eyes now, Roarke thought. But the avenging angel.

"There was no passion, just sheer delight." She closed her eyes again, bringing that image back, clearly, and when she opened them again, the fire was banked, smoldering deep. "It made me sick."

Annoyed with herself, she picked up the

wine again, sipped once. "I had to tell the parents. I had to watch their faces when I did. And Vandoren, watching him go to pieces, seeing him try to understand that his world had just fallen apart. She was a nice woman, a nice simple woman who was happy in her life, about to get engaged, and she opens the door to someone who's symbolically a figure of innocence. Now she's dead."

Because he knew her, he took her hand, unballing the fist she'd made. "It doesn't make you less of a cop because it touches you."

"Too many of them touch you and the edges get blurred. You get closer to the limit, to the time you know you're not going to be able to face another of the dead."

"Did it ever occur to you to take a break?" When her brows drew together, he only smiled. "No, of course not. You'll face the next, Eve, because that's what you do. That's who you are."

"I might be facing one sooner than I'd like." She linked fingers with the hand that held hers. "Was she the one, Roarke? His true love? Or are there eleven more?"

# CHAPTER THREE

Eve circled the parking deck at the sky mall a second time. And ground her teeth.

"Why aren't these people at work? Why don't they have lives?"

"For some," Peabody said solemnly, "shopping is life."

"Yeah, yeah." Eve passed a section where cars were stacked like poker chips, six high in their slots. "Screw this." She whipped the wheel, threaded through the stacks, skinning by bumpers close enough to have Peabody closing one eye. "You know, you can buy anything you want right on screen in the privacy of your own home. I don't get this."

"Screen shopping doesn't give you the same buzz." Peabody braced a hand on the dash as Eve jerked to a stop in the fire lane right outside of Bloomingdale's. "You can't use the senses, or your elbows to jab people out of the way. There's no sport in screen shopping."

With a snort, Eve engaged her On Duty sign and stepped out of the car. Immediately her ears were assaulted with a blast of music. Christmas carols pumped, full blast, into the air. She decided that people ran inside, ready to buy anything, just to escape the noise.

Though the temperature in the computer-controlled environment hovered at a pleasant seventy-two, a light, synthetic snow swirled in the enormous dome. The windows of the department store were filled with costumed droids. Santas and elves labored away in a workshop, reindeer flew or danced on rooftops, young, golden-haired children with angelic faces unwrapped bright packages.

Behind another window, a teenage boy, decked out in the latest fashion trend of black unisuit and neon checked overshirt, did circles and flips on his new Flyer 6000 airskate — this year's hot-ticket item. A push of the button beside the glass would engage the recording of his excited voice hawking the skate's options and virtues, as well as its price and location in the store.

"I'd like to try one of those suckers," Peabody said under her breath as she followed Eve to the door.

"Aren't you a little old for toys?"

"It's not a toy, it's an adventure," Peabody said, reciting the tag line for the airskate.

"Let's get this over with. I hate these places."

The doors slid smoothly open and greeted them with a soothing promise: *Welcome to Bloomingdale's. You're our most important customer.*

Inside, the music continued to play, but at a lower volume. But the voice level rose, dozens of people speaking at once making a cacophony of sound that rose up and up, to echo off the ceiling, where angels soared in graceful circles.

It was a palace of consumption, with merchandise displayed temptingly on twelve glossy floors.

Droids and staff swept through the crowds modeling fashions, accessories, the hair- and body-styles that could be purchased in the salons. The electronic map just inside the door stood ready to guide customers to their heart's desire.

Licensed child, pet, and elderly care facilities were located handily on the main level for those who didn't care to shop with Junior, Fido, or Grandpa underfoot.

Mini-carts to carry customers, their purchases, or both were available for a small rental fee. Hourly or daily rates available.

A droid with hair in snaking, flame-colored ropes approached with a small crystal bottle.

"Keep that thing away from me," Eve ordered.

"I'd like some." Obligingly, Peabody tilted back her head so the droid could spritz some perfume on her throat.

"It's called Do Me," the droid purred. "Wear it, and prepare to be ravished."

"Hmm." Peabody angled her head toward Eve. "What do you think?"

Eve took one sniff, shook her head. "It's not you."

"Could be me," Peabody muttered, trudging after her.

"Let's try to keep our focus here." Eve took Peabody's arm as her aide paused at a cosmetic counter where a woman was being painted with sparkling gold from the neck up. "Let's hit the men's department, see if we can find out who waited on Hawley day before yesterday. She used credit so they'd have her address."

"I could finish up my Christmas shopping in about twenty minutes."

"Finish it?" Eve turned back as they stepped on the people guide going up.

"Sure, I've only got a couple of little

things left." Peabody pursed her lips, then bit the inside of her cheek to hold back the grin. "Haven't started yet, have you?"

"I've been thinking about it."

"What are you getting Roarke?"

"I've been thinking about it," Eve said again and jammed her hands in her pockets.

"They've got great clothes here." Peabody nodded toward the display droids as they turned left on the glide toward Men's Casual Wear.

"He's got a closet the size of Maine full of clothes already."

"Have you ever bought him any?"

Eve felt her shoulders hunch defensively and straightened her spine. "I'm not his mother."

Peabody paused by a droid modeling a dull silver silk shirt and black leather trousers. "He'd look good in this." She fingered the sleeve. "Of course, Roarke would look good in anything." She wiggled her brows at Eve. "Guys really love having a woman buy them clothes."

"I don't know how to buy clothes for somebody else. I barely know how to buy them for myself." When she caught herself trying to imagine Roarke's face and body in place of the droid's, she hissed out a breath. "And we're not here to shop."

Scowling, she strode straight to the first checkout counter, then slapped her badge on it under the nose of the clerk.

He cleared his throat and tossed his long black hair over his shoulder. "Is there something I can do for you, Officer?"

"Lieutenant. You had a customer a couple of days ago, Marianna Hawley. I want to know who waited on her."

"I'm sure I can check on that for you." His eyes, a trendy gold, shifted right, then left. "Lieutenant, would you mind putting your identification away, and perhaps, uh, buttoning your jacket over your weapon. I believe our customers would be more at ease."

Saying nothing, Eve jammed her shield back in her pocket, then hitched her jacket over her side arm.

"Hawley," he said, obviously relieved. "Would you know if her transactions were made with cash, credit, or store accounts?"

"Credits. She bought two men's shirts — one silk, one cotton — a cashmere sweater and jacket."

"Yes." He stopped running the scan on his register. "I remember. I waited on her myself. An attractive brunette of about thirty. She was selecting gifts for her partner. Ah . . ." He closed his eyes. "Shirts in fifteen and a half, thirty-one-inch sleeves. Sweater and jacket, forty-two chest."

"Good memory," Eve commented.

"It's my job," he said, opening his eyes to smile. "Remembering customers, their tastes and needs. Ms. Hawley had excellent taste, and the foresight to bring along a wallet hologram of her young man so that we could program a color chart for him."

"Did she deal with anyone but you?"

"Not in this department. I gave her my full time and attention."

"You have her address on record?"

"Yes, of course. As I recall I offered to have her purchases sent, but she said she wanted to take them with her. She laughed and said that it added to the fun. She enjoyed her shopping experience very much." His eyes clouded. "Does she have a complaint?"

"No." Eve looked him in the eye and knew in her gut she was wasting her time. "She isn't complaining. Did you notice anyone hanging around while she was shopping, talking to her, watching her?"

"No. We were quite busy, though. Oh, I hope she wasn't accosted in the parking area. We've had a number of incidents in the last few weeks. I don't know what's wrong with people. It's Christmas."

65

"Um-hm. You sell Santa suits?"

"Santa suits?" He blinked. "Yes, that would be in Seasonals and Novelties, sixth floor."

"Thanks. Peabody, check it out," Eve ordered as she turned away. "Get names and locations for anyone buying or renting a suit in the last month. I'm going down to Jewelry, see if anyone can make the hairpin. Meet me there."

"Yes, sir."

Knowing her aide, Eve laid a warning hand on her arm. "In fifteen minutes. Any longer, and I bust you down to mall guard."

Peabody moved her shoulders as Eve strode off. "She's so strict."

Having to elbow her way to a spot at the counter on the third floor didn't improve Eve's mood. Beneath the glass was an ocean of sparkling body accessories, from earrings to nipple rings. Gold, silver, colored stones, elaborate shapes, varying textures all vied for attention under the glass.

Roarke was always buying her things to drape around her neck, pin to her ears. She didn't get it. Absently she fingered the diamond under her shirt. But he seemed to enjoy seeing her wear the things he chose for her.

Because she was running out of patience, and being roundly ignored by the staff manning the counter, she simply leaned over and snagged a clerk by the collar.

"Madam." Outraged, the clerk scorched her with a hot blue scowl.

"Lieutenant," she corrected, pulling out her shield with her free hand. "Got a minute for me now?"

"Of course." He eased back, straightened his needle-thin silver tie. "What can I do for you?"

"Do you sell anything like this?" She opened her bag and took out the sealed pin.

"I don't believe that's one of ours." He stooped until his gaze was level with the pin. "Very nice work. Festive." He leaned back. "We won't be able to take this as a return unless you have a receipt. I don't recognize it as being of our stock."

"I'm not looking to return it. Got any ideas where it might have come from?"

"I'd suggest a specialty shop. The craftsmanship appears to be quite fine. There are six jewelers in the mall. Perhaps one of them will recognize it."

"Great." She dropped it back in her bag and blew out a breath.

"Is there something else I can do for you?"

Eve shifted her feet and scanned the

display under her nose. A set of three chained ropes with clashing colored stones the size of her thumb caught her eye. It was ridiculously flashy, edging toward tacky. And just screamed Mavis.

"That," she said and pointed.

"Ah, you'd like to see the Heathen Neck Ornament. Very unique, very —"

"I don't want to see it. I'll take it. Just wrap it up, and make it fast."

"I see." Training kept him from goggling. "And how would you like to pay for that?"

Peabody marched up just as Eve was accepting the festive red and silver bag. "You shopped," she said accusingly.

"No, I bought. There's a difference. The pin didn't come from here. The guy seemed to know his stuff and was pretty definite. I don't want to waste any more time here."

"Doesn't look like you wasted it," Peabody muttered.

"We'll run the pin through the computer. I'll see if Feeney's got time to do a trace."

"What did you buy?"

"Just something for Mavis." She caught Peabody's pout as they walked through the doors. "Don't worry, Peabody, I'll get you something."

"Really?" She brightened immediately. "I've already got your present. It's wrapped and everything."

"Show-off."

Cheered now, Peabody hopped into the car. "Want to guess what it is?"

"No."

"I'll give you a hint."

"Pull yourself together. Start running the names you got on the Santa suits, see if you get a hit on anyone with a sheet."

"Yes, sir. Where are we heading?"

"Personally Yours." She sent Peabody a sidelong glance. "And you're not doing any shopping there either."

"Spoilsport. Sir," Peabody added dutifully and began to run the names on her hand unit.

In the heart of midtown, towering over Fifth Avenue in polished black marble, was a palace of pleasure. The exterior was a sleek spear ringed on the upper floors with gilded balconies and silvered glides. Sheer glass tubes slid up and down at the four corners of the compass.

Inside there were salons for body sculpting, mood enhancement, sexual orientation. Without leaving the premises a client could be buffed, polished, molded, remodeled, or sexually satisfied in the manner of their choice.

Several gyms were outfitted with the newest equipment for those who preferred a little do-it-yourself. For those who chose a more passive road to fitness and beauty, licensed consultants were available to wield laser and toning tubes to rid a client of those pesky extra pounds and inches.

One floor was dedicated to the holistic approach, which included everything from chakra balancing to coffee enemas. As she scanned those particular offerings, Eve wasn't certain whether to laugh or shudder.

Mud baths, algae scrapes, injections of the placenta of sheep raised on Alfa Six, tranquility sessions, VR trips, vision adjustments, face-lifts, tucks, and morphs — all could be done on the premises, with a number of package deals offered.

Once your body and mind were perfected, you were invited to explore the possibility of finding the right mate for the new you with the trained staff of Personally Yours.

The firm encompassed three floors of the building, with its staff uniformed in simple black suits with small red hearts embroidered on the breasts. With the path of beauty on the doorstep, attractive faces and bodies were every bit as much a part of the dress code.

The lobby area was done in Grecian

temple, with small musical ponds glinting with the flash of goldfish, and white marble columns decked with trailing vines separating areas. The seating arrangements were low to the tiled floor, cushy and plentiful. A check-in desk was discreetly tucked between fanning palms.

"I need information on one of your clients." Eve held up her badge and watched the receptionist's eyes flicker with nerves.

"We're not allowed to give out client information." The woman bit her lip and brushed her fingers over the tiny heart that was tattooed under her eye like a pretty red tear. "All our services are strictly confidential. We guarantee to protect our clients' privacy."

"One of your clients isn't worried about privacy anymore. This is police business. I can have a warrant transmitted in about five minutes, or you can give me what I need and avoid having the department go over every file."

"If you'd just wait a moment." The receptionist indicated the closest seating area. "I'll get the manager for you."

"Fine." Eve turned away as the receptionist slipped on a headset.

"It smells great in here," Peabody commented. "The whole building smells great."

She took in a deep sniff of air. "They must pump something through the air vents. Nice and soothing." She settled her rump on one of the golden cushions near a tinkling fountain. "I want to live here."

"You're annoyingly chipper these days, Peabody."

"The holidays do that to me. Wow, look at that." She swiveled her head, her eyes lighting appreciatively as a man with a stream of streaked blond hair swaggered in. "Now, why would a guy who looked like that need a dating service?"

"Why does anybody? It's creepy."

"I don't know, could save time, trouble, wear and tear." Peabody leaned forward to look around Eve and keep the man in view. "Maybe I should try it out. I could get lucky."

"He's not your type."

Peabody's face clouded exactly as it had when Eve had rejected the perfume. "How come — I like looking at his type."

"Sure, but try to have a conversation with him." Eve dipped her hands in her pockets and rocked back on her heels. "Guy's in love with himself and figures every woman who gets a load of him has to go moony-eyed — just like you're doing. He'd bore you to death in ten minutes because all he'd talk about is himself — how he looks, what he does, what he likes. You'd just be his latest accessory."

Peabody considered, watching as the gold-tipped Adonis posed at the check-in counter. "Okay, so we won't bother to talk. We'll just have sex."

"He'd be a lousy lay — wouldn't give a damn if you got off or not."

"I'm getting off just looking at him." But she sighed when he took out a small silver-backed mirror and examined his face with obvious delight. "It's times like this I hate it when you're right."

"Look at this," Eve said under her breath. "These two are so polished I need my sun-shades."

"Ken and Barbie on the town." At Eve's blank look, Peabody sighed again. "Man, you didn't have a Barbie doll. What kind of kid were you?"

"I was never a kid," Eve said simply and turned back to greet the magnificent couple gliding her way.

The woman was slim-hipped and full-breasted as the current fashion demanded. Her silvery blond hair fell in a straight streaming waterfall over her shoulders to flick across the big, beautiful breasts as she walked. Her face was smooth and white as alabaster, with deep-set eyes of rich emerald-green surrounded by long lashes dyed to match those jewel-like irises. Her mouth was full and red, curved in a polite smile of greeting.

Her companion was every bit as dazzling, her twin in coloring, with his moonlight hair swept back into a long braid twined with thin gold ribbon. His shoulders were wide, his legs long.

Unlike the rest of the staff, they weren't dressed in black, but wore slim white skin-suits. The woman had draped a transparent red scarf cleverly over her hips.

She spoke first, in a voice as soft and silky as the scarf. "I'm Piper, and this is my associate, Rudy. What can we do for you?"

"I need data on one of your clients." Once again, Eve took out her badge. "I'm investigating a homicide."

"A homicide." The woman put a hand to her heart. "How dreadful. One of our clients? Rudy?"

"We'll certainly cooperate in any way we can." He spoke quietly in a creamy baritone. "We should discuss this upstairs, in private."

He gestured toward the clear tube of an elevator guarded by enormous white azaleas in full bloom. "You're sure the victim was one of our clients?"

"Her lover met her through your service." Eve stepped directly to the middle of the tube and ignored the view as they whisked up. Heights had never appealed to her.

"I see." Piper sighed. "We have an excellent success rate in matching couples. I hope it wasn't a lover's quarrel that ended in tragedy."

"We haven't determined that."

"I can't believe that could be it. We screen very carefully." Rudy gestured toward the opening of the tube as the elevator stopped.

"How?"

"We're connected to ComTrack." As he spoke, he escorted them down a quiet corridor in hospital white with soft, dreamy watercolors in gold frames and banquets of fresh flowers in clear vases. "Every applicant is put into the system. We look at marital history, credit ratings, criminal records, of course. Our applicants must also take the standard personality test. Any violent tendencies are rejected. Sexual preferences and desires are recorded, analyzed, and matched."

He opened the door to a large office done in blinding whites and screaming reds. The window wall was filtered against both the glare of the sun and the noise of sky traffic.

"What's your percentage of deviants?"

Piper's perfect mouth thinned. "We don't consider personal sexual preferences deviant unless the partner or partners involved object."

Eve merely lifted her brows. "Why don't we use my definition instead? Bondage, S and M? You get any in here who like to doll up their partner after sex?"

Rudy cleared his throat and moved behind a wide, white console. "Certainly some applicants look for what we might call adventurous sexual experiences. As I said, those preferences would be matched with like applicants."

"Who did you match up with Marianna Hawley?"

"Marianna Hawley?" He glanced at Piper.

"I'm better with faces than names." She turned to the wall screen as Rudy fed the name into the computer. Seconds later, Marianna smiled out at them, her eyes bright and alive.

"Oh yes, I remember her. She was charming. Yes, I very much enjoyed working with her. She was looking for a companion, someone fun who she could enjoy art — no, no, it was theater, I believe." She tapped one perfectly shaped nail against her bottom lip. "She was a romantic, rather sweetly old-fashioned."

It seemed to come to her all at once, and Piper's hand dropped limply to her side. "She's been murdered? Oh, Rudy."

"Sit down, dear." He came gracefully around the console to take her hand, pat it, to lead her to a long sofa with deep air cushions. "Piper becomes very personally involved with our clients," he told Eve. "That's why she's so marvelous at her work. She cares."

"So do I, Rudy."

Though her voice was flat, his eyes flicked over her face and whatever he saw had him nodding. "Yes, I'm sure you do. You suspect that someone in our system, someone she might have met through our service, killed her."

"I'm investigating. I need names."

"Give her whatever she needs, Rudy." Piper patted her fingers under her eyes to dry tears.

"I'd like to, but we have a responsibility to our clients. We guarantee privacy."

"Marianna Hawley was entitled to privacy," Eve said shortly. "Someone raped her, sodomized her, and strangled her. I'd say they pretty much violated her privacy. I doubt any of your clients would enjoy sharing in that experience."

Rudy took a deep breath. His face was

paler now, if that was possible, so that his eyes seemed to burn against a field of glossy white. "I trust you'll be discreet."

"You can trust I'll be good," Eve said in return and waited for him to call up the list of matches.

# CHAPTER FOUR

Sarabeth Greenbalm wasn't having a good day. First off she hated working the afternoon shift at the Sweet Spot. The clientele from noon to five consisted primarily of junior execs looking for a long lunch and cheap thrills. With the emphasis on cheap. The climbing-the-corporate-ladder crowd didn't have a lot of money to toss to a stripper.

They just liked to gawk and hoot.

Five hours of hard work had netted her just under a hundred in cash and credit chips, and a half a dozen drunken propositions.

None of which included marriage.

Marriage was Sarabeth's Holy Grail.

She wasn't going to find a rich husband in the afternoon set of a strip club. Even a high-class club like the Sweet Spot. There was potential in the night hours, when the VPs and CEOs sauntered in, bringing important clients for an hour or two of titillation. She could make a thousand easily, and when you added in some lap dancing, double that. But the best was collecting business cards.

Sooner or later one of those corporate suits with their big, white smiles and perfectly manicured and grabby hands was going to put a ring on her finger for the privilege of groping her.

It was all part of the career plan she'd carefully mapped out when she'd moved from Allentown, Pennsylvania, to New York City five years before. Stripping in Allentown had been a dead-end situation, netting her just enough per week to keep her from becoming another sidewalk sleeper. Still, moving to New York had been risky. There was more competition for the same recreation dollar.

Younger competition.

The first year she'd worked two shifts, three if she could still stand. She'd worked as a roamer, sliding from club to club and shelling out the hard-line forty percent of take to the managers. It had been a gruesome year, but she'd earned her nest egg.

The second year she'd focused on nailing a regular spot at an upscale club. It had taken nearly all of those twelve months, but she'd carved her niche at the Sweet Spot. During her third year she'd fought her way up the food chain to shift headliner, cagily investing her profits. And, she admitted, she had wasted nearly six months considering the cohabitation offer of the club's head smasher.

She might have done it, too, if he hadn't gone and gotten himself sliced into six separate pieces in a bar fight at a dive where he'd been moonlighting because Sarabeth had insisted he needed a bigger bank account if he wanted her to sleep with him on a permanent basis.

She'd decided to consider it a lucky escape. Now, well into year four, she was forty-three years old and running out of time.

She didn't mind naked dancing. Hell, she was a damn good dancer and her body — she studied it as she turned in front of her bedroom mirror — was her meal ticket.

Nature had been generous, gifting her with high, full breasts that hadn't required augmentation. So far. A long torso, long legs, a firm ass. Yes, she had all the necessary weapons.

She'd had to put money into her face, and considered it a good investment. She'd been born with thin lips, a short chin, and a heavy forehead. But a few trips to a beauty enhancement center had fixed that. Now her mouth was full and ripe, her chin sassily pointed, and her brow high and clear.

Sarabeth Greenbalm looked, in her opinion, damn good.

The problem was she was down to her last five hundred, the rent was due, and some overeager bozo in the lunch crowd had ripped her best G-string before she could slither out of it.

She had a headache, her feet hurt, and she was still single.

She should never have plunked down the three thousand for Personally Yours. In retrospect what had seemed like a clever investment now appeared to be good money down the sewer. Losers used dating services, she thought as she tugged on a short purple robe. And losers attracted losers.

After meeting the first two men on her match list, she'd gone straight down to Fifth Avenue and asked for her money back. The blond ice queen hadn't been so friendly then, Sarabeth thought now. No refunds, no way, no how.

With a philosophical shrug, Sarabeth walked from the bedroom into the kitchen — a short walk in an apartment barely bigger than the communal dressing room at the Sweet Spot.

The money was gone, a write-off. And a lesson had been learned: She had to depend on herself, and herself only.

The knock on her door interrupted her hopeful scan of the limited offerings of her AutoChef. Absently she tugged her robe closed, then beat a fist on the wall. The couple next door fought like cats and fucked like minks most every night. Her pounding wouldn't change the noise level by a decibel, but it made her feel better.

She turned one suspicious brown eye to the security peep, then grinned like a girl. Hurriedly she disengaged the locks and swung the door wide.

"Hey there, Santa."

His eyes twinkled merrily. "Merry Christmas, Sarabeth." He shook the big silver box he carried, then winked at her. "Have you been good?"

Captain Ryan Feeney sat on the end of Eve's desk and munched on candied almonds. He had the lived-in, vaguely morose face of a basset hound and a wiry thatch of russet hair sprinkled with thin, steely threads of silver. There was a rust-colored splotch on his rumpled shirt — a memory of the bean soup he'd had for lunch — and

83

a small nick on his chin where he'd cut himself shaving that morning.

He looked harmless.

Eve would have gone through any door with him. And had.

He'd trained her, and taught her. Now as captain of the Electronic Detective Division, he was an invaluable resource to her.

"Wish I could tell you the bauble was a one of a kind." He popped another nut into his mouth. "Still there's only a dozen stores in the city that sell it."

"And how many do we have to trace?"

"Forty-nine of them were sold in the last seven weeks." He scratched his chin, worrying at the tiny scab. "The pin runs about five hundred. Forty-eight were credit deals, only one cash transaction."

"That would be him."

"More than likely." Feeney pulled out his memo book. "The cash deal was at Sal's Gold and Silver on Forty-ninth."

"I'll check it out, thanks."

"Nothing to it. Got anything else? McNab's willing and able."

"McNab?"

"He liked working with you. The boy's good and sharp and you could toss him any grunt work."

Eve considered the young detective with

his colorful wardrobe, sharp mind, and smart mouth. "He gives Peabody the fish eye."

"You don't think Peabody can handle him?"

Eve frowned, tapped her fingers, shrugged. "Yeah, she's a big girl, and I could use him. I contacted the victim's ex-husband. He's relocated in Atlanta. His alibi for the period in question looks fairly solid, but it wouldn't hurt to look closer. See if he booked any travel to New York, made any calls to the victim."

"McNab can do that in his sleep."

"Tell him to stay awake and do it." She reached for a disc file, handed it over. "All the data I have on the ex is here. I'll be running the names of the matches from Personally Yours. I'll pass those to him after I've taken a look."

"Don't understand places like that." Feeney shook his head. "In my day you met women the old-fashioned way. You picked them up in a bar."

Eve lifted an eyebrow. "Is that how you met your wife?"

He grinned suddenly. "It worked, didn't it? I'll pass this on to MacNab," he said as he rose. "Aren't you off the clock, Dallas?"

"Yeah, just. I think I'll run those names

before I head out."

"Suit yourself. Me, I'm out of here." He started for the door, stuffing his bag of nuts into his pocket. "Oh, we're looking forward to the Christmas party."

She was already focused on her computer and barely glanced over. "What party?"

"Your party."

"Oh." She searched her mind, found it blank as far as parties went. "Yeah, great."

"Don't know a thing about it, do you?"

"I must." And because it was Feeney, she smiled. "It's just in another compartment. Look, if you see Peabody out in the bullpen, tell her she's off duty."

"Will do."

Party, she thought with a sigh. Every time she turned around, Roarke was giving a party or dragging her off to one. The next thing she knew Mavis would pounce on her about getting her hair done, having face and body work, trying a new outfit designed by her lover Leonardo.

If she had to go to a damn party, why couldn't she just go as she was?

Because she was Roarke's wife, she reminded herself. And as such she was expected to attend social functions looking slightly better than a cop with murder on the brain.

But that was . . . whenever it was. And this was now.

"Computer, list matches through Personally Yours for Hawley, Marianna."

*Working . . .*

*Match one of five . . . Dorian Marcell, single, white, male, age thirty-two.*

While the computer listed his statistics, Eve studied the image on screen. A pleasant face — a shy look around the eyes. Dorian liked art, theater, and old videos, claimed to be a romantic at heart looking for a mate for his soul. His hobbies were photography and snowboarding.

Nothing special about Dorian, she thought, but they would see what he'd been up to on the night Marianna had been murdered.

*Match two of five . . . Charles Monroe, single, white, male —*

"Whoa, whoa, hold it. Stop." With a half laugh Eve peered at the face on screen. "Well, Charles, fancy meeting you here."

It was a fine face smiling back at her, and she remembered it. She'd met Charles Monroe nearly a year before while investigating another murder — the case that had brought her and Roarke together. Charles was a licensed companion, slick and charming. And what, she wondered, was a well-heeled LC doing in dating service?

"Trolling, Charlie? Looks like you and I are going to have to have another talk. Computer go to third match."

*Match three of five, Jeremy Vandoren, divorced —*

"Lieutenant."

"Computer pause. Yeah?" She glanced over as Peabody hovered at the door.

"Captain Feeney said you're finished with me for the day."

"Right. I'm just running some names before I go."

"He, uh, mentioned that you were going to use McNab for some of the e-work."

"That's right." Eve angled her head, then kicked back in her chair as Peabody struggled to keep her face controlled. "You got a problem with that?"

"No — that is . . . Dallas, you don't really need him. He's such a pain in the ass."

Eve smiled cheerfully. "He's not a pain in mine. I guess you'll just have to work on making your ass a little tougher, Peabody. But buck up, he'll do most of what I give him over in EDD. He won't be around here much."

"He'll find a way," Peabody muttered. "He's such a show-off."

"He does good work. And anyway —" She

broke off as her communicator beeped. "Shit, I should have gotten out of here on time." She pulled it out. "Dallas."

"Lieutenant." Commander Whitney's wide, stern face filled the small screen.

"Sir."

"We have a homicide that appears to be connected to the Hawley case. There are uniforms on the scene now. I want you as primary. Report to 23B West One Hundred and Twelve, apartment 5D. Contact me at my home office after you've confirmed the status."

"Yes, sir. I'm on my way." She spared Peabody a glance as she rose and grabbed her jacket. "You're back on duty."

The uniform standing guard at Sarabeth's door had eyes that told Eve she'd seen the likes of what was inside before, and expected to see it again.

"Officer Carmichael," Eve began, scanning the nameplate. "What have we got?"

"White female, early forties, dead at scene. Apartment's in the name of Sarabeth Greenbalm. No sign of forced entry or struggle. There's no video security in this building other than on the main door. My partner and I were on our cruise when Dispatch sent the call at sixteen thirty-five.

A 1222 anonymous report at this address. We responded, arriving at sixteen forty-two. The entrance door and the door of the reported unit were unsecured. We entered and found the deceased. We then secured the scene and alerted Dispatch of a suspicious death at this location."

"Where's your partner, Carmichael?"

"Locating the building manager, sir."

"Fine. Keep this hallway clear. Stand until relieved."

"Sir." Carmichael slid her eyes over Peabody as they passed. Among the uniforms Peabody was regarded as Dallas's pet, with varying degrees of envy, resentment, and awe.

Feeling a combination of all three from Carmichael, Peabody twitched her shoulders as she followed Eve through the door.

"Recorder on, Peabody?"

"Yes, sir."

"Lieutenant Dallas and aide, on scene at 23B West One Hundred Twelve Street, apartment of Sarabeth Greenbalm." As she spoke, Eve took a can of Seal-It from her field kit and sprayed her hands and boots before handing it off to Peabody. "Victim, yet to be identified, is white female."

She approached the body. The bedroom area was no more than an alcove off the main room, the bed a narrow bunk style that could be folded up to afford more room. It had plain white sheets and a brown blanket worn at the edges.

He'd used red garland this time, wrapping it around her boa style from neck to ankle so that she resembled a festive mummy. Her hair, a shade of violet Eve imagined Mavis would admire, had been neatly brushed and styled into an upswept cone.

Her lips, slack in death, had been painted a rich purple, her cheeks a tender pink. Pale gold glitter shadow had been carefully applied to her eyelids all the way to the brow line.

Pinned to the garland just at the center of her throat was a circle of glossy green. Within it two birds, one gold, one silver, nested, beak to beak.

"Turtledoves, right?" Eve studied the brooch. "I looked up the song. The second day his true love gives him two turtledoves." Gently, Eve pressed a hand to the painted cheek. "She's fresh. I'd bet it hasn't been more than an hour since he finished her."

Stepping back, she took out her communicator to contact Whitney and request a Crime Scene team.

It was nearly midnight when she got home.

Her shoulder was throbbing a little, but she could ignore that. What annoyed her was the fatigue. It came too quickly and too intensely these days.

She knew what the department's orifice poker would say about it. Not enough recovery time. She'd been entitled to another ten days injury leave. Her return to full duty had been too soon.

Because it tended to sour her mood to think of it, she blocked it out.

She'd forgotten to eat, and the minute she stepped inside the warmth of the house the first pangs of hunger hit. Just need a candy bar, she told herself and scrubbed her hands over her face before turning to the scanner near the door.

"Where is Roarke?"

*Roarke is in his home office.*

Figures, she decided as she started up the stairs. The man didn't seem to need sleep like a normal human. She imagined he'd look as fresh as he had when she'd left him that morning.

He'd left his door open, so it only took one quick glance inside to confirm her suspicions. He sat at the wide, glossy console, scanning screens, giving orders into his 'link while his laser fax hummed behind him.

And he looked sexy as sin.

She thought if she could get her hands on that candy bar, she might just have the energy to jump him.

"Don't you ever quit?" she demanded as she stepped into the room.

He glanced over, smiled, then turned back to his 'link. "All right, John, see that those alterations are made. We'll go over this in more detail tomorrow." He broke transmission.

"You didn't have to stop," she began. "I just wanted to let you know I was home."

"I was entertaining myself while I waited for you." He angled his head as he studied her face. "Forgot to eat, didn't you?"

"I'm hoping for a candy bar. Got any?"

He rose and moved across the polished floor to the AutoChef. Moments later he took out a thick green bowl, steaming with soup.

"That's not a candy bar."

"You can feed the child after you take care of the woman." He set the soup on a table, then poured himself a brandy.

She walked over, sniffed the soup. Nearly drooled. "Smells pretty good," she decided and sat down to devour. "Did you eat?" she asked with her mouth full, and nearly groaned with joy as he set a plate of hot

93

bread on the table. "You have to stop taking care of me."

"It's one of my little pleasures." He sat beside her, sipping brandy, watching the hot food put color back in her cheeks. "And yes, I've eaten — but I wouldn't say no to a bit of that bread."

"Umm." Obligingly, she broke a hunk in half and passed it to him. It was sort of homey, she decided. The two of them sharing soup and bread after a long day.

Just like, well, normal people.

"So . . . Roarke Industries rose, what, eight points yesterday?"

His brow winged up. "Eight and three-quarters. Have you developed an interest in the stock market, Lieutenant?"

"Maybe I'm just keeping an eye on you. Your stock goes down, I might have to dump you."

"I'll bring that point up at the next share-holders' meeting. Do you want some wine?"

"Maybe. I'll get it."

"Sit, eat. I haven't finished taking care of you yet." He rose and selected a bottle already open and chilling in the cold box cabinet.

While he poured, she scraped the last of the soup from the bowl, barely resisting licking it clean. She felt warm, settled. Home.

"Roarke, are we having a party?"

"I imagine. When?"

"I don't know when." A line formed between her eyebrows as she looked up at him. "If I knew when, why would I ask? Feeney said something about our Christmas party."

"December twenty-third. Yes, we're having a party."

"Why?"

"Darling Eve." He bent down and kissed the top of her head before he sat again. "Because it's the holidays."

"How come you didn't tell me?"

"I believe I did."

"I don't remember."

"Do you have your date book handy?"

Grumbling, she tugged it out of her pocket and plugged in the date. There, clear as crystal, was the information, followed by her initials to indicate she'd logged it in herself.

"Oh."

"The trees are being delivered tomorrow."

"Trees?"

"Yes. We'll have a formal one in the parlor, several in the ballroom upstairs. But I thought we'd have a smaller, more personal one in our bedroom. We'll decorate that one ourselves."

Her brows shot high. "You want to decorate a tree?"

"I do."

"I don't know the first thing about it. I've never decorated a Christmas tree before."

"Neither have I, or not in years. It'll be our first."

The warmth that moved through her now had nothing to do with a hot meal or vintage wine. Her lips curved. "We'll probably make a mess of it."

He took the hand she held out to him. "No doubt. Feeling better?"

"A lot, yeah."

"Do you want to tell me about tonight?"

Her fingers tightened on his. "Yeah, I do." She released his hand and rose because she would think more clearly on the move.

"He got another one," she began. "Same MO. Outside security cameras tagged him. The Santa suit, the big silver box with the fussy bow. He left her a pin, two birds in a circle."

"Turtledoves."

"Right — or close enough. I don't know what a damn turtledove looks like. No sign of forced entry, no sign of struggle. I imagine the tox report will show she was tranq'd. She'd been restrained, probably gagged as the unit wasn't soundproofed. There were some fibers on her tongue and in her mouth, but he didn't leave whatever he gagged her with behind."

"Sexually assaulted?"

"Yes, same as the first. There was a fresh temp tattoo on her right breast. My True Love. And he'd wrapped her up in red garland, painted her face, brushed her hair. The bathroom was the cleanest place in the apartment. I'm guessing he scrubbed it down himself after he was done cleaning himself up. She'd only been dead an hour by the time I got there. The anonymous call came in from a pay slot a half a block from her house."

He could see the frustration working back into her. Rising, he took her glass and his own. "Who was she?"

"A stripper, lap dancer, worked at the Sweet Spot — an upscale club on the West Side."

"Yes, I know where it is." When she turned, eyes narrowed, he handed her the wine. "And yes, it happens to be one of my properties."

"I really hate when that happens." When he only grinned at her, she blew out a breath. "Anyway, she had the afternoon shift, got off just before five. From what we can tell, she went straight home — she ran a scan on her AutoChef at six, just about the time the outside camera picked up this bastard going into the building."

Eve stared into her wine. "I'd say she missed dinner, too."

"He's working quickly."

"And having a jolly old time with it. Looks to me like he wants to make his quota by New Year's. I need to run her 'link, her finances, her personal records. I've got to check out the pin. I'm getting nowhere with the Santa suit or the garland. How the hell do I connect a sweet administrative assistant to a lap dancer?"

"I know that tone." With that he turned and moved to his console. "Let's see what we can do."

"I didn't say anything about you running scans."

He flicked a glance in her direction. "It was implied. What was her name?"

"It was not implied. Sarabeth — one word, no *h* — Greenbalm." She walked over to stand with him behind the console. "I was simply running through my thoughts out loud. The address is 23B West One Hundred and Twelve."

"Got it. What do you want first?"

"I can run her 'link in the morning. Go with either personal or financial."

"Financial would take you longer, let's start with that."

"No showing off," Eve warned, then laughed when he snaked a hand around her waist and pulled her against his side.

"Of course I'm going to show off. Subject, Sarabeth Greenbalm," he began, then nuzzled at Eve's throat. "Residing West One Hundred and Twelve." His hand slid up to cup her breast. "All financial records, latest transactions first."

*Working . . .*

"Now," he murmured, and turned Eve until their bodies meshed. "I should just have enough time to . . ." His mouth swooped down, drawing deeply from hers and sending the top of her head spinning somewhere near the lofty ceiling.

*Data complete.*

"Well." He nipped her bottom lip. "Maybe not quite enough time. Your data, Lieutenant."

She cleared her throat, exhaled. "You're good." Exhaled again. "I mean you're really good."

"I know." And because she was just a bit off balance yet, he sat, pulling her until she tumbled into his lap.

"Hey, I'm working here."

"Me, too." Swiveling her to face front, he

began to nibble at the back of her neck. "I'll work on this, you work on that."

"I can't while you're . . ." She hunched her shoulders, stifled a chuckle, and tried to concentrate on the data on screen. "Rent's her biggest expense, followed by clothes. She's got most of them marked costume for taxes. Stop it!" She slapped at the clever fingers that had already unbuttoned her blouse to the navel.

"You don't need your shirt to read data," he said reasonably and began sliding it off her shoulders.

"Look, pal, I'm still wearing my clutch piece, so —" She sprang to her feet, making him mutter an oath. "Shit, shit. There it is. Son of a bitch. There's the link."

Resigned, he tucked away thoughts of seducing her and turned his attention to the screen. "Where?"

"There. Three thousand to Personally Yours by electronic transaction, six weeks ago."

Her eyes were hot now, not with passion but power, as she swung around to face him. "She and Hawley used the same dating service. That's not a coincidence. That's a connection. I need her matches," she murmured, then catching Roarke's inquiring look, she shook her head. "No, we'll do it the right way. By the book. I'll go in tomorrow and get them."

"It wouldn't take me long to access."

"It's not legal." She struggled to keep her face stern when that grin of his beamed at her. "And it's not your job. But I appreciate it."

"How much?"

She stepped back, stood between his legs, and looked down at him. "Enough to let you finish taking care of me." She sat, straddling him. "After I take care of you, that is."

"How about . . ." He fisted a hand in her hair and brought her mouth within a breath of his, "we take care of each other?"

"That's a deal."

# CHAPTER FIVE

Settled in her home office with weak winter sunlight dribbling through the window wall at her back, Eve organized her data. She intended to feed a report to her commander by midmorning and had several blanks she wanted to fill in first.

"Computer engage. Detail data on dating service enterprise known as Personally Yours located on Fifth Avenue in New York."

*Working . . . Personally Yours, established 2052 in Fifth Avenue location, owned and operated by Rudy and Piper Hoffman.*

"Stop, confirm. Business in question is owned by Rudy and Piper Hoffman?"

*Affirmative. Rudy and Piper Hoffman, fraternal twins, age twenty-eight. Residence 500 Fifth Avenue. Continue scan on Personally Yours?*

"No, search and report, full data on owners."

*Searching . . .*

While her computer juggled its chips, she rose to get a cup of coffee. Fraternal twins, she thought as the AutoChef filled her request. Brother and sister. She'd tagged them as lovers. And now, thinking back, remembering the way they'd touched, moved together, the looks exchanged, she wondered if both she and the computer were right.

It was a thought that didn't sit well in her gut.

A movement in the adjoining doorway caught the corner of her eye an instant before Roarke stepped into full view.

"Good morning. You're up and about early."

"I want to get my prelim report to Whitney first thing." She took her coffee from the AutoChef, shook back her hair. "You want a cup of this?"

"Yes, I do." He took hers, smiling when she frowned at him. "I'll be in meetings most of the day."

"What else is new," she muttered and programmed the unit for a second cup of coffee.

"But you can reach me, if you need."

She grunted, then glanced over as her computer signaled data search was complete. "Good. Okay, I've got —" She yelped in surprise as he grabbed the front of her shirt and tugged. "Hey, what — Hold data," she called out and shoved at her husband.

"I like the way you smell in the morning." He leaned in and sniffed at her hair as he spoke.

"It's just soap."

"I know."

"Get ahold of yourself." But damn it, he had her blood up and pumping fast. "I've got work," she muttered even as her arms came around him.

"So do I. I miss you, Eve." He set his cup aside so he could hold her, just hold her.

"I guess we've both been busy the last couple of weeks." It felt so good to lean against him and just be. "I can't back off this case now."

"I don't expect you to." For the pleasure of it, he rubbed his cheek against hers. "I wouldn't want you to." But it was the last case, what it had done to her, that weighed on his mind and his heart. "I'm content to steal a moment here and there." He eased back, brushed his lips over hers. "I've always had a good hand at stealing . . . whatever."

"You're not supposed to remind me." And, smiling, she framed his face with her hands.

From the doorway, Peabody watched

them. It was too late to step back, too soon to step forward. Though they were only standing, his hands on Eve's shoulders, hers on his cheeks, Peabody found it a wrenchingly intimate moment that had her face heating and her heart sighing with envy.

At a loss, she did the only thing she could think of and worked up the fake, faintly embarrassed cough of the intruder.

Roarke ran his hands down Eve's arms, and smiled toward the doorway. "Good morning, Peabody. Coffee?"

"Um, yeah. Thanks. Uh . . . it's pretty cold out."

"Really?" Roarke said as Eve moved back toward her desk.

"Yeah, it's not supposed to get up to freezing. We might get some snow flurries this afternoon."

"What are you, the National Weather Service?" Eve demanded, then took a good look at her aide. Peabody's face was flushed, her eyes soft, her hands busily plucking at her brass buttons. "What's wrong with you?"

"Nothing. Thanks," she said when Roarke brought her a cup of coffee.

"You're welcome. I'll leave you to work."

When he walked through the adjoining doorway and closed it off, Peabody sighed. "I don't know how you can remember your name when he looks at you the way he does."

"If I forget it, he reminds me."

Though she heard the wry humor in Eve's voice, Peabody stepped closer. "What's it like?"

"What?" Glancing up, Eve caught the intensity in her aide's eyes and shrugged uncomfortably. "Peabody, we've got work here."

"Isn't that what it's about?" Peabody interrupted. "Isn't what you've got what those two women were looking for?"

Eve opened her mouth, then shut it again. She glanced toward the connecting doors, saw that Roarke had closed them, but hadn't engaged locks on either side. "It's more than you think it can be," she heard herself say. "It changes everything, and fixes everything that matters. Maybe you're never going to be the same, and maybe part of you is always afraid of what will happen if . . . but he's always going to be there. All you have to do is reach out, and he's going to be there."

Surprised at herself, she slipped her hands into her pockets. "Can you find that by pumping data into a computer system and letting it run personality and lifestyle matches? I don't know. But we've got two dead women who thought it was worth a try. Pull up a chair, Peabody, and we'll see what we've got."

"Yes, sir."

"We'll run a full search of Jeremy Vandoren. Instincts aside, we need to confirm or eliminate. Once we have full data on all five matches on the Hawley list, we'll pay another visit to Personally Yours."

"Detective McNab, reporting for duty."

Eve looked over and saw Ian McNab swagger into the room. He had a big, satisfied grin on his pretty face, a knee-length vest in eye-searing fuchsia over his Christmas-green jumpsuit, and a striped ribbon of both colors binding back his long sweep of glinting gold hair.

Feeling Peabody stiffen like a flagpole beside her, Eve nearly sighed.

"How's it going, McNab?"

"It's going good, Lieutenant. Hey there, Peabody." He winked cockily then set a hip on the desk. "Captain Feeney said you could use me on this Santa case. I'm here to serve. Got anything to eat?"

"See what's in the AutoChef."

"Mag. Working for you, Dallas, has rocking benefits." He wiggled his brows suggestively at Peabody then walked over to forage breakfast.

"If you were going to use that pinhead," Peabody muttered under her breath, "why can't he work out of EDD?"

"Because I wanted to irritate you, Peabody. It's my main goal in life. Since you're here, McNab," Eve continued, "you can take over these searches. Peabody and I need to go out in the field."

"Just line them up," he said, taking a huge bite of a blueberry Danish. "I'll knock them back."

"When you've finished stuffing your face," Eve said mildly, "run the names in the Hawley file — all data."

"Took care of the ex last night," he said with his mouth full. "Can't find any break in his alibi so far."

"Okay." She appreciated the fast return, but decided not to mention it and have Peabody pouting all day. "I'll be sending you another list from the field — run those names, then do a cross-check between the lists. Take a good look at the Hoffman twins, Rudy and Piper. I want anything that pops. And run this."

She turned back to her computer, called up the evidence file, and shot out a hologram of the second brooch. "I want to know who made this piece, how many were manufactured, where they were sold, how many were sold, and to whom. Cross-check that with the first pin found on Hawley's body. You getting this, McNab?"

"Sir." He swallowed hastily, then tapped a finger to his temple. "Every bit."

"You get me a name that matches both lists and the bauble, and I'll see to it you've got fresh Danishes every morning for the rest of your life."

"That's a hell of an incentive." He wiggled his fingers. "Let me at it."

"Let's ride, Peabody." Eve rose, grabbed her bag. "Don't bother Roarke, McNab," she warned and headed out.

"Looking good, She-body," McNab called just as Peabody hit the doorway. She snarled, hissed, stomped out, and left him feeling gratified.

"EDD's full of detectives with class, you know," Peabody complained as they trooped downstairs. "How come we're stuck with the one asshole in the division?"

"Just lucky, I guess." Eve snagged her jacket off the newel post, and swung it on as they walked outside. "Christ, it's fucking freezing out here."

"You really ought to have a warmer coat, Lieutenant."

"I'm used to this one." But she slid into the car quickly. "Heat, for God's sake," she ordered. "Seventy-five degrees."

"I love this unit." Peabody snuggled into the seat. "Everything works."

"Yeah. But it lacks character." Still Eve glanced down with pleasure as her 'link signaled an incoming. "Catch this," she told Peabody. "Screen incoming," she ordered as she drove through the gates.

"Dallas? Dallas? Damn it." The attractive and irritated face of ace screen reporter Nadine Furst came on screen. "I just missed you at home. Summerset said you're on route somewhere. Answer the damn 'link, will you?"

"I don't think so."

"Hell, those city-issue units you cops drive never work."

Peabody and Eve exchanged cheerful grins while Nadine continued to mutter. "I guess she got wind of the case."

"Sure she did," Eve confirmed. "Now she wants to hit me up for information for her midmorning report, and she'll hound me for a one-on-one for the noon edition."

"Dallas, I need more data on these women who were killed. Are the cases linked? Come on, Dallas, be a pal. I need to bump up my midmorning."

"Told you," Eve said complacently as she twisted through traffic.

"Get in touch, will you? We can set up a one-on-one. I'm on deadline here."

"My heart bleeds." Eve yawned as Nadine signed off.

"I like her," Peabody commented.

"So do I. She's fair, she's accurate, and she's good at what she does. But that doesn't mean I'm going to take time out to give her ratings a goose. If I avoid her for a couple of days, she'll be digging on her own. Let's see what she can feed *us* for a change."

"You're sneaky, Lieutenant. I like that about you. But about McNab —"

"Live with it, Peabody," Eve suggested and whipped up and into a second-level parking slot on the curb on Fifth.

Inside she went directly to a tube, stepped in, hooked her thumbs in her pockets, and tolerated the ride up to the office level of Personally Yours.

Manning the greeting desk was a young god with shoulders the size of mountains, skin the color of rich Swiss chocolate, and eyes like antique gold coins.

"Stop vibrating," Eve muttered, and Peabody only grunted in response.

"Tell Rudy and Piper Lieutenant Dallas and aide are here."

"Lieutenant." His smile was dreamy and slow. "I'm sorry, but Rudy and Piper are in client consultations."

"Tell them I'm here," Eve repeated. "And that they're minus another client."

"Of course." He gestured to the waiting area to the left. "Please make yourselves comfortable. Feel free to order up some refreshment while you wait."

"Don't keep me waiting long."

He didn't. Within five minutes, and before Peabody could weaken enough to order up something called a Raspberry Cream Froth, both Rudy and Piper stepped into the lobby area.

They were in white again, ankle dusters this time, with Piper jazzing hers up with a blue silk sash. Each wore a single gold hoop in the right ear — one the mate of the other.

It made Eve's skin crawl.

"Lieutenant." Rudy spoke, keeping a hand on Piper's shoulder. "We're a bit rushed this morning. Our schedule's very full."

"It just got fuller. You want to do this here, or in private?"

The faintest hint of irritation flickered in Rudy's exotic eyes, but he gestured gracefully toward the hallway leading to their offices.

"Sarabeth Greenbalm," Eve began the minute the door shut at her back. "She was

112

found murdered yesterday. She was one of yours."

"Oh God, oh my God." Instantly Piper collapsed in a wide white chair and covered her face with her hands.

"Hush now." Rudy ran a hand over Piper's hair, caressed the back of her neck. "You're certain she was a client?"

"Yes. I want her matches. Which one of you worked with her?"

"I would have." Piper dropped her hands in her lap. The deep green eyes glinted with threatening tears, her pale gold mouth trembled. "I work with the female applicants, Rudy with the male unless otherwise requested. In general we find that people are more comfortable discussing romantic and sexual needs with a member of the same sex."

"Okay." Eve kept her eyes on Piper's face and tried not to notice the way her hand crept up until it was swallowed by her brother's.

"I remember her. Sarabeth. I remember her because she was dissatisfied with the first two matches. She wanted a full refund."

"Did she get one?"

"We have a firm policy against refunds once the client has begun to explore the matches." Rudy gave his sister's hand a reassuring squeeze, then walked to his console.

"I see. Neither of you mentioned that you owned the company."

"You didn't ask," Rudy said simply as he called up the data Eve had requested.

"Who besides the two of you would have access to client data?"

"We have thirty-six consultants," Rudy began. "After the initial screening, which Piper and I deal with personally, applicants are assigned to the consultant who most suits their needs. Our consultants are screened, trained, and licensed, Lieutenant."

"I want their names, full data."

His eyes shuttered, seemed to frost. "I can't agree to that. That kind of invasion into the privacy of our staff is insulting."

Eve angled her head. "Peabody, request a warrant, search and seizure of all records, personnel and client lists, for Personally Yours. Log in reports on the Hawley and Greenbalm cases, and request warrant be issued directly to me through my communicator. And put a rash on it."

"Right away, Lieutenant."

"Rudy." Rubbing her hands together, Piper rose. "Is this necessary?"

"I think it is." He held out a hand, taking

hers when she crossed to him. "If our records are to be part of a police investigation, I want it all to be documented. I apologize for what might seem like a lack of cooperation and compassion, Lieutenant Dallas, but I have a great many people to protect."

"So do I." When the communicator beeped, Piper jolted. "Excuse me." Eve turned her back to them and slipped it out of her pocket. "Dallas."

"We tagged the makeup used on Hawley." Dickie scowled out of the screen. "Brand name's Natural Perfection. High-dollar shit, like I figured."

"Nice work, Dickie."

"Yeah, it cost me overtime, and I got Christmas shopping to do. Prelim indicates the stuff on Greenbalm was the same brand. You gotta buy this crap through salons or an enhancement center. Can't get it in regular stores, even high-end ones, or off screen."

"Good, that'll make it easier to trace. Who manufactures?"

His scowl transformed into a wide, wicked grin. "Renaissance Beauty and Health, a division of Kenbar, which is an arm of Roarke Industries. Don't you know what your old man's up to, Dallas?"

"Hell" was all Eve said, and she cut the transmission before she turned around. "Any of the salons in this building sell Natural Perfection products?"

"Yes." Piper leaned against Rudy in a way that made Eve's stomach roll over. "That line is showcased in All Things Beautiful on the tenth level."

"Are you connected with the salon?"

"It's a separate business, but we maintain relationships with all the salons and shops in the building." Rudy moved to the console, opened a compartment, and selected a glossy, foldout brochure and attached disc. "Packages including salon work and gift certificates are available with consults here," he said as he offered Eve the material.

"All Things Beautiful," he continued, "is the most exclusive salon in the building. They also offer packages which include a consult with us in their Diamond Day plan."

"Handy."

"It's good business" was Rudy's response.

"Warrant approved, Lieutenant." Peabody tucked her own communicator away again. "Processing transmission now."

"Feed all that data to McNab," Eve ordered Peabody when they were in the tube again.

"All of it?"

Eve didn't spare much sympathy despite Peabody's wide, shocked eyes. "All. Start with the matches on Greenbalm, then give him personnel. Go from there into client list, go back one year. I have a feeling our man is living pretty much in the present."

"That's going to take twenty or thirty minutes."

"Then find yourself a quiet spot and get started. I get off here. Meet me in the salon when you've finished uploading data."

"Yes, sir."

"And buck up, Peabody. Pouting's not attractive."

"I'm not pouting," Peabody said with some dignity. "I'm gritting. As in my teeth." She sniffed audibly as the tube whooshed shut again.

The salon level smelled of forests and meadows. The sound system piped in soft, tinkling music of lyres and flutes. Underfoot was a carpet the color and consistency of crushed rose petals. The walls were dull silver and drenched with the slowly streaming flow of water that fed into a narrow canal that circled the entire floor. Palm-sized swans in pastel hues glided over its surface.

There were six salons in all, each with glass-fronted archways arbored with exotic vines. Eve recognized the reproduction of the Immortal blossom that had been trained to spiral up a thin, gilded curve that haloed the entrance of All Things Beautiful.

Figures, she thought. That particular bloom had caused her quite a bit of trouble once upon a time.

The doors parted fluidly as she approached. Inside, the lobby area was wide and sumptuous, with deep, cushioned scoop chairs in pale greens. Each was fitted with its own mini-screen and communication system. Statuary and sculpture ran to bronze nudes.

Small serving droids scooted here and there, carrying refreshments, reading material, VR goggles, and whatever else clients ordered for their amusement while they were beautified.

Two of the chairs were occupied by women who chatted absently and sipped something that looked like seafoam while they waited for their treatments. Both wore plush shell-pink robes with the salon's name discreetly etched on the lapel.

"May I help you, madam?" The woman behind a U-shaped console gave Eve's battered jeans, scarred boots, and untidy hair a slow, measuring study out of glittering silver eyes. The eyes matched the S-shaped streaks snaking through her wedge of triangular magenta hair. "I assume you're looking for our Complete Woman package?"

Eve smiled pleasantly. "Is that a dig?"

The woman blinked with a flurry of silver lashes. "I beg your pardon?"

"Never mind, sister. I want to talk about your Natural Perfection line."

"Yes, of course. It's the very best cosmetic and enhancement line money can buy. I'll be happy to arrange for a consultant to speak with you. Would you care to make an appointment?"

"Yeah." Eve slapped her badge on the console. "Now would be good."

"I don't understand."

"I can see that. Get me whoever runs this place."

"Excuse me a moment." The woman shifted on her high stool and spoke softly into her 'link. "Simon, could you come up front please?"

With her thumbs in her front pockets, Eve rocked back on her heels and studied the elegant bottles and tubes in the revolving display behind the console. "What's all that?"

"Personalized scents. We feed your personality and physical traits into a program and create a scent that is uniquely you. The container is your choice. Each is one of a kind and, once selected, will never be made again."

"Interesting."

"They make thoughtful gifts," she arched a razor-thin brow, "but are quite exclusive and expensive."

"Really?" Irritated by the sarcasm, Eve sent her a tawny, slitted stare. "I want one."

"Naturally the purchase must be prepaid before programming."

Seriously riled, Eve imagined grabbing a handful of that stiff, streaked hair and rapping the perfect, sneering face firmly against the console. She took one step forward as hurried footsteps sounded on the floor behind her.

"Yvette, what seems to be the problem? I'm swamped back there."

"She's the problem," Yvette said with a thin smile, and Eve turned and got a full blast of the magnificent Simon.

The eyes caught her first. They were a pale, almost translucent blue framed by thick dark lashes and thin ebony brows that each peaked to a ruler-sharp point in the middle. His hair was a brilliant ruby red, swept high off his forehead and temples and styled to tumble in a snowfall of springy curls to the middle of his back.

His skin had the dull gold sheen indicating mixed-race heritage or complexion dyes. His mouth was painted a deep bronze, and riding along his prominent left cheekbone was a white unicorn with gold horn and hooves.

He swept back the electric-blue cape draped over his shoulders. Beneath he wore a skinsuit of chartreuse and silver stripes with a deeply scooped neckline. A tangle of gold chains gleamed against his impressive chest. He angled his head, sending the long gold dangles in his ears dancing as he set one hand on one slim hip and studied Eve.

"And what can I do for you, dear heart?"

"I want —"

"Wait, wait!" He threw up both hands, palms cut, revealing a chain of hearts and flowers tattooed there. "I know that face." With a dramatic toss of his head, he circled Eve and gave her a whiff of his scent.

Plums, she thought. The guy smelled like plums.

"Faces," he continued while Eve's eyes narrowed, "are, after all, my art, my business, my stock and trade. I've seen yours. Oh yes indeed, I have."

Abruptly, he grabbed Eve's face between his hands and leaned forward until they were nearly nose to nose. "Look, pal —"

"Roarke's wife!" He squealed it, then planted a loud, juicy kiss on her mouth, leaping back before she could follow through with the urge to punch him. "That's who you are! Darling," he crooned, turning with his hands crossed over his heart to the receptionist. "Roarke's wife is in our humble salon."

"Roarke's wife?" Yvette went bright red, then lost all color. "Oh," she muttered and looked ill.

"Sit, you must sit and tell me everything you desire." He scooped an arm around Eve's shoulders and began to nudge her toward a chair. "Yvette, be a lamb and cancel all my consultations. Dear lady, I am yours. Where shall we begin?"

"You can begin by stepping back, ace." She shrugged off his arm, and with some regret pulled out her badge instead of her weapon. "I'm here on police business."

"Oh my, oh my goodness." Simon patted his hands to his cheeks. "How could I have forgotten? Roarke's wife is one of New York's finest. Forgive me, dear heart."

"The name is Dallas, Lieutenant Dallas."

"Of course." Then he smiled sweetly. "Forgive me, Lieutenant. My enthusiasm . . . I tend to emote. Seeing you here, I lost my head, if you will. You see, you're on our top ten wish list, along with Madam President and Slinky LeMar — the video Queen," he added when Eve's eyes remained narrowed. "It's excellent company."

"Right. I need your client list for the Natural Perfection line."

"Our client list." He laid a hand on his heart again, and sat. He touched the video screen and had the menu popping on. "A sparkling lemon. Please, Lieutenant, allow me to offer you some refreshment."

"I'm fine." But because he looked chastised and didn't appear to be planning on grabbing her again, she sat across from him. "I need the list, Simon."

"Is it permissible to ask why?"

"I'm investigating a homicide."

"A murder." He whispered it, leaned closer. "I know it's dreadful, but I find that terribly exciting. I'm an avid fan of mystery and detective videos." He offered that sweet smile again, and despite herself Eve softened.

"This is a little different than a video, Simon."

"I know, I know. It's horrid of me. Ghoulish. But I can't imagine how a line of cosmetics and enhancements figure into a . . ." His eyes went wide and bright. "Poison? Was it poison? Someone added poison to the lip dyes. The victim prepared herself for a glorious night on the town — perhaps she used Radical Red, or no, no, Bombshell Bronze, then —"

"Get a grip on yourself, Simon."

His lashes fluttered, his color went bright, then he chuckled warmly. "I should be spanked." Without glancing over, he scooped a tall, slim glass of pale yellow liquid from the serving droid that zipped to his chair. "Of course, we'll cooperate, Lieutenant, in any way we can. I should warn you that our client list is quite extensive. If you could give me specific products, we could whittle it down considerably."

"Give me the whole shot for now, then I'll see what I can do."

"At your command." He rose, bowed, then waltzed behind the console. "Yvette, give dear Lieutenant Dallas some samples while I perform this little task for her. There's a lamb."

"I don't need any samples." Eve smiled thinly at Yvette. "But I want the scent we were talking about."

"Absolutely." The receptionist nearly knelt at Eve's feet. "Would this be for yourself?"

"No, it's a gift."

"And a very thoughtful one." Yvette took a personal palm computer out of her pocket.

"Male or female?"

"Female."

"Could you give me three of her strongest personality traits? As in bold or shy or romantic."

"Intelligent," Eve said, thinking of Dr. Mira. "Compassionate. Thorough."

"Very good. Now something of the physical?"

"Medium height, slender, brown hair, blue eyes, light complexion."

"That's very nice," Yvette said. For a police report, she thought in disgust. "What color brown is her hair? How does she wear it?"

Eve hissed between her teeth. This Christmas shopping was tough stuff. Doing her best, she focused and described the city's top profiler and shrink.

By the time Peabody walked in, she was choosing the bottle and waiting for Simon to generate hard copy and disc.

"You shopped again."

"No, I bought again."

"Should we have this delivered to your home or office, Lieutenant?"

"Home."

"Would you like it gift wrapped?"

"Hell. Yeah, yeah, wrap it up. Simon, how about that data?"

"Just coming, Lieutenant dear." He looked up, beamed at her. "I'm so happy we could help you in that matter." He slipped the papers and disc into a gold foil shopping bag. "I added some samples. I think you'll find them perfect. Naturally." He chuckled at his own joke as he passed the bag to Eve. "And I hope you'll keep me informed. Please come back, any time, any time at all. I'd love to work on you."

# CHAPTER SIX

An ocean of humanity swamped Fifth Avenue. People swarmed on the sidewalks, the people glides, clogged the intersections and crowded at display windows, all in a flurry to get into stores and buy.

Some, already burdened like pack mules with shopping bags, elbowed and shoved their way through the waves of pedestrians to fight the hopeless fight for a cab.

Overhead advertising blimps encouraged the masses toward a shopping frenzy with competing announcements of sales and products no consumer could live without.

"They're all insane," Eve decided as she watched a ministampede toward a maxibus heading downtown. "Every one of them."

"You bought something twenty minutes ago."

"In a civilized and dignified manner."

Peabody shrugged. "I like crowds at Christmastime."

"Then I'm about to make you very happy. We're getting out."

"Here?"

"It's as close as we're going to get in a vehicle." Eve nosed her car through the stream of people and inched it toward the curb at Fifth and Fifty-first. "The jeweler's just a few blocks down. We'll make better time on foot."

Peabody shoehorned her way out, and caught up with Eve's long strides on the corner. The wind rushed down the street like a river through a canyon and turned the tip of her nose pink before they'd managed a block.

"I hate this shit," Eve muttered. "Half these people don't even live here. They come in from all over hell and back to clog the streets every damn December."

"And drop a nice ton of money in our economy."

"Cause delays, petty crime, traffic accidents. You try to get uptown at six o'clock some night. It's ugly." Scowling, she walked through the roasting meat-scented steam of a corner glide-cart.

A shout had her flicking her glance to the left in time to see a scuffle. She lifted a brow in mild interest as a street thief on airskates toppled a pair of women, snatched what bags he could reach, snagged both purses, and skimmed away through the crowd.

"Sir?"

"Yeah, I've got him." Eve noted his grin of triumph as he weaved through the crowds of people, gaining speed as they leaped out of his path.

He ducked, swiveled, dodged, then veered around toward Eve's right. Their eyes met for one brief second, his bright with excitement, hers flat and level. She pivoted and took him out with one short-armed, back-fisted punch. Had there been less of a crowd, she thought he would have sailed nicely for ten feet or so. Instead he barreled back into a group of people, upended with his skates still humming and facing the sky.

Blood gushed out of his nose. His eyes rolled back white.

"See if you can get a beat cop in here to take care of this jerk." Eve flexed her fingers, rolled her shoulder, then absently put one booted foot on the thief's midriff as he began to moan and squirm. "You know what, Peabody? I feel a lot better now."

Later, Eve thought busting the thief had been the high point of her day. She didn't learn squat from the jeweler. Neither he nor his sour-faced clerk remembered anything about the customer who'd paid cash for the partridge pin. It was Christmas, the jeweler had complained, even while his clerk rang up sales with the speed and precision of an accounting droid. How was he supposed to remember one transaction?

Eve suggested he think harder, and contact her when his memory cleared. Then ended up buying a copper ear chain for Mavis's lover, Leonardo — much to Peabody's disgust.

"You catch some transpo, go back to the house, and work with McNab."

"Why don't you just punch me in the face with a bare fist?"

"Handle it, Peabody. I'm going into Central. I'll need to give Whitney an update, and I want to see Mira, start her working on a profile."

"Maybe you'll pick up a few more Christmas presents on the way."

Eve stopped by her car. "Was that sarcasm?"

"I don't think so. It was too direct for sarcasm."

"Find me a match on those lists, Peabody, or we start interviewing lonely hearts."

Eve left Peabody elbowing her way toward Sixth to catch a maxibus uptown. She engaged her 'link as she headed in the opposite direction, and set up the two meetings.

She scanned the incoming, listened to Nadine's harried voice, and decided to give the reporter a break. "Stop whining, Nadine."

"Dallas, Christ, where have you been?"

"Keeping the city safe for you and yours."

"Look, there's just enough time to plug something into my noon report. Give me a line here."

"I just busted a mugger on Fifth."

"Don't be droll, I'm up against the wall. What's the connection between the two murders?"

"Which two murders? We got a lot of bodies this time of year. Christmas brings out that wacky holiday spirit."

Nadine snarled audibly. "Hawley and Greenbalm. Come on, Dallas. Two women strangled. I've got that much. You're primary on both. I hear there was sexual molestation. Will you confirm?"

"The department will not confirm or deny at this time."

"Rape and sodomy."

"No comment."

"Damn it, why the hardball?"

"I don't have any breathing room right now. I'm trying to stop a killer, Nadine, and

I just can't be too worried about the ratings for Channel 75."

"I thought we were friends."

"I guess we are, and because of that when I've got something to give, you'll get it."

Nadine's eyes brightened. "First, exclusive?"

"Don't keep tying up my 'link."

"A one-on-one, Dallas. Let me set it up. I can be at Cop Central by one."

"No. I'll let you know when and where, but I don't have time for you today." And time, Eve thought, was the biggest factor. No one she knew researched as fast or as deep as Nadine Furst. "You're not seeing anybody in particular these days, are you, Nadine?"

"Seeing anyone — as in dating or sleeping with? No, not in particular."

"Ever try one of those dating services?"

"Please." Nadine's eyelashes fluttered as she lifted her hand to examine her manicure. "I think I can find my own men."

"Just a thought. I hear they're popular." Eve paused and watched Nadine's eyes narrow and glitter. "You might want to give it a try."

"Yeah, I might do that. Thanks. Gotta run. I'm on in five."

"One thing. Do I have to buy you a

Christmas present?"

Nadine's brows went up, her lips curved in a wide smile. "Absolutely."

"Damn, I was afraid of that." Frowning, Eve broke transmission and steered into the garage at Cop Central.

On the way to Whitney's office, she snagged an energy bar and a tube of Extra-Zing Coke from a vending machine. She wolfed down the bar, chugged the soft drink, and as a result stepped into Whitney's office feeling slightly ill.

"Status, Lieutenant?"

"I have McNab from EDD working with my aide at my home office, Commander. We have the lists from Personally Yours for each victim. We're hoping to get a match. We're still working on the jewelry he left with the victims, and have the brand and projected source for the enhancements he used."

He nodded. Whitney was a powerfully built man with a smooth, dark complexion and tired eyes. Through the window at his back, Eve could see the city — the constant flow of air traffic around the spears of buildings; people moving around offices behind other windows. She knew if you stepped up to that window, you could look down and see the street below. All the people rushing to or away. All the lives that needed protect-ing.

As always she thought she preferred her cramped office and limited view.

"Do you know how many tourists and out-of-state consumers come into the city in the weeks before Christmas?"

"No, sir."

"The mayor gave me the estimated num-ber this morning when he called to inform me the city couldn't afford a serial killer scaring away holiday dollars." His smile was thin and humorless. "He didn't seem, at that point, to be overly concerned with residents of the city being raped and strangled, but with the distressing side ef-fects such events could cause if the media plays the Santa killer angle."

"The media isn't aware of that angle at this time."

"How long before it leaks?" Whitney leaned back, kept his eyes level and on Eve's.

"Maybe a couple of days. Channel 75 has already been tipped that they're sexual homicides, but their data is patchy at this point."

"Let's see if we can keep it that way. How long before he hits again?"

"Tonight. Tomorrow at the latest." No way to stop it, she thought, and saw by Whitney's face he understood.

"The dating service is the only connection you've got."

"Yes, sir. At this time. There's no indication that the victims knew each other. They lived in different parts of the city, moved in widely different circles. They weren't of a type, physically."

She paused, waiting, but Whitney said nothing. "I'm going to consult with Mira," Eve continued. "But in my opinion he's already established a pattern and a goal. He wants twelve on or before the end of the year. That's less than two weeks, so he has to move quickly."

"So do you."

"Yes, sir. The source of his victims has to be Personally Yours. We've tagged the cosmetics used on the victims. Sources of purchase for them in the city are fairly limited. We have the pins he left at both sites." Then she exhaled. "He knew we could trace the cosmetics; he left the pins deliberately. He feels secure that his tracks are covered. If we don't find a match within the next twenty-four hours, our best defense might be the media."

"And tell them what? If you spot a fat man in a red suit, call a cop?" He pushed back from his desk. "Find a match, Lieutenant. I don't want twelve bodies under my tree this Christmas."

Eve pulled out her communicator as she left Whitney's office. "McNab, make me happy."

"I'm doing my best, Lieutenant." He gestured with what appeared to be a slice of pineapple pizza. "I've pretty well eliminated the ex-husband of the first victim. He was at an arena ball match with three friends on the night of the murder. Peabody's going to check on the three pals, but it looks solid. No transpo to New York was issued under his name. He hasn't been to the east coast in over two years."

"One down," Eve said as she hopped a glide. "Give me more."

"None of the names on Hawley's list match any on Greenbalm's, but I'm checking finger- and voiceprints to make sure nobody tried to pull a fast one there."

"Good thinking."

"And two on Hawley's list look clear so far. Need to follow up, but they're alibied. I'm just going into Greenbalm's now."

"Run the names on the cosmetics first." She dragged a hand through her hair as she stepped off the glide and squeezed into an elevator. "I should be back within two hours."

She got off the elevator, crossed a small lobby area, and entered Mira's offices. There was no one at the reception desk, and Mira's door stood open. Poking her head in, Eve saw Mira reviewing a case file on video and nibbling on a thin sandwich.

It wasn't often she caught Mira unaware, Eve mused. Mira was a woman who saw almost everything. Too much, Eve often thought, when it came to herself.

She wasn't sure what had caused the bond to form between them. She respected Mira's abilities — though they sometimes made her uncomfortable.

Mira was a small, cleanly built woman with soft sable hair waving elegantly around a cool, attractive face. She habitually wore slim suits in quiet colors. Eve supposed that Mira represented all she, Eve, thought a lady should be: self-contained, quietly elegant, well spoken.

Dealing with mental defectives, violent tendencies, and habitual perverts never seemed to ruffle Mira's composure or her compassion. Her profiles of madmen and murderers were invaluable to the New York Police and Security Department.

Eve hesitated at the door just long enough for Mira to sense her. The psychiatrist turned her head, and her blue eyes warmed when they met Eve's.

"I didn't mean to interrupt. Your assistant isn't at her station."

"She's at lunch. Come in, close the door. I was expecting you."

Eve glanced at the sandwich. "I'm cutting into your break."

"Cops and doctors. We take our breaks where we find them. Would you like something to eat?"

"No, thanks." The energy bar wasn't sitting well in her stomach, which made her wonder just how long it had been since the vending machine had been serviced.

Despite Eve's refusal, Mira rose and ordered tea from the AutoChef. It was a ritual Eve had learned to live with. She'd sip the faintly floral-tasting brew, but she didn't have to like it.

"I've reviewed the data you were able to transmit, and the copies of your case reports. I'll have a complete and written profile for you tomorrow."

"What can you give me today?"

"Probably little you haven't gleaned for yourself." Mira settled back in one of the blue scoop chairs similar to those in Simon's salon.

Eve's face, she noted, was a bit too pale, a bit too thin. Mira hadn't seen her since

Eve's return to duty, and her doctor's eye diagnosed that the return had been rushed.

But she kept that opinion to herself.

"The person you're looking for is likely a male between the ages of thirty and fifty-five," she began. "He's controlled, calculating, and organized. He enjoys the spotlight and feels he deserves to be the focus of attention. He may have had some aspirations toward acting or a connection to the field."

"He showed off for the camera, played to it."

"Exactly." Mira nodded, pleased. "He employed costumes and props, and not just, in my opinion, as tools and disguises. But for the flair of it, and the irony. I wonder if he sees his cruelty as irony."

She took a breath, shifted her legs, and sipped at her tea. If she'd believed Eve would actually drink the cup she'd given her, Mira would have added some vitamins to it. "It's possible. It's a stage, a show. He enjoys that aspect very much. The preparation, the details. He's a coward, but a careful one."

"They're all cowards," Eve stated and had Mira tilting her head.

"Yes, you would see it that way, because to you the taking of a life is only justifiable in defense of another. For you murder is the ultimate cowardice. But in this case, I would say he recognizes his own fears. He drugs his victims quickly — not to save them pain but to prevent them from fighting, and perhaps overcoming him physically. He needs to set the stage. He puts them in bed, restrains them before cutting off their clothes. He doesn't strip them in a rage, and he makes certain they're bound before he goes to the next step. Now they're helpless, now they're his."

"Then he rapes them."

"Yes, when they're bound. Naked and helpless. If they were free they would reject him. He knows this. He's been rejected. But now he can do as he wishes. He needs them awake and aware for this so that they can see him, so they know he has the power, so they struggle but can't escape."

The words, the images, had Eve's already uneasy stomach pitching. Memories danced too close to the surface. "Rape's always about power."

"Yes." Because she understood Mira wanted to reach out and take Eve's hand. And because she understood, she didn't. "He strangles them because it's personal, an extension of the sexual act. Hands to the throat. It's intimate."

Mira smiled a little. "How much of this

had you already concluded?"

"Doesn't matter. You're confirming my take on him."

"All right then. The garland is trimming. Props again, show, irony. They're gifts from himself to himself. The Christmas theme may have some personal meaning to him, or it may simply be the symbolism."

"What about the destruction of Marianna Hawley's tree and ornaments?" When Mira only cocked a brow, Eve shrugged. "Breaking the symbol of the holiday in the tree, the eradication of purity in the angel ornaments."

"It would suit him."

"The pins and tattoos."

"He's a romantic."

"A romantic?"

"Yes, he's very much the romantic. He brands them as his love, he leaves them a token, and he takes the time and the trouble to make them beautiful before he leaves them. Anything less than that would make them an unworthy gift."

"Did he know them?"

"Yes, I would say he did. Whether they knew him is another matter. But he knew them, he'd observed them. He'd chosen them and for the length of time he had them, they were his true love. He doesn't mutilate," she added, leaning forward. "He decorates, enhances. Artistically, perhaps even lovingly. But when he is finished, he is done. He sprays the body with disinfectant, erasing himself. He washes, scrubs, erasing them from him. And when he leaves, he is jubilant. He's won. And it's time to prepare for the next."

"Hawley and Greenbalm were nothing alike physically, nor in their lifestyles, their habits, or their work."

"But they had one thing in common," Mira put in. "They were both, at one time, lonely enough, needy enough, interested enough, to pay for help in finding a companion."

"Their true love." Eve set her untouched tea aside. "Thanks."

"I hope you're well." Aware that Eve was braced to rise and leave, Mira stalled. "Fully recovered from your injuries."

"I'm fine."

No, Mira thought, not quite fine. "You only took what, two or three weeks off to recover from serious injuries."

"I'm better off working."

"Yes, I know you think so." Mira smiled again. "Are you ready for the holidays?"

Eve didn't squirm in her chair, but she

wanted to. "I've picked up a couple of presents."

"It must be difficult finding something for Roarke."

"You're telling me."

"I'm sure you'll find something perfect. No one knows him better than you."

"Sometimes I do, sometimes I don't." And because it was in the back of her mind, she spoke without thinking. "He's getting into all this Christmas stuff. Parties and trees. I just figured we'd hand each other something and be done with it."

"Neither of you have the memories of childhood everyone's entitled to — of anticipation and wonder, of Christmas mornings with pretty boxes stacked under the tree. I'd say Roarke intends to start making those memories, for the two of you. Knowing him," she added with a laugh, "they won't be ordinary."

"I think he's ordered a small forest of trees."

"Give yourself a chance at that anticipation and wonder, as a gift for both of you."

"With Roarke you don't have a choice." She did stand now. "I appreciate the time, Dr. Mira."

"One last thing, Eve." Mira got to her feet as well. "He's not dangerous at this point to anyone other than the person he's focused on. He won't kill indiscriminately or without purpose and planning. But I can't say when that might change, or what might trigger a shift in pattern."

"I've got some thoughts on that. I'll be in touch."

Peabody and McNab were bickering when she walked into her home office. They sat side by side at her workstation snarling at each other like a couple of bulldogs over the same bone.

Ordinarily it might have amused Eve, but at the moment it was only one more irritation. "Break it up," she snapped and had both of them shooting to attention with grim, resentful faces. "Report."

When they both began to talk at once, she seethed for approximately five seconds then bared her teeth. That shut both of them up. "Peabody?"

Risking one smug sidelong glance at her nemesis, Peabody began. "We have three matches with the cosmetics. Two from Hawley's list and one from Greenbalm's. One from each bought the works, from skin care to lash dye. The second from Hawley's purchased eye and brow pencils and two lip dyes. We got a hit on what was used on

144

Greenbalm's mouth. That's Cupid's Coral. All three purchased that shade."

"Problem." McNab lifted a finger like an instructor halting an overzealous student. "Both Cupid Coral lip dye and Musk Brown lash enhancer are routinely given as samples. In fact," he gestured to the counter where the samples Eve had been given were lined up, "you have both here."

"We can't track every stupid sample," Peabody said with a dangerous edge to her voice. "We have three names, and a place to start."

"The Fog Over London eye smudger used on Hawley is one of the pricier products and it isn't given out as a sample. You only get it as a separate or when you buy the whole shot in the deluxe package. We follow the smudger, we'll be closer to the mark."

"And maybe the son of a bitch lifted the smudger when he was buying the rest of the stuff." Peabody turned on McNab. "You want to track every shoplifter in the city now?"

"It's the only product we can't trace so far. So it's the one we have to find."

They were nose to nose when Eve stepped forward and gave them both a shove. "The next one who speaks, I'm taking down. You're both right. We interview the matches, and we look for the eye gunk. Peabody, get the names, go down to my vehicle, and wait for me."

Peabody didn't have to speak, not when a ramrod-stiff spine and hot eyes could say volumes. The minute she stalked out, Mc-Nab shoved his hands in his pockets. But when he opened his mouth, he caught the warning glint Eve shot him, and closed it again.

"You run Personally Yours again, client and personnel, find who on there bought that smudger, and see how many more of the products used on the victims you can match." She lifted her eyebrows. "Say yes, sir, Lieutenant Dallas."

He heaved a sigh. "Yes, sir, Lieutenant Dallas."

"Good. While you're at it, McNab, see if you can wiggle into Piper and Rudy's credit account. Let's find out what brand of enhancements they use." She waited, brows still high. One thing McNab wasn't was slow.

"Yes, sir, Lieutenant Dallas."

"And stop pouting," she ordered as she strode out.

"Females," McNab muttered under his breath, then caught a movement out of the corner of his eye. He spotted Roarke standing in the open doorway between the offices, grinning at him.

"Marvelous creatures, aren't they?" Roarke stepped in.

"Not from where I'm standing."

"Ah, but you'll be a hero, won't you, if you can match your product with the right name." He strolled over, scanned the lists and documents that they both knew were official business, and none of his. "I find I have an hour or two free. Want some help?"

"Well, I . . ." McNab glanced toward the door.

"Don't worry about the lieutenant." Roarke pleased himself and sat at the computer. "I can handle her."

Donnie Ray Michael wore a ratty brown bathrobe and a silver nose ring with an emerald cabochon. His eyes were a bleary hazel, his hair the color of butter, and his breath ferocious.

He studied Eve's badge, expelling air in a yawn that nearly knocked her flat, then scratched his armpit.

"What?"

"Donnie Ray? Got a minute?"

"Yeah, I got plenty of minutes, but what?"

"I'll tell you after we come in, and you gargle with a gallon or two of mouthwash."

"Oh." He went slightly pink and stepped back. "I was asleep. Wasn't expecting visitors. Or cops." But he waved them inside, then disappeared down a short hallway.

The place was as tidy as your average pigsty, with clothes, empty and half-empty take-out containers, overflowing ashtrays, and a litter of computer discs strewn over the floor. In the corner beside a threadbare sofa was a music stand and a brightly polished saxophone.

Eve caught a drift in the air of very old onions and the shadow of an illegal usually consumed by smoking. "If we decide a search is in order," Eve told Peabody, "we've got probable cause."

"What, suspicion of toxic waste?"

"There's that." Eve toed what might have been underwear aside. "He's been pumping Zoner, probably as a bedtime soother. You can just smell it."

Peabody sniffed. "I just smell sweat and onions."

"It's there."

Donnie Ray walked back in, his eyes slightly clearer, his face red and damp from a quick splash. "Sorry about the mess. Droid's year off. What's this about?"

"Do you know Marianna Hawley?"

"Marianna?" His brow wrinkled in

thought. "I dunno. Should I?"

"You matched with her through Person-ally Yours."

"Oh, the dating gig." He kicked clothes out of the way then dropped into a chair. "Yeah, I gave that a shot a few months back. I was in a drought." He smiled a little, then shrugged. "Marianna. Was she a big redhead — no, that was Tanya. We hit it off pretty well, but she moved to Albuquerque for Christ's sake. I mean what rocks there?"

"Marianna, Donnie Ray. Slim brunette. Green eyes."

"Yeah, yeah, now I get her. Sweet. We didn't click, too much like, well, a sister. She came to the club where I was blowing and heard me, we had a couple of drinks. So?"

"You ever watch the screen, read the paper?"

"Not when I've got a steady gig. I'm booked with a group downtown at the Empire. Been doing the ten-to-four slot for the last three weeks."

"Seven nights on?"

"No, five. You blow seven nights, you lose the edge."

"How about Tuesday night?"

"I'm off Tuesday. Mondays and Tuesdays are clear." His eyes were focused now and just beginning to go wary. "What's the deal?"

"Marianna Hawley was murdered Tuesday night. You got an alibi for Tuesday from nine to midnight?"

"Oh, shit. Shit. Murdered. Jesus H." He sprang up, stumbling over debris as he paced. "Man, that bites. She was a sweetheart."

"Did you want her to be your sweetheart? Your true love."

He stopped pacing. Eve found it interesting that he didn't look frightened or angry. He looked sorry. "Look, I had a couple of drinks with her one night. A little talk, tried to convince her to take a harmless roll, but she wasn't into it. I liked her. You couldn't help but like her."

He pushed his fingers against his eyes, then ran them back into his hair again. "That was, hell, six months ago, maybe more. I haven't seen her since. What happened to her?"

"Tuesday night, Donnie Ray."

"Tuesday?" He rubbed his hands over his face. "I don't know. Hell, who remembers? I probably did a few clubs, some hanging. Lemme think a minute."

He closed his eyes, blew out a couple of breaths. "Tuesday I went down to Crazy

150

Charlie's and heard this new band."

"Did you go with anybody?"

"A few of us started out together. I don't know who ended up at Crazy's. I was pretty wasted by then."

"Tell me, Donnie Ray, what did you buy the full product line of Natural Perfection for? You don't look like the type to paint up."

"What?" He looked baffled, then dropped into the chair again. "What the hell is Natural Perfection?"

"You ought to know. You spent over two thousand on the line. Cosmetics, Donnie Ray. Enhancements."

"Cosmetics." He shoved his hands through his hair until it stood up in buttery spikes. "Oh shit, yeah. The jazzy stuff. My mother's birthday. I bought her the works."

"You spent two large on your mother's birthday?" With doubt obvious in her eyes, Eve glanced around the cramped, messy room.

"My mother's the best. The old man ditched us when I was a kid. She worked like three dogs to keep a roof over my head, and to pay for music lessons." He nodded toward the sax. "I make good money blowing. Fucking good. Now I'm helping to pay for the roof over her head, in Connecticut.

A decent house in a decent neighborhood. This . . ." he gestured to encompass the room, "it don't matter a damn to me. I'm hardly here except to flake out."

"How about I call your mother, right now, and ask her what her boy Donnie Ray gave her for her last birthday?"

"Sure." Without hesitation he jerked a thumb toward the 'link on a table by the wall. "Her number's programmed. Just do me a favor, okay? Don't tell her you're a cop. She worries. Say you're doing a survey or something."

"Peabody, ditch the uniform jacket and call Donnie Ray's mom." Eve moved out of transmission range and sat on the arm of a chair. "Rudy at Personally Yours do your profile?"

"No, well, I talked to him first. I got the feeling everybody does. Like an audition. Then some joker did the consult. What do you like to do for entertainment, what do you dream about, what's your favorite color. You take a physical, too, to make sure you're clean."

"They didn't turn up traces of Zoner."

He had the grace to look abashed. "No. I was clean."

"I bet your mother would want you to stay that way."

152

"Ms. Michael received a complete line of Natural Perfection Cosmetics and Enhancers from her son on her birthday." Peabody shrugged back into her uniform jacket, then gave Donnie Ray a smile. "She was really happy with the gift."

"She's pretty, isn't she?"

"Yes, she is."

"She's the best."

"That's what she said about you," Peabody told him.

"I got her diamond earrings for Christmas. Well, they're really just chips, but she'd get a large charge." He was eyeing Peabody with interest now, having seen her without the stiff jacket. "You ever get down to the Empire?"

"Not yet."

"You ought to drop in. We really blow."

"Maybe I will." But she caught Eve's owlish look and cleared her throat. "Thank you for your cooperation, Mr. Michael."

"Do your mother a favor," Eve said as they headed for the door. "Shovel out this garbage heap and lay off the Zoner."

"Yeah, sure." And Donnie Ray gave Peabody a suggestive wink before he closed the door.

"It's unseemly to flirt with suspects, Officer Peabody."

"He's not really a suspect." Peabody glanced over her shoulder. "And he was really cute."

"He's a suspect until we confirm his alibi. And he's a pig."

"But a really cute pig. Sir."

"We've got two more interviews to conduct, Peabody. Try to control your hormones."

"I do, Dallas, I do." She sighed as she climbed back into the car. "But it's so nice when they control me."

# CHAPTER SEVEN

Spending most of the day doing interviews without making a crack in a case didn't put Eve in the best of moods. Finding McNab packed and gone when she returned to her home office darkened her mood a bit more.

She considered it fortunate for his future well-being that he'd left her a memo, and a nibble.

"Lieutenant. Logged off at sixteen forty-five. List of names and products under case file, subhead E for Evidence Two-A. Couple of pops might interest you. I got hits on both Piper and Rudy on the smudger, another on Piper for the lip dye. By the way, the two of them are rolling in credits. Not that they'd give Roarke a run, but they aren't hurting. Interesting, too, all their assets are held jointly, down to the last penny. Report also in file."

All their assets held jointly, Eve mused. Her impression had been that Rudy manned the business end of things. It had always been Rudy who'd made the decisions, gone to the console when she'd been there.

It followed that he handled the money, too.

He had the control, Eve decided. He had the power.

And the opportunity, the access.

"One other hit on smudger," McNab's voice continued. "Two on lip dye, with Charles Monroe popping on both. Missed him first pass because he put another name on the credit slip for the mailing list of new products and specials. Profile on Monroe included."

Eve frowned as the memo ended. Her instincts might have been steering her toward Rudy, but it looked as though she was going to pay Charles Monroe a visit.

Glancing over, she saw the light over the door that adjoined Roarke's office was on. If he was busy, it was as good a time as any to check on a more personal matter.

She moved quietly, using the stairs rather than the elevator, keeping an eye out for Summerset as she lengthened her strides toward the library.

The walls of the two-level room were lined with books. It always baffled her that a man who could buy a small planet at the snap of a finger preferred the weight and bulk of a book rather than the convenience of reading on screen.

One of his quirks, she supposed, though she could appreciate the rich smell of leather from the bindings, the glossy look of the spines as they marched along the dark mahogany shelves.

There were two generous seating areas, more leather in the wood-trimmed deep burgundy sofas and chairs, jewels of colors on glass lamp shades, the sheen of brass, the shine of old wood in cabinets deeply carved by craftsmen from another century.

Drapes were open to the night around a wide window seat dressed with thick pillows in tones that picked up the multihues of the lamps. Enormous and ancient rugs with intricate patterns over a red-wine background stretched over the wide and polished chestnut planks of the floor.

She knew a full-range multitask computer system was hidden behind the antique cabinet. But everything in view in the room spoke of age and wealth and a taste for both.

She didn't come here often, but she knew Roarke did. She might find him sitting in one of the leather chairs in the evening, his long legs stretched out, a brandy by his elbow and a book in his hands. Reading relaxed him, he'd told her. And she knew it was a skill he'd taught himself as a boy in the slums of Dublin when he'd found a tattered copy of Yeats in an alley.

She crossed to the cabinet and opened the doors rich with inlays of lapis and malachite. "Engage," she ordered and cast a cautious glance over her shoulder. "Search library, all sections, for Yeats."

*Yeats, Elizabeth; Yeats, William Butler?*

Her brows came together, her hand scooped through her hair. "How the hell do I know? It's some Irish poet."

*Yeats, William Butler, confirmed. Searching stacks . . .* The Wanderings Of Oisin, *Section D, shelf five.* The Countess of Cathleen, *Section D —*

"Wait." She pinched the bridge of her nose. "Shift search. Tell me what books by this guy aren't in the library."

*Adjusting . . . Searching . . .*

He probably had every damn thing anyway. Stupid idea, she decided, and jammed her hands in her pockets.

"Lieutenant."

And nearly jumped out of her boots. She whirled around and stared at Summerset. "What? Damn it, I hate when you do that."

He merely continued to eye her blandly. He knew she hated when he came up on

158

her unawares. It was one of the reasons he so enjoyed doing it. "May I help you find a book — though I didn't realize you read anything but reports and the occasional disc on aberrant behavior."

"Look, pal, I've got a perfect right to be in here." Which didn't explain why being found in the library made her feel like a sneak. "And I don't need your help."

*All works by subject author, Yeats, William Butler, are included in library. Do you require locations and titles?*

"No, damn it. I knew it."

"Yeats, Lieutenant?" Curious, Summerset moved into the room, closely followed by Galahad, who padded over to Eve, scissored between her legs, then deserted her to leap onto the window seat and stare out at the night as if he owned it.

"So what?"

He only raised his eyebrows. "Was there a play you were interested in, a collection, a particular poem?"

"What are you, the library police?"

"These books are quite valuable," he said coolly. "Many are first editions and quite rare. You'll find all of Yeats's work in the disc library as well. That method, I'm sure, would suit you better."

"I don't want to read the damn thing. I

just wanted to see if there was something he didn't have, which is stupid because he has every damn thing, so what the hell am I supposed to do?"

"About what?"

"Christmas, you moron." Incensed, she turned back to the computer. "Disengage."

Summerset pursed his lips and followed the train of thought. "You wished to purchase a volume of Yeats for Roarke as a Christmas gift."

"That was the idea, which turns out to suck."

"Lieutenant," he said as she started to storm out.

"What?"

It annoyed him when she did or said something that touched him. But it couldn't be helped. And he owed her for risking, nearly losing, her life to save his. That simple fact, Summerset knew, made them both uncomfortable. Perhaps he could even the scales, by a small weight.

"He does not own, as yet, a first edition copy of *The Celtic Twilight*."

The mutinous glare faded, though some suspicion remained. "What is it?"

"It's a prose collection."

"By this Yeats guy?"

"Yes."

A part of her, a small, nasty part, wanted to shrug and walk away. But she jammed her hands in her pockets and stuck. "The search said he had everything."

"He owns the book, but not in a first edition. Yeats is particularly important to Roarke. I imagine you know that. I have a connection to a rare book dealer in Dublin. I could contact him and see if it can be acquired."

"Bought," Eve said firmly. "Not stolen." She smiled thinly when Summerset's spine snapped stiff. "I know something about your connections. We keep it legal."

"I never intended otherwise. But it won't come cheap." It was his turn to smile, just as thinly. "And there will, no doubt, be a charge for securing the acquisition in time for Christmas, as you've waited until the eleventh hour."

She didn't wince, but she wanted to. "If your connection can find it, I want it." Then because she couldn't figure a way around it, she shrugged. "Thanks."

He nodded stiffly, and waited until she'd left the room before he grinned.

This, Eve thought, was what being in love did to you. It made you have to cooperate with the biggest annoyance in your life. And, she thought sourly as she took the elevator to the bedroom, if the skinny son of a bitch actually pulled it off, she was going to owe him.

It was mortifying.

Then the elevator doors opened, and there was Roarke with a half smile on his lost angel face, his eyes impossibly blue with pleasure.

What was a little mortification?

"I didn't know you were home yet."

"Yeah, I was . . . doing stuff." She cocked her head. She knew that look. "Why are you looking so smug?"

He took her hand, drew her into the room. "What do you think?" he asked and gestured.

Centered in the deeply recessed window on the far side of the raised platform that held their bed was a tree. Its boughs fanned out into the room and rose up and up until the tip all but speared the ceiling.

She blinked at it. "It's big."

"Obviously you haven't seen the one in the living area. It's twice this tall."

Cautious, she moved closer. It had to be ten feet. If it toppled, she mused, while they were sleeping, it would drop like a stone on the bed and pin them like ants. "I hope it's secure." She sniffed. "Smells like a forest in here. I guess we're going to hang stuff on it."

"That's the plan." He slipped his arms around her waist, drew her back against him. "I'll deal with the lights later."

"You will?"

"It's a man's job," he told her and nipped at her neck.

"Who says?"

"Women throughout the ages who were sensible enough not to want to deal with it. Are you off duty, Lieutenant?"

"I thought I'd get some food, then run a few probability scans." His mouth was cruising up to her earlobe. She thought he could do the most interesting things to an earlobe. "And I want to see if Mira sent through her profile."

Her eyes were already half shut as she angled her head to give him fuller access to the side of her neck. When his hands slid up to cup her breasts, her mind went wonderfully foggy.

"Then I've got a report to write and file." His thumbs flicked over her nipples and sent a spear of heat lancing straight to her gut.

"But I probably have an hour to spare," she muttered, and turning, she fisted her hands in his hair and pulled his mouth to hers.

A sound of pleasure hummed in his throat and his hands glided down her back. "Come with me."

"Where?"

He bit her bottom lip. "Wherever I take you."

Circling her, he guided her back into the elevator. "Holoroom," he ordered, then backed her into the corner and cut off her question with one long, mind-numbing kiss.

"Something wrong with the bedroom?" she asked when she could breathe again.

"I have something else in mind." Keeping his eyes on hers, he drew her out. "Engage program."

The large, empty room, with its stark black mirrored walls, shimmered, shifted. She smelled smoke first, fragrant, faintly fruity, then the tang of some spicy scented flower. The lights dimmed and wavered. Images formed.

A crackling fire in a big stone hearth. A window wide as a lake with a view of steel-blue mountains and deep, feathery snow that gleamed icily in the moonlight. Urns of hammered copper filled to bursting with flowers in whites and rusty hues. Candles, hundreds of candles, white as the snow, burning with flickering flames out of polished brass holders.

Under her feet the mirrored floor became wood, dark, nearly black, with a dull sheen.

Dominating the room was an enormous bed with head- and footboards fashioned of complicated curves and loops of thin, sparkling brass. Spread over it was a cover of dull gold that looked thick enough to drown in, and dozens of pillows in shades of precious gems.

Scattered over all were white rose petals.

"Wow." She looked toward the window again. The view, those towering peaks, the miles of white, did something odd to her throat. "What are those?"

"A simulation of the Swiss Alps." One of his greatest delights was watching her reaction to something new. The initial wariness that was the cop, the slow bloom of pleasure that came from the woman. "I've never managed to take you there in reality. A holographic chalet is the next best thing."

Turning, he picked up a robe that was draped over a chair. "Why don't you put this on?"

She reached for it, frowned. "What is it?"

"A robe."

She shot him a bland look. "I know that. I meant what's it made of? Is this mink?"

"Sable." He stepped forward. "Why don't I help you?"

"You're in a mood, aren't you?" she murmured as he began unbuttoning her shirt.

His hands skimmed over her bare shoulders as he brushed the shirt aside. "It seems I am. In a mood to seduce my wife. Slowly."

Need was already kindling, spreading. "I don't need seduction, Roarke."

He laid his lips on her shoulder. "I do. Sit." He nudged her down so he could tug off her boots. Then, bracing his hands on the arms of the chair, he leaned over and took her mouth again.

Just mouth to mouth, warm and soft, a skillfully tender sliding of lips and tongue, a cleverly gentle scrape of teeth. Her muscles quivered, then went lax. Feeling her surrender was his own seduction.

Drawing her to her feet, he unhooked her trousers. "The wanting of you never stops." His fingers skimmed over her hips; the trousers pooled at her feet. "The loving of you never peaks. There's always more."

Undone, she leaned against him, her face buried in his hair. "Nothing's the same for me since you."

He held her a moment, for the simple pleasure of it. Then, reaching down, he lifted the robe and draped the soft pelt over her shoulders. "For either of us."

He picked her up and carried her to the bed.

And her arms reached out for him.

She knew what it would be like. Overwhelming, unsettling. Glorious. She'd come to crave each separate sensation he could bring her, to crave the feel of him against her the way she did air or water.

Without thinking of it, and unable to survive without it.

There was nothing she couldn't give, or take, when their bodies came together. Sunk deep in the feather bed she met his mouth eagerly, reveling in the slow burn of her blood. Sighing, she tugged at her shirt, helping him shrug it aside so flesh could meet flesh.

The long and lovely slide of it. A slow roll, a low moan. The silk of the petals, the satin of the spread, the ripple of muscle under her hands — all tangled together in an exotic mix of textures.

The quick, bounding leap of the heart. A delicious shiver, a soft sigh. The flicker of candlelight, the spill of the moon, the shifting shimmer from the fire melded into one sumptuous glow.

She tasted and was tasted. She touched

and was touched. Aroused and was aroused. And trembled her way up the long curve of a peak as smooth as polished silver.

He felt her rise up, shudder, then slide lazily down again. Their limbs tangled as they rolled over the bed, to touch again, to adjust the fit of bodies. He could see the lights flicker over her face, her hair, in her eyes, the rich brandy of them. Eyes he could watch go glassy as he nudged her, inch by inch, toward that peak again.

Her hands, strong, capable, and beautifully familiar, moved over him, a grip, a caress. Quiet sounds of pleasure hummed in her throat, sighed into his mouth, whispered over his skin.

His breath began to quicken, and need became a thunder in the blood. Warmth turned to heat and heat to a dangerous flash.

Then she was rising over him, her body slim and silvered in the shift of light and shadow. Her moan was long, a throaty sound of greed as she lowered to him, enclosed him, took him in. When his fingers dug into her hips, she arched back into a gleaming curve, rocking, rocking, with her eyes golden brown slits, her breath rushing between parted lips.

She tightened around him when the orgasm slashed through her, then curled into him when he reared up, when his mouth fixed hungrily on her breast.

Lost now, captured, he pushed her back so both her mind and body went spinning. And he drove into her, one wild animal thrust after another, with a sudden pounding greed that ripped her past control. Her fingers wrapped around the thin, curving tubes of the headboard, gripping hard as if to anchor herself, a scream of mindless pleasure strangling in her throat as he pushed her knees back to go deeper.

When her body erupted beneath him, his mouth swooped down to hers. And he let himself go.

She was covered with rose petals and nothing else. Those slim, disciplined muscles were as lax as the melted candle-wax pooled fragrantly beneath the white tapers.

As her breathing slowed to normal, Roarke nibbled at her shoulder, then he rose to get the robe and draped it over her.

Her response was a grunt.

Both amused and pleased that that was the best she could do, he moved to the far corner of the room and ordered the jet tub to fill at one hundred and one degrees. He popped the cork on a bottle of champagne, set it back in its bucket of ice, then snatched his limp wife off the bed.

"I wasn't asleep." She said it quickly and with the slurred tone that told him that's just what she'd been.

"You'll blame me in the morning if I let you sleep and you don't do your probability scan." With this, he dumped her in the hot, frothing water.

She yelped once, then moaned in sheer, sensual delight. "Oh God. I want to live here, right here in this tub, for about a week."

"Arrange for some time off and we'll go to the Alps for real and you can soak in a tub until you turn into one big pink wrinkle."

It was exactly what he wanted — to take her away, to see that she was completely healed and recovered. And he imagined he had as much chance of doing so as he had of convincing her to kiss Summerset on the mouth.

The image of that even made him grin.

"Joke?" she asked lazily.

"Oh, it would be a delightful one." He handed her a flute and, taking his own, climbed in to join her.

"I have to get to work."

"I know." He let out a long breath. "Ten minutes."

The combination of hot water and icy champagne was just too good to refuse. "You know, before you, my breaks used to consist of a cup of bad coffee and a . . . a cup of bad coffee," she decided.

"I know, and they still do entirely too often. This," he said and sank a little deeper, "is a much superior way to recharge."

"Hard to argue." She lifted her leg, examined her toes for no particular reason. "I don't think he's going to give me much time, Roarke. He's working on a deadline."

"How much do you have?"

"Not enough. Not nearly enough."

"You'll get more. I've never known a better cop. And I've known more than my share."

She frowned into her wine. "It's not out of rage, not yet. It's not for profit. It's not, that I can find, for revenge. He'd be easier to track if I had a motive."

"Love. True love."

She cursed softly. "My true love. But you can't have twelve true loves."

"You're being rational. You're thinking a man can't love more than one woman with equal degrees of fervor. But he can."

"Sure, if his heart is in his dick."

With a laugh, Roarke opened one eye. "Darling Eve, it's often impossible to separate the two. For some," he added, mistrusting the quick glint in her eye, "physical attraction most usually proceeds the finer emotions. What you may not be considering is that he might very well believe each of them the love of his life. And if they didn't agree, the only way he can convince them is to take their lives."

"I have considered it. But it isn't enough to give me a full picture. He loves what he can't have, and what he can't have he destroys." She jerked her shoulder. "I hate all the goddamn symbolism. It muddles things up."

"You have to give him points for theatrical flare."

"Yeah, and I'm counting on that to be what trips him up. When it does, I'm tossing jolly old St. Nick in a cage. Time's up," she announced and rose out of the water.

She'd just flicked a towel from a heated bar when she heard the muffled beep on her communicator. "Shit." Dripping, she dashed across the room to snatch up her trousers and pull it from the pocket.

"Block video," she muttered. "Dallas."

"Dispatch, Dallas, Lieutenant Eve. DAS at 432 Houston. Apartment 6E. Report to scene immediately as primary."

"Dispatch." She dragged a hand through

her damp hair. "Acknowledged. Contact Peabody, Officer Delia as adjutant."

"Affirmative. Dispatch out."

"DAS?" Roarke picked up the robe to drape it over her again.

"Dead at scene." She heaved the towel aside and, bending, tugged on the trousers. "Damn it, goddamn it, that's Donnie Ray's apartment. I just interviewed him today."

Donnie Ray had loved his mother. That was the first thing Eve thought of as she looked at him.

He was on the bed, draped in green garland that sparkled with gold flecks. His buttery hair had been carefully styled to flow against the pillow. His eyes were shut so that lashes, lengthened and dyed a deep, antique gold lay against his cheeks. His lips matched the tone perfectly. Around his right wrist, just over the raw and broken skin, was a thick bracelet with three pretty birds etched into hammered gold.

"Three calling birds," Peabody said from behind her. "Shit, Dallas."

"He changed sexes, but he's keeping to pattern." Eve's voice was flat as she shifted aside so that the body would be in full view for the record. "There's bound to be a tattoo on him, and probable signs of sexual

173

abuse. Ligature marks hands and feet, as with previous victims. We need any security discs from the hallway and the outer building."

"He was a nice guy," Peabody murmured.

"Now he's a dead guy. Let's do the job."

Peabody stiffened, the slightest of movements that had her shoulders going straight as a ruler. "Yes, sir."

They found the tattoo on his left buttock. If that and the clear signs of sodomy affected her, Eve didn't let it show. She did the preliminary, had the scene secured, ordered the initial door-to-doors, and had the body bagged for transport.

"We'll check his 'link," she told Peabody. "Get his date book, any data you can find on Personally Yours. I want the sweepers in here tonight."

She moved down the short hall to the bathroom, pushed the door open. Walls, floor, and fixtures sparkled like the sun. "We can assume our man cleaned this. Donnie Ray wasn't too concerned about cleanliness being next to godliness."

"He didn't deserve to die this way."

"Nobody deserves to die this way." Eve stepped back, turned. "You liked him. So did I. Now put it away, because it doesn't do a damn thing for him now. He's gone, and we have to use what we find here to help us get to number four before we lose another."

"I know that. But I can't help feeling. Jesus, Dallas, we were in here joking with him a few hours ago. I can't help feeling," she repeated in a furious whisper. "I'm not like you."

"You think he gives a damn what you feel now? He wants justice not grief, not even pity." She marched into the living area, kicking away scattered cups and shoes to vent a little of her frustration.

"Do you think he cares that I'm pissed off?" She whirled back, eyes blazing. "Being pissed off doesn't do anything for him, and it clouds my judgment. What am I missing? What the hell am I missing? He leaves it all here, in front of my face. The son of a bitch."

Peabody said nothing for a moment. It wasn't, she thought, the first time she'd mistaken Eve's cool professionalism for a lack of heart. After all the months they'd worked together, she realized she should know better. She drew a deep breath.

"Maybe he's giving us too much, and it's scattering our focus."

Eve's eyes narrowed, and the fists she'd jammed in her pockets relaxed. "That's good. That's very good. Too many angles, too much data. We need to pick a channel and zoom in. Start the search here, Peabody," she ordered as she pulled out her communicator. "It's going to be a long night."

She stumbled home at four a.m. riding on the high-octane, low-quality faux caffeine of Cop Central coffee. Her eyes felt sticky, her stomach raw, but she thought her mind was still sharp enough to do the job.

Still, she jerked and had a hand on her weapon when Roarke came into her home office a few paces behind her.

"What the hell are you doing up?" she demanded.

"I might ask the same, Lieutenant."

"I'm working."

He lifted a brow and took her chin in his hand to study her face. "Overworking," he corrected.

"I ran out of real coffee in my AutoChef, had to drink that sewage they brew at Central. A couple of hits of the good stuff and I'll be fine."

"A couple of hours unconscious, you'll be better."

Though it was tempting, she didn't shove his hand away. "I've got a meeting at oh eight hundred. I have to prep."

"Eve." He shot her a warning glance when she hissed at him, then calmly laid his hands on her shoulders. "I'm not going to interfere with your work. But I will remind you that you won't do your job well if you're asleep on your feet."

"I can take a booster."

"You?" And he smiled when he said it, making her lips twitch.

"I may have to hit the departmental-approved drugs before it's over. He's not giving me any time, Roarke."

"Let me help."

"I can't use you every time it gets tough."

"Why?" His hands began to knead the tension out of her shoulders. "Because I'm not on the departmental-approved list?"

"That would be one." The shoulder massage was relaxing her a bit too much. She felt her mind drift, and wasn't able to snap it back to clarity again. "I'll take two hours downtime. Two hours to prep should be enough. But I'll crash in here."

"Good idea." It was simple enough to guide her to the sleep chair. Her bones were like rubber. He slipped down with her, ordered the chair to full recline.

"You should go to bed," she murmured, but turned her body into his.

"I prefer sleeping with my wife when the

opportunity arises."

"Two hours . . . I think I have an angle."

"Two hours," he agreed, and shut his eyes when he felt her go limp.

# CHAPTER EIGHT

"There's something I should tell you." Roarke waited until Eve scooped up the last of an egg-white omelette, and smiled at her as he topped off her coffee. "About the Natural Perfection beauty products."

She only stared at him as she swallowed. "You own the company."

"It's a line of a company that's part of an organization that's a branch of Roarke Industries." He smiled again as he sipped his coffee. "So, in a word, yes."

"I already knew it." She jerked a shoulder, gaining some satisfaction at seeing his eyebrows lift at her careless reaction. "I actually thought I might get through a case without you being connected."

"You really have to get over that, darling. And since I do own it," he continued as she bared her teeth at him, "I should be able to help you track the products used on the victims."

"We're stumbling along there on our own." She pushed away from the little table and paced to her desk. "Logically, the products were purchased at the location where the victims were chosen. Going on that assumption, I can whittle down the choices to a short list. Those enhancements are obscenely expensive."

"You get what you pay for," Roarke said easily.

"Lip dye at two hundred credits a tube for Christ's sake." She shot him a narrow-eyed glance. "You ought to be ashamed of yourself."

"I don't set the price." Now he grinned at her. "I just manage the profit."

A couple of hours of sleep and a hot meal had recharged her, he noted. She wasn't pale now, or quite so heavy-eyed. He rose, walking to her to skim his thumbs over the faint shadows under her eyes. "Would you like to sit in on a board meeting and lobby for a price adjustment?"

"Ha ha." When he brushed his lips over hers, she struggled to keep her own from curving. "Go away, I need to focus."

"In a minute." He kissed her again, nudging a sigh out of her. "Why don't you tell me about it? It'll help you to think out loud."

She sighed again, leaned for a moment, then drew back. "There's an ugliness to this because he's using something that symbolizes hope and innocence. This kid last night . . . damn it, he was harmless."

"The others were women. What does it tell you?"

"That he's bisexual. That his idea of true love crosses genders. The male victim was raped, just as the women were, bound like them, marked like them, and painted up like them after he'd finished."

She moved away, idly picking up her coffee to drink. "He's getting them from Personally Yours, obviously scanning their videos and personal data. He might have dated the women, but not Donnie Ray. Donnie was straight hetero. The shift makes me think he hasn't met any of the victims face-to-face, at least not in a romantic sense. It's all fantasy."

"He chooses people who live alone."

"He's a coward. Doesn't want any real confrontation. He tranqs them right off, gets them restrained. It's the only way he can be sure he'll have the power, the control."

Her thoughts veered back and settled once again on Rudy. Setting the coffee down again, she dragged a hand through her hair. "He's smart, and obsessive. He's even predictable on several levels. That's how I'll nail him."

"You said you had an angle."

"Yeah, a couple of them. I have to run them by the brass. I've got to dodge Nadine for a while. I can't give her the Santa suit. We'll have people whipping up on every store and street corner Santa in the city."

"There's an image," Roarke murmured. "Serial Santa Strangles Singles . . . Details at noon. Nadine would love that lead."

"She's not getting it. Not until I don't have a choice. I'm toying with leading the Personally Yours connection. It'll keep her off my back and get the word out to anyone who's used the service. And Rudy and Piper will scream harassment." Her smile spread slow and wicked. "It would be worth it. Couple of protocol droids — I need to shake them up."

"You don't like them."

"They give me the creeps. I know they're fucking each other. Sick."

"You don't approve?"

"They're brother and sister. Twins."

"Oh, I see." However worldly he was, Roarke found himself mirroring his wife's reaction. "That's very . . . unattractive."

"Yeah." The thought of it ruined her appetite and had her pushing the plate of flaky croissants aside. "He's running the show, and her. Right now, he's top of my list. He has access to every client file, and if I can confirm the incest, we add a bent toward deviant sexual behavior. I need someone inside." She drew a deep breath as she heard bootsteps marching down the hallway. "And there she is now."

Both Eve and Roarke turned as Peabody stepped into the doorway. She looked from one to the other, rolled her shoulders as if shrugging off something vaguely uncomfortable. "Something wrong?"

"No, come in." Eve jerked a thumb toward a chair. "Let's get started."

"Coffee?" Roarke offered. He'd already figured out what Eve had in mind for her aide.

"Yeah, thanks. McNab isn't here yet?"

"No. I'll brief you first." Eve shot Roarke a look, waited.

"I'll just get out of your way." He passed Peabody a cup, turned and kissed his wife despite — or perhaps because of — the fact that she scowled at him, then walked into his adjoining office and shut the door.

"Does he always look like that in the morning?" Peabody wanted to know.

"He always looks like that period."

Peabody sighed deeply. "Are you sure he's

human?"

"Not always." Eve angled a hip on the corner of her desk and studied Peabody carefully. "So . . . want to meet some guys?"

"Huh?"

"Want to broaden your social circle, meet some men who share similar interests?"

Certain Eve was joking, Peabody grinned. "Isn't that why I became a cop?"

"Cops make lousy life partners. What you need, Peabody, is a service like Personally Yours."

Sipping coffee, Peabody shook her head. "Nope. I did a dating service a few years back, right after I moved into the city. Too regimented. I like picking up strange men in bars." When Eve only continued to stare at her, Peabody slowly lowered her cup. "Oh," she said as realization struck. "Oh."

"I'd have to clear it with Whitney. I can't put a uniform undercover without the commander's okay. And before you agree, I want you to know just what you'd be getting into."

"Undercover." Despite the fact that she had been a cop long enough to know better, the phrase conjured up images of excitement and glamour.

"Get the stars out of your eyes, Peabody. Christ." Eve straightened, scooped both hands through her hair. "I'm talking about putting your ass on the line here, using you as bait, and you're grinning like I've just given you a present."

"You think I'm good enough for it. You trust me to handle it. That's a pretty good present."

"I think you're good enough," Eve said, dropping her arms. "I think you can handle it because you know how to follow orders, exactly. And that's what I'd expect. Following orders to the letter. No grandstanding. If I get it cleared, and if I can get the fucking budget to stretch enough for the consultant fee for that place, you'll go in."

"What about Rudy and Piper? They're not off the suspect list, and they've seen me."

"They saw a uniform. People like that don't pay attention to who's wearing it. We'll get Mavis and Trina to deck you out."

"Cool."

"Get a grip, Peabody. We'll work out a cover, an identity. I've gone over the victims' videos and personal data. We'll cull out the similarities and work them into your profile. The idea is to tailor make you."

"That's bullshit."

McNab stood in the doorway. His face was flushed with a fury that had his eyes glittering, his mouth tight, and his hands fisted at his side. "That's fucking bullshit."

"Detective," Eve said mildly. "Your opinion is noted."

"You're going to stick her like a worm on a line and drop her into the pool? Goddamn it, Dallas. She's not trained for undercover."

"Mind your own business," Peabody snapped as she lunged to her feet. "I know how to handle myself."

"You don't know squat about undercover." McNab strode forward, turning on his heel so that they were nose to nose. "You're a goddamn aide, a button pusher, next up from a droid."

Eve saw the intent flash in Peabody's eyes and managed to shove between them before her aide's fist plowed into McNab's nose. "That's enough. Your opinion is noted, Mc-Nab, now shut up."

"The son of a bitch isn't going to stand there and call me a droid and get away with it."

"Suck it in, Peabody," Eve warned, "and sit down. Both of you sit the hell down and try to remember who's in charge before I put the pair of you on report. The last thing I need on this case is a couple of hotheads. If you can't maintain, you're off."

"We don't need Detective Data Bank," Peabody muttered.

"We need what I say we need. And we need inside information and bait. Bait," she added, shifting her eyes from face to face, "of both sexes. You up for it, McNab?"

"Wait a minute. Wait." Peabody was out of her chair again, as rattled as Eve had ever seen her. "You want him to go under, too? With me?"

"Yeah, I'm up for it." McNab smiled thinly at Peabody as he agreed. It would be the perfect way to keep an eye on her — and keep her out of trouble.

"This is going to be mag!" Mavis Freestone danced around Eve's home office in thigh-high boots. The material was clear and snug, molding her legs and showing them off while she balanced on their three-inch glittery red heels. The heels matched the slither dress that barely met the top of the boots.

Her hair was the exact same glittery Christmas red and fell in Medusa-like coils to her shoulders. She had a tiny heart tattoo under the peak of her left eyebrow.

"You're on the departmental payroll." Eve knew the reminder that this was official business was wasted. But she felt obliged to get it in as Mavis beamed at Peabody out of newly toned grass-green eyes.

"Pays shit." This was from Trina. The

beauty consultant circled Peabody as a sculpture might with a flawed piece of marble — with interest, caution, and faint derision.

Trina was wearing eyebrow rings today, a fact that made Eve wince when she looked at the tiny gold hoops pinned to the outer line. Her hair, a deep plum purple, was slicked up in a foot-high cone. Her choice of outfit was a somewhat conservative black jumpsuit with the holiday touch of naked Santas dancing over each breast.

And this, Eve thought as she pressed her fingers to her eyes, this was the pair she'd convinced Whitney to budget into the case account.

"I want to keep it simple," she told them. "I just don't want her to look like a cop."

"What do you think, Trina?" Mavis leaned over Peabody's shoulder, pulling at her own curls so they lay over Peabody's cheeks. "This color'd rock on her. Festive, right? Holiday time. And wait till you see the wardrobe I got Leonardo to lend us." She bounced back, grinning. "There's this peekaboo skinsuit that's really you, Peabody."

"Skinsuit." Peabody paled, thinking of bulges. "Lieutenant."

"Simple," Eve said again, ready to desert

her aide.

"What do you use on your skin?" Trina demanded, taking a firm hold of Peabody's chin. "Sandpaper?"

"Um —"

"You got pores like moon craters here, girlfriend. You need a full facial treatment. I'm starting with a peeler."

"Oh God." Panicked, Peabody tried to jerk her chin free. "Listen —"

"Are those tits yours or enhanced?"

"Mine." Instantly, Peabody crossed her arms over her chest and grabbed her own breasts before Trina could. "They're mine. I'm really happy with them."

"They're good tits. Okay, strip. Let's have a look at them, and the rest of you."

"Strip?" Peabody swiveled her head until her terrified eyes latched onto Eve's. "Dallas, Lieutenant. Sir?"

"You said you could handle undercover, Peabody." After one sympathetic shudder, Eve turned and started out. "You've got two hours with her."

"I need three," Trina called out. "I don't rush my art."

"You got two." Firmly Eve shut the door on Peabody's shocked squeak.

It seemed best all around, Eve thought, if she stayed as far away from what was happening to her aide as possible. She decided to pay a visit to an old friend.

Charles Monroe was a licensed companion, as slick and attractive a prostitute as Eve had encountered, on or off the force. He'd once helped her with a case — and then offered her his services for free.

She'd taken the help, and politely refused the offer.

Now she pressed the buzzer outside his elegant apartment in a high-priced midtown building. A building Roarke owned, she thought with a roll of her eyes.

When the security beam blinked green, she lifted a brow, aiming a look at the peephole and holding up her badge in case Charles had forgotten her.

When he opened the door, he proved she needn't have worried about his memory. "Lieutenant Sugar." He caught her off guard with a strong hug and a quick, slightly too intimate kiss.

"Hands off, pal."

"I never got to kiss the bride." He winked at her, a sleepy-eyed, handsome man with an elegant face. "So how do you like being married to the richest man in the universe?"

"He keeps me in coffee."

Charles cocked his head, studied her. "You're in love with him, all the way. Well, good for you. I see the two of you on screen now and then. At some glitzy do. I wondered how it was with you. Now I see, and I have to assume you're not here to take me up on that offer I made some months back."

"I need to talk to you."

"Okay, come on in." He stepped back, gesturing. He wore a black unisuit that showed off a very well-disciplined body. "Want a drink? I doubt my blend of coffee compares to what Roarke can supply. How about a tube of Pepsi?"

"Yeah, fine."

She remembered his kitchen. Neat, spartan, clean lined. A great deal like its tenant. She took a seat while he took two tubes out of the cold box and poured each into a tall clear glass. He rolled the tubes, slipped them into the recycle slot, then sat down across from her.

"I'd drink to old times, Dallas, but . . . they sucked."

"Yeah. Well, I've got some new times for you, Charles. They suck, too. Why is a successful LC using a dating service? Before you answer," she continued, lifting her glass, "I'll inform you that using such services for professional solicitations is illegal."

He blushed. She wouldn't have believed it possible, but his strong, handsome face colored painfully and his gaze dropped to his glass. "Jesus, do you know everything?"

"If I knew everything, I'd know the answer. Why don't you give it to me?"

"It's private," he muttered.

"I wouldn't be here if it was. Why have you gone to Personally Yours for consults?"

"Because I want a woman in my life," he snapped. His head came up, and now his eyes were dark and angry. "A real woman, not one who buys me, all right? I want a goddamn relationship, what's wrong with that? In my line of work, they don't happen. You do what you're paid to do, and you do it well. I like my job, but I want a personal life. There's nothing illegal about wanting a personal life."

"No," she said slowly, "there's not."

"So I lied about what I do on the form." He moved his shoulders restlessly. "I didn't want to match up with the kind of woman who'd get some prurient thrill out of dating an LC. You going to arrest me for lying on a fucking dating video?"

"No." And she was sorry, sincerely, to have embarrassed him. "You matched up with a woman. Marianna Hawley. Do you remember her?"

"Marianna." He struggled to regain his composure, drank deeply of the iced drink.

"I remember her video. Pretty woman, sweet. I contacted her, but she'd already met someone." Now he smiled, shrugged again. "Just my luck. She was exactly the type I was looking for."

"You never met her?"

"No. I went out with the other four from my first match list. Hit it off with one of them. We saw each other off and on for a few weeks." He blew out a breath. "I decided if it was going to go anywhere, I had to tell her what I really did. And that," he finished, toasting Eve with his glass, "was the end of that."

"I'm sorry."

"Hey, there are more where she came from." But his cocky smile didn't reach his eyes. "Too bad Roarke took you out of the running."

"Charles, Marianna is dead."

"What?"

"Haven't you caught the news lately?"

"No. I haven't been watching any screen. Dead?" Then his eyes sharpened, focused in on Eve. "Murdered. You wouldn't be here if she'd died quietly in her sleep. She was murdered. Am I a suspect?"

"Yeah, you are," she said because she liked him enough to be straight with him. "I'm going to want to do a formal interview, just to keep it all official. But tell me now, can you clear yourself for last Tuesday night, for Wednesday, and for last night?"

He stared at her for a long time, just stared with eyes dull with horror. "How do you do what you do?" he demanded. "Day in and day out?"

She met those eyes levelly. "I could ask you the same thing, Charles. So let's not get into career choices. Can you alibi?"

He broke the stare, pushed away from the table. "I'll get my book."

She let him go, knowing she could trust her gut on this one. He wasn't a man who had murder inside him.

He came back carrying a small, elegant date book. Opening it, he plugged in the dates she'd asked for. "Tuesday, I had an overnight. Regular client. It can be verified. Last night I had a theater, late supper, and seduction here. The client left at two-thirty a.m. Got thirty minutes overtime out of it. And a handsome tip. Wednesday I was home, alone."

He slid the book across the table to her. "Take the names, check it out."

She said nothing, merely copied the names and addresses into her own book. "Sarabeth Greenbalm, Donnie Ray Michael," she said at length. "Either ring for you?"

"No."

She looked at him then, steadily. "I've never seen you use enhancements. Why did you purchase lip dye and eye smudger from the Natural Perfection line at All Things Beautiful?"

"Lip dye?" He looked blank for a moment, then shook his head. "Oh, I picked them up for the woman I was seeing. She asked me to get her a couple of things since I was going into the salon for the styling that came with my package."

Obviously confused, he smiled a little. "And why, Lieutenant Sugar, should you care if I buy lip dye?"

"Just another detail, Charles. You did me a favor once, so I'm doing you one. Three people who used the services of Personally Yours are dead, killed in the same manner and by the same hand."

"Three? God."

"In less than a week. I'm not going to give you many details, and what I do give can't be passed on to anyone. It's my opinion that he's using the data from Personally Yours to select his victims."

"He's killed three women in less than a week."

"No." Eve leveled her gaze. "The last victim was a man. You're going to want to watch your step, Charles."

When he understood, the edge of resentment faded. "You think I could be a target?"

"I think anyone in the Personally Yours data bank could be a target. At this point I'm concentrating on the victims' match list. I'm telling you not to let anyone in your apartment you don't know. Anyone." She drew another breath. "He dresses up like Santa Claus and carries a large gift-wrapped box."

"What?" He set down the glass he'd just lifted. "Is this a joke?"

"Three people are dead. It's not very funny. He gets them to let him inside, he drugs them, restrains them, and he kills them."

"Jesus." He rubbed his hands over his face. "This is bizarre."

"If this guy comes to your door, keep it secured and call me. Stall him if you can, let him go if you can't. Don't, under any circumstances, open your door. He's smart, and he's deadly."

"I won't be opening the door. The woman I was seeing — from the service — I need to tell her."

"I've got your match list. I'll tell her. I need to keep this out of the media as long as I can."

"I'd rather the press didn't get ahold of the story of the lonely-hearts LC, thanks very much." He grimaced. "Can you get to her right away, to Darla McMullen? She lives alone, and she's . . . naive. If Santa came knocking, she'd open the door and offer him milk and cookies."

"She sounds like a nice woman."

"Yeah." Now his eyes were bleak. "She is."

"I'll go see her." Eve rose. "Maybe you ought to call her again."

"No good." He rose and worked up a smile. "But you be sure to let me know if you decide to ditch Roarke, Lieutenant Sugar. My offer's open-ended."

The heart, Eve thought as she drove, was a strange and often overworked muscle. It was hard to connect the sophisticated, smooth-talking LC with the quiet, intellectual woman she'd just left. But, unless her instincts were way off, Darla McMullen and Charles Monroe were halfway in love.

They just didn't know what to do about it.

On that score, they had her full sympathy. Half the time, she didn't know what to do about the impossible feelings she had for her own husband.

She made three more stops on the way

back to her home office, doing interviews with people on the match lists, giving them the basic and specific warning and instructions she had written up and had approved by the commander.

If Donnie Ray had been warned, she thought, he might still be alive.

Who was next in line? Someone she'd spoken with, or someone she'd missed? Driven by that, she accelerated and blew through the gates toward home. She wanted Peabody and McNab to sign up with Personally Yours and get their profiles in before the end of the business day.

She saw Feeney's vehicle parked in front of the house. The sight made her hope her campaign to add him to the investigative team had been successful. With Feeney and McNab doing the e-work, she'd be freed up for the streets.

She headed straight up to her home office, wincing when she heard the blast of music — if it could be called music — searing the air of the hallways.

Mavis had one of her video clips on screen. She sang along with herself, screaming out lyrics that seemed to have something to do with ripping out her soul for love. Feeney sat behind Eve's desk, looking bemused and slightly desperate. Roarke stood behind a chair, looking completely comfortable and politely attentive.

Knowing her chances of being heard over the din were nil, Eve waited until the last notes clashed out and Mavis, flushed with effort and pleasure, giggled and took her bows.

"I wanted you to see the rough cut right away," she said to Roarke.

"It looks like a winner."

"Really?" Obviously delighted, Mavis rushed him, threw her arms around his neck, and squeezed. "I just can't believe it's really happening. Me, cutting a disc for the top recording company on the planet."

"You're going to make me lots of money." He kissed her forehead.

"I want it to work. I really want it to work." When she spotted Eve, Mavis grinned. "Hey! Did you catch any of the cut?"

"The tail end. It was great." And because it was Mavis, she meant it. "Feeney, are you on?"

"Officially assigned." He leaned back in her chair. "McNab's doing his prelim consult at Personally Yours. We profiled him as a computer droid for one of Roarke's companies. His data's been inputted, and his new ID is in place."

"Roarke's company?"

"Seemed logical." Feeney grinned at her. "You got weight, you use it. Appreciate your help, boy-o."

"Anytime," Roarke told him, then smiled at his wife. "We cut a few corners as you're in a bit of a hurry. Peabody's profiled as a security guard at one of my buildings. Feeney thought it would be simplest to keep the profiles somewhat in line with truth."

"Oh yeah, let's keep it simple." But blowing out a breath, she nodded. "Good enough. You own half the damn city anyway, and nobody's going to question it, or find any holes in your personnel files if you had your hand in it."

"Exactly."

"Where's Peabody?"

"Trina's just finishing her."

"I need her now. She's got to get over here and put in her app, get the consult going. She looked okay, for God's sake. How long does it take to primp her up and put some street clothes on her?"

"Trina had some mag ideas," Mavis assured her with such enthusiasm Eve's blood chilled. "Wait till you see. Oh yeah, Trina wants you to plug in a session before your party. She wants to glam you some for it, since it's the holidays."

Eve merely grunted. She had no intention of being glammed — now or ever.

"Sure, right. Where the hell . . ." Her voice trailed off as she heard them coming. She turned toward the doorway and blinked. Gaped.

"I have to say," Trina announced, "I'm good."

Peabody snorted, flushed, then smiled hesitantly. "Okay, so do you think I'll pass the audition?"

Her bowl-cut hair had been sheened and fluffed into a dark halo. Her face glowed with deep color smudged around her eyes to accent their shape and size, and her lips were dyed a soft coral pink.

Her body, which appeared so sturdy in a uniform, took on lusher, more feminine curves in a sweeping ankle duster of deep pine green. A tangle of chains in jewel hues were draped around her neck. Peeking out between the layers was a small, wistful tattoo of a gold-winged fairy.

Peabody had selected the tattoo herself after Trina had caught her up in the spirit of things. She hadn't flinched when the quick, capable hands had cupped her left breast to apply the temp. By that time she'd begun to enjoy the sensation of being re-made.

But now, as Eve stared at her, Peabody began to shift her feet — they were clad in toothpick heels that matched the wings of her mystical tattoo. "It doesn't work?"

"You sure as hell don't look like a cop," Eve decided.

"You look beautiful." Amused by his wife's reaction, Roarke stepped forward and took both of Peabody's hands. "Absolutely delicious." So saying, he kissed her fingers and had Peabody's susceptible heart stuttering.

"Yeah, really? Wow."

"Get over it, Peabody. Feeney, you've got twenty minutes to brief her on her profile. Peabody, where's your stunner, your communicator?"

"Here." Still flushed, she slipped a hand into a hidden pocket in the hip of the dress. "Handy, huh?"

"It's not going to replace uniforms," Eve said, then pointed to a chair. "You need to commit the data Feeney's going to give you to memory. Record it. You can replay it on the drive over. We can't afford any slipups. I want you in by end of day, and on match lists by tomorrow."

"Yes, sir." But Peabody fingered the material of the dress lovingly as she walked over to sit with Feeney.

"You're next," Trina said, running a quick,

assessing hand through Eve's hair.

"I don't have time for a treatment." Eve backed up. "Besides, you just did me a few weeks ago."

"You don't get regular treatments, you ruin my work. She makes time before the party, or I'm not responsible for how she looks," Trina warned Roarke.

"She'll make time." And to placate her, he took her arm, steering her out as he praised her brilliance with Peabody.

# CHAPTER NINE

Finding Nadine Furst lazily filing her nails at Eve's desk wasn't the welcome Eve was looking for when she arrived at Cop Central.

"Get your butt out of my chair."

Nadine merely smiled sweetly, tucked her nail file away in her enormous calf-colored bag, and uncrossed her smooth legs. "Hello, Dallas. So good to see you. Doing a lot of work out of your home office these days? I can't blame you." As she rose, Nadine skimmed her sharp cat's eyes over the cramped, dingy, dusty room. "This place is a dump."

Saying nothing, Eve marched directly to her computer, checked the last log-on time, then did the same with her 'link.

"I didn't touch anything." Nadine added just enough insult to her voice for Eve to be sure the reporter had considered it.

"I'm busy, Nadine. I don't have time for the media. Go chase an MT van or harass one of the droids in Booking."

"You might want to make time." Still smiling, Nadine moved to the only other chair in the office and daintily crossed her legs again. "Unless you want me to go on an air with what I've got."

Eve jerked a shoulder — and found that her muscles had tensed as she sat — stretched out her own denim-covered legs, and crossed her battered boots at the ankles. "What you got, Nadine?"

"Singles seeking romance find violent death. Personally Yours: dating service or death list? Ace homicide lieutenant, Eve Dallas, investigating."

Nadine watched Eve's face as she spoke. She gave Eve full points — her eyes didn't flicker — but Nadine was gut sure she had her full attention.

"You want me to go on with a no comment from the investigating officer on that lead?"

"The investigation is proceeding. A task force has been formed. The NYPSD is pursuing all leads."

Nadine leaned forward, slipping a hand into her bag to turn on her recorder. "Then you confirm that the murders are connected."

"I'm not confirming anything with your

recorder on."

Irritation flickered over Nadine's pretty, triangular face. "Give me a break here."

"You turn that recorder off, put it here on my desk in plain view, or I'll give you a break. I'll confiscate it and anything else you have in that suitcase you're hauling around. Recording devises aren't permitted in official areas of Cop Central without authorization."

"Christ, you're strict." Annoyed, Nadine took out her mini, plunked it on the desk, then set her bag aside. "Off the record?"

"Off the record." Because Nadine had said the words, Eve nodded. Nadine could be irritating, tenacious, and a general pain in the ass, but she had integrity. There was no need to search the bag for another recorder.

"The homicides under my investigation were committed by the same person. Personally Yours appears to be the source of the victims. You can go on air with that."

"The dating service." All traces of annoyance faded as Nadine smiled. Eve's subtle hint had nudged her into research on every dating service in the city. She would be able to plug in the correct data and flesh out her report with the flick of a couple of buttons.

"That's right."

"What can you give me on it?"

"Most of my notes are on my office unit." But Nadine pulled out her PPC and called up data. "You have all the standard already: owners, length of time in business, requirements. They do some pricey ads on our station. Shelled out . . . a cool two mil last year on screen ads. Our credit checks showed they can afford it, that's less than ten percent of their gross."

"Romance is profitable."

"Damn right. I did an informal poll at the station. About fifteen percent of the talent and crew have used services. Informing the public takes a toll on the personal life," she added lightly.

"Anybody you like use Personally Yours?"

"Probably." Nadine cocked her head. "I like a lot of people, being the friendly, sociable sort. Should I be worried about them?"

"All three victims used the dating service, two knew each other casually through it. As yet, we've found no other connection among them."

"So . . . your guy's trolling for lonely hearts." And that was a hell of a lead, Nadine decided, already running copy in her head.

"We suspect that Personally Yours is his source." Eve wanted that one element hammered in. She didn't intend to give Nadine much more. "The task force, formed today, is pursuing all avenues of investigation."

"Leads?"

"Are being checked out. I'm not giving you specifics on this, Nadine."

"Suspects?" Nadine said doggedly.

"Interviews are under way."

"Motive?"

Eve considered a moment. "They're sexual homicides."

"Ah. Well, that would fit. You got a bisexual killer? One of the victims was male, two were female."

"I can't confirm or deny the killer's sexual preferences." She thought of Donnie Ray, and guilt scraped along her stomach. "The victims have admitted the killer into their homes. There was no sign of forced entry in any case."

"They opened the door to him? They knew him?"

"They thought they did. You can advise your viewing audience to think twice before opening their door to anyone they don't know on a personal level. I can't give you any more without compromising the investigation."

"He's killed three times in less than a week. He's in a hurry."

"He has a program," Eve said. "That's not for on air. He has a schedule, a pattern, and that's how we'll get him."

"Give me a quick one-on-one remote, Dallas. I can have a camera in here in ten minutes."

"No. Not yet," she added before Nadine could bitch about it. "You've got more than I've given anyone. Take it and be grateful. I'll give you a one-on-one if and when I can. I'd be more inclined if, after you corner Piper and Rudy, you tell me what you get."

Nadine arched a brow. "Quid pro quo. Fine. I'm heading over there now. Once I —" She broke off, her mouth dropping open as Peabody rushed in the door.

"Dallas, you wouldn't believe — Hi, Nadine."

"Is that you, Peabody?"

Though Peabody struggled to maintain a casual air, her lips twitched up in a smile. "Yeah, I just had a little work done."

"A little. You look fabulous. Is that one of Leonardo's designs? It's just absolutely mag." She was up, circling Peabody.

"Yeah, it's one of his. It really works on me, doesn't it?"

"Peabody, you rock." Laughing, Nadine stepped back. Then her smile began to sharpen; her eyes narrowed. "You let your aide play dress-up in the middle of a murder investigation?" Nadine began, turning to Eve. "I don't think so. I'd say what we have here is a very slick undercover scam. Trying the wonders of computer dating, Peabody?"

"Close the door, Peabody." At Eve's flat command, Peabody inched in and shut the door at her back. "Nadine, if you leak this, I'll cut you off. I'll see to it that there isn't a cop here at Central who gives you the day of the week much less a story lead. Then I'll get nasty."

Nadine's fox-sly smile faded. Her eyes went dark and dull. "You think I'd fuck with your investigation? You think I'd go on with data that could put Peabody in a jam? Go to hell, Dallas." She scooped up her bag and swung toward the door. But Eve was quicker.

"I put her ass on the line." Furious with herself, Eve yanked the purse out of Nadine's hands and tossed it. "I made the call, and if anything goes wrong, it's on me."

"Dallas —"

"Shut up," she snapped at Peabody. "If it hurts your feelings to know just how far I'd go to protect her cover and this case, that's too damn bad."

"Okay." Nadine took a deep breath and reeled in her own temper. It was a rare thing for her to detect even a shadow of fear in Eve's eyes. "Okay," she repeated. "But you should remember Peabody's a friend of mine. And so are you."

She bent down to pick up her bag, shouldered it. "Nice hair, Peabody," she said before she opened the door and walked out.

"Fuck" was all Eve could think to say. Turning, she stepped to the stingy window and stared out at miserable air traffic.

"I can handle this, Dallas."

Eve stared at an airbus that blatted fiercely at an advertising blimp in its airspace. "I wouldn't have put you on if I didn't think you could handle it. But the fact remains I'm the one who put you on. And you've got no undercover experience."

"You're giving me a chance to get some. I want to make detective. I won't get the grade without undercover work on my record. You know that."

"Yeah." Eve stuck her hands in her back pockets. "I know that."

"Uh . . . I know my ass is a little bigger than it ought to be — even though I'm working out — but I know how to cover it."

With a half laugh, Eve turned back. "Your ass is fine, Peabody. Why don't you sit on it and give me your report?"

"It went great." Grinning now, Peabody

211

dropped into a chair. "I mean frigid. They didn't have a clue I was a cop, that I'd been in there just a couple days ago. I got the royal treatment." She fluttered her newly darkened and lengthened lashes.

Eve cocked her head. "If you've got that out of your system, Officer, I'd like your report."

"Sir." Peabody straightened in the chair, sobered. "As ordered, I reported to the subject location, requested a consult. After a brief interview I was escorted to a lounge where Piper continued the interview personally. The data I offered was logged on her personal palm computer. I was offered refreshment." A quick flicker of amusement lighted in her eyes. "I accepted, believing this to be in character. Dallas, they have hot chocolate. I mean the genuine stuff, and sugar cookies. Christmas style. I ate three reindeer before I got ahold of myself."

"Keep that up and you'll need a tarp to cover your ass."

"Yeah." But Peabody sighed in memory. "I indicated that I wanted to proceed immediately. Gave her a line about not wanting to be alone during the holidays. She was very sympathetic, personable. I can see why people who go in there trust her to fix them up. She wanted to pass me off to a consultant, but I balked. Said how I was so comfortable with her, and that this process was somewhat embarrassing for me. I offered to pay more, if necessary, to have her stick with me."

"Good thinking."

"She was sweet about it. Patted my hand. She walked me through the video herself, even coached me a little. Rudy came into it toward the end because she had a meeting to go to. He didn't make me either. He flirted with me."

"In what way?"

"In an automatic way. It was just part of the job, if you ask me. Approving smiles, compliments, hand holding. He is way not my type," she added, "but I played along. He offered me more hot chocolate, but I managed to resist. I also got a tour of the place, was shown a club area they have where matches can meet if they feel awkward about making the connection outside. Very tasteful, leaning toward elegant. They've got a small coffee shop, too, for the same purposes. That's casual. There were several couples linking up in there." She wrinkled her nose. "I saw McNab getting the run-through, too."

"Then we're in, and on schedule. What about your match list?"

"I can go in tomorrow morning. They prefer you come in person rather than arranging for a transmission on a first go. They screened me in about an hour. Roarke's new data held up, and from what I could see, they really dig. If I was going into this for real, I'd feel safe."

"Okay, you get the match list, go through the routine. But you set up meets outside." She considered a moment. "We'll use one of Roarke's places — medium-sized club or bar. We'll put a couple cops on the inside. I'll need to stay out. If Rudy or Piper are in on this, they'd make me. We'll get a surveillance vehicle. I want you to set up at least two, try for three, of the meets tomorrow night. We can't sit on this."

She glanced at her wrist unit, tapped her fingers. "Let's find an empty conference room. I need to pull in McNab and Feeney for an update. I want this to go smooth."

"If McNab starts on me, I'm flattening him."

"Wait till the case is closed," Eve advised. "Then flatten him."

She could see the lights from the end of the long drive the minute she was through the gates. At first, Eve wondered if the house was on fire, they were so bright and bril-

214

liant. As she sped closer, she saw the outline of a tree in the wide window of the front parlor. It was alive with white light, shimmering and glowing, sparking like little flames off the branches ladened with shiny globes of red or green.

Dazzled, she parked her car and jogged up the steps. Heading straight for the parlor, she stopped under the archway and stared. The tree had to be twenty feet high, at least four feet across. Miles of silver garland were artfully draped to set off the hundreds of colored balls. Atop, nearly brushing the ceiling, was a crystal star, each point pulsing with light. Beneath was a blanket of white that stood in for snow. She couldn't begin to count the elegantly wrapped gifts stacked there.

"Jesus, Roarke."

"Pretty, isn't it?"

He came in silently behind her, made her jolt before she turned to shake her head at him. "Where the hell did you get it?"

"Oregon. It has a treated root ball. We'll donate it to a park after the New Year." He slipped an arm around her waist. "Them, I should say."

"Them? You have more of these?"

"There's one a bit bigger than this in the ballroom."

"Bigger?" she managed.

"Another in Summerset's quarters, and the one in our bedroom. I thought we'd trim that one tonight."

"It'll take days to trim one of these."

"It only took the crew I hired four hours to do this one." And he laughed. "Ours is more manageable." He turned his head to brush his lips over her forehead. "I need to share this with you."

"I don't know how to do any of this."

"We'll figure it out."

She looked back at the tree and couldn't for the life of her determine why it made her nervous. "I've got work," she began, and would have stepped away. But he shifted, laid his hands on her shoulders, and waited for her eyes to meet his.

"I don't intend to interfere with your work, Eve, but we're entitled to a life. Our life. I want an evening with my wife."

Her brows came together. "You know I hate it when you say 'my wife' in that tone."

"Why do you think I do it?" He laughed when she tried to shrug his hands away. "I've got you, Lieutenant, and I'm keeping you." Knowing how quickly she could counter a move, he scooped her off her feet. "Get used to it," he advised.

"You're going to piss me off."

"Good, then we'll have sex first. It's such an adventure to make love with you when you're annoyed with me."

"I don't want to have sex." She might have, she thought irritably, if he wasn't so damn smug about it.

"Ah, a challenge and an adventure. It just gets better."

"Put me down, you jackass, or I'll have to hurt you."

"And now threats. I'm definitely getting excited."

She refused to laugh. And when he stepped into the bedroom, she was braced and ready for a bout. Later, she would think Roarke knew her thought process entirely too well.

He dropped her on the bed, then dived onto her before she could shift into offensive mode. With one hand he handcuffed her wrists and drew her hands over her head.

She shot him one hot, narrow-eyed look. "I won't go down easy, pal."

"God, I hope not."

She scissored her legs, clamped them around his waist, and managed to buck until they rolled. Galahad, who'd been enjoying a nap on the pillow, gave one ferocious hiss and leaped off.

"Now you've done it." Eve grunted as he

rolled on top of her again. "You annoyed the cat."

"Let him find his own woman," Roarke muttered, then crushed his mouth to Eve's.

He felt the pulses in her wrists give two quick, hard bumps, felt the head-to-toe shudder her body gave beneath his, but she didn't yield, wasn't ready to, he thought. There were times, he knew, Eve liked a hot, fast war.

By God, he was in the mood for one himself.

He bit her bottom lip, triumphing on the moan she couldn't quite swallow. With his free hand he released her weapon harness, tugged it down her shoulder. Then, because he could, because heat was already pouring off her in waves, he hooked a hand in the opening of her skirt and ripped it down the center.

Now her body strained toward his, demanding, daring, even as she twisted under him in an attempt to evade or take control.

"Christ, I want you. It's never enough." His mouth clamped onto her breast.

No, never enough, was her last clear thought. She cried out, her strong body bowing up as those fierce pulls and tugs on her breast vibrated through her like wild music set to a furious beat.

Heat seemed to roar from her center out.

Freed, her hands dragged at his shirt, ripping at the silk until she found flesh with her fingers, with her mouth, with her teeth.

Rolling again, they yanked at clothes, tormented skin with greedy nips and bruising strokes. When she reached for him, closed her fist around him, he was iron hard and smooth as satin.

"Now, now, now." She arched her hips, and came violently the instant he drove into her.

He held there, buried deep, panting as he blinked his vision clear to look at her. The fire that blazed in the hearth across the room shot flashes of light and shadow over her face, glinted into her hair, flickered in her eyes, which had gone dark and blind with what they brought to each other.

"It's me who has you." He drew back, thrust again. "Always." He shifted, lifted her hips with his hands. "Go up again," he demanded and began to destroy her with long, hard strokes.

She fisted her hands in the bedclothes as if to anchor herself. In the firelight she could see him over her, dark hair gleaming, eyes too blue to be real, muscles sleek, skin pale gold and dewed with sweat.

Need rose like a flood, and pleasure

swamped her. Her vision blurred, turning him into a shadow, gilded at the edges. She heard herself choke out his name as her body shattered.

"And again." He lowered himself, taking her mouth with his, linking his fingers with hers, pounding his body into hers. "Again," he managed, as his blood rioted. "With me."

And it was "Eve" he said, just "Eve," when he emptied himself into her.

She lost track of time as she lay under him, firelight dancing on the ceiling. She wondered vaguely if it could be normal to need someone this much, to love to the point of pain.

Then he turned his head, his hair brushing her cheek, his lips brushing her throat. And she wondered why she should care.

"I hope you're satisfied." Her mutter wasn't as snippy as she'd hoped it would be, and she caught herself stroking a hand down his back.

"Mmmm. I seem to be." He nuzzled her throat again before lifting his head and looking down at her. "It seems to be mutual."

"I let you win."

"Oh, I know."

The twinkle in his eyes had her snorting. "Get off me, you're heavy."

"Okay." He obliged, then scooped her up again. "Let's take a shower, then we can do the tree."

"Just what is this obsession you have with trees?"

"I haven't decorated one in years — not since Dublin when I lived with Summerset. I want to see if I can still do it." He stepped into the shower with her, and she clamped a hand over his mouth, knowing his baffling preference for cold showers.

"Water on, at one hundred degrees."

"Too hot," he mumbled against her hand.

"Live with it." And she sighed long and deep when the hot water began to pulse out from all directions. "Oh yeah, this is good."

Fifteen minutes later she stepped out of the drying tube with her muscles warmed and limber, her mind clear and alert.

Roarke toweled off — another of his habits she couldn't understand. Why waste time rubbing yourself with cotton when a quick spin in the drying tube took care of it? She was reaching for her robe when she noticed it wasn't the one she'd left hanging there that morning.

"What's this?" She took down the long flow of scarlet.

"Cashmere. You'll like it."

"You've bought me a million robes. I don't

see . . ." But her voice trailed off as she slipped it on. "Oh." She hated it when she lost herself in something as shallow as textures. But this was soft as a cloud, warm as a hug. "It's pretty nice."

He grinned, belting a black robe in the same material. "Suits you. Come on, you can fill me in on the case while I tackle the lights."

"Peabody and McNab are in. They'll have their match lists by tomorrow." She wandered back into the bedroom, and spotted the silver bucket with champagne; a silver tray with canapés was waiting. What the hell, she decided, and stuffed something glorious into her mouth as she poured two flutes. "Your covers for them passed screening."

"Of course." From a large box, Roarke took a long string of tiny lights.

"Don't get cocky, we've got a long way to go. Nadine was in my office when I got to Central," Eve added, and set Roarke's champagne on the table by the bed. "She got a load of Peabody so I had to fill her in more than I wanted. Off the record."

"Nadine is one of those rare reporters you can trust." Roarke studied the tree, the lights, and decided to dive straight in. "She won't leak sensitive data."

"Yeah, I know. We got into that a bit." Frowning, Eve circled the tree while Roarke worked. She had no idea if he knew what he was doing. "If Piper and Rudy hadn't seen me, I'd have done the inside work myself."

Roarke lifted an eyebrow as he secured the first string and took out another. "I might have some mild objection to my wife dating strange men."

She went back to the tray, took another pretty canapé at random. "I wouldn't have slept with any of them . . . unless the job called for it." She grinned at him. "And I would have thought of you the whole time."

"It wouldn't have taken very long — since I'd have cut off his balls and handed them to you."

He kept stringing lights as she choked on her wine. "Jesus, Roarke, I'm only kidding."

"Mmm-hmm. Me, too, darling. Hand me another string of these."

Not at all sure of him, Eve pulled out another string of lights. "How many of these are you going to use?"

"As many as it takes."

"Yeah." She blew out a breath. "What I meant — before — was I've done under-cover before, Peabody's green."

"Peabody's had good training. You should

trust her. And yourself."

"McNab's still kicking about it."

"He's smitten with her."

"He really — What?"

"He's smitten with her." Roarke stepped back, pursed his lips. "Tree lights on," he ordered, then nodded, satisfied as the tiny diamond points blinked on. "Yes, that'll do it."

"What do you mean, smitten? Like he's got a case on her? McNab? No way."

"He's not sure he likes her, but he's attracted." Wanting to see his work from another angle, Roarke walked over, picked up his wine, and sipped as he studied. "Ornaments, next."

"He irritates the hell out of her."

"I believe you felt the same way about me initially." He toasted his wife in the glow of tree and fire lights. "And look where we ended up."

Eve stared at him for a full ten seconds, then sat heavily on the side of the bed. "Oh Christ, this is perfect. This is just perfect. I can't have the two of them working together like this if there's a thing there. Annoyance I can deal with; sexual shit, no way."

"Sometimes you have to let your children go, darling." He opened another box, chose an antique porcelain angel. "You put the first one on. It'll be our little tradition."

Eve stared at it. "If anything happens to her —"

"You won't let anything happen to her."

"No." She let out a breath, and rose. "No, I won't. I'm going to need your help."

He reached out, stroked a fingertip over the shallow dent in her chin. "You have it."

She turned, picked her branch, and hung the angel. "I love you. I guess that's turning out to be our little tradition, too."

"It's my favorite."

Late, very late, when the tree lights were off and the fire burned low, she lay awake. Was he out there, now? Would her 'link beep, announcing another body, another soul lost because she was too many steps behind?

Whom did he love now?

# CHAPTER TEN

The snow started to spit out of the sky at dawn. No pretty postcard snow, but thin, mean needles that hissed nastily as they hit pavement. By the time Eve settled in her office at Cop Central, there was a slick layer of ugly gray over the city streets, sidewalks, and glides that would certainly keep the MTs and traffic cops busy.

Outside her window, two weather copters from rival channels dueled in a war to pass the bad news to viewers and report on the latest fender bender or pedestrian spill.

All they had to do, Eve thought bad-temperedly, was open their own fucking doors and see for themselves.

It was going to be a lousy day.

Keeping her back to the arrow-slit view of her window, she fed data into her computer with little hope that she'd get a decent probability match.

"Computer, probability program. Using

known data, analyze and compute. List in order of probability which names most likely to be targeted by True Love killer."

*Working . . .*

"Yeah, you do that," she muttered. While her machine whined and clunked, she took copies of photos confiscated from Personally Yours and, rising, fixed them to a board over her desk.

Marianna Hawley, Sarabeth Greenbalm, Donnie Ray Michael. Faces smiling hopefully. Putting their best side forward. The lonely, looking for love.

The desk clerk, the stripper, and the sax blower. Different lifestyles, different goals, different needs. What else did they have in common? What was she missing that linked them all to a killer?

What did he see when he looked at them that attracted and enraged? Ordinary people, living ordinary lives.

*Probability percentages even for all subjects.*

Eve glanced over at her machine and snarled. "The hell with that. There has to be something."

*Insufficient data for further analysis. Current pattern is random.*

"How the hell am I supposed to protect two thousand people, for Christ's sake?" She closed her eyes, reeled in her temper.

"Computer, eliminate all subjects who live with a companion or family member. Recalibrate remaining."

*Working . . . Task complete.*

"Okay." Rubbing her fingers over her eyes, she nodded. All three victims had been white, she thought. "Eliminate all subjects not Caucasian. Recalibrate remaining."

*Working . . . Task complete.*

"Number remaining?"

*Six hundred twenty-four subjects remaining . . .*

"Shit." She turned back to study the photos. "Eliminate all subjects over the age of forty-five and under the age of twenty-one."

*Working . . . Task complete.*

"Okay, all right." She began to pace as she thought it through. Grabbing her hard-copy file, she pushed through paperwork. "First-timers," she muttered. "They were all first-timers. Eliminate all subjects with repeated consults from Personally Yours. Recalibrate remaining."

*Working . . .*

This time the machine bogged and rattled. Eve gave it an impatient smack with the heel of her hand.

"Piece of shit," she muttered, and set her teeth as the machine whined again.

*Task . . . complete.*

"Don't you start stuttering on me. Number remaining?"

*Two hundred six names remaining.*

"Better. Much better. Print amended list."

While her machine chewed and spit out data, Eve turned to her 'link and contacted EDD. "Feeney, I've got just over two hundred names. I need them checked out. Can you run them? See how many have left the city, how many got themselves matched or married, died in their sleep, are on vacation at Planet Disney?"

"Shoot them over."

"Thanks." She glanced up as she heard a stream of whistles and catcalls from the detective's bull pen. "It's a priority," she told him and logged off just as a flushed and flustered Peabody walked in.

"Jesus, you'd think those morons hadn't seen me out of uniform before. Henderson offered to leave his wife and kids for a weekend with me in Barbados."

But, from the gleam in her eye, Peabody didn't appear to be too displeased by the reaction.

Eve frowned. Her aide's face was painted and polished, her hair fluffed. Her legs were showcased in a short, snug skirt and stiletto-heeled boots, both the color of ripe raspberries.

"How the hell do you walk in that getup?" Eve wanted to know.

"I practiced."

Eve inhaled deeply, then blew out air. "Sit down, let's go over the plan."

"Okay, but it takes me a couple of minutes to get down in this skirt." Cautious, Peabody braced a hand on the edge of the desk and began to lower her butt.

"You going to do squats or sit the hell down?"

"Just a second." She sucked in air, winced a little. "Little tight in the waist," she managed as she eased down.

"You should have thought of your internal organs before you poured yourself into that thing. You've got an hour before you're due at Personally Yours. I want you to —"

"What the hell are you doing in that?" McNab stopped at the doorway, his eyes bugged out as they skimmed along Peabody's legs.

"My job," she said with a sniff.

"You're just asking to get hit on. Dallas, make her wear something else."

"I'm not a fashion consultant, McNab. And if I were" — Eve took the time to study his baggy red and white striped trousers and

230

butter-yellow turtleneck — "I might have something to say about your wardrobe choices."

At Peabody's snicker, Eve narrowed her eyes. "Now, children, you may be aware that we're working multiple homicides at this time. If you can't be friends, I'm afraid I'll have to limit your playground time this afternoon."

Peabody immediately squared her shoulders, and though she slid a sneering look toward McNab, she was wise enough to say nothing.

"Peabody, I want you to convince Piper to stick with you through the consult. McNab, you take Rudy. Once you have the match lists, you'll browse through the retail areas. Make yourselves obvious."

"Do we have a budget for purchases?" McNab wanted to know, and at Eve's bland stare, he shrugged and dipped his hands into the wide pockets of his trousers. "It'd make more of an impression if we bought some things. Chatted up the clerks."

"You've got two hundred credits apiece departmental funds. Anything over, it's your worry. McNab, we know Donnie Ray used the salon to buy enhancements for his mother. Make sure you spend time there."

"He could use a month," Peabody said

under her breath, then folded her lips innocently when Eve scowled at her.

"Peabody, Hawley used credits in the salon and in Desirable Woman, lingerie place on the floor above. Check it out."

"Yes, sir."

"You'll both need to contact as many names on your match lists as possible. Set up meets. I want this to start tonight. Arrangements are being made to use the Nova Club on Fifty-third. The earlier in the evening, the better to start. Try for the first meet at four — then book the rest an hour apart. Get in as many as you can. We don't know if he hit last night. We may have gotten lucky. But he won't wait."

She glanced over at the photos again. "We'll have cops inside. Feeney and I will be out on the street, in constant contact. You'll both be wired. Neither of you are to leave with anyone. If you have to take a pee, you signal and one of the inside cops goes with you."

"It isn't his pattern to hit in a public place," Peabody pointed out.

"I don't take chances with my people. You follow the steps, no deviations, or you're out. Get Feeney and me the match lists as soon as you have them. Any member of the staff at Personally Yours or in any of the outlets shows undo interest in you, you report. Questions?"

Eve lifted her eyebrows as both of them shook their heads. "Then get started."

She didn't grin when Peabody levered herself, with some difficulty, out of the chair. But she wanted to. McNab rolled his eyes and showed his teeth as she marched by him and out of the office.

"She's green," he said to Eve.

"She's good," Eve countered.

"Maybe, but I'm keeping my eye on her."

"I can see that," Eve muttered as he strode out.

She turned back to the photos. They haunted her, those three faces. What had been done to them crawled inside her and refused to let go.

Too close, she reminded herself. Too focused on what and not enough on why.

She closed her eyes a moment, rubbed them as if to erase the images of her own memories.

Why these three? she asked herself again and moved closer to study the cheerfully smiling face of Marianna Hawley.

Office professional, she mused, trying out the same system that she'd used to select Mira's scent. Reliable, old-fashioned, romantic. Pretty in a safe, comfortable sort of way. Close family ties. Interested in theater. A tidy woman who enjoyed pretty things around her.

Hooking her thumbs in her pocket, she turned her gaze to Sarabeth Greenbalm. The stripper. A loner who was careful with money and collected business cards. Reliable, too, in her chosen career. Lived sparely, horded her take-home pay and calculated her tips. No apparent hobbies, friends, or family connections.

And Donnie Ray, she mused, the boy who'd loved his mother and had blown sax. Lived like a pig and had a smile like an angel. Puffed a little Zoner but never missed a gig.

And suddenly she had it, staring at the three faces of victims who never met.

The theater.

"Oh yes! Computer, bring up Personally Yours, data on Hawley, Marianna; Greenbalm, Sarabeth; Michael, Donnie Ray. Tile on screen, highlight professions and hobbies/interests."

*Working . . . On screen, requested subjects. Hawley, Marianna, administrative assistant, Foster-Brinke. Hobbies and interests, theater. Member West Side Community Players. Other interests —*

"Stop, continue next subject."

*Greenbalm, Sarabeth, dancer . . .*

"Stop. And Donnie Ray, sax player." She took a minute, letting it process in her own mind. "Computer, run probability scan on killer selecting current subjects due to mutual connection or interest in theater and entertainment."

*Working. . . . With current data, probability index is ninety-three point two percent.*

"Good, damn good." And huffing out a breath, she answered her communicator's beep. "Dallas."

"Dispatch, Dallas, Lieutenant Eve. See the couple at 341 West Eighteen, unit 3. Possible assault attempt. Probability incident linked to current homicide investigations, ninety-eight point eight percent."

Eve was already up and snagging her jacket. "On my way, Dallas, out."

"It was just weird." The woman was tiny, as delicate as the fairies that danced on the tiny white glass tree centered in the wide window of the old rehabbed loft. "Jacko gets too up about things."

"I know what I know. That flake was wrong, Cissy."

Jacko scowled as he tightened his arm around the woman's shoulder. He'd have made four of her, Eve thought. He had to

235

be six-three and two-fifty. An arena ball player's build, a face tough as mountain rock. Scars dug in at the lantern jaw and over the right eyebrow.

She was pale as a moonbeam, he dark as midnight. His big hand swallowed hers.

The loft had been sectioned off into three main areas. Eve got a peek at the bedroom suite through the opening in wavy glass walls the color of peaches. The bed was enormous and unmade.

In the living area the long U-shaped sofa could have fit twenty people comfortably. Jacko took up space for three.

What she could see indicated easy money, feminine taste, and masculine comfort.

"Just tell me what happened."

"We told the policeman last night." Cissy smiled, but her eyes were shadowed with obvious annoyance. "Jacko insisted on calling them. It was just a silly prank."

"Hell it was. Look." He leaned forward, his tight scalp curls bobbing a bit. "This guy comes to the door, dressed like Santa Claus, carrying this big box all wrapped and ribboned. Does the ho-ho, merry Christmas deal."

Anticipation curled in Eve's gut, but she spoke coolly. "Who opened the door?"

"I did." Cissy fluttered her hands. "My

daddy lives in Wisconsin. He usually sends me something fun for Christmas if I can't get out for the holidays. I can't take the time this year, so I thought he'd arranged for Santa to drop in. I still think —"

"That guy wasn't from your daddy," Jacko said dampeningly. "She goes to let him in. I'm in the kitchen. I hear her laughing, and I hear this guy's voice —"

"Jacko's much too jealous for his own good. It hurts our relationship."

"Bullshit, Cissy. You can't tell a guy's making you until he's got his hand up your skirt. Jesus." Obviously disgusted, Jacko hissed out a breath. "He's moving in on her when I walk out."

"Moving in?" Eve repeated while Cissy pouted.

"Yeah, I could see it. He's moving in, got this big smile, this gleam in his eyes."

"Twinkle," Cissy muttered. "Santa's eyes are supposed to twinkle for Lord's sake, Jacko."

"They sure as hell stopped twinkling when he saw me. He went statue, just stood there, gaping at me. Scared the ho-ho right out of him, I tell you. Then he takes off, like a fucking rabbit."

"You yelled at him."

"Not until after he started to run." Jacko

threw up his enormous hands in frustration. "Yeah, damn right I yelled then, and I took off after him. Would've had his ass, too, if Cissy hadn't gotten in the way. But by the time I shook her off and got out to the street, he was gone."

"Did the uniform who took the initial call take the security discs?"

"Yeah, he said it was routine."

"That's right. What did he sound like?"

"Sound like?" Cissy blinked.

"His voice. Tell me what his voice was like."

"Um . . . It was jolly."

"Jesus, Cissy, do you practice being stupid? It was put on," Jacko said to Eve while Cissy, obviously insulted, sprang up and flounced — Eve could think of no other word for it — into the kitchen. "You know that fake cheer. Deep, rumbling. He said something like . . . 'Have you been good little girl? I've got something for you. Only for you.' Then I stepped out and he looked like he'd swallowed a live trout."

"You didn't recognize him?" Eve asked Cissy. "There was nothing about him, under the costume, under the makeup, that looked familiar? Nothing about his voice, the way he moved?"

"No." She walked back in, rigidly ignoring

Jacko and sipping from a glass filled with fizzy water. "But it was only a couple of minutes."

"I'm going to have you review the discs, take a look at them when we enlarge and enhance. If there's anything familiar, I want to know."

"Isn't this a lot of trouble for something so silly?"

"I don't think so. How long have the two of you lived together?"

"On and off for a couple years."

"A lot of off lately," Jacko mumbled.

"If you weren't so possessive, if you didn't punch every man who looks at me sideways," Cissy began.

"Cissy?" Eve held up a hand, hoping to forestall the domestic dispute. "What do you do for a living?"

"Me, I'm an actor — teach acting when I can't land a part."

There's one, Eve mused.

"She's terrific." With obvious and shameless pride, Jacko grinned at Cissy. "She's rehearsing for a play off-Broadway right now."

"Way off," Cissy said, but she moved back to Jacko with a smile and sat beside him again.

"It's going to be a huge hit." He kissed

one of her pretty hands. "Cissy beat out twenty other women at the auditions. This one's her big break."

"I'll be sure to watch for it. Cissy, have you used the services of Personally Yours?"

"Um . . ." Her gaze skidded away. "No."

"Cissy." Eve put all cop in her voice, in her eyes, and leaned forward. "Do you know the penalty for lying during an interview?"

"Well, for goodness' sake, I don't know what business it is of yours."

"What's Personally Yours?" Jacko wanted to know.

"A computer dating service."

"Oh, for Christ's sake, Cissy! For Christ's sake." Furious, Jacko shoved off the couch, rattling knickknacks as he stomped around the living room. "What the hell is wrong with you?"

"We broke up!" All at once the little fairy managed to out-shout the giant. "I was mad at you. I thought it would be fun. I thought it would teach you a lesson, you dummy. I've got a perfect right to see who I want when I want when we aren't cohabitating."

"Think again, honey." He swung back, black eyes glinting.

"See, see?" Cissy jabbed a finger at him as she appealed to Eve. All the flirty softness in her eyes had turned to flint. "This is what

I put up with."

"Calm down, both of you. Sit," Eve ordered. "When did you have your consult, Cissy?"

"About six weeks ago," she mumbled. "I went out with a couple of guys —"

"What guys?" Jacko demanded.

"A couple of guys," she repeated, ignoring him. "Then Jacko came back around. He brought me flowers. Pansies. I caved. But I'm rethinking that decision."

"That decision might have saved your life," said Eve.

"What do you mean?" Instinctively Cissy cringed into Jacko. His arm came back around her.

"The incident last night matches the pattern of a series of homicides. In the other cases, the victims lived alone." Eve glanced at Jacko. "Lucky for you, you don't."

"Oh God, but . . . Jacko."

"Don't worry, baby, don't worry. I'm here." He all but folded her into his lap as he stared at Eve. "I knew that guy was off. What's going on?"

"I'll tell you what I can. Then I need both of you to come down to Cop Central, review the disc, make another report, and tell me everything you can remember, Cissy, about your experience at Personally Yours."

■ ■ ■ ■

"The witnesses are giving the investigation their full cooperation." Eve stood in Commander Whitney's office. Too wired to sit, she barely resisted pacing as she gave him her report.

"The woman's shaken, can't give us much to go on. The man's holding it together. Nothing about the perpetrator is familiar to either. I've interviewed both of the matches Cissy Peterman dated. Both are alibied for at least one of the murders. I think they're clear on this."

Lips pursed, Whitney nodded and began to scan the hard copy of Eve's report. "Jacko Gonzales? *The* Jacko Gonzales? Number twenty-six with the Brawlers?"

"He plays professional arena ball, yes, sir."

"Well, hell." Whitney's faced creased in one of his rare smiles. "I'll say he plays. He's a killer out there. Scored three goals his last game and took out two defensive blocks."

He cleared his throat as Eve only watched him. "My grandson's a big fan."

"Yes, sir."

"Too bad Gonzalez didn't get his hands on this guy. He wouldn't be walking, I promise you."

242

"I got that impression, Commander."

"Ms. Peterman's a fortunate woman."

"Yes, sir. The next one might not be. This threw him off schedule. He's bound to hit again. Tonight. I ran this by Dr. Mira. Her opinion is he'll be angry, emotionally distraught. To me that means he might be sloppy as well. McNab and Peabody have three meets each set up for tonight. Everything's in place there. I have their lists and reports."

She hesitated, then decided to speak her mind. "Commander, what we're doing tonight is a necessary step. But he's going to be out there while we're on this surveillance. He's going to move."

"Unless you've got a crystal ball, Dallas, you've got to take the steps."

"I've got a probability list of victims down to just over two hundred. I think I've found another connection, the theater, that can carve that number down. I'm hoping with the new data Feeney can get us a short list of probables. The potential victims need to be protected."

"How?" Whitney spread his hands. "You know as well as I do the department can't spare that many officers."

"But if he fines it down —"

"If he quarters it, I can't spare them."

"One of those people is going to die tonight." She stepped forward. "They need to be warned. If we go to the media, put out an alert, whoever he's targeted might not open the damn door."

"If we go to the media," Whitney said coolly, "we start a panic. How many street-corner Santas ringing their bells for charity get assaulted as a result? Or killed. You can't play trade the victim here, Dallas. And," he added before she could speak, "if we go to the media, we risk scaring him off. He goes under, we might never find him. Three people are dead, and they deserve better."

He was right, but knowing it didn't ease her gut. "If Feeney fines down the list to a workable number, we can contact each name. I'll put together a team to make the calls."

"It'll leak, Lieutenant, and we'll be back to panic."

"We can't just leave them open this way. The next one he kills is on us." *On me,* she thought, but knew better than to say it. "If we do nothing to alert the victim, it's on us. He knows we've got his pattern. He knows we've got the number of targets. And he knows we can't do anything but juggle names and wait for him to hit again. He loves it. He performed for the security camera at Peterman's. Stood in the damn foyer and posed. If Gonzales had been out making goals last night, she'd be dead. That's four in a week, and it's too damn many."

He heard her out, his face calm and set. "It's a hell of a lot easier where you're standing, Lieutenant. Maybe you don't think so, but it's a hell of a lot easier on that side of the desk. I can't give you what you want. I can't let you stand in front of every victim and take the hit the way you stood in front of Roarke's man a few weeks ago."

"This has nothing to do with that." Battling frustrated fury, she set her teeth. "That incident is closed, Commander. And my current investigation is against the wall. Information is already leaking to the media. Another one dies, it's going to blow up in our faces."

Whitney's eyes flattened. "How much have you given Furst?"

"No more than I had to, and most of that off the record. She'll hold back. But she's not the only reporter with a good nose, and not many of them have her integrity."

"I'll take that matter up with the Chief. That's the best I can do. You get me Feeney's amended list, and I'll ask for individual contacts. I can't authorize the budget for that kind of operation, Dallas. It's out of my control."

He leaned back, studying her. "Come up with something tonight on this surveillance. End this thing."

Eve found Feeney scanning the monitor in her office. "Good, you saved me a trip to EDD."

"Heard you had Jacko Gonzales in." He glanced wistfully over her shoulder. "Guess he's gone, huh?"

"I'll get you his autographed hologram, for God's sake."

"Yeah? Appreciate it."

"I need you to run these names and data." She pulled out a copy of a disc. "My machine's stuttering again and it takes me too damn long. I need victim probability whittled down as far as it'll go." She dragged open a drawer, pawing through and ignoring the vague headache behind her eyes. "Just the top fifty, okay? I can push Whitney into contacting fifty. God help the others. Where the goddamn hell is my candy bar?"

"I didn't take it." Feeney jostled his bag of nuts. "McNab was in here. He's a known candy thief."

"Son of a bitch." Desperate for fuel, she

snagged Feeney's bag and downed a handful of nuts. "I had the security disc from Peterman's enhanced and enlarged, but I figure you can do better. I want the frame of him when he's most himself — when he's turned to run. You can see the panic."

She jabbed at the AutoChef hoping for coffee to wash down the nuts. "I've got photos of the match lists, the personnel at Personally Yours. You got the equipment to scan them, see how many might pop as far as facial shapes, eye shape, that kind of thing. Even with enhancements, something's got to come through. Most of his mouth's hidden by the beard."

"We can do most-likely shapes on that if we have a good enough image."

"Yeah. Build isn't going to work, but height should. See how close you can come to height. From the images he didn't appear to be wearing lifts, so I think we can get close. The gloves screw up the shape of his hands."

She gulped coffee, eyes narrowing. "Ears," she said abruptly. "Would he have bothered to change the shape of his ears? How much of them show?"

She leaped to her machine, called up the program, the file, the images. "Shit, nothing, nothing, nothing. Here!" Scanning through she came up with a side view. "That's good, that's pretty damn good. Can you work with it?"

Feeney nibbled, considered. "Yeah, maybe. The hat covers the top of the ear, but maybe. Nice call, Dallas. It would've slipped by me. We'll work feature by feature, see what jumps. It's not going to be quick. Something this complex is going to take days. Maybe a week."

"I need the bastard's face." She closed her eyes, concentrated. "We'll go back, work the jewelry angle again, the disinfectant, the cosmetics. The tattoos were hand drawn. Maybe we can shake out something there."

"Dallas, two-thirds of the salons and clubs in the city have freehand tattoo artists."

"And maybe one of them knows that design." She blew out a breath. "We've got two hours before the meets at Nova. Let's do what we can."

# CHAPTER ELEVEN

The one thing that really irritated Peabody was that McNab was on her match list. It didn't matter that it was most likely due to the fact that her profile and his had been altered to fit those of the victims'.

It just griped her.

She didn't like working with him, with his ridiculous clothes, cocky grins, and know-it-all attitude, but figured she was stuck as long as Eve found him an asset.

There was no one on the force Peabody admired as much as Eve Dallas, but she figured even the smartest of smart cops could make one mistake. Eve's, in Peabody's opinion, was McNab.

She could see him across the snazzy little bar. He and the six-foot blonde he'd matched with were directly in her line of vision. A deliberate move on McNab's part, Peabody imagined, just to annoy her while they worked.

If he hadn't been there, she might have been able to enjoy the quietly elegant atmosphere. The bar had pretty silver-topped tables, pale blue privacy booths, and clever art prints of New York street scenes decorating the warm yellow walls.

Classy, she thought, glancing over at the long, shiny bar with sparkling mirrors and tuxedo-decked servers. But you'd expect classy from something that belonged to Roarke.

The padded chair where she sat was designed for comfort; the drinks were glorious. The table was equipped with hundreds of musical and video selections and individual headsets if a customer wanted entertainment while he or she waited for a friend or enjoyed a quiet, solitary drink.

Peabody was sorely tempted to try out the headset, as her first match was a blistering bore. The guy's name was Oscar and he was a teacher who specialized in physics on at-home screens. So far, he'd mostly been interested in sucking down rippers and bad-mouthing his recent ex-wife.

She was, Peabody was told, a nonsupporting, self-centered bitch who was frigid in bed. After fifteen minutes, Peabody was fully on the bitch's side.

Still, she played the game, smiling and

chatting while she crossed Oscar off her mental lists of suspects. The guy had a serious problem with alcohol, and their man was too clear-headed to spend his time with the awesome hangovers a few rippers produced.

Across the room, McNab erupted with delighted laughter that ran along Peabody's nerve endings like a dull razor. While Oscar guzzled the last of his third ripper, she glanced over, and caught the quick, eyebrow wiggle McNab sent her.

It made her want to do something cool and mature. Like sticking out her tongue.

With great relief, she parted ways with Oscar, making vague plans to hook up again.

"When they sell iced rippers in hell," she muttered and winced as she heard Eve's voice in her earpiece.

"Maintain, Peabody."

"Sir." Peabody hissed the word, covering it by lifting her own virgin blitzer. She sighed, noting by her wrist unit that she had ten minutes before the next meet.

"Goddamn it!"

Peabody jolted when Eve's voice exploded in her ear. "Sir?" she said again, choking.

"What the hell is he doing here? Damn it!"

Baffled, one hand sliding down to where

her weapon was snug inside her left boot, Peabody scanned the room. And caught herself grinning widely as Roarke strolled in.

"Now, that's a match made in heaven," Peabody murmured. "Why can't I get one of those?"

"Don't talk to him," Eve ordered in a snap. "You don't know him."

"Okay, I'll just stare and drool, like every other woman in the place."

She chuckled out loud at Eve's snarling string of curses, and the couple at the next table glanced over. Peabody cleared her throat, lifted her drink again, and settled back to admire her lieutenant's husband.

He walked by the bar, and the bartenders came to attention like soldiers on parade for the general. He stopped by a table to speak briefly with a couple. Leaned down to brush his lips over the woman's cheek, then moved to the end of the bar to lay a friendly hand on a man's shoulder.

Peabody wondered if he moved just that beautifully in bed, then flushed. It was a damn good thing, she decided, that the wire wasn't transmitting her thoughts to the surveillance van.

Outside, Eve scowled at the screen that

252

projected the view from the microcamera in Peabody's collar button. She watched Roarke work the room, very casual, very easy, and vowed to pound him into dust at the first opportunity.

"He's got no business walking into an operation," she said to Feeney.

"It's his place." Feeney hunched his shoulders, an automatic defense against a marital tiff.

"Right, he came by to check the liquor levels at the bar. Fuck." She dragged both hands through her hair, then made low, feral sounds in her throat as she watched Roarke wander over to Peabody's table.

"Enjoying your drink, miss?"

"Um, yeah, I . . . Shit, Roarke" was the best Peabody could manage.

He only smiled, leaned down. "Tell your lieutenant to stop swearing at me. I won't get in her way."

Peabody's eye twitched as Eve's voice exploded in her ear. "Uh, she suggests you get your fancy ass out of here. She'll, um, kick it for you later."

"Looking forward to it." Still smiling, he lifted Peabody's fingers, kissed them. "You look fabulous," he told her, then strolled away while the equipment in the van reported a sharp spike in her blood pressure and pulse rate.

"Down, Peabody," Eve warned.

"I can't control an involuntary physical reaction to outside stimuli." Peabody blew out a breath. "Sure does have a fancy ass. Respectfully, sir."

"Match Two approaching. Pull it together, Peabody."

"I'm ready."

She glanced toward the door, her company smile ready. One of the perks for the operation, as far as she was concerned, had just walked in. She remembered him from her first visit to Personally Yours. The trim bronzed god who'd caught her attention — then given his own to his pocket mirror.

He was going to be a pleasure to look at for the next hour.

He posed at the door, head up, profile turned to the room as he scanned tables. His eyes, a tawny gold that matched his hair, flickered, then settled on Peabody. His mouth turned up as he gave a quick, practiced head toss to allow his hair to flow. He crossed directly to her table.

"You must be Delilah."

"Yes." Great voice, she thought with an inward sigh. Better in person than on his video profile. "And you're Brent."

Across the room it was McNab's turn to

scowl. The man preening for Peabody was all plastic, he decided, with a thick layer of spray gloss. Probably just her type.

Asshole had his face tailor-made, McNab decided. Body, too. He doubted there was an inch on the man that hadn't been paid for.

*And just look! Just look at the way she's fawning all over him,* McNab thought in disgust, tinged with a vicious dose of jealousy. The woman was practically lapping up every word the guy dropped through his collagen-enhanced lips.

Women were so pitifully predictable.

His gaze slid over as Roarke stopped by the table. "She's looking particularly appealing tonight, isn't she?"

"Most guys find it appealing when a woman has half her tits out of her shirt."

Roarke grinned, enjoying himself. McNab's eyes were on fire and his fingers were beating a rapid and angry tattoo against the tabletop. "But obviously you're above such things."

"Wish I were above them," McNab muttered as Roarke moved on. "Those are some superior tits."

"Keep your eyes off Peabody's tits," Eve ordered. "Your second match is at the door."

"Yeah." McNab glanced over at a tiny

redhead in a spangled skinsuit. "I'm on it."

Inside the van, Eve frowned at the screen. "Give me the run on the guy with Peabody, will you, Feeney? Something about it seems off to me."

"Brent Holloway, commercial model. Works for Cliburn-Willis Marketing. Thirty-eight, twice divorced, no kids."

"Model?" Her eyes narrowed. "On screen? That's sort of like entertainment, right?"

"Shit. You haven't watched much commercial screen lately. Nothing entertaining about those ads, you ask me. He's originally from Morristown, New Jersey. New York resident since 2049. Current address Central Park West. Income in middle eighties. Shows nothing on yellow sheets — no arrests. Got a mountain of traffic violations."

"We saw him — Peabody and me — at Personally Yours on our first trip there. How many consults has he had?"

"This is his fourth match group this year."

"Okay, why does a guy who looks like that, has credits, a strong career, and a high-dollar address become a dating service addict? Four match groups in a year, five matches per group. That's twenty women, and nothing sticks. What's wrong with him, Feeney?"

Feeney pursed his lips and studied the

screen. "From my view he looks like a conceited asshole."

"Yeah, but a lot of women aren't going to care about that. He's got looks and bucks. Something should've stuck." She drummed her fingers on the narrow console. "No complaints to the service pop out?"

"Nope. His sheet there's clean, too."

"Something's off," she said again an instant before she watched her aide rear back and plow a fist directly in Brent Holloway's perfect nose. "Jesus Christ. Jesus, did you see that?"

"Busted it," Feeney said placidly as he studied the quick gush of blood. "Nice short-armed jab."

"What the hell was she thinking? What the hell's going on? Peabody, have you lost your mind?"

"Son of a bitch stuck his hand up me under the table." Flushed and furious, Peabody was on her feet, hands fisted. "Bastard's talking about the new play at the Universe and he grabs my crotch. Pervert. You pervert, get up."

"McNab, stay the hell where you are!" Eve shouted as McNab surged to his feet with murder in his eyes. "Stay the hell where you are, or you're off. That's an order. A goddamn order! Maintain. Peabody, for Christ's sake, put that guy down."

Even as Eve was pulling the hair out of her head, Peabody hauled Holloway to his feet and hit him again. She'd have gone for three, even though his gold eyes were rolling back white, if Roarke hadn't stepped through the excited crowd and pulled the rubber-legged Holloway back.

"Was this man bothering you, miss?" Coolly, Roarke hauled Holloway out of reach, kept his eyes level on Peabody's glinting ones. "I'm terribly sorry. I'll take care of it. Please, let me get you another drink." With one hand on Holloway, he lifted Peabody's glass with his free one, sniffed. "Blitzer, virgin," he ordered and all three bartenders rushed to comply as he dragged the now struggling Holloway to the door.

"Get your fucking hands off me. That bitch broke my nose. My face is my living, for Christ's sake. Stupid cunt. I'm suing her crazy ass off. I'm reporting —"

The minute they were outside, Roarke slammed him against the side of the building. Holloway's head hit the wall with a sound reminiscent of pool balls cracking on the break.

The gold eyes rolled back white a second time.

"Let me give you a clue: This is my place."

Roarke accented the information by rapping Holloway's head against the bricks again, while, in the van, Eve could only watch and swear. "Nobody paws a woman in my place and walks away on his own legs. So unless you want to try crawling with your limp dick in your hand, you'll start moving now and thank Jesus only your nose is broken."

"The bitch asked for it."

"Oh, now then, that was the wrong thing to say. Entirely."

"His Irish comes out when he's pissed. Listen to the music of it," Feeney said sentimentally as Eve only continued to make violent sounds in her throat.

On what might have been a sigh, Roarke hammered a fist into Holloway's stomach, kneed him handily in the balls, and let him drop.

He flicked one glance toward the van with what certainly was a quick and wicked grin, then strolled back inside.

"Nice tidy job," Feeney decided.

"Let's call a cruiser to pick up that stupid bastard and get him to a health center." Eve rubbed her eyes. "This is going to look wonderful on the report. McNab, Peabody, maintain positions. Do not — repeat — do not break cover. Christ. When this little party is over, report to my home office so we can try to salvage something."

At just past nine, Eve paced her home office. No one spoke. They knew better. But Roarke gave Peabody's shoulder a reassuring squeeze.

"We hit six meets between you, so that's something. The last two, one for each of you, is scheduled tomorrow noon. Peabody, you'll report this . . . incident with Match Two to Piper in the morning. Play it up. I want to see how they handle it. His sheet with them is clear up to now. We have recordings on all meets, but I want both of you to work up individual reports. When we've finished the debriefing tonight, you'll both go home and stay there, keeping your communicators open at all times. Both Feeney and I will be monitoring."

"Yes, sir. Lieutenant." Bracing herself, Peabody got to her feet. She swallowed hard, but kept her chin lifted. "I apologize for my outburst during the operation. I realize my behavior could compromise the investigation."

"The hell with that!" McNab exploded out of his chair. "You should've broken his fucking legs. The son of a bitch deserved
—"

"McNab," Eve said mildly.

"The hell with it, Dallas. The bastard got what he deserved. We should —"

"Detective McNab." Eve snapped off the words and moved forward until they were toe to toe. "I don't believe your opinion in this matter was requested. You're now off duty. Go home and cool off. I'll see you in my office at Central at oh nine hundred."

She waited while he fought the war between training and instinct. In the end he turned on his heel and stormed out without another word. "Roarke, Feeney, would you give me a moment with my aide?"

"Glad to," Feeney said under his breath, more than happy to desert the field. "Got any Irish, Roarke? It's been a long day."

"I think we can find you a glass." He sent Eve one quiet look before guiding Feeney out of the room.

"Sit down, Peabody."

"Sir." Peabody shook her head. "I let you down. I promised you I would handle myself and the responsibilities you gave me. Then I broke at the first turn. I realize you have every right and reason to take me off the investigation, at least the undercover op, but I'd like to respectfully request another chance."

Eve said nothing, let Peabody wind down.

Her aide was still sheet-pale, but her hands were steady, her shoulders straight. "I don't believe I mentioned any plans to remove you from the undercover op, Officer. But I did tell you to sit down. Sit down, Peabody," she said more gently, then turned away to dig up a bottle of wine.

"I understand that when you're under you have to keep to your cover, to handle any curves without breaking."

"I didn't see you break your cover, just that asshole's nose."

"I didn't think, I just reacted. I understand during that kind of op you have to think at all times."

"Peabody, even an LC has the right to protest if some jerk grabs her crotch in a public place. Here, have a drink."

"He stuck his fingers in me." Her hand did shake now as Eve pressed the glass into it. "We were just sitting there talking and all of a sudden I feel him jam his fingers in me. I know I was flirting, and I let him get a good look at my boobs so maybe I deserved —"

"Stop it." Eve's control wavered enough for her to put her hands on Peabody's shoulders and shove her into a chair. "You didn't deserve it, and it pisses me off to hear you think it. The son of a bitch didn't have any right to touch you that way. Nobody has a right to push themselves on you that way."

*To hold you down, to tie your hands, to hammer himself into you when you're begging him to stop. And it hurts, it hurts, it hurts.*

The sickness rose up, all but gagging her, until she turned, laid her hands on her desk, and ordered herself to breathe.

"Not now," she murmured. "For Christ's sake."

"Dallas?"

"It's nothing." But she had to stay as she was, hands braced, for another moment. "I'm sorry you were put in that kind of position. I knew something was off about him."

Peabody lifted her glass with both hands. She could still feel the sudden sharp shock of Holloway's fingers digging into her. "He passed their screening."

"And now we know their screening isn't as good as they claim." She drew a deep breath and, steadier, turned back. "I want you to hit Piper with this in the morning, in person. Go in, demand to see her. A little hysteria wouldn't hurt; you can threaten to sue or go to the press. I want her to get it full in the face. Let's see what shakes. Can you do it?"

"Yeah." Appalled that tears were perilously

close, Peabody sniffed. "Yeah, the way I'm feeling, it'll be easy."

"Keep your communicator open. We can't use anything you get on the inside, but I want you in constant contact. You can delay your report on tonight until tomorrow afternoon. I'm going to have Feeney take you home, okay?"

"Yeah."

Eve waited a beat. "Peabody?"

"Sir?"

"Damn good punch. Next time, though, follow it through with a groin shot. You want to completely disable, not just annoy."

Peabody let out a long sigh, then managed a half smile. "Yes, sir."

Because she wanted the position of command, Eve sat behind her desk and waited for Roarke. She knew he'd walk Feeney and Peabody out, probably add a few comfort strokes for Peabody. Which would set the poor woman up for sweaty, erotic dreams if Eve knew her aide.

Better, she thought, than ugly nightmares about groping hands and helplessness.

And that, she realized, was part of her problem with this case. Sexual homicides, bondage, the gleeful cruelty in the name of love. Too close to home. Too close to the past she'd spent most of her life running from.

Now it was hitting her in the face. Each time she looked at a victim, she saw herself.

And she hated it.

"Get past it," she ordered herself. "And find him."

She looked over as Roarke walked in, kept her eyes on him as he crossed the room. He poured two glasses of the wine she'd gotten out for Peabody, set one on her desk, then took the other with him and sat in the chair facing her.

He sipped, took out one of his increasingly rare cigarettes, lighted it. "Well," he said and left it at that.

"What the hell did you think you were doing?"

He drew in smoke, blew it out in a thin, fragrant stream. "At which point?"

"Don't get cute with me, Roarke."

"But I do it so well. Easy, Lieutenant." He lifted his glass in salute as she growled low in her throat. "I didn't infringe on your operation."

"The point is you had no business being near the scene."

"Pardon me, but I *own* the scene." There was arrogance in his tone now, and a dare. "I often drop in on my properties. Keeps the employees on their toes."

"Roarke —"

"Eve, this case is choking you. Do you think I can't see it?" His composure cracked just enough to have him rising to pace.

Feeney was right, she thought fleetingly, the Irish came out when he was pissed.

"It disturbs your sleep — what little you allow yourself. It haunts your eyes. I know what you go through." He turned back, temper alive in those wonderfully blue eyes. "Christ, I admire you. But you can't expect me to stand back and pretend I don't see, don't understand, and not do whatever it is I can do to ease what's inside you."

"It isn't about me. It can't be about me. It's about three dead people."

"They haunt you, too." He crossed to the desk and sat on the edge close to her. "That's why you're the best cop I've ever run up against. They're not names and numbers to you. They're people. And you have the gift — or curse — of being able to imagine too well what they saw and felt and prayed for in those last minutes of life. I won't back away."

He leaned forward, a quick move that caught her unguarded, and gripped her chin. "Damn it. I won't back away from what you are or what you do. You'll take me, Eve, every bit as fully as I take you."

She sat very still, absorbing his words, searching his eyes. She could never resist the things she found in his eyes. "Last winter," she began slowly, "you pushed yourself into my life. I didn't ask for you. I didn't want you."

His brow cocked, an irritated challenge. "Thank God you didn't give a damn what I asked for or what I thought I wanted," she murmured and watched the dare slide into a smile.

"I didn't ask for you either. A *ghra*."

My love. She knew what it meant, in the tongue of his birth, and couldn't stop her heart from opening to it. To him. "Since then I've rarely had a case that hasn't tangled you into it. I didn't want it to be that way. I've used you when it was expedient. That bothers me."

"It pleases me."

"I know it." She sighed and, lifting a hand, curled her fingers briefly around his wrist. His pulse beat there, strong and steady. "You get too close to pieces of me I don't like to look at, then I don't have any choice but to look at them."

"You look at them with or without me, Eve. But maybe with me they won't hurt you so much. I look back," he said and surprised her enough to have her eyes flicking up to his, holding there. "And it's easier, those moments are easier to stand since you. You can't ask me, can't expect me not to stand with you when your moments close in."

She stood now, taking her wine and moving away from him. He was right, she thought. What she too often saw as dependence should have been accepted as unity.

And she could tell him.

"I know what they felt. I know what went through them — the fear, the pain, the humiliation. Each one of them when they were helpless and naked and he was raping them. I know what their bodies felt, what their minds felt. I don't want to remember what it's like to be torn into that way. Ripped, invaded. But I do. Then you touch me."

She turned back, realizing she'd never really given him this. "Then you touch me, Roarke, and I don't. I don't feel that. I don't remember that. It's that simple. It's just . . . you."

"I love you," he murmured. "Outrageously."

"So you're here when you should be off planet seeing to your business." She shook her head before he could speak, could slide some smooth excuse by her when she knew better. "You were there tonight, knowing I'd be pissed off, because you thought there might be a chance I'd need you. You're here right now ready to argue with me just to take my mind off what's ripping at it. I know you, damn it. I'm a cop. I'm good at knowing people."

He only smiled. "Busted. So what?"

"So . . . thanks. But I've been on the job eleven years now and I can handle myself. On the other hand . . ." She studied her wine, then took a long swallow. "It sure gave me a nice feeling to watch you beat the puss out of that creep who jumped Peabody. I had to sit there in the fucking van. Couldn't risk getting out to smear him onto the pavement myself and blow cover. So it felt pretty good to watch you do it for me."

"Oh, it was absolutely my pleasure. Is she all right?"

"She will be. He shook her — that's the human part. She'll take a hot shower, a tranq if she's smart, and sleep it off. The cop part will maintain. She's a good cop."

"She's a better one because of you."

"No, don't put that on me. She's what she is." Uncomfortable with that topic, she shot him a cool stare. "I bet you hugged her, stroked her hair, and gave her a kiss good night."

That gorgeous eyebrow lifted again. "And if I did?"

"Her little heart's still pitty-patting over it, which is just fine. She's got a thing for you."

"Really?" He grinned widely. "How . . . interesting."

"Don't play with my aide. I need her focused."

"How about you unfocus for just a little while, and I see if I can make your heart pitty-pat?"

She ran her tongue around her teeth. "I don't know. I've got a lot on my mind. It'd be a lot of work."

"I enjoy my work." With his eyes on hers, he stubbed out his cigarette, set down his glass. "And I'm damned good at it."

She was facedown on the bed, naked and still vibrating, when the call came in. She grunted, blocked video, and answered. Thirty seconds later, she was rolling over and looking for her clothes. The call had been for her response to an anonymous tip on a domestic dispute. The address was all too familiar.

"That's Holloway's place. It's not a 1222.

He's dead. It followed pattern."

"I'll go with you." Roarke was already out of bed and reaching for his trousers.

She started to protest, then shrugged. "Okay. I have to tag Peabody for this, and she might not handle it well. I'm counting on you to give her the strokes because I'm going to have to be hard on her to keep her in line."

"I don't envy your job, Lieutenant," Roarke said as he dressed in the dark.

"Right now, neither do I." She dug out her communicator and called Peabody.

# CHAPTER TWELVE

Brent Holloway had lived well, and died badly. The furnishing of his town house spoke of a man who was ruled by both trends and comfort. A lake-sized sofa dominated the living area and was pooled with triangular black pillows that appeared wet to the touch. A view screen was recessed in the ceiling above. In a cabinet, shaped like a well-endowed female from neck to knee, was an expansive collection of porn discs, some legal, some bootlegged.

A silver serving bar stretched across one wall and was stocked with expensive liquor and cheap illegal drugs.

The kitchen was fully automated, soulless, and appeared to have been used rarely. There was an office with a high-end computer system and holophone and a playroom equipped with VR and a mood tube. A servant droid stood in the corner, shut down and blank-eyed.

Holloway was in the master suite, stretched over a water-to-air mattress, trussed in sparkly silver garland and staring blindly at his own reflection in the mirrored canopy. The tattoo had been painted low on his belly, and four plump birds flew on the silver choke chain around his neck.

"Looks like he'd been to a health center," Eve commented. His nose was only slightly swollen. Whatever bruising there might have been was expertly concealed with cosmetics.

Roarke stood back, knowing he wasn't permitted in the room. He'd seen her work before. Competent, thorough, with a gentleness under the professional moves as she tended the dead.

He watched her run the standard field test to establish time of death, recording it herself until Peabody and the Crime Scene techs arrived.

"Ligature marks, both wrists, both ankles indicate victim was restrained prior to death. Death occurred twenty-three fifteen. Bruising on throat indicates cause of death to be strangulation."

She glanced up as the buzzer sounded.

"I'll let her in," Roarke said.

"Okay. Roarke?" She hesitated only a moment. He was here, after all, and he was able. "Can you reactivate the droid? Bypass the programmed commands?"

"I think I could handle that."

"Yeah." There was very little he couldn't do to bypass security systems. She tossed him a can of Seal-It. "Coat your hands. I can't have your prints on it."

He gave the can a mild look of distaste, but carried it with him.

She turned back to the body, continuing her work. She could hear the muted conversation in the other room as Roarke spoke to Peabody. Moving to the doorway, she waited.

Peabody was back in uniform, her recorder pinned to her lapel, her hair ruthlessly slicked down in its usual straight bowl around her face. And her face was pale, her eyes horrified.

"Oh shit, Dallas."

"Tell me if you can't deal with it. I have to know now before you go in."

She'd asked herself the same question over and over since she'd received the call. Because she still wasn't sure of the answer, she kept her eyes on Eve's. "It's my job to handle it. I know that."

"I tell you what your job is. There's a droid. You can work that. You can check the 'links, the security discs. You can start the door-to-doors."

It was an out. She hated herself for wanting to take it. Wanting to do anything but step inside the room. "I prefer to work the scene. Sir."

Eve studied her another moment, then nodded. "Engage your recorder." She turned and walked back to the side of the bed. "The victim is Holloway, Brent, ID established by investigating officer. Preliminary on body recorded by Dallas, Lieutenant Eve. Subsequent record by Peabody, Officer Delia. Time and apparent cause of death established."

Peabody's stomach jittered when she forced herself to study the body. "It's just like the others."

"Apparently. Sexual molestation has not yet been established, nor has the victim been tested for drugs. The exposed skin shows signs of disinfectant. I can still smell it."

She took a visor out of her field kit, fit it over her head, adjusted the power on the eyepieces. "Crime Scene techs are late," she muttered. "Lights out," she commanded, and the spotlight beams trained on the bed went dark.

"Yeah, he's been sprayed down. The brushstrokes on the tattoo coincide with those on previous victims. It's damn good freehand," she added, with her nose all but pressing on Holloway's belly. "What have we got here? Give me the tweezers, Peabody. I got hair or fiber here."

Without looking back, Eve held out a hand, felt the small metal tool when Peabody passed it. "It's white, doesn't look man-made." Holding up the thin strand, she studied it through the magnified visor. "He's got several of these on him. I need a bag." Even as she said it, Peabody was holding one out. "I'd guess Santa's beard is shedding, and he wasn't as careful cleaning up after himself this time."

Carefully Eve plucked white strands from the body, bagged them. "He just made his first mistake. Take the visor." Eve pulled it off. "Check the bathroom, every corner. Pull the drains and bag the contents. I want everything. Lights on," she added. "Missing Cissy last night shook him, Peabody. He's getting sloppy."

By the time Eve turned the room over to the Crime Scene team, she'd found more than a dozen hairs, and minute traces of fiber. Her eyes were dark with purpose when she found Roarke with the droid in the playroom.

"Did you get it on?"

"Of course." Staying comfortably in the body-mold chair, he gestured toward the droid. "Rodney, this is Lieutenant Dallas."

"Lieutenant." The droid was short and squat, with a homely face and a clipped voice. Obviously Holloway hadn't wanted any competition, even in his electronics.

"What time were you disengaged tonight?"

"At ten oh three, shortly after Mr. Holloway returned for the evening. He prefers that I remain off unless he requires my services."

"He didn't require them tonight."

"Apparently not."

"Did he have any visitors from the time he returned and you were disengaged?"

"No. If I may say, Mr. Holloway didn't appear to be in the mood for companionship this evening."

"How so?"

"He appeared upset," the droid claimed, then folded his lips.

"Rodney, this is a police investigation. You're required to answer my questions fully."

"I don't understand. Has there been a burglary?"

"No, your employer is dead. Did anyone come to the door before Holloway returned?"

"I see." Rodney took a moment, as if adjusting his circuits to the news. "No, there were no visitors this evening. Mr. Holloway had an outside engagement. He returned home at nine fifty. He was angry. He swore at me. I noticed he had some facial bruises and I asked if I could be of assistance. He suggested that I fuck myself, which is a function I am not programmed to perform. He ordered me to go to hell, which was not possible, then countermanded that order with one to come into this room and shut down for the night. I was programmed to reengage at seven a.m."

Out of the corner of her eye, Eve could see Roarke grinning. She ignored him. "Your employer has illegal drugs and pornographic materials on the premises."

"I am not programmed to comment on those matters."

"Did he entertain sexual partners here?"

"Yes."

"Male or female?"

"Both, occasionally at the same time."

"I'm looking for a man, approximately six feet tall. I believe he has long hands, long fingers. He's likely Caucasian. Over thirty years of age, but probably not more than fifty. He has some artistic talent, and interest in theater."

"I'm sorry." Rodney inclined his head politely. "That is insufficient data."

"You're telling me," Eve muttered.

Eve waited until the body was bagged and removed. "There's more to this guy than we have on record," she said to Roarke. "Look around here, you can see. He had money, and liked to spend it on his face and body. He liked to look at himself." Her gaze scanned the room, noting mirrors on nearly every surface. "He uses a dating service, claiming to be straight hetero, but his droid says he was bi. The dating service screens better than the Candidate Control Division out of East Washington, but he slips all this by them. He finger rapes Peabody on their first meet. If he did it once, he did it before, but he gets by with it."

She paced the living room while Roarke said nothing. Nothing was required, he knew. She was using him as a bounce for her thoughts. "Maybe he's connected to either Rudy or Piper. A lover. Or he's helping to fund the place, or he's got something on them so they let it all slide. This guy wasn't a lonely heart, he was a pervert. They had to know it. At least one of them had to know it."

She paused by the cabinet, empty now of the discs already taken into evidence. "Some of those were homemade jobs. I wonder who we'll find doing nasty things with Holloway."

She looked back at Roarke. They were alone for the moment, but Peabody would be back shortly. She struggled with the decision, then thought of four body bags. "I have to go in with this. I don't know when I'll be home."

He knew her very well. He moved close, touched a hand to her cheek. "Do you want to ask, or do you want me to just do it and tell you after it's done?"

She blew out a breath. "I'll ask." She jammed her hands in her pockets as she did. "You can dig beneath the surface of what Holloway put on record. You can find out in hours what it would take Feeney days. He can't cut the corners you can. I don't have days. I don't want this bastard to give me another body to be bagged."

"I'll call you when I have something."

He was making it simple, and that only made it worse. "I'll transmit his file when I get into Central," she began, then shut her mouth firmly when he grinned.

"No point in wasting time when I can get it myself." Leaning down, he kissed her. "I

280

enjoy helping you."

"You just like screwing Compuguard and running illegal programs."

"There is that added benefit." He laid his hands on her shoulders, rubbed briefly at the tension there. "If you work until you fall on your face, I'm going to be annoyed."

"I'm still standing. I need the car and I don't have time to take you back home."

"I think I can manage to get there." He kissed her again before starting toward the door. "Oh, by the way, Lieutenant, you have an appointment with Trina at six tonight. She and Mavis will come to the house."

"Oh, for Christ's sake."

"I'll entertain them if you're running a bit late." Ignoring her next curse, he slipped outside.

She ended with a hiss, then gathered her field kit, called to Peabody, and sealed the scene. "I want to run the hair and fiber to the lab and light a fire under Dickhead," she said as they climbed into her vehicle. "We'll push the ME, too, though I don't think we're going to find out anything from the postmortem that we don't already know."

She slid a sidelong glance at her aide as she drove. "It's going to be a long day, Peabody.

You might want to take some approved ups to get through. You can requisition some Alert-All."

"I'm okay."

"I need you sharp. I want you transformed and under by nine. You have to pull off your bit with Piper. We'll hold the release of Holloway's name as long as possible."

"I know what to do." Peabody stared out the window, watching the night sweep by. There was a lone glide-cart on the corner at Ninth, the operator warming himself in the steam from his grill.

"I'm not sorry I broke his goddamn nose," she said abruptly. "I thought I would be. I thought when I saw him there, saw what had been done to him, that I'd be sorry."

"One doesn't have anything to do with the other."

"I thought it would. I thought it should. I was afraid to go in that room. But once I was in there, doing the job, I didn't feel all the stuff I thought I would."

"You're a cop. A good one."

"I don't want to be the kind who stops feeling." She turned her head, studied Eve's profile. "You're not. They're not just slabs to you, they're people. I don't want to stop remembering they're people."

Eve glanced right and left as she approached a red light, then seeing her way clear, breezed through it. "You wouldn't be working with me if I thought you would."

Peabody took a long, slow breath and felt her stomach settle. "Thanks."

"Since you're grateful, contact Dickhead. Tell him I want his skinny ass in the lab within the hour."

Peabody grimaced, shifted in her seat. "I don't know if I'm that grateful."

"Make the call, Peabody. If he balks, I'll take over and bribe him with a case of Roarke's Irish beer. Dickie's got a weakness for it."

It took two cases and a threat to tie his tongue around his neck, but at three a.m. Dickie was in his labcoat and testing hair and fiber.

Eve paced the lab, barking into her communicator as the assistant ME claimed a holiday backup on autopsies. "Look, you little drone, I can call Commander Whitney and fry your ass. This is Priority One. You want me to let it drop to the media that my investigation was delayed because some AME wanted to read his Christmas cards instead of doing a cut?"

"Come on, Dallas, I'm working a double.

I got stiffs stacked like bricks in the drawers here."

"Put my brick on the table and have the report to me by oh six hundred or I'm coming over there and I'm going to show you what a Y cut feels like."

She cut transmission and turned around. "Gimme, Dickie."

"Don't crowd me, Dallas. You don't scare me. I don't see no Priority One tab on this evidence."

"There will be by nine." She walked over and gave his hair a hard quick yank. "I haven't had my fucking coffee, Dickie. You don't want to mess with me here."

"Jeez, get some then." Behind his microgoggles, his eyes were as big as an owl's. "I'm running the damn stuff, aren't I? You want it quick or you want it right?"

"I want it both." Because she was desperate, she walked over and ordered a cup of the lab sludge pretending to be coffee and forced down a swallow.

"Hair's human," he called out. "Treated with a salon fixer and an herbal disinfectant."

That perked Eve up enough to have her drinking more coffee as she crossed to him. "What kind of fixer, what's it for?"

"To preserve color and texture. It'll keep

the white from yellowing or getting stiff. Two of your samples have some adhesive on one end. These hairs likely came from a wig. A good, expensive one. This is real human hair, and that puts it high-end. I'll have to run more to tag the adhesive. Might be able to get you a brand name on the fixer after some more tests."

"What about the fibers, the stuff Peabody got from the drains?"

"I haven't done it yet. Jesus, I'm not a droid."

"Okay." She pressed her fingers to her eyes. "I need to go to the morgue, make sure Holloway's on the table. Dickie." She laid a hand on his shoulder. He was a pain in the ass, but he was the best. "I need everything you can get me, and I need it fast. This guy's taken out four, and he's already looking for number five."

"I'll get it to you a hell of a lot faster if you stop breathing down my neck."

"I'm leaving. Peabody."

"Sir." Peabody jerked from her doze in a lab chair and blinked blindly.

"We're moving," Eve said shortly. "Dickie, I'm counting on you."

"Yeah, yeah. You know I don't think I got my invite to your big party tomorrow night." He smiled thinly. "Musta gotten lost."

"I'll make sure we find it. After you give me what I need."

"You got it." Pleased, he turned back and bent over his work.

"Greedy little bastard. Here." Eve pushed the coffee into Peabody's hand as they headed back out to the car. "Drink this. It'll either wake you up or kill you."

Eve badgered the AME until she had confirmed cause of death. She stood over his shoulder until he'd run the tox test and reported the over-the-counter tranq in Holloway's system.

Back at Central she ordered Peabody to the cramped area commonly known as the Resort. It consisted of one dark room with three two-level bunks.

While her aide slept, Eve settled into her office and wrote up the reports. She transmitted the necessary copies, and fueled herself with more coffee and what might have been a cranberry muffin from the vending machine.

It was still shy of dawn when her 'link beeped and Roarke's image swam onto her screen.

"Lieutenant, you're pale enough to see through."

"I'm solid enough."

"I have something for you."

Her heart bumped once. He'd know to say nothing more on a logged call. "I'm going to try to swing home shortly. Peabody's down for a couple of hours more."

"You need to go down yourself."

"Yeah. I've about done all I can here. I'm coming in."

"I'll wait up for you."

She broke the call, and left a brief memo for Peabody, should she wake before Eve returned. Once she was in her car and headed out, she put in another call to the lab.

"Anything more for me?"

"Jesus, you're relentless. Tagged your fiber. It's a sym-poly blend, trade name Wulstrong. Simulated wool, commonly in coats and sweaters. This was dyed red."

"Like a Santa suit?"

"Yeah, but not one of your bell-ringing suits. Those poor bastards can't afford this kind of weight and quality. This is good shit, next best thing to real wool. The manufacturers claim it's better — warmer, more durable, and blah blah blah. That's bullshit, 'cause nothing's better than genuine. But this is good, pricey. Just like the hair. Your guy isn't worried about spending credits."

"Good. Nice work, Dickie."

"You find my invitation, Dallas?"

"Yeah, it fell behind my desk."

"Those things happen."

"Get me the results of the drain lift, Dickie, and I'll have it messengered over."

She watched dawn flirt with the eastern sky as she turned toward home.

She knew where to find Roarke. In a room that shouldn't have existed, manning equipment that she shouldn't know about. She ignored the knee-jerk reaction, a cop's reaction, as she approached the room and laid her palm on the plate.

"Dallas, Lieutenant Eve."

Her palm- and voiceprints were analyzed quickly, and she was cleared inside.

He'd left the curtains open on the wide glass. The glass itself was treated. No one could see inside. The room was large, the floor a fancy marble, the walls accented with art — but for one, which was dominated by several screens.

All but one screen was blank now. On that, Roarke ran stock reports while he sat behind the slick U-shaped console toying with an unregistered computer.

"You were faster than I figured."

"There weren't that many layers to go through." He gestured to a chair beside him. "Sit down, Eve."

"Were they thin enough that I can slide it through? Indicate I found it myself without falsifying my report?"

His cop, Roarke thought fondly, would always worry about such niceties. "If you'd know just where to look, just what to question — which I imagine you would have, given another day or two. Sit," he repeated, and this time took her hand and pulled her into the chair.

He'd tied his hair back — which always made her want to tug it free of the thin leather band. He'd pushed up the sleeves of his black sweater. She found herself looking at his hands, thinking about his hands. Gorgeous, clever hands. She realized she was drifting and snapped herself back.

When she blinked her vision clear, his face was close, and one of those gorgeous, clever hands held her chin, his thumb brushing over the shallow dent in its center. "Nearly went out, didn't you?"

"I was just . . . thinking."

"Uh-huh. Thinking. I'm going to make a trade with you, Lieutenant. I'll give you what I've found if, in exchange for it, you'll be here at six tonight. You'll take a soother —"

"Hey, I'm not bargaining for information."

"You are if you want the information. I can wipe it." He reached out a hand and let it hover over some controls she couldn't identify. "You'll be here, take a soother," he repeated, "and let Trina give you a full treatment."

"I haven't got time for a stupid haircut."

It wasn't the hair styling he was thinking of, but the body massage and relaxation program he was going to arrange. "That's the deal. Take it or leave it."

"I've got four murder discs on my desk."

"Right at this moment, I don't give a damn if you have four hundred. Whatever your priorities, you happen to be mine. That's my price. Do you want the data?"

"You're as bad as Dickhead."

"I beg your pardon?"

She snorted out a laugh at the insult in his voice, then rubbed her hands over her face. She really hated when he was right. She was running on fumes. "Okay, I'll take the deal. What did you find?"

He frowned at her for a moment, then dropped his hand and turned to the screen wall. "Save data on screen four, screen off. Holloway file up, on all screens. Our friend here had a costly ID change four years ago. Under his birth name . . ."

"John B. Boyd. Shit." She got to her feet

and walked closer to the screens to read the first of several police reports. "Sexual offender, rape charges. Dropped by victim. Coerced sexual partnership, convicted. Six months psych treatment and community service. Bullshit. Possession of illegal sexual paraphernalia, pleaded out. Voluntary treatment for sexual obsessions. Treatment complete, records sealed. Fuck that. This guy was twisted and the system let him slide."

"He had money," Roarke pointed out. "It's easy to buy your way out of mid-level sex charges. He slithered his way clear, then ends up sodomized and strangled. Irony, Eve, or justice?"

"He should have gotten his justice in the courts," she snapped. "I don't give a damn about irony. Would Personally Yours have found this during screening?"

"I would have." He moved his shoulders. "It depends on how deep they go, but as I said, it was only a few layers down. Any full-security screen would have popped it. Sealing the records only protects him from a standard employee or credit screen."

"Did you get his financials?"

"Of course. Subject financials, screen six. You can see he did very well monetarily at his work. Had a decent broker who invested well. He liked to spend, but he had it to spend. There are, however, several reasonably good deposits which are over and above his modeling fees or investment dividends. Ten thousand at three-month intervals over a two-year period."

"Yeah." Again, she stepped closer to the screen. "I see them. Were you able to trace?"

"I wonder why I tolerate these small insults." He only sighed when she turned back and scowled at him. "Naturally. They were e-transfers, swung through a variety of sources in a decent attempt to conceal the original source. However, all of them bounce back to one location."

She nodded her head. "Personally Yours."

"You're an excellent detective."

"So, he was blackmailing them. Or one of them. Do you have initials of the name authorizing transfer?"

"The account is under both names. It could have been either Piper or Rudy. Their account uses a passcode rather than a signature."

"Okay, it gives me enough to bring them into Interview and cook them awhile." She drew a long breath. "I'm going to let Peabody have a go at them first, shake them up. Then I'll move in."

"Just make sure you're home by six."

Impatient, she turned back to him. The morning was breaking, light slipping through the treated glass and accenting her pale cheeks and shadowed eyes. "I made the deal. I'll keep it."

"Of course you will." If he had to go down to Cop Central and carry her out personally.

# CHAPTER THIRTEEN

Eve decided the best strategy was to hit her targets hard and clean while they were already bruised. If Peabody played it right, Rudy and Piper would be shaken, working frantically to avoid bad publicity and a potential lawsuit brought by a horrified client.

And when Peabody moved out, Eve thought, she would move in.

At nine thirty she was in the salon, showing Holloway's picture to the reception clerk. If it went as timed, she would be finishing up when Peabody came in and gave her the go signal.

"Sure, I know Mr. Holloway. He had a regular once a week, and a standing monthly."

"Once a week for what?"

"Hair style, facial, manicure, massage, and aroma-relax." Yvette, friendly and helpful now, leaned over the counter and let out a little sigh as she studied Holloway's picture again. "This guy's got a mag shell, and he knew how to maintain. Once a month he got the works, full day of treatments."

"Same consultant?"

"Oh sure, he wouldn't settle for anybody but Simon. A few months ago, Simon took a vacation. Mr. Holloway pitched a big one right here in the wait area. We gave him a free spin in the mood tube and a Deluxe O to chill him down."

"Deluxe O?"

"O for orgasm, honey. Privacy room, with his choice of VR, holo, or droid LC. We aren't set up for human licensed companions, but we have all the alternatives. The Deluxe runs five hundred, but it was worth it to take him down. You gotta keep your regulars happy. A client like Holloway drops like five thousand a month in here, not counting product purchases."

"And there's nothing like a Deluxe Orgasm to keep the customer satisfied."

"You got it." She grinned, grateful that Eve didn't appear to hold grudges. "So, did he do something?"

"You could say that. But he won't be doing it again. Simon around?"

"He's back in Studio Three. You don't

want to go back there," she began when Eve turned.

"Yes, I do."

Eve walked down a short hallway and through frosted glass doors etched with silhouettes of perfect human forms.

There were muted voices and music, the sounds of water splashing tunefully, birds chirping, breezes blowing. She could smell eucalyptus, rose, musk.

Pastel-colored doors lined both sides. Through an open one she could see a long padded table and complicated equipment, tubes, mirrors, a small computer station. All of which reminded her uncomfortably of a health center.

As she continued down, another door opened and a consultant in a white uniform led a woman covered from head to toe in green glop toward another area.

"Studio Three?"

"Corridor to the left, the door's marked."

"Uh-huh." Eve watched while the consultant drew her client away, telling her that ten minutes in the Desert Room would make her a new woman.

It took all Eve's willpower not to shudder.

When the corridor forked, she saw the large bubbling spa framed with miniature weeping cherry trees. Three women were already relaxing in it, breasts bobbing cheerfully on the surface of the sugar-pink froth.

Another woman drifted alone, submerged to the chin in the thickened green fluid of a sensory tube. Just beyond it, in what Eve supposed was the wet area, was a narrow pool called the Plunge, where the sharply blue water was held at a temperature of thirty-six degrees. Even looking at it made her teeth chatter.

She turned left. After a quick knock on the Easter-egg-blue door marked Three, she stepped in. It was a toss-up who was more surprised, herself, Simon, or McNab, who reclined in a relaxation chair with his face coated with what appeared to be black mud.

"This is a treatment area." Hands flapping, Simon rushed to block her way. "You're not allowed in here while I'm consulting. Out, out, out."

"I need to talk to you. It'll only take a couple minutes."

"I'm working here." Simon spread his hands, sending a few blobs of mud sailing.

"Two minutes," she said and had to clamp down on the urge to laugh as McNab rolled his eyes dramatically behind Simon's back.

"Out, out," he said again, snagging a towel. "I do apologize," he said to McNab. "Your slather needs to set in any case.

Please, just relax, let your mind rest. I'll just be a moment."

"No problem," McNab muttered.

"No, no, shh!" With a benign smile, Simon tapped a finger to his lips. "No talking. Let your face relax completely, let your mind empty. This is your time. Now, close your eyes, imagine all impurities flowing out. I'll be just outside."

His smile fell away the minute he shut the door and looked at Eve. "I won't have you disturbing my clients."

"Sorry. But one of your clients was really disturbed last night. He won't be coming in for his standing monthly anymore."

"What are you talking about?"

"Holloway. Brent Holloway. He's dead."

"Dead? Brent?" Simon leaned back against the glossy wall. The hand he hadn't quite wiped clean pressed against his heart. "But I saw him only a few days ago. There must be a mistake."

"I saw him this morning, in a drawer at the morgue. There's no mistake."

"I can't . . . breathe." Cape fluttering, Simon dashed down the hall. Eve found him in a plush waiting area, collapsed on a silk settee, his head between his knees.

"I didn't know you were that close."

"I'm his — was his consultant. No one,

not even a spouse, is more intimate."

She tried to think of intimacy with Trina and had to block off another shudder. "I'm sorry for your loss, Simon. You want something. Water?"

"Yes, no. Oh dear God." He lifted his head and reached out with a trembling hand to engage the pop-up refreshment screen on the table beside him. His face was a sickly gray framed by the brilliant red of his hair. "I need a soother. Camomile, chilled." Then he leaned back, shut his eyes. "How did it happen?"

"We're investigating. Tell me about him, tell me who he was involved with."

"He was a very exacting man. I respected that. He knew precisely how he wanted to appear, and was dedicated to maintaining his face, his body. Oh God." He snagged the tall, slim glass from the server droid the minute it scooted in. "I'm sorry, dear heart. Give me just a moment."

He drank deeply, taking slow, even breaths between sips. Some of the color that had washed away from his face came back. "He never missed an appointment, and sent me many referrals. He appreciated my work."

"Did he hook up with anyone around here on a personal level? Stylists, consultants, other clients?"

"Our staff isn't permitted to date the clientele. As to other clients, I don't recall him mentioning any. He enjoyed women. He had a varied and satisfying sexual life."

"He told you about that?"

"What is discussed between consultant and client is absolutely sacred." Simon sniffed once, then set his empty glass aside.

"Did he go for men, too?"

Simon's mouth flattened. "He never mentioned an interest in same-sex relationships. I don't feel comfortable with these questions, Lieutenant."

"Holloway's not real comfortable now either." She waited a beat, saw Simon pause, take it in, then nod.

"You're right. Of course you're right. I apologize. It's just such a shock."

"Did any of your male staff members show an interest in him, a romantic or sexual interest?"

"No. At least . . . I honestly never noticed any signals or vibrations, if you will. Such behavior is soundly discouraged here. We're professionals."

"Right. Who have you got on staff who does freehand tattoos?"

He sighed long and loud. "We have several consultants who are excellent freehand body artists."

"Names, Simon."

"Ask Yvette at the desk. She'll give you what you need. I must get back to my client." He pressed his fingers to his eyes. "I can't allow my personal feelings to interfere with my work. Lieutenant . . ." Simon dropped his hands back into his lap, and his eyes were dark and damp. "Brent had no family. What will happen to his . . . What will happen to him?"

"The city will take care of it, if there's no one."

"No, that wouldn't be right." He pressed his lips together, then pushed himself to his feet. "I'd like to make the arrangements if that's allowed. It would be the last thing I could do for him."

"We can work it that way. You'll have to come down to the morgue, fill out the paperwork."

"To the . . ." His mouth trembled, but he drew in a breath and nodded. "Yes, I will."

"I'll let them know to expect you." Because he looked so devastated, she added, "You won't have to see him, Simon. We've done an ID already. You just make the application, and they'll release the body to whatever mortuary or memorial center you choose."

"Oh." His breath came out in a rush.

"Thank you. My client's waiting," he said dully. "He hasn't been caring for his skin. Fortunately, he's young, so there's a great deal I can do to help. It's our obligation to present an attractive appearance. Beauty soothes the soul."

"Yeah. Go take care of your client, Simon. I'll be in touch."

She headed back out and was just taking the printout of names from Yvette when Peabody came in. She looked flushed and hollow-eyed. But she gave Eve a quick nod before turning to the desk clerk.

"I have a chit from Personally Yours," she began. "For the Diamond Day Plan."

"Oh, that's our very best." Yvette beamed at her. "And, honey, you look exhausted. This is just what you need. We'll fix you right up."

"Thanks." She wandered off, ostensibly to study the glass cabinet full of colorful bottles that guaranteed beauty and vitality with regular use. In a fast whisper, she gave Eve her report.

"They were both shaken, tried to cover it. Worked on convincing me I'd misinterpreted." She bit back a snort. "Went into placate-the-client mode, like it was programmed. Promised to look into the matter right away, offered me a free second consult and this deal here. I saw the brochure. The Diamond Day goes for five thousand. I didn't let them off the hook. Told them I was going to take the day to calm down before I spoke to my lawyer."

"Good work. Talk to as many of the consultants as you can while you're getting slathered and rubbed. Bring up Holloway's name. I want reactions, gossip, opinions. Make sure you get some male consultants in there."

"Anything for the job, sir."

"Ms. Peabody?"

Peabody turned, and thought her mouth must have hit her shoes as she stared at the polished golden god. "I'm uh . . . Yes?"

"I'm Anton. I'll be assisting you with your herbal detox. If you'd like to come with me now?"

"Oh yeah." Peabody managed to shoot Eve one sidelong eyeroll before Anton took her hand and gently led her away.

Hoping for the best, Eve tucked the printout in her bag and headed up to the office level of Personally Yours.

"Rudy and Piper are unavailable," the receptionist announced with just enough snip in her voice to put Eve's back up.

"Oh, they're going to want to become available." She slapped her badge on the counter. "Trust me."

"I'm aware of who you are, Lieutenant. Rudy and Piper aren't available. If you'd care to make an appointment, I'd be happy to schedule one for you."

Eve leaned companionably on the counter. "Ever hear the term obstruction of justice?"

The woman's eyes flickered. "I'm just doing my job."

"Here's what we've got. You clear me through to your bosses now, or I take you down to Cop Central and charge you with obstruction, for impeding an officer, and for being basically stupid. You got ten seconds to decide how you want to play it."

"Excuse me." The woman turned, switched on her headset, and murmured into it quickly. Her face was stiff when she turned back. "You're to go right in, Lieutenant."

"There, that wasn't such a tough choice, was it?" Pocketing her badge, Eve strode back through the glass doors, and met Rudy and Piper at the doorway of their office.

"Was it necessary to bully our receptionist?" Rudy demanded.

"Yeah. You got a reason for wanting to dodge me this morning?"

"We're very busy."

"You're about to get busier. You'll have to

come with me."

"Come with you?" Piper put a hand on Rudy's arm. "Why? Where?"

"To Cop Central. Brent Holloway was murdered last night, and we have a lot to talk about."

"Murdered?" Piper swayed and might have fallen if Rudy's arm hadn't whipped up to support her. "Oh God. Oh dear God. Like the others? Was it like the others? Rudy."

"Hush now." He drew his sister closer while his eyes held Eve's. "It isn't necessary to go into Central."

"Well, that's where we disagree. Your choice is to come voluntarily, or for me to call a few uniforms up here and have you escorted."

"You can't possibly have cause to arrest either one of us."

"You're not being arrested or charged at this time. But you're required to come in, upon demand, for formal interview."

With Piper trembling against him, Rudy let out a careful breath. "I'm going to contact our attorneys."

"You can do that downtown."

"Okay, we keep them separated," Eve said to Feeney as they studied Piper through the glass. Piper sat at the little scarred table in Interview A, rocking herself as one of the attorneys murmured to her. "We could double team them, but I think we can get more done if we each take one. You want her or Rudy?"

Feeney considered, lips pursed. "I'll start with him. I say we switch off, toss them out of balance once they get used to the rhythm. If either of them shake enough, then we go in double."

"Good enough. Did McNab check in?"

"Just did. He's about finished at the salon. He'll be in and have his report up before we're done here."

"Tell him to stand by. If we get enough here, we may be able to juggle a warrant for their computer system. If he can work on their machine, he might dig something out."

Otherwise, she thought, she was going to have to ask Roarke to work his magic again.

"Buzz when you want to switch," she told Feeney.

"Same goes."

Eve pulled open the door of the interview room and stepped inside. The lawyer immediately got to his feet, puffed out his chest, and went into the expected song and dance.

"Lieutenant, this is an outrage. My client

is overwrought, emotionally distressed. You have no cause to demand this interview at this time."

"You want to block it, get a court order. Record on. Dallas, Lieutenant Eve, ID 5347BQ, interviewer. Subject Piper Hoffman. Initial date and time. Interviewer has requested representation. Attorney is present. These proceedings are being recorded. Subject Hoffman has been read the revised Miranda. Do you understand your rights and obligations, Ms. Hoffman?"

Piper looked at her lawyer, waited for him to nod.

"Yes."

"You knew Brent Holloway?"

She jerked her head into a nod.

"Let the record show interviewee answered in the affirmative. He was a client of your service, Personally Yours."

"Yes."

"Through that service, you matched the deceased with female clients."

"That's — that's the purpose, to match couples with common interests and goals, to afford them an opportunity to meet and explore relationships."

"Romantic and/or sexual relationships?"

"The tone of the relationships is up to each individual couple or client."

"And these clients are screened before their application is accepted, before they pay the fee, before they are put on any match lists."

"Carefully screened." Piper seemed to breathe a sigh of relief at the avenue of questioning. She straightened a bit, skimmed back her silvery hair with long fingers. "It's our responsibility to see that our clientele meets certain standards."

"Do those standards include sexual offenders? Convicted sexual offenders?"

"Certainly not." She went prim, head lifting, mouth firming.

"That's your company policy?"

"A very firm policy."

"But you made an exception for Brent Holloway."

"I —" The hands Piper had folded neatly on the table clenched to whiten the knuckles. "I don't know what . . ." Her voice trailed off, and she stared helplessly at her lawyer.

"My client has explained her company's policy in this area, Lieutenant. Please move on."

"Brent Holloway was convicted of sexual coercion, was charged more than once with sexual molestation, harassment, perversions." Eve spoke briskly as every ounce of color in Piper's cheeks drained. "You've established for the record that your clientele is screened carefully, you've explained your policy in this area. I'm asking you why you exempted Holloway from this policy."

"We — I — we didn't." Her hands began to twist, and something like fear moved into her eyes. "We have no record of that information on Brent Holloway."

"Maybe you recognize the name John B. Boyd." Because her eyes were trained on Piper's face, she saw it. The flicker of knowledge, the shadow of guilt. "Your system is top of the line. So you told me. It would be your responsibility to do a search for this kind of information on an applicant. Is your company irresponsible or inept, Ms. Hoffman?"

"I don't like the tone of that question," the lawyer protested.

"So noted for the record. Your answer, Piper?"

"I don't know what happened." Her breath came quickly now, and both hands were crossed over her beautiful breasts. "I don't know."

Oh yes, Eve thought. Yes, you do, and he scared the hell out of you.

"Four clients of your service are dead. Four. Each one of them came to you, and each one of them was terrorized, raped, and strangled."

"It's a terrible, terrible coincidence. Just a coincidence." Piper began to shake, with her breath hitching out in little forced gasps. "Rudy said so."

"You don't believe that." Eve said it softly as she leaned closer. "You don't believe that for a minute. They're dead." Brutally, she laid four photos on the table. The crime scene shots were vivid and cruel. "These don't look coincidental, do they?"

"Oh God. Oh God." She covered her face with her hands. "Don't, don't, don't. I'm going to be ill."

"That was uncalled for." Red-cheeked with fury, the lawyer sprang up.

"Murder's uncalled for," Eve tossed back and got to her feet. "I'll give your client a few minutes to compose herself. Record, off." She turned her back and walked out.

As she watched through the glass, she buzzed Feeney's communicator.

"I've got her on the edge," she said when he joined her. "You can push her over. I'd go in light, sympathetic, be her uncle."

"You always get to be the bad cop," Feeney complained.

"I'm better at it. Pat her hand, then ask her why they were paying Holloway off. I didn't get there yet."

"Okay. Rudy's holding tight. He's got a snippy attitude you ask me. Arrogant little putz."

"Good. I'm in the mood to kick some putz." Since it was there, she reached into Feeney's bag of nuts and popped a handful. "She claims they didn't know about Holloway's record. She's lying, but that might get us into their system. I'll try for the warrant before I hit Rudy."

She took time for that and one quick jolt of coffee before going into Interview B. "Record on," she ordered. "Interview continuing with Dallas, Lieutenant Eve. Initialize time and date."

She sat, smiled at Rudy and the lawyer at his side. "Well, boys, let's get started."

She ran him through a pattern similar to what she'd used on Piper. Rather than paling and shaking, Rudy seemed to go stiffer, harder.

"I'd like to see my sister," he said abruptly, interrupting her rhythm.

"Your sister is being interviewed."

"She's delicate. Her emotions are very close to the surface. This entire ugly business will damage her."

"I've got four people a lot more damaged, ace. Are you worried what Piper has to say in there? I talked to her just a bit ago." Instinct had her leaning back, shrugging a shoulder. "She's not holding up real well. She'll do better once you clear things up."

Eve watched his hands fist and wondered what Mira would conclude about his violence potential.

"She should be allowed to rest." He bit off the words, his exotic green eyes flat as a cat's. "To have a soother and a meditation break."

"We're not big on meditation breaks around here. And she's got her lawyer in there, just like you've got yours. I guess you're pretty close, being twins."

"Naturally."

"Holloway ever make a move on her?"

Rudy's mouth thinned. "Of course not."

"On you maybe?"

"No." He reached for his glass of water with a steady hand.

"Why were you paying him off?"

The water slopped toward the rim before he hastily set it down. "I don't know what you're talking about."

"Regular payments, ten thousand each, over a two-year period. What did he have on you, Rudy?"

His eyes stormy, he whirled to his lawyer. "They have no right to access financial records, do they?"

"Certainly not." The lawyer leveled his shoulders, hooking a hand pompously in his lapel, where trendy medallions dangled. "Lieutenant, if you've searched my client's financials without probable cause and proper warrant —"

"Did I say that?" Eve only smiled. "I don't have to explain how I came by certain information that pertains to this homicide. You won't find a departmental search of financials. But you paid him, didn't you, Rudy?" She swung back, hitting low and fast. "You paid him time after time, let him blackmail you into putting him on match lists when you knew he was a sexual deviant. How many clients did you have to placate, or pay, or intimidate to keep the wraps on it?"

"I don't know what you're talking about." But his hand wasn't quite so steady now as he picked up the water in front of him. Dark red streaks of emotion began to burn along the milk-white skin.

Eve knew if she'd had him on a truth tester, the graft would have cracked through the screen.

"Yes, you do. And I bet it wouldn't be too tough for me to dig out a couple of your clients who Holloway jumped during one of those nice, polite meets you recommend. Once I do, I can charge you and your sister for soliciting, for fraud, for accessory to several types of sex crimes." She shot a look over. "And your lawyer knows I can make at least some of that stick, and it'll stick long and hard enough to put your business in the sewer, to put your face, and Piper's, on every screen in the city for newsflashes."

"We can't be held responsible. She can't be held responsible for what that . . . that deviant did."

"Rudy." The lawyer held up a hand, then laid it on Rudy's shoulder. "I'd like a moment to confer, Lieutenant."

"No problem. Record off. You got five," she warned and left them alone.

With her eyes on them through the glass, she pulled out her communicator. "McNab."

While she waited for response, she rocked back and forth on her heels, judging the body language inside the room. Rudy had his arms crossed, his fingers digging into his biceps. The lawyer was hunched over, talking fast.

"McNab. I'm heading in, Dallas."

"Then head back. I'm getting a warrant to put you into the system at Personally Yours. Wait for it."

"Can I take a six-eight? Grab some lunch?"

"Hit a glide-cart on the way back. I want you in place the minute the authorization comes in." She heard his sigh and smiled thinly. "How was the facial, McNab?"

"Great. I got cheeks like a baby's ass. And I saw Peabody naked. Well, mostly. She was coated with green shit, but I got the picture."

"Just put that picture out of your mind and get ready to dig."

"I can do both. Hell of a picture. She's really pissed, too."

Eve did her best not to grin back at him, and shut him off before she lost the battle.

"Time's up, pal," she murmured and walked back into Interview. After resetting the record, she sat down, lifted a brow. Sometimes silence worked a subject better than hammering.

"My client wishes to make a statement."

"That's what we're here for. So, what do you have to say, Rudy?"

"Brent Holloway was extorting money from my company, through me. I did my best to protect my clients, but he was blackmailing me and part of what he demanded was regular consultations and matches. He was, in my opinion, difficult and irritating, but not dangerous to the women we matched him with."

"That's your professional opinion?"

"Yes, it is. We advise all our clients to meet their matches in a public place. Any who agreed to meet him privately subsequent to that were making their own decision. All clients sign a waver."

"Uh-huh, so you figure that covers your ass, ethically speaking. I'm pretty sure the courts may have a different view. But let's get to the meat first. What did he have on you?"

"It's not relevant."

"Oh yeah, it is."

"It deals with my personal life."

"It deals with homicide, Rudy. But if you don't want to tell me about it, I'll go back and talk to your sister." She started to rise, but Rudy's hand flew out and gripped her arm.

"Leave her alone. She's delicate."

"One of you will talk to me. Your choice."

His fingers tightened on her arm, dug in hard before he released it and sat back. "Piper and I have a unique and special relationship. We're twins. We're connected." He kept his eyes level. "We're matched."

"You and your sister have a sexual relationship."

"It's not for you to judge," he snapped. "Nor do I expect you to understand the bond between us. No one can. And though what we have together isn't strictly illegal, society disapproves."

"Incest isn't a pretty word, Rudy." The image of her father, his face red with effort, his eyes hard with purpose, flashed into her mind. Under the table she clenched her hands into fists and forced the image, and the sickness it caused, back.

"We're matched," he said again. "For most of our lives we refused to act on what was in our hearts. We tried to be with other people, to live separate lives. And we were miserable. Are we supposed to be unhappy, unfulfilled, because people like you say it's wrong?"

"It doesn't matter what I say, or what I think. How did Holloway find out?"

"It was in the West Indies. Piper and I had taken a vacation. We'd been careful. We're discreet. We understand that we'd lose clients if they knew. We'd gone away where we could have a little time alone together, to be free to be together openly as any other couple can. Holloway was there. He didn't know us, nor we him. We had registered under different names."

He paused, sipped his water. "A few

months later he came in for a consult. It was just . . . fate. I didn't even recognize him at first. But after his screening, when the data on him showed up and we refused his application, he reminded us where we'd met, and how."

Rudy stared into his water, shifted the glass from hand to hand. "He was very clear as to how it would be handled, what he wanted. Piper was destroyed, terrified. We both believe very strongly in the service we provide. You see, we know just what it means to be matched with someone who fills your life, who makes the difference in it. We're dedicated to helping others find what we have."

"Your dedication's earned you a nice fat portfolio."

"Making a profit doesn't negate the worth of the service. You live well, Lieutenant," he said quietly. "Does that negate the worth of your marriage?"

Walked into that one, she told herself, but only lifted her eyebrows. "Let's talk about you and how you handled Holloway."

"I wanted to stand against him, but she couldn't." He closed his eyes. "He managed to get her alone, to threaten her. He even tried to induce her to . . ."

He opened his eyes again, and they were

brimming with fury. "He wanted her. His kind, they want what belongs to someone else. So we paid, we did everything he demanded. Still, if he came in and caught her alone, he would touch her."

"You must have hated him for that."

"Yes. Yes, I hated him for that. For everything, but most of all for that."

"Enough to kill him, Rudy?"

"Yes," he said evenly before his lawyer could stop him. "Yes, enough to kill him."

# Chapter Fourteen

"We don't have enough to charge him."

She knew it. Damn it, she knew it, but Eve went to battle with the assistant prosecuting attorney anyway.

"He's got the means, he's got the opportunity, and God knows he had a motive with Holloway. He had access to the enhancements used on all four victims," she continued before APA Rollins could speak. "He knew all of them."

"You don't even have a decent circumstantial case against him." Carla Rollins held her ground. She was barely five-two, despite the skyscraper heels she habitually wore. Her eyes were the color of blackberries, exotically slanted in a round face. Her complexion was creamy and smooth, her figure neat, her hair a ribbon-straight ebony that fell precisely one inch above her slim shoulders.

She looked, and sounded, like a child care

professional, and had a core as tough as moon rock. She liked to win, and didn't see a victory in *The State* v. *Hoffman.*

"You want me to bag him when he's got his hands around the next victim's throat?"

"That would be handy," Rollins said evenly. "Barring that, get me a confession."

Eve paced the length of Whitney's office. "I can't get you a confession if we spring him."

"So far all he's guilty of is banging his sister," Rollins said in her soft, sweet voice. "And paying blackmail. Maybe we could cook him on illegal and unlicensed solicitation since he knew Holloway's predilections, but it's a stretch. I can't give you murder, Dallas, without more evidence or a confession."

"Then I need to sweat him longer."

"His lawyer's called for a humane break. We can't hold him any longer today," she added as Eve snorted. "You can pick him up again tomorrow, after the standard twelve hours out."

"I want a bracelet on him."

This time Rollins sighed. "Dallas, I don't have cause to order a security bracelet on Hoffman at this time. At this point he's only a suspect, and not a solid one at that. He's entitled, under the law, to his privacy and freedom of motion."

"Christ, give me something." Eve dragged both hands through her hair. Her eyes were burning from lack of sleep, her stomach raw from caffeine. Her still-healing wound was throbbing. "I want him tested and profiled. I want Mira to do him."

"It'll have to be voluntary." Rollins held up one delicate hand before Eve could swear at her. She was used to cops swearing at her, and it didn't particularly bother her. But she was thinking, and didn't want the interruption. "I might be able to convince his attorney it's in his best interest. Co-operation in this area would influence the PA's office not to pursue the solicitation charges."

Satisfied with the idea, Rollins rose. "Clear it with Mira, and I'll see what I can do. But spring him, Dallas, within the hour."

Whitney waited until Rollins breezed out, then shifted in his chair. "Sit down, Lieutenant."

"Commander —"

"Sit," he repeated and jabbed a finger at the chair across from his desk. "I'm concerned," he began when she took her seat.

"I need more time to squeeze him. Mc-Nab's working the system at Personally Yours. We could have something by the end of the day."

"You concern me, Lieutenant." He leaned back as Eve frowned. "You've been on this case nearly twenty-four/seven for more than a week."

"So has the killer."

"It's unlikely the killer is still recovering from life-threatening wounds received in the line of duty."

"My health chart's clear." She heard the edge of resentment in her own voice and took a careful breath. If she couldn't maintain with Whitney, she'd only prove his point. "Your concern is appreciated, sir, but unnecessary."

"Is it?" He lifted his brows as his sharp eyes scanned her face. Pale, shadowed, running up fast on exhaustion, was his considered opinion. "Then you're willing to go down to the clinic and take a physical?"

The resentment bounced back, all but vibrating down to the fingers she fought not to curl into fists. "Is that an order, Commander Whitney?"

He could make it so. "I'll give you a choice, Dallas. Take the physical, abide by the results, or go off duty until oh nine hundred tomorrow."

"I don't consider those viable options at this time."

"One or the other, or I take you off the case."

She nearly sprang from the chair. He saw her bunch and brace then vibrate. But she stayed in her seat. Color rushed into her face, but it didn't stay long. "He's killed four times, and I'm the only one who's close to knowing him. You take me off, we lose time. And we lose people."

"It's your choice, Dallas. Go home," he said more quietly. "Get a decent meal and some sleep."

"And while I'm doing that, Rudy walks."

"I can't hold him, I can't bracelet him. But that doesn't mean I can't put a tag on him." Now Whitney smiled a little. "He'll be watched. And tomorrow, we'll hold a press conference. You called that right, Dallas. The mayor and the chief will bare the brunt of it, but you'll get flack."

"I can handle it."

"I know. We'll release as many details as we can to alert the public." He lifted his hand, rubbing the back of his neck. "Peace on Earth, goodwill toward men." He let out a short laugh. "Go home, Dallas. You're going to need to be fresh tomorrow."

She went because the alternatives were unacceptable. She couldn't back off from the case, and she couldn't risk a departmental physical. Whatever she said out loud, she had a suspicion she wouldn't pass one at the moment.

She ached all over, enough to warn her she was going to have to break down and take a painkiller to get through. Worse, she couldn't quite focus, not now that she was in the car and heading home. Her head insisted on floating somewhere inches above her shoulders.

When she nearly clipped a glide-cart while making the turn onto Madison, she shifted into auto and let the program guide her through traffic.

Okay, so maybe she needed a nap and a little fuel. But being off duty didn't mean she couldn't run some more scans and searches; it didn't mean she couldn't work on her own from her home office.

She needed more coffee and something solid in her stomach, that was all.

And she nearly nodded off as the car slid through the gates and up the drive toward the house.

The lights in the windows blazed against the dark and made her eyes smart. Her head pounded like the back beat in one of Mavis's more enthusiastic numbers. Her shoulder thrummed.

When she stepped out of the car, her legs

felt rubbery and disconnected. Because she felt weak, her mood was foul as she pushed through the grand front door.

And there was Summerset.

"Your guests have already arrived," he announced. "You were expected twenty minutes ago."

"Kiss my ass" was her best suggestion as she stripped off her jacket and deliberately dropped it over the newel post.

"The prospect holds no appeal for me. One moment of your time, however, Lieutenant." He simply stepped in front of her before she could head up the stairs.

"Life's too short to spend a moment with you. Out of the way or I'll take you out."

She looked ill, he thought, and her threat lacked its usual bite. "The book you requested for Roarke has been located," he said stiffly, but his eyes were narrowed as he studied her face.

"Oh." She braced a hand on the newel post as she tried to get through the fog in her brain to think. "Fine. Good."

"Shall I order it to be shipped?"

"Yeah, yeah. That's the idea."

"You'll need to transfer the price, plus shipping, to the book searcher's account. As the book searcher knows me, he's agreed to send the item immediately and trust that

326

you'll transfer the appropriate funds within twenty-four hours. I noted the details on your E-mail."

"Okay, fine. I'll take care of it." She had to swallow pride. "Thank you." And she turned toward the stairs. Looked up. She thought it would be like climbing a mountain, but she couldn't swallow another gulp of pride and take the elevator while he was watching.

"You're quite welcome," he murmured, then stepped away to the in-house screen while she moved up the steps. "Roarke, the lieutenant is home and on her way up." He hesitated, then sighed. "She looks unwell."

She was going to take a hot shower, fuel up, and get to work. Eve calculated she could at least run a probability scan on Rudy with the data she had. If it clicked, she might be able to pressure the PA into slapping a surveillance bracelet on him.

But when she stepped into the bedroom, Roarke was already waiting.

"You're late."

"I hit traffic," she said as she unhooked her weapon harness.

"Strip."

She knew she was punchy, but she was pretty sure this was a first. "Well, that's real romantic, Roarke, but —"

"Strip," he said again and picked up a robe. "Put this on. Trina's set up for you in the pool house."

"Oh for Christ's sake." She raked her hands through her hair. "Do I look in the mood for a goddamn beauty session?"

"No, you look like you're in the mood for a goddamn hospital session." Temper snapping, he tossed down the robe. "Take care of yourself here, or that's where you're going."

Her eyes went dark and dangerous. "Don't push me. You're my spouse, not my keeper."

"A fucking keeper's just what you need." He grabbed her arm and, because her reflexes were slow, shoved her into a chair. "Stay down," he warned in a voice that sizzled with barely restrained fury. "Or I'll tie you down."

She gripped the arm of the chair, fingers digging in as he stalked across the room to the recessed AutoChef. "What the hell's gotten into you?"

"You. Have you looked at yourself recently? You stand over bodies that have more color than you do right now. There are shadows under your eyes thick enough to hide in. And you're hurting." That was what snapped it for him. "Do you think I can't see it?"

He came back with a tall glass filled with amber liquid. "Drink it."

"You're not tranqing me."

"I can pour it down your throat. I've done it before." He leaned over until their faces were close, and the bitter anger in his eyes made her want to shrink away. "I won't let you make yourself sick. You'll drink this, Eve, and you'll do what I tell you, or I'll make you. We both know you're too damn tired to stop me."

She snatched the glass, and though she thought there would be lovely satisfaction gained from heaving it across the room, she didn't think she was up to dealing with the consequences. Her eyes burned into his over the rim as she gulped it down.

"There. Happy now?"

"You'll have something solid later." He bent down to tug off her boots.

"I can undress myself."

"Shut up, Eve."

For form's sake, she tried to tug her foot free, but he simply held on and pried off her boot. "I want a shower and a meal, and I want you to leave me alone."

He pulled off the other boot, then started on the buttons of her shirt.

"Did you hear me? I said leave me alone." The fact that she could hear the petulance in her own voice only added depression to exhaustion.

"Not in this or any other lifetime."

"I don't like to be taken care of. It irritates me."

"Then you're going to be irritated for quite a while."

"I've been irritated since I met you." She closed her eyes on that, but thought she caught a flicker of a smile around his mouth.

He undressed her quickly, efficiently, then bundled her into the robe. The limpness of her muscles told him the painkiller he'd added to the nutri-drink he'd made her was already at work. The mild tranq he'd laced it with should have done no more than relax her, but in her current state he imagined it would knock her out very shortly.

All for the best.

Still she slapped at him as he lifted her. "Don't carry me."

"I hate to repeat myself, but shut up, Eve." He walked to the elevator and stepped inside with her.

"I don't wanna be babied." Her head spun once, one long, lilting circle that forced her to let it drop on his shoulder. "What the hell was in that drink?"

"All manner of things. Just relax."

"You know I hate tranqs."

"I know." He turned his head, brushed his lips over her hair. "You can give me grief about it tomorrow."

"Will. I let you push me round, you'll get used to it. I'm gonna lie down for a minute."

"That's right." He felt her head loll back, and the arm around his neck slid off and dangled as he stepped out into the pool house.

Mavis raced out from under the fanning fronds of a palm. "Jesus, Roarke, is she hurt?"

"I tranqued her." He moved through the lush flowering plants, skirted the side of the shimmering waters of the pool, and laid his wife on the long, padded table Trina had already set up.

"Man, she'll be pissed royal when she comes out of it."

"I imagine so." Gently, he brushed the untidy hair back from Eve's forehead. "Not so tough now, are you, Lieutenant?" He bent down and kissed her lightly on the lips. "Don't worry about the styling, Trina. She needs relaxation therapy."

"Can do." Trina, decked out in a flesh-colored skinsuit with a shimmering purple duster, rubbed her hands together. "But since she's out anyway, why don't I give her the works? She's always bitching about treatments. This way she'll be nice and quiet."

Roarke lifted a brow at the gleam in the woman's eye, and laid a protective hand on Eve's shoulder. "Keep it simple." Then remembering who he was dealing with, he cleared his throat. He didn't mind facing his wife's wrath, but not over his passive agreement to having her hair dyed pink. "Why don't I order us down some dinner? I'll just stick around."

She heard voices, laughter. All so distant and disconnected. In part of her mind Eve knew she was fogged out by the drug. Roarke would pay for that.

She wished he would hold her again, just hold her in that way that made everything inside her stretch and yearn.

Someone was rubbing her back, her shoulders. The moan of pleasure was trapped in her mind, but it was low and it was long.

She smelled him, just a whiff in passing of the scent that was Roarke.

Then there was water, warm, bubbling, swirling around her. She was floating in it, weightless, mindless as a fetus in the womb. She drifted there, endlessly, feeling nothing but peace.

A flash of heat on her shoulder. A shock.

Someone was whimpering inside her head. Then cool, cool liquid over the heat, soothing as a kiss.

And under she went again, sliding down and down until she rocked on the soft bottom and curled there, sleeping deep.

When she surfaced, it was dark. Disoriented, she lay very still, counting her own breaths. She was warm and naked, stretched flat on her stomach under the billowing cloud of the duvet.

Home in bed, she realized, as the last hours of her life slipped in and out of focus. Trying to bring it clear, she rolled over, and her legs tangled with Roarke's.

"Awake?"

His voice sounded alert — a little skill of his that was a mild irritation to her. "What —"

"It's nearly morning."

She was indeed warm, and naked, her skin soft as dewed petals thanks to Trina, and she smelled like the cool juice of hothouse peaches.

"How do you feel?"

She wasn't entirely sure. Everything in her was so loose and smooth. "I'm fine," she said automatically.

"Good. Then you're ready for the final

phase of your relaxation program."

His mouth took hers, whisper-soft, his tongue already sliding in to tangle. Her mind, which had just started to clear, clouded again. This time with pure and healthy lust.

"Hold on. I'm not —"

"Let me taste you." His mouth skimmed down her throat to nibble and destroy. "Touch you." His hand glided up to her hip, down, parted her legs. "Have you."

When he slipped inside her, slowly, she was already hot and ready.

She couldn't see. The predawn light was like ink. He was a shadow moving over her, a steady, glorious force moving inside her. She tripped over the first peak before she could find the rhythm.

With long, slow, torturous strokes he pleasured them both. Her breathing thickened to match his, her hips lifted and fell until their paces meshed. Now when their mouths met, they swallowed each other's groans.

Warm, soft waves of sensation cradled her, then swept her up and over silky crests. When she felt his body tense, she enfolded him, wrapping herself around him, welcoming that final thrust that pinned them both to peak.

He buried his face in her hair and breathed her in.

"You are feeling better." He murmured it, his breath tickling her skin and making her smile.

Then her mind cleared.

"Goddamn it."

"Uh-oh." Chuckling, he rolled, taking her with him until her body was sprawled over his.

"You think it's funny." She shoved up and away, blowing at her hair as she sat up. "You think it's a joke? You push me around, bully me into taking some tranq."

"I wouldn't have been able to bully you into anything if you hadn't been ready to drop." He sat up as well. "Lights, ten percent." At his order the room filled with a soft glow. "You look good," he said after a moment's study of her furious — and rested — face. "Despite her rather extreme personal taste, Trina knows what suits you."

The way her mouth dropped open and her eyes bugged out had Roarke fighting back a roar of laughter. "You let her work on me while I was out? You sadistic, treacherous son of a bitch." She might have taken a swing at him, but she was already leaping out of bed toward the mirror.

The relief that she looked normal, fairly

much the way she looked every other morning wasn't quite enough to cut through the
temper. "I ought to throw you both in a
cage for this."

"Mavis was in on it, too," he said cheerfully. She hadn't moved that quickly or easily in several days, he noted. And her eyes
were free of shadows. "Oh, and Summerset."

Now she had no choice but to sit down.
She staggered back to the bed and dropped
down on the edge. "Summerset." It was a
horrified croak.

"He worked on your shoulder after I ran a
quick diagnostic. The muscles had flamed
up. Why the hell don't you take normal
steps to deal with discomfort?"

"Summerset" was all she could say.

"He's had medical training, as you know.
He simply treated your shoulder. How does
it feel?"

Maybe it was pain free for the first time in
days. Maybe her entire body felt gloriously
energized and fresh. That didn't make
Roarke's methods acceptable.

She pushed off the bed, snagged the robe
that was draped over a chair, and shoved
her arms into the sleeves. "I'm going to kick
your ass."

"All right." He got up agreeably and

found a robe for himself. "It'll be a fairer match than it was last night. You want to go at me here, or down in the gym?"

Before the last word was of his mouth, she sprang. She came in low. He had time to start a pivot, but not to complete it, and ended up sprawled on the bed, his wife on top of him, with her knee planted firmly, worrisomely, between his legs.

"Ah, I'd say you're back, Lieutenant."

"Damn right. I ought to knock your balls up to your ears, smart guy."

"Well, at least we both got one last use of them first." He grinned and risked serious damage. Then he reached up and feathered his fingers over her cheek. And distracted her just enough to allow him to counter the move. He flipped her over and pinned her down.

"Now, you listen." The grin was gone. "Whatever it takes is what I'll do. Whenever it's needed is when I'll do it. You don't have to like it, but you'll damn well live with it."

He pushed off, shifting to the balls of his feet when he saw her eyes narrow with purpose. Then he let out a sigh and jammed his hands into his pockets. "Bloody hell. I love you."

She'd been poised to spring. Those two sentences, said with equal parts frustration and weariness, arrowed straight to her heart. He stood there, his hair tousled from sleep and sex and struggle, his eyes deeply blue and filled with annoyance and love.

Everything inside her shifted, then settled into the pattern she supposed it was fated for. "I know. I'm sorry. You were right." She tunneled her fingers through her hair, distracted enough not to see the flicker of surprise on his face. "I don't like your methods, but you were right. I was pushing too hard before I was a hundred percent. You've been telling me to recharge for days, and I didn't want to hear it."

"Why?"

"I was scared." It was hard to admit it, even to a man she knew she could tell every secret.

"Scared?" He crossed to her, sat down, and took her hand in his. "Of what?"

"That I wouldn't be able to go back, not all the way back. That I wouldn't be strong enough, or sharp enough to be back on the job. And if I couldn't . . ." She squeezed her eyes shut. "I've got to be a cop. I have to do the job. If I can't — I've lost myself."

"You could have talked to me about this."

"I wouldn't even talk to myself about it." She rubbed her fingers over her eyes, irritated that there were tears brewing behind them. "Since I went back, I've been mostly doing paperwork, court dates. This is my first homicide since I got off disability leave. If I can't handle it . . ."

"You are handling it."

"Whitney ordered me home last night — either that or he was taking me off the case. I get here and you threaten to pour drugs down my throat."

"Well." He gave her hand a sympathetic squeeze. "That was lousy timing. But I believe, in both cases, it was a matter of wanting you to rest, rather than a criticism of your abilities."

He took her chin in his hand, rubbing his thumb over the center dent. "Eve, there are times when you are astonishingly unaware of self. You push yourself to the wall on every case. The only difference with this is that you were physically shaky to begin with. You're the same cop you were when I met you last winter. And occasionally that's a frightening thought."

"Yeah, I'm counting on that." She studied their joined hands. "But I'm not the same person I was last winter." With her fingers linked with his, she lifted her head, looked into his eyes. "I don't want to be. I like who I am now. Who we are now."

"Good." He leaned over to kiss her.

"Because we're stuck."

She fisted a hand in his hair to deepen the kiss. "It's turned out to be a pretty good deal. But . . ." She nibbled lightly at his bottom lip then bit it sharply enough to make him yelp in surprise and pain. "If you ever again let Summerset put his hands on me when I'm out . . ." She rose, breathed deeply, and decided she felt incredible. "I'll shave you bald in your sleep. I'm starving," she said abruptly. "Want breakfast?"

He considered her for a moment, then ran a considering hand over his long black hair. He was, fortunately, a very light sleeper. "Yeah. I could eat."

# CHAPTER FIFTEEN

Armed with the results of the probability scan on Rudy, Eve paced Dr. Mira's outer office. She needed the weight of Mira's profile on him to yank him back into Interview and, hopefully, into a cell.

Time was passing. With or without the tag, she expected him to move on to number five that night.

"Does she know I'm out here?" Eve demanded of Mira's assistant.

Well used to impatient cops, the woman didn't bother to glance up from her own work. "She's in a session. She'll be with you as soon as possible."

Pumped by refreshed energy, Eve paced to the far wall and eyed with suspicion a dreamy watercolor of some seacoast town. She paced back and scowled at the mini AutoChef. She knew it wouldn't be stocked with coffee. Mira preferred her patients and associates to sip soothers or tea.

The minute Mira's door opened, Eve whirled and pounced. "Dr. Mira —" She broke off when she spotted Nadine Furst.

The reporter flushed, then straightened her shoulders and met Eve's annoyed glare dead on.

"If you start going around me to pump my profiler for data, you're going to find yourself without a departmental source, and up on charges, pal."

"I'm here on personal business," Nadine said stiffly.

"Save the bullshit for your viewing audience."

"I said I'm here on personal business." Nadine held up a hand before Mira could interfere. "Dr. Mira counseled me after the . . . incident last spring. You kept me alive, Dallas, but she kept me sane. Now and again I need a little help, that's all. Now if you'll get the hell out of my way —"

"I'm sorry." Eve wasn't sure if she was more surprised or ashamed, but neither sensation sat well. "It was rough on you. I know what it's like to carry around bad memories. I'm sorry, Nadine."

"Yeah, right." She jerked a shoulder, striding out quickly. Her heels tapped on tile, and the sound echoed away.

"Please come in, Eve." Mira, her face

carefully blank, stepped back, then shut the door behind Eve.

"Okay, I jumped and I shouldn't have." She jammed her hands in her pockets to keep from squirming under the air of disapproval Mira created with a quiet look. "She's been nagging me about this case, and we've got a press conference set up in a couple of hours. I figured she was trying to cut some corners."

"You have difficulty trusting, even after a measure of trust has been established." Mira sat, smoothed her skirt. "You were also quick with an apology that came from the heart. You are, and always have been, a study of contradictions, Eve."

"I'm *not* here on personal business." Eve's tone was flat and dismissive, but she glanced back toward the door with concern in her eyes. "Is she okay?"

"Nadine is a strong and determined woman — traits you should recognize. I can't discuss this with you, Eve. It's privileged."

"Yeah." She blew out a breath. "She's pissed at me now. I'll give her a one-on-one and smooth her out again."

"She values your friendship. Not only the information you give her. Are you going to sit down? I don't intend to scold you."

Eve grimaced, then cleared her throat and held out the file she carried. "I have the probability scan on Rudy. With current data he comes out at eighty-six point six percent. That's high enough to poke at him again, but I can tie him up tighter after you test him. Rollins said Rudy's lawyer popped to it."

"Yes, I have him scheduled for this afternoon as you flagged it Priority One."

"I need to know his head, his violence potential, so I can put him away long enough for me to dig up evidence. I don't think he's going to break, or deal. If the sister knows anything, I can work on her. She'll fold eventually."

"I'll give you what I can, as soon as I can. I understand the pressure you and your team are under. However," she added, tilting her head, "you look well. Rested. The last time I saw you I was a little concerned. I still think you came back to full duty sooner than was wise."

"You and everyone else." Then she shrugged. "I feel good. Better. I had a top-level relaxation therapy session last night, and about ten hours sleep."

"Really?" Mira's lips curved. "And how did Roarke manage that?"

"He drugged me." At Mira's delighted

burst of laughter, Eve scowled. "Figures you'd be on his side."

"Oh, completely. How well you suit each other, Eve. It's a pleasure to watch what grows between you. I look forward to seeing you both tonight."

"The party, right." Whoopee, she thought irritably, but her mouth twitched when Mira laughed again. "Get me that profile, and maybe I'll be in a party mood."

But she wasn't when she walked into her office and found McNab rifling through her desk.

"I don't keep my candy stash there anymore, ace."

He straightened so quickly his hip hit the drawer, and shoved it closed on his fingers. His pained yelp greatly lifted Eve's mood.

"Jesus, Dallas." Pouting, he sucked his throbbing fingers. "You might as well blast me as scare me to death."

"I ought to give you a jolt. Stealing a superior officer's candy bars is no small matter, McNab. I need my candy fix."

"Okay, okay." Trying for contrite, he smiled and pulled out her desk chair for her. "Looking good this morning, Dallas."

"Don't suck up, McNab. It's pathetic." She dropped down in her chair and stretched her legs out, which bumped her boots against the wall. "You want to make points, give me some news."

"I verified the financials, and found eight complaints lodged against Holloway buried in the FI file."

"FI?"

"Fuck It file," he said with a quick grin. "It's a place businesses stick cranks and other shit they don't intend to deal with. But all eight women were given free perks, just like Peabody. Salon treatments or free match lists, credit in the boutiques."

"Who authorized?"

"Both of them, depending. She knew what was up, all right I got her initials on three of the complaints."

"Okay, that puts Piper in, but it doesn't win us a prize. I can use it to squeeze her some."

"Something else's a little interesting," he said and sat down on the corner of her desk.

Eve eyed him balefully. "Interesting enough for me not to kick your ass off my desk?"

"Well, lets find out. I found a memo on Donnie Ray, dated six months ago and updated the first of December."

Eve felt a little tickle under her heart. "What kind of memo?"

"From Rudy to the consulting staff. Donnie Ray was not to be put through to Piper. Rudy would do his consults personally, or oversee them. The update was a little slap, restating the original notice and reprimanding some drone who didn't shield a call."

"That's fairly interesting. So he didn't want Donnie Ray sniffing around Piper. I can use that. Anything on the other two victims?"

"Nothing that popped out."

She drummed her fingers on the desk. "Medical? Mental or physical treatments?"

"They're both sterilized." McNab squirmed on the desk as he imagined the cold tongue of the laser on his own genitals. "They opted out of the reproductive market about five years back."

"That follows."

"Piper's had regular shrink work, weekly sessions at Inner Balance for as long as they have records on file. Last year, she did a month at one of their retreats on Optima II. I hear they do colonics, sleep in mood tubes, and eat nothing but grain noodles."

"What a party. What about him?"

"Zip."

"Well, he's going to get some shrink work this afternoon. Decent job, McNab." She looked over as Peabody came in. "Good timing. The two of you nail down that last piece of jewelry. I want to know where he bought those four calling birds. He got a little sloppy at the scene; maybe he tripped up with the necklace, too."

Peabody studiously avoided looking at McNab. "But, sir —"

"I'm going to squeeze Piper, so I can't take you with me. If you leave the building, either of you, you leave together." She rose. "If he hasn't picked out number five by now, he's looking. I want you both where I can find you."

"Relax, She-Body," McNab sneered as Eve headed out. "I'm a professional."

"Bite me."

Though Eve managed to swallow a chuckle at her aide's use of her own standard response to annoyances, she didn't quite make it over McNab's cheerful, "Where?"

Eve's timing was well calculated. If Rudy's lawyer had any brains, he'd have his client in some locked room being prompted on the upcoming tests. She had, she decided, at least an hour to rattle Piper before she had to get back to Central for the press conference.

This time, the receptionist didn't bother

to stall, but simply cleared her through.

"Lieutenant." Pale, hollow-eyed, Piper stood at the doorway of the office. "My lawyer informs me that I'm not under any obligation to speak with you, and advises me against it unless it's in formal interview with my counsel present."

"You can play it that way, Piper. We can go in right now, or we can stay here, be comfortable, and you can tell me why Rudy didn't want you dealing with Donnie Ray Michael."

"That was nothing." Distress shimmered into her voice as she linked her hands. "That was nothing at all. You can't make anything bad out of it."

"Fine. Why don't you just clear it up for me so we can put it away?"

Without waiting for an invitation, Eve slipped into the room and took a chair. She waited, saying nothing, and let the little war so obvious on Piper's face play out.

"It was just that Donnie Ray had a little crush on me. That's all. It was nothing. It was harmless."

"Then why the staff memos?"

"It was just a precaution. To avoid any . . . unpleasantness."

"Is there often unpleasantness?"

"No!" Piper shut the door and hurried

over. There were spots of agitated color in her cheeks. The silvery hair had been twisted back today, leaving her face unframed, adding a contrast of sophistication and fragility.

"No, not at all. We're dedicated to helping people find pleasantness, in companionship, romance, often marriage. Lieutenant . . ." She steepled her hands, folded the fingers down. "I could show you dozens of endorsements from satisfied clients. From people we helped to find each other. Love, true love, matters."

Eve kept her eyes level. "You believe in true love, Piper?"

"Absolutely, completely."

"What would you do for your true love, to keep him?"

"Whatever I had to do."

"Tell me about Donnie Ray."

"He asked me out, a couple of times. He wanted me to hear him play." She sighed, then seemed to melt into a chair. "He was just a boy, Lieutenant. He wasn't . . . It wasn't the way it was with Holloway. But Rudy felt, rightly so, that in order to fulfill our obligation to him as a client, it would be best if contact with me was eliminated."

"Were you interested in hearing Donnie Ray play?"

A smile ghosted around her mouth. "I

might have enjoyed that, if that was all. But it was clear that he had hopes for more. I didn't want to hurt his feelings. I can't bear to bruise a heart."

"And what about yours? How does your relationship with your brother sit on your heart?"

"I can't — won't discuss that with you." She sat straight again, folded her hands.

"Who made the decision that you'd be sterilized, Piper?"

"You go too far."

"Do I? You're twenty-eight years old." She pushed because she'd seen Piper's lips tremble. "And you've eliminated the chance to have children because you can't risk conceiving one with your own brother. You've been in therapy for years. You've been cut off from developing a relationship with another man. You conceal the relationship you do have, paid a blackmailer to insure it continued to be concealed because incest is a dark and shameful secret."

"You can't possibly understand."

"Oh yes, I can." But she'd been forced, Eve reminded herself. She'd been a child. She'd had no choice. "I know what you're living with."

"I love him! If it's wrong, if it's shameful, if it's wretched, that doesn't change. He's

351

my life."

"Then why are you afraid?" Eve leaned forward. "Why are you so afraid that you'll cover for him even when you wonder if he's killed? Anything for true love? You let Holloway prey on your clients, and that makes you the same as a pimp for an unlicensed whore."

"No, we did our best to find him like-minded women."

"And when you didn't, and they complained, you paid them off," Eve finished. "Is that what you wanted to do, or was it Rudy?"

"It was business. Rudy understands the business better than me."

"Is that how you live with it? Or maybe neither one of you could live with it anymore. Was he with you the night Donnie Ray was killed? Can you look at me and swear he was with you all that night?"

"Rudy couldn't hurt anyone. He couldn't."

"Are you so sure, so sure, you'll risk another death? If not tonight, then tomorrow."

"Whoever is killing these people is insane — vicious, cruel, and insane. If I thought it could be Rudy, I couldn't live. We're part of each other, so it would be in me the way it's in him. I couldn't live." She covered her face with her hands. "I can't stand any more of this. I won't talk to you. If you accuse Rudy, you accuse me, and I won't talk to you."

Eve rose, but paused by the chair for a moment. "You're not half of a whole, Piper, whatever he's told you. If you want a way out, I know someone who can help you."

Though she felt it was a useless attempt, she took one of her own cards and noted Dr. Mira's name and number on the back. She left it on the arm of the chair and walked away.

Her emotions were in upheaval when she got into her car. She took a moment to settle them, then glanced at her wrist unit. Not much time, she mused, but enough.

She used her personal porta-'link rather than her car unit and tagged Nadine.

"What do you want, Dallas? I'm under the gun here. The press conference is in an hour."

"Meet me at the D and D, bring your crew. Fifteen minutes."

"I can't —"

"Yeah, you can." Eve broke transmission and drove downtown.

She'd picked the Down and Dirty Club partly for sentiment, partly because it would be fairly private on a midweek afternoon. And the proprietor was a friend who would see that she wasn't hassled.

"What you doing here, white girl?" Crack, all six and a half feet of him, grinned at her. His face was dark and homely, his scalp recently shaved and oiled to a mirror gleam. He sported a vest of peacock feathers, leathers so snug she wondered his balls weren't bruised, and shin-breaking boots in cherry red.

"Got a meet," she told him and did a quick scan of the club. It was mostly empty, but for the six dancers practicing a routine on stage and a scatter of customers who — being what they were — marked her as a cop in the time it takes to pick a tourist's pocket in Times Square.

She imagined several ounces of illegals would shortly be swimming into New York's sewer system.

"You bringing more cops into my place?" He glanced over as two skinny dealers made a beeline for the johns. "Somebody's business gonna suffer tonight."

"I'm not here for a bust. I got press coming. Got a privacy room we can use?"

"You got Nadine coming down? Now, she be fine. You use room three, honeypot. I look out for you awhile."

"Appreciate it." She glanced over her shoulder as the door opened, letting in sunlight, Nadine, and a camera operator. "It won't take long."

Eve pointed toward the room and strode over and in without waiting for Nadine's assent.

"You frequent such interesting places, Dallas." Wrinkling her nose, Nadine stared at the stained walls and rumpled bed — the only piece of furniture the room could boast.

"You liked the place well enough, as I recall. Enough to strip down to your undies and dance on stage."

"I was impaired at the time," Nadine said with some dignity when her operator snickered. "Shut up, Mike."

"You got five minutes." Eve sat on the side of the bed. "You can either hit me with questions or I'll give you a straight statement. I'm not going to give you more than what we'll release at the press conference, but you'll have it on a good twenty minutes before anyone else. I'm also giving you the go-ahead to use data already discussed."

"Why?"

"Because," Eve said quietly, "we're friends."

"Step outside a minute, Mike." Nadine

waited until he'd finished grumbling and had closed the door behind him. "I don't want any pity favors."

"That's not what this is. You kept the deal, holding information until I cleared it. I'm keeping my end. That's professional. I trust you to report the truth. That's professional. I like you, even when you're irritating. That's personal. Now, do you want the one-on-one or not?"

Nadine's smile bloomed slowly. "Yeah, I want it. I like you, Dallas, and you're always irritating."

"Give me a quick rundown of your take on Rudy and Piper."

"Charming, absolutely. They can spout their company line like champs. Every button I pushed, they came back with the perfect reaction. Well programmed."

"Who's in charge?"

"Oh, he is. No question. He's a little overprotective of her for a brother, if you ask me. And it's mildly creepy the way they dress alike down to their lip dye. But it's probably a twin thing."

"Did you interview any of the staff?"

"Sure, picked a few consultants at random. They've got a very slick operation going there."

"Gossip about the owners?"

"Nothing but praise. I couldn't elbow out one spiteful sentence." She cocked a brow. "Is that what you're looking for?"

"I'm looking for a killer," Eve said flatly. "Let's get this going."

"Fine." Nadine reached back, rapping her knuckles on the door to signal Mike. "Straight statement with follow-up questions."

"One or the other."

"Don't be so pissy. Start with the statement." Nadine glanced at the bed, calculating the varied body fluids that might have been spent there, and opted to stand.

An hour later, Eve listened to Chief of Police and Security Tibble run nearly the identical statement she'd given Nadine. He had a more impressive style, she mused, shivering a bit in the cold, as he'd chosen to give the statement on the steps of the Tower, where his offices spanned the top of the building.

Air traffic had been rerouted for the thirty-minute event so that only a scatter of sky-cams and traffic choppers disturbed the sky overhead.

Eve was certain he already knew she'd gone on-air with the data. He could slap her down for it. But as she had not been officially barred from preceding him with a statement, it would be a waste of time.

Eve knew Tibble rarely wasted anything.

She respected him, and respected him more when he managed to give a complete statement while withholding vital pieces of evidence they would need for trial.

As questions began to bullet out of the crowd of reporters, he held up both hands. "I'll turn questions over to the primary investigating officer, Lieutenant Eve Dallas."

He turned, then bent down to her ear. "Five minutes, and don't give them any more than they already have. Next time, Dallas, wear a goddamn coat."

She huddled in her jacket and stepped forward.

"Do you have any suspects?"

Eve didn't sigh, but she wanted to. She hated facing the media. "We're questioning several individuals in connection with these cases."

"Were the victims sexually assaulted?"

"The cases are being handled as sexual homicides."

"How are they connected? Did the victims know each other?"

"I'm not free to discuss that area of the investigation at this time." She held up a hand to cut off the vicious barrage. "We are, however, treating the cases as connected. As Chief Tibble stated, the investigation, thus far, points to one killer."

"Santa Claus is coming to town," some comedian called out, and set off a wave of laughter in the crowd.

"Yeah, make a joke of it." Temper warmed her blood and made her forget her hands were freezing. "That's easy enough when you haven't seen what he leaves behind. When you haven't had to tell mothers and partners that the person they loved is dead."

The crowd fell quiet enough that she heard the swish of copter blades overhead. "I imagine the person responsible for this misery, for these deaths, will get a big charge out of being played up in the media. Go ahead and give him what he wants. Make the murder of four people small and foolish, and turn him into a star. But inside Cop Central we know what he is. He's pathetic, even more pathetic than you. I've got nothing more to say."

She turned, ignoring the shouts, and all but bumped into Tibble.

"Inside one moment, Lieutenant." He took her arm, steering her quickly through guards and through the reinforced doors. "Well done," he said briefly. "And now that we're done with that annoying spectacle, I have to play politics with the mayor. Go do your job, Dallas, and get me this son of a bitch."

"Yes, sir."

"And find some gloves, for Christ's sake," he added as he stalked away.

Eve jammed one hand in her pocket to warm it, and took out her communicator with the other. She tried Mira first, and was told the doctor was still in testing. She put in the next call to Peabody.

"Anything pop on the necklace?"

"We got a possible. Baubles and Bangles on Fifth. Their jeweler designed and made the necklace. This was a one of a kind — commissioned. They're checking records now, but the clerk said she thought she remembered the customer coming in personally to pick it up. They've got security cameras."

"Meet me there. I'm on my way."

"Lieutenant?"

She glanced over and into the hollow eyes of Jerry Vandoren. "Jerry, what are you doing here?"

"I heard about the press conference. I wanted . . ." He lifted his hands, then helplessly let them fall. "I wanted to hear what you had to say. I listened. I want to thank you . . ."

He trailed off again, looking around as if he'd turned a corner and found himself on another planet.

"Jerry." She took his arm, guiding him away before the reporters scented fresh meat and pounced on him. "You should go home."

"I can't sleep. I can't eat. I dream about her every night. Marianna's not dead when I dream about her." He drew in a shuddering breath. "Then I wake up, and she is. Everyone says I need grief counseling. I don't want to be counseled out of my grief, Lieutenant Dallas. I don't want to stop feeling what I feel for her."

It was out of her element, she thought, this raw desperation that looked to her for an answer. But she couldn't turn away from it. "She wouldn't want you to go on hurting. She loved you too much for that."

"But when I stop hurting, she'll really be gone." He squeezed his eyes shut, then opened them. "I wanted — just to say I appreciated what you said out there. That you weren't going to let them turn this into a joke. I know you'll stop him." The plea swam in his eyes. "You will stop him, won't you?"

"Yeah. I'm going to stop him. Come on."

Gently, she led him toward a side exit. "Let's get you a cab. Where did you say your mother lived?"

"My mother?"

"Yeah. Go see your mother, Jerry. Go stay with her for a while."

He blinked at the sunlight when they stepped outside. "It's almost Christmas."

"Yeah." She signaled to a uniform leaning against his cruiser. A better bet, she decided, than a cab. "You go spend Christmas with your family, Jerry. Marianna would want you to."

Eve had to put Jerry Vandoren and his grief out of her mind and focus on the next step. After fighting through traffic, she parked illegally in front of the jewelry store, switched her On Duty sign to active, then bulled her way through the crowd jamming the sidewalk.

Eve imagined it was the kind of place where Roarke might breeze in, have a glitter catch his eye, and drop a few hundred thousand.

The shop was all pink and gold, like the inside of a seashell. Music, the quiet, deep sort that made her think of churches, hummed in the rarified air.

The flowers were fresh, the carpet thick,

the guard at the door discreetly armed.

Because he gave her jacket and boots a sneer of disdain, she badged him. It gave her a petty pull of satisfaction to see the sneer vanish.

She breezed by him, her battered boots silent on the shell-pink carpet. A quick scan showed her a woman wrapped in miles of mink seated on a thickly padded chaise, debating over diamonds or rubies; a tall man with silvered hair with a topcoat folded neatly over his arm, perusing gold wrist units; two more guards; and a giggling blonde being treated to a shopping spree by a pouchy man old enough to be her grandfather. He obviously had more money than sense.

She tagged the security cameras, little pinhole lenses tucked in the carved molding that framed a coffered ceiling. A fluid spiral of stairs arched to the right. Or if madam was too weary from carting around pounds of gold and stones, she was welcome to use the shining brass elevator.

Only the weight of the diamond between her breasts prevented Eve from a sneer of her own. It was faintly embarrassing to know that Roarke could buy everything in the place, and the building it was housed in.

She approached a beveled glass counter where bracelets studded with colored gems were artfully draped, and sized up the clerk behind the counter. He didn't appear particularly thrilled to see her. He was as polished as his wares, but his mouth was pinched, his eyes bored, and his voice, when he spoke, dripped with sarcasm.

"May I help you, madam?"

"Yeah, I need the manager."

He sniffed, inclining his head so that the lights gleamed on his gilt hair. "Is there a problem?"

"That depends on how quickly you get me the manager."

Now his mouth drew in as if something not quite fresh had landed on his tongue. "One moment. And please, don't touch the display case. It's just been cleaned."

Little bastard, Eve thought mildly. She managed to put half a dozen fingerprints on the sparkling glass by the time he came back with a slim, attractive brunette.

"Good afternoon. I'm Ms. Kates, the manager. May I help you?"

"Lieutenant Dallas, NYPSD." Because the woman's smile was a great deal warmer than her clerk's, Eve held her badge at counter level and blocked it from the clientele with her back. "My aide called in earlier regarding a necklace."

"Yes, I spoke with her. Shall we talk in my office?"

"Fine." She glanced around as Peabody and McNab came in. Saying nothing, she signaled them to follow.

"I remember the necklace distinctly," Kates began as she led them into a small, feminine office. She gestured toward two high-backed chairs before taking a seat behind a desk. "My husband designed it, on commission. I haven't been able to reach him, I'm sorry, but I believe I can give you any information you need."

"You have the paperwork on it?"

"I do. I looked up the disc and printed out a hard copy for you." Efficiently, she opened a file, checked the contents, then passed it to Eve. "The necklace was done in fourteen-carat gold, interlinked chain, choker length, with four stylized birds. A charming piece."

It hadn't looked so charming, Eve mused, wrapped around Holloway's bruised neck.

"Nicholas Claus," she murmured, reading the customer's name. She supposed he'd thought of it as irony. "Did you get ID?"

"It wasn't necessary. The customer paid in cash, a twenty percent deposit on order, the remainder on completion."

Kates folded her hands. "I recognize you, Lieutenant. Am I to assume this necklace is part of a murder investigation?"

"You can assume that. This Claus, he came in personally?"

"Yes, three times that I recall." Kates lifted her folded hands, tapped her fingers against her mouth, then lowered them again. "I spoke to him myself on his first visit. About average height, I suppose, perhaps a little taller. Slender, but not thin. Graceful," she said after a moment's thought. "Very well presented. Dark hair, rather long, with silver streaks. I remember him as very elegant, very polite, and very specific about his needs."

"Give me his voice."

"His voice?" Kates blinked a moment. "I . . . Cultured, I'd say. Faintly accented. European, I suppose. Quiet. I'm sure I'd recognize it again. I remember taking a call from him and knowing who it was the minute he spoke."

"He called in?"

"Once or twice, I think, to check on the progress of the necklace."

"I'm going to need your security discs, and your 'link logs."

"I'll get them for you." She got immediately to her feet. "It may take a little time."

"McNab, give Ms. Kates a hand with that."

"Sir."

"He had to know we'd check," Eve said to Peabody when they were alone. "He left the necklace at the scene, a one of a kind he commissioned himself. He had to know we'd track it here."

"Maybe he didn't think we'd move this fast, or that Kates would have such a good memory."

"No." Dissatisfied, Eve rose. "He knew. This is just where he wants us to be. It's another show. He played a role here, and he doesn't look like the man we're going to see on those discs any more than he looks like Santa Claus."

She paced to the door, back again. "Different props, different costume, different stage, but it's just his show. He covered his ass, Peabody, but he's not as smart as he thinks he is. The voice prints from the 'link logs are going to nail him."

# Chapter Sixteen

"Jesus, Dallas." Feeney shrugged the shoulder she was leaning over. "Stop breathing down my neck."

"Sorry." She leaned back one stingy inch. "How long does it take to program the print into this thing?"

"Twice as long as it would if you weren't nagging on me."

"Okay, okay." She backed off, stalked to the window of the conference room. "It's sleeting," she said more to herself than him. "Traffic's going to be ugly later."

"Traffic's always ugly this time of year. Too many damn tourists. I tried to do a little shopping last night. Wife wants this sweater thing. People are like wolves on a dead deer out there. I'm not going back."

"Video shopping's easier."

"Yeah, but the fucking circuits are jammed. Everybody and his cousin's on trying to scoop up bargains. I don't come up with a dozen pretty boxes under the tree for her, I'm bunking in the den till spring."

"A dozen?" Mildly horrified, she swung back around. "You have to buy her more than one?"

"Man, Dallas, are *you* green in the marriage area." He snorted, working manually on the programming. "One present don't mean dick. Quantity, pal. Think quantity."

"Great, terrific. I'm sunk."

"You got a couple of days left. And here we are."

Her shopping dilemma cleared from her mind as she rushed back. "Run it."

"I'm getting to it. Here's our man on the 'link."

*Is Mr. or Mrs. Kates available?*

"I cut out the other voices. That's your pauses," Feeney explained.

*Good morning, Ms. Kates. This is Nicholas Claus. I wondered how the work on my necklace is progressing.*

"I can run the rest, but that's enough for a match."

"The accent's vague," Eve mused. "He doesn't put a lot on it. That's smart. You got Rudy in there?"

"Coming up. This is from the interview tape. Just him."

*We advise all our clients to meet their*

*matches in a public place. Any who agreed to meet him privately subsequent to that were making their own decision.*

"Now we got prints. This baby computes everything: pitch, inflection, cadence, tonal quality. Don't matter a damn if you disguise your voice. It's as reliable as fingerprints and DNA. You can't fake it. Shift to Subject A, graft style, on screen and on audio."

*Working . . .*

Eve listened to the 'link call, watched the lines of color skim and jump along the screen. "Split the screen," she told him, "put the interview blurb up under that one."

"Just hold on." Feeney ordered the function, then pursed his lips. "Got a problem here."

"What? What's wrong with it?"

"Meld prints on screen," he ordered, then sighed as the points and valleys clashed. "They don't match, Dallas. They aren't even close. You got two different voices here."

"Shit." She tunneled her fingers through her hair. Because she could see it for herself, her stomach started to burn. "Let me think. Okay, what if he used a distorter on his end of the 'link?"

"He could mess it up a little, but I'd still get match points. Best I can do is run a scan, search for any electronic masking, clean it out if I find it. But I've seen enough of these to know when I'm looking at two different guys."

He sighed and sent her one of his mournful looks. "Sorry, Dallas. This sets things back a ways."

"Yeah." She rubbed her eyes. "Run the scan anyway, will you, Feeney? How about the feature-by-feature from the videos?"

"It's coming — coming slow. I can run Rudy's ear shape, eye shape against it."

"Let's go that route, too. I'm going to check with Mira, see if the profile's done."

To save herself time, Eve called Mira's office. The doctor was gone for the day, but a preliminary report had been transmitted to Eve's office 'link. She headed over, trying to pick apart the voice prints as she went.

The guy was smart, she mused. Maybe he'd figured on a voice print analysis. Anticipated it and found a way around it. What if he'd had someone else call the jeweler's?

And that was reaching, she admitted. But it wasn't impossible.

She heard what she would have sworn was a giggle, and stepped inside her office to see Peabody chatting amiably with Charles Monroe.

"Peabody?"

"Sir." Peabody sprang instantly to her feet and to attention. "Charles, ah, Mr. Monroe has some . . . wanted to . . ."

"Restrain your hormones, Officer. Charles?"

"Dallas." He smiled, rising from his seat on the arm of her one pathetic chair. "Your aide kept me company, charmingly, while I waited for you."

"I bet. What's the deal?"

"It might be nothing, but —" He shrugged. "One of the women from my match list got in touch a couple of hours ago. It seems her date for a jaunt upstate this weekend hit a snag. She thought I might like to substitute, though we didn't really connect before."

"That's fascinating, Charles." Impatient to get on with her work, Eve dropped into a chair. "But I don't feel qualified to give you advice on your social life."

"I can handle that on my own." As if to prove it, he winked at Peabody and had her going rosy pink with pleasure. "I was toying with the idea of taking her up on it, but knowing how things can go, I chatted her up awhile to get a feel for it."

"Is there a point to this?"

He leaned forward. "I like my moment in the sun, Lieutenant Sugar." Both of them ignored Peabody's gasping snort at the term. "She started unloading. She'd had a big bustup with the guy she'd been seeing. Dumped all the crap on me. She caught him cheating on her with some redhead. Then she tells me how he thought he could make up for it by having Santa bring her a present last night."

Eve sat up slowly, and now her attention focused in. "Keep going."

"I thought that would do it." With satisfaction, Charles leaned back. "She says the doorbell rings about ten last night, and when she looks out there's Santa with a big silver box." He shook his head. "I have to tell you, with what I knew, my heart just about stopped. But she's rambling on about how she wouldn't give the cheating bastard the satisfaction of opening the door. She didn't want his pitiful makeup gift."

"She didn't let him in," Eve murmured.

"And I figure that was why she was alive to call me and bitch."

"You happen to know what she does for a living?"

"She's a dancer. Ballet."

"Yeah, that works," Eve murmured. "I need a name and address. Peabody?"

"Ready."

"Cheryl Zapatta, she's on West Twenty-eighth. That's all I've got."

"We'll find her."

"Look, I don't know if I did the right thing, but I told her. Your one-on-one with Nadine Furst had just run, so I figured it was out. I told her to turn on her screen, and I filled her in." He blew out a breath. "She panicked. Big time. Said she was getting out. I don't know if you're going to find her for a while."

"If she's scrambled, we can get an order to enter and search. You did the right thing, Charles," Eve said after a moment. "If she hadn't heard the report, she might have had a change of heart and opened the door the next time. I appreciate you coming in."

"Anything for you, Lieutenant Sugar." He got to his feet. "Can you let me know what happens?"

"Watch your screen," Eve advised.

"Yeah. Uh, would you mind showing me the way out, Officer?" He sent a killer smile at Peabody. "I'm a little turned around."

"Sure. Lieutenant?"

"Go ahead." Eve waved them away, then dived into Mira's report. Engrossed and frustrated, she didn't notice that it took Peabody twenty minutes to show Charles to his choice of people glide or elevator.

"She's cleared the son of a bitch." Eve sat

back, scrubbing her hands over her face when Peabody came back in. "I've got nothing to hang on him."

"Rudy?"

"His personality index doesn't fit the profile. His capacity for physical violence runs low on the scale. He's devious, intelligent, obsessive, possessive, and sexually limited, but in the doctor's opinion, he isn't our man. Damn it. His lawyer gets a copy of this, I won't be able to touch the little creep."

"Are you still looking at him for it?"

"I don't know what I'm looking at." She tried to keep her head and her temper clear. "We go back and we start over. From the beginning. We reinterview, starting with the first victim."

At eight forty-five, Eve charged up the steps. She was already irked, as Summerset had greeted her in the foyer with his bilious stare and the comment that she had precisely fifteen minutes to make herself presentable before guests began to arrive.

It didn't help to race into the bedroom and find Roarke showered and dressing. "I'll make it," she blurted out and dashed into the bath.

"It's a party, darling, not an endurance

test." He wandered in behind her, mainly for the pleasure of watching her strip. "Take your time."

"Yeah, like I'm going to walk in late and give that butt-face another reason to complain about me. Shower, all heads full, one-oh-one degrees."

"You aren't required to meet Summerset's approval." He leaned idly against the wall to watch her. She showered as she did nearly everything: quickly and efficiently, no wasted time or moves. "In any case, people traditionally arrive late for affairs like this."

"I'm just running a little behind." She hissed as shampoo ran into her eyes and stung. "I lost my prime suspect, and I'm starting from scratch." She sprang out, took a step toward the drying tube, then stopped. "Shit, am I supposed to put that glop on my hair when it's wet or when it's dry?"

Having a fairly good idea which glop she referred to, Roarke plucked a tube from the shelf and poured a dab in his palm. "Here, allow me."

The way his hands moved through her hair made her want to purr, but she eyed him narrowly. "Don't mess with me, pal. I don't have time for you."

"I have no idea what you mean." Enjoying himself, he chose another tube and poured a generous pool of body lotion into his hands. "I'm simply helping you get ready," he began as he slid his slickened hands over her shoulders, her breasts. "Since you seem frazzled."

"Look —" Then she closed her eyes and sighed when his hands slithered down to her waist, slipped over her butt. "I think you missed a spot."

"Careless of me." He lowered his head, sniffed at her throat. And bit. "Want to be very, very late?"

"Yeah. But I'm not going to." She wiggled away and leaped into the drying tube. "But don't forget where you left off."

"A pity you didn't get here twenty minutes ago." Having decided that watching her wasn't going to help his blood cool, he strolled back into the bedroom.

"I just have to gunk up my face some." She whipped out of the tube and dashed for the mirror without bothering with a robe. "What am I supposed to wear to something like this?"

"I have it."

She stopped fumbling ineptly with her lash dye and scowled. "Do I pick out your clothes?"

"Eve, please."

She had to laugh. "Okay, bad example,

but I don't have time to think of another one." Solving the problem of hairstyle by skimming her fingers briskly through what she had, she turned into the bedroom to see Roarke studying what she supposed some people would call a dress.

"Get out of here. I'm not wearing that."

"Mavis brought it by the other night. Leonardo designed it for you. It'll look very good on you."

She frowned at the fluid panels of silver held together on the sides by thin sparkling straps. The straps were repeated at the shoulders, catching a drape of fabric in the front and much, much lower in the back.

"Why don't I just go naked and save time?"

"Let's see how it looks."

"What do I wear under it?"

He tucked his tongue in his cheek. "You're wearing it."

"Jesus Christ." With ill grace, she stepped into it, wiggled it up.

The material was soft as a waterfall and clung like a lover, the seductive side slashes exposing smooth skin and slender curves.

"Darling Eve." He took her hand, turning it over to nuzzle the palm in one of the gestures he used to turn her legs to putty. "Sometimes you take my breath away. Here, try these."

He took a pair of diamond drop earrings from the dresser and handed them to her.

"Were these already mine, or what?"

Now he grinned. "You've had them for months. No more presents until Christmas."

She fastened them on, and decided to take it philosophically when he selected her shoes. "There's no place in this thing to keep my communicator. I'm on call."

"Here." He offered her the ridiculously small evening bag that matched the shoes.

"Anything else?"

"You're perfect." He smiled when he heard the beep that signaled the first car arriving at the gate. "And prompt. Let's go down so I can show off my wife."

"I'm not a poodle," she muttered and made him laugh.

Within an hour, the house was full of people and music and light. Scanning the ballroom, Eve could only be grateful Roarke never expected her to have any input into the preparations.

There were huge tables groaning under silver platters of food: honied ham from Virginia, glazed duck from France, rare beef from Montana; lobster, salmon, oysters harvested from the rich beds on Silas I; an array of fresh vegetables picked only that morning and cleverly arranged in patterns. Desserts that would tempt a political prisoner from a hunger strike surrounded a three-foot tree fashioned out of sinfully rich cake and hung with gleaming marzipan ornaments.

She wondered that it could still amaze her what the man she had married could conjure.

A soaring pine decorated with thousands of white lights and silver stars stood at either end of the ballroom. The floor-to-ceiling windows showed not the nasty sleet that hissed over the city, but a hologram of a dreamy snowscene where couples skated on a silver pond and young children raced down a gentle slope on shiny red sleds.

Such details, she thought, were so utterly Roarke.

"Hey, sweetheart. All alone in this palace?"

She arched a brow when she felt the hand on her bottom and turned her head slowly to stare at McNab.

He went red, then white, then red again. "Christ! Lieutenant. Sir."

"Your hand's on my ass, McNab. I don't think you want it to be there."

He snatched it away as if scorched. "God. Man. Shit. Beg your pardon. I didn't recognize you. I mean . . ." He jammed the hand he sincerely hoped she'd allow him to keep in his pocket. "I didn't know it was you. I thought . . . You look . . ." Words failed him.

"I believe Detective McNab is trying to compliment you, Eve." Roarke slipped up beside them and, because it was too much to resist, stared hard into McNab's panicked eyes. "Weren't you, Ian?"

"Yeah. That is . . ."

"And if I believed he'd realized it was your ass he was fondling, I'd just have to kill him. Right here." Roarke reached out and flicked at the strings of McNab's snazzy red tie. "Right now."

"Oh, I'd have already taken care of that myself," Eve said dryly. "You look like you could use a drink, Detective."

"Yes, sir. I could."

"Roarke, why don't you take care of him? Mira just came in. I want to talk to her."

"Delighted." Roarke draped an arm around McNab's shoulder and squeezed just a little harder than comfort allowed.

It took longer than Eve liked to make her way across the room. It amazed her how much people wanted to talk at parties. And about nothing in particular. That was delay enough, but she caught sight of Peabody, looking very un-Peabody-like in sweeping evening pants of dull gold and a trim sleeveless jacket. Her bare arm was tucked comfortably through Charles Monroe's.

Mira, Eve decided, could wait. "Peabody."

"Dallas. Wow, the place looks amazing."

"Yeah." Eve shifted her gaze and pinned Charles with angry eyes. "Monroe."

"Fabulous home you've got, Lieutenant."

"I don't recall your name on the guest list."

Peabody colored, stiffened. "The invitation said I was free to bring a date."

"Is that what this is?" she asked, keeping her eyes on Charles's. "A date?"

"Yes." He lowered his voice as a flicker of hurt clouded his eyes. "Delia is aware of my profession."

"Are you giving her the cop's standard discount?"

"Dallas." Horrified, Peabody stepped forward.

"It's all right." Charles tugged her back. "I'm on my own time, Dallas, and hoping to spend a pleasant evening with an attractive woman whose company I enjoy. If you'd rather I leave, it's your house, your call."

"She's a big girl."

"Yes, she is," Peabody murmured. "Just a second, Charles," she added, then gripped Eve's arm and tugged her aside.

"Hey!"

"No, you hey." Fury bubbled into her voice as Peabody boxed Eve into a corner. "I don't have to clear my personal time or relationships with you, and you have no right to embarrass me."

"Wait a minute —"

"I'm not done." Later, Peabody would recall the look of speechless shock on Eve's face, but at the moment she was too revved to notice or react to it. "What I do off duty has nothing to do with the job. If I want to take on table dancing in my personal time, it's my business. If I want to pay six LCs to fuck me blind on Sundays, it's my business. And if I want to have a civilized date with an interesting, attractive man who for some reason wants to have one with me, it's my business."

"I was only —"

"I'm not done," Peabody said between clenched teeth. "On the job, you're in charge. But that's where it ends. If you don't want me here with Charles, then we'll leave."

As Peabody turned on her heel, Eve snagged her wrist. "I don't want you to leave." Her voice was quiet, controlled, and stiff as a petrified board. "I apologize for stepping into your personal life. I hope it doesn't spoil your evening. Excuse me."

Hurt, unbelievably hurt, she walked away. Her stomach was still jittering with it when she found Mira. "I don't want to take you away from the party, but I'd like a few minutes. In private."

"Of course." Concerned by the dark eyes and pale cheeks, Mira reached out. "What is it, Eve?"

"In private," she repeated, and ordered herself to bury her feelings as she led the way out. "We can talk in the library."

"Oh." The minute she stepped inside, Mira clasped her hands in sheer pleasure. "What a marvelous room. Oh, what absolute treasures. Not enough people appreciate the feel and the smell of a real book in their hands any longer. The delight of curling into a chair with the warmth of one instead of the cool efficiency of a disc."

"Roarke's into books," Eve said simply and shut the door. "The testing on Rudy. I question some of your findings."

"Yes, I thought you might." Mira wandered through, admiring, then settled onto a soft leather chair, smoothing the skirt of her rose-pink cocktail suit. "He's not your killer, Eve, nor is he the monster you want him to be."

"It has nothing to do with what I want."

"His relationship with his sister disturbs you on a deep and personal level. She isn't like you, though; she isn't a child, she isn't defenseless, and while I do believe he has an unhealthy measure of control over her, she isn't being forced."

"He uses her."

"Yes, and she him. It's mutual. I agree that he is obsessive when it pertains to her. He is sexually immature. The very thing that eliminates him from your lists, Eve, is the fact that I strongly believe he is impotent with anyone but his sister."

"He was being blackmailed and the black-mailer is dead. A client was hitting on his sister; that client is dead."

"Yes, and I admit that with that evidence I was prepared to find him capable of those murders. He isn't. He has some potential for physical violence. When roused, when threatened. But it's a flash, it's immediate. It isn't in his makeup to plan, to orchestrate, to complete the kind of killings you're dealing with."

"Then we just turn him loose?" Eve walked away. "Let him go?"

"Incest is against the law, but it has to be proven to be coerced. This isn't the case. I understand your need to punish him, and to, in your mind, release his sister from his hold."

"This isn't about me."

"Oh, I know that, Eve." Because it hurt her heart to watch, she reached up to take Eve's hand and stop the restless pacing. "Don't keep punishing yourself."

"I focused on him because of this. I know I did." Suddenly weary, she sank down beside Mira. "And because I did, I might have missed something, some detail, that would have led to the killer."

"You followed very logical, very clear-cut steps. He had to be eliminated from the list."

"But I took too long to do it. And every time my gut told me I was looking at the wrong man, I ignored it. Because I kept seeing myself. I'd look at her and I'd think, way back in my mind, I'd think, *That could be me. If I hadn't killed the son of a bitch, that could be me.*"

She lowered her head into her hands, then dragged them back through her hair. "Christ, I'm messing up. All over the damn place."

"How?"

"There's no point in getting into this."

Mira merely stroked Eve's hair. "How?"

"I can't even seem to handle a perfectly ordinary holiday. Just the thought of trying

386

to figure out what to do, what to buy, how to act makes my stomach ache."

"Oh, Eve." Laughing lightly, Mira shook her head. "Christmas drives nearly everyone half crazy with just those problems. It's absolutely normal."

"Not for me, it isn't. I never had to worry about it before. I didn't have so many people in my life."

"Now you do." Mira smiled, indulged herself by stroking Eve's hair again. "Who do you want to get rid of?"

"I think I just managed to kick Peabody out." Disgusted, Eve shot to her feet again. "She comes in with an LC. Oh, he's basically okay, but he's a goddamn whore, a great looking, slick, amusing one."

"It disturbs you," Mira suggested, "that you like him on one level and despise him for what he does for a living."

"This isn't about me. It's about Peabody. He says he wants a real relationship, and she's got stars in her eyes over him and she's majorly pissed at me because I said something about it."

"Life's messy, Eve, and I'm afraid you've gone and carved yourself out a life, with all the conflicts and problems and hurt feelings that entails. If she's angry with you, it's because there's no one she admires or respects more."

"Oh, Christ."

"Being loved is a heavy responsibility. You'll mend your fences with her, because she matters to you."

"I'm getting damn crowded with people who matter."

The house screen across the room blinked on. Summerset's pinched face filled it. "Lieutenant, your guests are inquiring about you."

"Fuck off." She smiled thinly as Mira swallowed a laugh. "At least that's one person I don't have to worry about mattering. But I shouldn't have busted up your evening."

"You haven't. I enjoy talking with you."

"Well . . ." Eve started to stick her hands in her pockets, remembered she didn't have any, and sighed. "Would you mind hanging out here for a minute? There's something I want to get from my office."

"All right. May I look through the books?"

"Sure, help yourself." Not wanting to take the time to go out and down the stairs, Eve slipped into the elevator. She was back in less than three minutes, but Mira was already cozied into a chair with a book.

"*Jane Eyre.*" She sighed as she set it aside. "I haven't read it since I was a girl. It's so wrenchingly romantic."

"You can borrow it if you want. Roarke wouldn't mind."

"I have my own copy. I just haven't taken the time. But thank you."

"I wanted to give you this. It's a couple of days early, but . . . I might not see you." Feeling ridiculously awkward, she held out the elegantly wrapped box.

"Oh, how sweet of you." With obvious delight, Mira clasped the box in her hands. "May I open it now?"

"Sure, that's the deal, right?" She shifted her feet, then rolled her eyes as Mira delicately untied the fussy bow and painstakingly unfolded the corners on the paper.

"Drives my family crazy, too," she said with a laugh. "I just can't bear to rip in; then I save the paper and ribbon like a pack rat. I have a closet full of it which I constantly forget to reuse. But . . ." She trailed off as she opened the lid and found the bottle of scent inside. "Why, it's lovely, Eve. It has my name etched on it."

"It's this personalized sort of fragrance. You give the guy physical and personality traits, then he creates an individual fragrance."

"Charlotte," Mira murmured. "I wasn't sure you knew my first name."

"I guess I heard it somewhere."

Mira blinked at sentimental tears. "It's wonderfully thoughtful." She set the bottle down and turned to draw Eve into a hug. "Thank you."

Swamped with warmth, and embarrassment, Eve let herself be held. "I'm glad you like it. I'm pretty new at this kind of thing."

"You did very well." She drew back, but caught Eve's face in her hands. "I'm so fond of you. Now I need the powder room because another of my Christmas traditions is to weep a little over my gifts. I know where it is," she added, patting Eve's cheeks lightly. "You go dance with your husband and drink a little too much champagne. The world outside will still be there tomorrow."

"I need to stop him."

"And you will. But tonight, you need your life. Go find Roarke and take it."

# CHAPTER SEVENTEEN

Eve did what the doctor ordered. It wasn't such a bad deal, she decided, getting a little light-headed, swaying in Roarke's arms to some sort of dreamy music in a room filled with color and scent and light.

"I can live with it," she murmured.

"Hmm?"

She smiled as his lips skimmed her ear. "I can live with it," she repeated, drawing back enough to look at his face. "All the Roarke stuff."

"Well." His hands stroked up her back, then down again. "That's good to know."

"You got a whole bunch of stuff, Roarke."

"I do, indeed, have a whole bunch of stuff." And a wife, he thought with an amused glint in his eyes, who was heading toward drunk.

"Sometimes it's spooky. But not now. Now it's pretty nice." Sighing, she rubbed her cheek against his. "What kind of music is this?"

"Do you like it?"

"Yeah, it's sexy."

"Twentieth century, primarily the nineteen forties. It was called Big Band. That's a hologram of Tommy Dorsey's band doing this little number. 'Moonlight Serenade.' "

"That's a million years ago."

"Almost."

"How do you know all that stuff anyway?"

"Maybe I was born out of my time."

She sighed in his arms as the music swelled. "No, you hit your time just right." She tilted her head on his shoulder so she could watch the room. "Everybody looks happy. Feeney's dancing with his wife. Mavis is sitting on Leonardo's lap in the corner over there with Mira and her husband. They're all laughing. McNab's hitting on every woman in the room, and giving Peabody the hairy eyeball while he sucks down your Scotch."

Idly, Roarke glanced over, lifted a brow. "Trina's got him now. Jesus, she'll eat that boy alive."

"He doesn't look worried about it." She leaned back again. "It's a nice party."

The music changed, a quick beat bouncing out. Eve's mouth dropped open. "Holy shit, look at Dickhead. What's he doing?"

Grinning, Roarke slipped a hand around Eve's waist, turning so they were hip to hip. "I believe it's called jitterbug."

Stunned, she watched the lab chief tug and pull Nadine Furst around the room, spinning her out, whipping her back. "Yeah, I can see why. I can never get him to move that fast in the lab. Whoa!" Her eyes widened as Dickie shoveled Nadine through his legs. Nadine let out a burst of laughter as her feet hit the floor again, and the crowd roared with approval.

Eve found herself grinning, leaning companionably against Roarke. "Looks like fun."

"Want to try it?"

"Oh no." But she laughed and began to tap her foot. "Watching's just fine."

"Is that mag or what?" Mavis bounced over, pulling Leonardo after her. "Who'da thought Nadine could move like that? Frigid party, Roarke. It's iced."

"Thanks. You're looking festive, Mavis."

"Yeah. We call it my gay apparel." She laughed and did a quick twirl to show off the multicolored panels that fluttered from breast to ankle. The movement parted them, revealing flashes of skin that had been dusted with gold and matched her hair, which fountained out from a wild topknot.

"Leonardo thought yours should be more refined," she told Eve.

"No one shows off my designs as well as you and Mavis." Towering over them, Leonardo smiled his gorgeous smile. "Merry Christmas, Dallas." He bent down to kiss her cheek. "We have something for you, both of you. Just a token."

He took a package from behind his back and put it in Eve's hands. "Mavis and I are having our first Christmas together, thanks in a large part to you." His gold eyes misted.

Because she couldn't think of what to say, Eve set the package on one of the banquet tables and began to unwrap it.

Inside was a box of carved and polished wood, its brass hinges gleaming. "It's beautiful."

"Open it up," Mavis prompted, all but bouncing. "Tell them what it means, Leonardo."

"The wood's for friendship, the metal for love." He waited until Eve opened the lid to reveal the two silk-lined compartments within. "One part is for your memories, the other for your wishes."

"He thought of it." Mavis squeezed Leonardo's big hand. "Isn't he mag?"

"Yeah." Eve managed to nod. "It's great, really great."

Understanding his wife, Roarke touched a hand to her shoulder, then stepped forward to extend the other to Leonardo. "It's a lovely gift. A perfect one. Thank you." And with a smile he kissed Mavis. "Both of you."

"Now you can make a wish together on Christmas Eve." Delighted, Mavis threw her arms around Eve, held hard, then swung back to Leonardo. "Let's dance."

"I'm going to get sloppy," Eve murmured when her friends moved off.

"It's the season for it." He lifted her chin, smiled into her swimming eyes. "I love watching you feel."

Riding the emotion, she cupped a hand around the back of his neck and drew his mouth down to hers. A long, warm kiss that soothed rather than excited.

She was smiling when she drew back. "That's the first memory for our box."

"Lieutenant."

Eve turned, clearing her throat as she looked at Whitney. Embarrassment fluttered as she thought of him catching her with her eyes wet and her mouth still soft from Roarke's. "Sir."

"I'm sorry to disrupt things." He offered Roarke an apologetic glance. "I've just received word that Piper Hoffman has been attacked."

The cop snapped back into place. "Do you have her location?"

"She's on her way to Hayes Memorial Hospital. Her condition is unknown at this time. Is there a private place I can fill you and your team in on known details?"

"My office."

"I'll take the commander down," Roarke said. "Get your people."

"She was attacked in the living quarters above Personally Yours," Whitney began. Out of habit, he'd placed himself behind the desk, but he didn't sit. "At this time, it's believed she was alone. The responding uniform reports that it appears her brother walked in during the assault. The assailant fled."

"Was the witness able to ID?" Eve demanded.

"Not as yet. He's at the hospital with his sister. The scene has been secured. I've ordered the uniforms to leave it undisturbed and await your arrival."

"I'll take Feeney. We'll go to the hospital first." She caught Peabody's quick jolt of shock, but kept her eyes on Whitney. "I don't want to break Peabody's and Mc-Nab's cover at this time. I prefer for them to remain here, in contact, until I move on the scene."

"It's your call," Whitney said simply, and it was one he agreed with.

"We've got witnesses this time, and he's on the run. He's scared. He can't be sure he wasn't made. And, if Piper stays alive, this makes his third miss." She turned to her team. "I've got to change out of this thing. Feeney, I'll be downstairs in five minutes. Peabody, contact the hospital and see what you can find out on the victim's status. McNab, I'll have a uniform bring you the security discs. I want them run before we get back."

"Dallas," Whitney said as she strode to the elevator, "let's cage this bastard in."

"One of these days," Feeney said as they walked down the hospital corridor, "I'm going to leave one of your parties with my wife."

"Cheer up, Feeney. We might've just caught the break that will put this away and give you a nice cozy Christmas."

"Yeah, there's that." Someone moaned behind an opened door as they passed, and had Feeney hunching his shoulders. "Too many broken bodies around here to suit me. The way the roads are tonight, they've probably been hauling in traffic accidents all night."

"Cheerful thought. There's Rudy. I'll take him. See if you can find her attending and an update."

One look at the man slumped in a chair with his head in his hands and Feeney couldn't have been happier to be somewhere else. "He's all yours, kid."

They parted ways, with Eve going straight ahead until she stopped in front of Rudy.

He lowered his hands slowly, staring at her boots first, then gradually lifting a face dominated by devastated eyes. "He raped her. He raped her and he hurt her. He tied her up. I heard her crying. I heard her begging and crying."

Eve sat beside him. "Who was he?"

"I don't know. I didn't see. I think — he must have heard me come in. He must have heard me. I ran into the bedroom, and I saw her. Oh God, oh God, oh God."

"Stop." Snapping out the order, she took his wrists to drag his hands away from his face again. "That won't help her. You came in and heard her. Where had you been?"

"Shopping. Christmas shopping." A single tear slid out of his eye and down his cheek. "She'd seen a sculpture, a fairy at a pond. She left hints around the apartment. A little sketch of it, the address of the gallery. Everything's been so confused that I hadn't had time to buy it until tonight. I never should have left her alone."

She could check on the gallery, the timing, and be certain, Eve thought. Be certain the man who'd put Piper in the hospital wasn't sitting beside her. She knew, she knew better than to let anyone in. Why would she have let her attacker in?

"Was the door secured when you got there?"

"Yes. I coded in. Then I heard her crying, calling out. I ran in." His breath hitched. He closed his eyes, fisted his hands. "I saw her on the bed. She was naked, her hands and feet tied. I think — I'm not sure — but I think I saw something out of the corner of my eye. A movement. Or maybe I just sensed it. Then someone shoved me, and I fell. My head."

Absently he lifted a hand to the side of his head. "I hit it on something, the footboard? I don't know. I might have been out for a few seconds. It couldn't have been long because I heard him running away. I didn't go after him. I should have, but she was lying there, and I couldn't think of anything but her. She wasn't crying anymore. I thought . . . I thought she was dead."

"You called for MTs, an ambulance?"

"I untied her first, covered her. I had to. I couldn't stand . . . Then I called. I couldn't wake her up. I couldn't. She never woke up. And now they won't let me see her."

This time when he covered his face with his hands, Eve let him weep. Spotting Feeney, she rose and met him halfway.

"She's in a coma," he began. "Doctors figure it for extreme shock rather than physical. She was raped, sodomized. Wrists and ankles abraded. A couple of bruises. They did a tox. She was tranq'd — same over-the-counter shit. The tattoo's on her right thigh."

"They got a prognosis?"

"They say they can't do anything. Lots of medical mumbo, but basically, the girl's closed herself up. She'll come back when and if she wants to."

"Okay, we're useless here. Let's put a uniform on her door, and another on the brother."

"You still looking at him, Dallas?"

She glanced back, watching him sob. The stir of pity surprised her. "No, but we'll put one on him anyway."

She took out her communicator, and sent out the orders as they headed toward the elevator.

"Guy's pretty busted up," Feeney commented. "Wonder if he's crying over his sister, or his lover."

"Yeah, it's a puzzle all right." She stepped into the elevator and requested the street level. "So, how did our man know she'd be alone tonight? He wouldn't have tried her if he'd thought Rudy was with her. Not his style. He knew she was alone."

"Someone she knew. Could've been watching the place. Could've called and checked."

"Yeah, he knew her. Knows them both. And I don't think she was one of his true loves." She stepped out into the lobby, turned toward the doors. "She breaks pattern there. Piper isn't on any of the match lists. He went for her to keep us focused on Rudy. Here's how it plays for me."

She paused while they climbed into the car, Eve taking the wheel. "He knows we've had Rudy into Interview, that I like him for the murders. He's got a couple to make up anyway, since he missed with Cissy and the ballet dancer. He's smart enough to know if he gets Piper, we're going to run Rudy again. It just follows. This wasn't for love, it was for insurance."

Feeney leaned back, reaching into his pocket for his nut bag before remembering his wife hadn't let him carry it to the party. He huffed once. "He knows her, she knows him. Maybe that's how he got in."

"She wouldn't have opened the door to a stranger, and she sure as hell wouldn't have opened it up to some guy in a Santa suit. We need McNab to run those discs."

"You know what I think, Dallas. I don't think we're going to find any discs."

Feeney was on the mark. The uniform on the scene reported that the security cameras had been shut off from the main control at nine fifty.

"No sign of forced entry," Eve said after an examination of the locks and palm plate. "She goes to the door, looks out, and sees a familiar face. Opens right up. We won't find any internal security discs either."

She stepped into the apartment. A white tree festooned with crystal ropes and balls stood in front of the windows that faced Fifth. There were stacks of prettily wrapped gifts under it and a single white dove where traditionalists would have put a star or an angel.

There were shopping bags scattered from just inside the doorway to the first arch off the main room's right. She could see Rudy coming in, hearing his sister, dropping the bags on the run. Following the trail, she crossed the soft white carpet and moved through a second seating area set up for screen viewing.

More white. Soft fabric chairs in ecru, tables with glossy surfaces in ivory tones. Clear bowls and urns were overflowing with white flowers.

It was, Eve thought, like stepping into a cloud.

Smothering.

Beyond the sitting area was a fitness room, equipped with sunken spa, air weights, a mood tube, and a multi-setting treadmill.

"Bedrooms are at the far end," she pointed out. "Even at a run it would take Rudy several seconds to get in from the front door."

She turned into a large bedroom. The privacy screen was drawn over the window, letting the night in, and keeping prying eyes out.

Along one wall was an enormous white counter where hundreds of colorful bottles and pots and tubes were arrayed. A queen of vanities, Eve mused, scanning the triple mirror and ring of lights. Two padded chairs, she noted, side by side.

They even painted their faces together.

The bed was heart shaped, which made

her want to roll her eyes. Scrolling chrome tubes framed it like icing on the side of a cake. Roped restraints dangled from four points.

"He didn't take his toys away with him." Eve crouched down to examine the opened silver box on the floor. "We've got all kinds of goodies, Feeney. Here's the pressure syringe." She tapped it with a sealed finger. "The tattoo works, and this is pretty special."

There was a box inside the box. It was simulated wood, about two feet in length. When she opened the lid, three tiers shuffled out. It was neatly packed with Natural Perfection enhancements.

"I don't know much about this kind of shit, but this doesn't look like civilian stuff. It looks like a pro's."

"Ho, ho, ho." Feeney bent down and picked up a snowy white beard. "Maybe he came dressed for the party after all."

"I say he got her down, then dressed himself up. Habit." Eve leaned back on her heels. "He gets in, tranqs her. Once he's got her in here, restrained, he takes the time to deck himself out. He does the tattoo, makes up her face the way he wants it, all the while neatly storing his tools away. No mess. When she comes around enough to know

404

what's going on . . ."

Eyes narrowed, Eve stared at the bed, brought the scene into her mind. "She comes around. She's disoriented, confused. She struggles. She knows who he is. It shocks her, scares her, because she knows what he's going to do. Maybe he talks to her while he's cutting off her clothes."

"Looks like this was a robe." Feeney lifted neat strips of a filmy white material.

"Yeah, she's home, comfortable, in for the night. She's probably excited knowing her brother's out buying her presents. Now she's naked, terrified, staring up at this face she knows. She doesn't want to believe it's happening. You never want to believe it."

But it happened, she thought as a clammy sweat sprung out on her skin. Couldn't be stopped.

"He takes off his clothes. My bet is he folds them neatly. He takes off the beard, too. No need for disguises with her."

So she would see his face, contorted, eyes burning.

"He's aroused now. It's really getting him off that she knows who he is. He doesn't need or want the disguise. Maybe he thinks he loves her after all by now. She belongs to him. She's helpless. He's got the power. More power because she calls him by name when she begs him to stop. But he doesn't stop. He won't stop. He just keeps ramming himself into her. Ripping her, ramming her."

"Hey, hey." Shaken, Feeney squatted down, put his hands on Eve's shoulders. Her eyes had gone glassy, her breath thick and uneven. "Come on, kid."

"Sorry." She closed her eyes.

"It's okay." He patted her awkwardly. He knew what had been done to her as a child, knew because Roarke had told him. But he wasn't sure if Eve was aware he knew. Better, he figured, for both of them, if they pretended he didn't know. "Sometimes you get too close, that's all."

"Yeah." She had to wipe her mouth with the back of her hand. She could smell the unlovely odor of sex going stale, of sweat. And, she thought, of helpless female terror.

"You want, uh, some water or something."

"No, I'm okay. I just . . . I hate sex crimes like this. Let's bag this stuff and finish going through. We might get lucky here and pick up some prints." Steadier, she got to her feet. "Then we'll see what the sweepers can suck up. Wait." Abruptly, she put her hand on Feeney's arm. "Something's missing."

"What?"

"Five, this is five — what is it?" She

juggled the song through her mind. "Where are the five golden rings?"

They did a thorough search, every room, but found nothing that fit the pattern of jewelry left at the scene. Eve's blood went cold.

"He took it with him. He still needs number five. But he doesn't have his tools. I'm going to check the salon downstairs, see if he broke into it. Can you finish here and call the sweepers?"

"Yeah. Watch your back, Dallas."

"He's gone, Feeney. He's back in his hole."

But she was careful as she made her way down to the store level. She could see no signs of forced entry on the elegant doors of the salon. Beyond the glass, it was black.

Following instinct, she used her master code to disengage the locks. And drew her weapon. "Lights on," she ordered, then blinked into the sudden glare.

When her eyes adjusted she saw the cash/credit drawer behind the reception counter standing open. And empty.

"Oh yeah, you stopped by."

She swept the room first, eyes and weapon, then sidestepped toward the display cases. The glass was whole, and she could spot no spaces between the neat lines of products. Moving left, she walked toward the treatment rooms.

Each was empty, and surgically neat.

She uncoded another door and stepped into the staff lounge and locker area. It was, like the rest of the salon, scrupulously clean. Almost obsessively so, she decided as her blood began to hum.

She scanned the lockers, wishing for Roarke's skill with manual locks. Her master wouldn't get her into the compartments. She'd need a warrant for that.

The next room was storage. And here the stringent tidiness was broken. Cases of products were upended, bottles and tubes scattered. She imagined he'd rushed in, desperate to replace his supply, furious that he'd panicked and left it behind upstairs.

He'd torn into the boxes, grabbing his choices, stuffing them into a bag, or another box.

Quickly now, she went out to check each consultant's station. Only one was disturbed, the drawers in the shiny white counter yanked out, rifled through. A thick blob of liquid of some kind had been spilled on the top and left to spread and gel.

Though she already knew, she stuck to routine and searched for the stylist's license. When she found it, she studied the photo.

"Didn't keep your area clean this time, Simon? And I've got your ass."

She whipped out her communicator, striding quickly toward the doors to secure the scene. "Dispatch, Dallas, Lieutenant Eve, all points required on Lastrobe, Simon, last known address 4530 East Sixty-third, unit 35. Subject may be armed and dangerous. Current photo will be transmitted immediately. Pick this guy up, suspicion of sexual homicide, multiple, first degree."

*Dispatch. Acknowledged and authorized.*

"Feeney." Eve shot a transmission to his communicator as she relocked the doors and pulled a crime scene tag out of her kit. "Secure up there. I'm calling Peabody in to handle the sweepers. We've gotta ride."

"Our guy's a face painter. Jesus." Feeney shook his head in disgust as Eve drove east like a bullet. "What's the world coming to, Dallas? Swear to God."

"Yeah, he painted their faces, their bodies, played with their hair, listened to the stories of their lives, fell in love, and killed them for it."

"You figure he worked on all of them in that salon?"

"Maybe, but if not, he saw them. Picked them out. He could have accessed the

409

match lists easy enough, gotten data on them."

"Doesn't explain the Christmas fetish."

"It'll come out once we have him." She squealed to a stop, fishtailing behind two cruisers already blocking the street. Her badge was in her hand as she jumped out. "You been up?" she shouted through the wind and sleet.

"Yes, sir. Subject doesn't answer the door. Men are posted on it, and on the rear exit. Windows are dark. No movement spotted."

"Feeney? The entry warrant come through yet?"

"Still waiting."

"We're going in. Hell with it." She started up, shoving through the grilled doors.

"You muck the case you go in without a warrant," he reminded her, grumping a bit when she pounded up the stairs rather than wait for the elevator.

"I could find the door unsecured." She sent one hot look over her shoulder as he rushed up behind her. "Couldn't I?"

"Shit, Dallas. Give me five here. I'll light a fire under the warrant."

He was puffing a bit when they reached the third floor, and his rumpled face was bright pink. But he shoved in front of her and stood in front of the door to 35. "Just hold on, damn it. Let's take him clean. You know the drill."

She wanted to argue, wanted the sheer, physical satisfaction of kicking the door in. Because it was personal, she thought, certain she felt her own bones vibrating against tensed muscles.

She wanted her hands on him, wanted him to feel fear and helplessness and pain. Wanted it, she realized with a sick jolt, much too much.

"Okay." With an effort, she pulled herself in. "When we go through the door, if we find him, you take him down, Feeney."

"Kid, it's your collar."

"You take him down. I can't swear it'll be clean if I do."

He studied her face, saw the strain, and nodded. "I'll take him for you, Dallas." He yanked out his communicator when it beeped. "Here's our pass. We're clean to move. You want high or low?"

Her lips curved, without humor. "You always wanted high in the old days."

"Still do. Low hurts my knees." They turned, a unit, drawing that hard breath together, then slamming the door. As hinges popped, she went low, crouching under Feeney's arm, weapon out.

Guarding each other's back, they did a

full sweep of the room, dimly lit by the backwash of streetlights.

"Tidy as a church," Feeney whispered. "Smells like a hospital."

"It's the disinfectant. I'm calling for lights. I'll take the left."

"Go."

"Lights on," she ordered then swung left. "Simon? This is the police. We're armed and warranted. All exits are blocked." She gestured toward a doorway, received Feeney's go-ahead nod.

Leading with her laser, she moved in, shoving the door with her elbow so that it bounced against the wall. "He's been here," she told Feeney, scanning the disordered room. "Packed up what he could. He's gone under."

# CHAPTER EIGHTEEN

"Here's what we've got," Eve began once her team had regrouped in her home office. "He's good at disguises. We can give his photo to the media, let them blast it every half hour, but he won't look like his picture. We suspect he has enough cash, loose credits, or alternate ID to travel freely. We'll put out the traces, but the odds of tagging him that way are slim."

She rubbed the fatigue out of her eyes and pumped more caffeine into her system. "I want Mira's take, but mine is that his being interrupted tonight, after the rape, before the payoff, will have him sexually frustrated, on edge, shaken. He's an obsessively neat individual, but he left his workspace and his living space upended in his rush to get what he needed and get out."

"Lieutenant." Though she didn't raise her hand for attention, Peabody felt as if she should. It was cop to cop and nothing else when Eve looked at her. "Do you think he's still in the city?"

"The data we've been able to gather so far indicates he was born here, raised here. He's lived here all of his life and it's unlikely he would seek safety elsewhere. Captain Feeney and McNab will continue to dig for personal data, but for now we assume he's still in the area."

"He doesn't own transpo," Feeney put in. "Never took any vehicle pilot tests. He has to depend on public for his movements."

"And public transpo, in, out, and around the city, is at peak usage right now." This was from McNab, who barely glanced up from his work at the computer. "Only way he's getting out of the city if he didn't have prebooked reservations is to sprout wings and fly."

"Agreed. Added to that, the other targets on his agenda are here. All previous victims have been in the city. Spooked or not, he's going to be compelled to go for number five. The Christmas holidays are his trigger."

Eve moved over to the wall screen. "Run Evidence Disc, Simon, 1-H," she ordered. "We confiscated dozens of video discs with holiday themes from his apartment," she continued as the first flashed on screen.

"This is vintage stuff. Some twentieth-century film —"

"*It's a Wonderful Life,*" Roarke said from the doorway. "Jimmy Stewart, Donna Reed." He only smiled pleasantly at Eve's scowl. "Am I interrupting?"

"This is police business," Eve told him. Didn't the man ever sleep?

Ignoring her, Roarke came in and sat on the arm of Peabody's chair. "You've put in a long night. Can I order some food for you?"

"Roarke —"

"Man, I could eat," McNab said over Eve's objections.

"There are several other like videos," she continued, turning back to the screen as Roarke rose and strolled into the kitchen area. "He collected them, and print discs such as *A Christmas Carol.* In addition, we found a large supply of porn, in both print and video, that follow the theme. Run Evidence Disc, Simon, 68-a. For example," she said dryly when the screen behind her filled.

Roarke stepped back just in time to see a woman, wearing nothing but reindeer antlers and a strap-on tail, purr "Just call me Dancer," as she took Santa's waiting dick into her mouth.

415

"Now, that's entertainment," he commented.

"There are more than a dozen of these, another dozen underground snuff films, also vintage, that aren't quite as cheery. But this one's the award winner. Run Evidence Disc, Simon, 72."

She flicked a glance at Roarke, then stepped away.

On screen Marianna Hawley struggled against restraints. Her head whipped frantically right and left. She was weeping. Simon stepped into view, still wearing his red suit and beard.

He mugged for the camera, then grinned at the woman in bed. "Have you been naughty or nice, little girl?"

*Be quiet, little girl.* The smell of candy on his breath with liquor under it. *Daddy's going to give you a present.*

The voice came into her mind, like a whisper in the ear. But Eve forced her hands steady and kept her eyes on the screen.

"Oh, I think you've been naughty, very, very naughty, but I'm going to give you something nice anyway."

He turned back to the camera, doing a stylish striptease. He left the wig and beard in place as he began to stoke himself.

"It's the first day of Christmas. My true love."

He raped her. It was quick and brutal. While her screams echoed through the room, Eve picked up her coffee. However bitter and foul it felt going down her throat, she swallowed it.

He sodomized her. And she stopped screaming and simply whimpered like a child.

His eyes were glassy when he'd finished, his well-toned chest heaving. He took something out of his enhancement case, swallowed it.

"We believe that he's ingesting an herb and chemical mix, partly Exotica, in order to maintain an erection." Eve's voice was flat, and her eyes stayed on the screen. It was, for her, a responsibility to the dead and a challenge to herself. She would look, she would see. And she would survive it.

Marianna didn't struggle through the next rape. She'd gone away, Eve knew. Away where it couldn't hurt any longer. Deep inside where she was all alone in the dark.

She didn't struggle as Simon began to weep, began to curse her as a whore, wrapping the pretty garland around her neck and yanking it taut until it snapped and he was forced to use his hands.

417

"Oh sweet Jesus." McNab's choked whisper was full of horror and pity. "Isn't that enough?"

"Now he decorates her," Eve continued in the same empty voice. "Pretties her face, styles her hair, drapes the garland. You can see as he lifts her here, the tattoo is already in place. He lets the camera linger on her. He wants this. Wants to be able to run this over and over again when he's alone. See her as he left her. As he made her."

The screen went blank.

"He didn't need a record of the cleanup. This disc ran thirty-three minutes and twelve seconds. That's how long it took him to accomplish this section of his goal. There are other discs of the subsequent murders. All follow the same pattern. He's a creature of habit and discipline. He'll find a comfortable place in the city he knows to recuperate, to hide. He won't go for a flop, but a good hotel, or another apartment."

"Booking a room this time of year won't be easy," Feeney put in.

"No, but it's where we start looking. Uptown to start. We'll question his friends and coworkers at start of business tomorrow. We might get a handle on where he'd go. Peabody, you'll meet me at the salon at nine hundred, in uniform."

"Yes, sir."

"The best we can do is get some sleep, for what's left of the night."

"Dallas, I can hang with this for another hour. If I could bunk right here, I could get an early roll on it in the morning."

"All right, McNab. Let's pack it in for now."

"I'm for that." Feeney rose. "I'll give you a lift home, Peabody."

"Don't play with my toys, McNab," Eve added as she walked out. "I get really cranky."

"You need a sleep inducement tonight." Roarke took her arm as they started toward the bedroom.

"Don't start on me."

"You don't need dreams tonight. You need to turn it off for a few hours, if not for yourself, for the sake of that woman we watched being brutalized."

"I can do my job." She began to strip the minute she was inside, peeling off her clothes in a rush. She needed a shower, viciously hot water to scrub the stench off her skin.

She left her clothes heaped on the floor, strode directly into the bath, and ordered water at blistering.

He just waited her out. She would, he

knew, need to fight it first. Even to fight him and his offer of comfort. That prickly, resistant shell was only one of the aspects of her that fascinated him.

And he knew, as if he'd been inside her head, inside her heart, what she had gone through viewing that disc.

So when she came out, bundled in a robe, her eyes too dark, her cheeks too pale, he simply opened his arms and took her in.

"Oh God, God!" She clung, her fingers digging into his back. "I could smell him on me. I could smell him."

It tore him to pieces to see her break, to feel her shudders and the quake of her heart against his. "He can't ever touch you again."

"He touches me." She buried her face in his shoulder, filled herself with the scent of him. "Every time he comes into my head he touches me. I can't stop it from happening."

"I can." He picked her up, and sat on the bed to cradle her. "Don't think any more tonight, Eve. Just hold onto me."

"I can do my job."

"I know." But at what cost? he wondered and rocked her like a child.

"I don't want drugs. Just you. You're enough."

"Then go to sleep. Let go." He turned his

head to kiss her hair. "And sleep."

"Don't go away." She burrowed into him and sighed once, long and deep. "I need you. Too much."

"Not too much. It can't be too much."

She'd put a memory into their box, he thought. Now he put a wish there. One night, or the few hours left in it, she would sleep in peace.

So he held her until she slipped away into dreamless slumber.

And was holding her still when she woke.

They were wrapped around each other, her head nestled into the curve of his shoulder. Sometime during the night he'd undressed and slipped them both into bed.

She lay still a moment, studying his face. It seemed impossibly beautiful in the soft light. Strong lines, long thick lashes, that dreamy poet's mouth. She had an itch to stroke his hair, the silky sweep of it, but her arms were pinned.

She kissed him instead, lightly, as much to thank him as to rouse him enough to allow her to wiggle free. But his hold merely tightened.

"Mmm. Another minute."

Her brows lifted. His voice was thick, slurry, and his eyes stayed closed. "You're tired."

"God, yes."

She pursed her lips. "You're never tired."

"I am now. Quiet down."

It made her chuckle, that edge of sleepy crossness in his tone. "Stay in bed awhile."

"Damn right."

"I have to get up." She pried an arm free and did stroke his hair. "Go back to sleep."

"I would if you'd shut up."

She laughed, then slithered free. "Roarke?"

"Oh Christ!" He rolled in defense and buried his face in the pillow. "What?"

"I love you."

He turned his head, heavy eyes slitting open with a lazy gleam that had her juices flowing. That, she thought, was the magic of him. That he could make her yearn for sex after what she'd seen, what she'd experienced.

"Well then, come back here. I can probably manage to stay awake long enough."

"Later."

His response was a grunt as he pushed his face back into the pillow.

Deciding not to take it the wrong way, she dressed, ordered up coffee, strapped on her weapon. He hadn't stirred a muscle when she left the room.

She decided to check in with McNab first

and found him sprawled out flat in her sleep chair with Galahad draped over his head like fat earmuffs. Both of them snored.

At her approach, the cat slitted one eye open, gave her a bored look, then offered her an irritable meow.

"McNab." When she got no response from him, Eve rolled her eyes and gave his shoulder a light punch. He only snorted and turned his head.

The slight shift had the cat drooping lower. Galahad retaliated by digging in with his claws. McNab snorted again and smirked in his sleep. "Watch the nails, honey."

"Jesus." Eve punched harder. "No sick sex dreams in my chair, pal."

"Huh? Come on, baby." His eyes opened, glazed and heavy, then focused on Eve's face. "Uh, Dallas, what? Where?" He lifted a hand to the weight on his shoulder and closed it over Galahad's head. "Who?"

"You forgot why, but don't ask me. Pull it together."

"Yeah, yeah. Man." He turned his head again and found himself eyeball to eyeball with Galahad. "This your cat?"

"He lives here. You awake enough to give me an update?"

"Okay, sure." Struggling to sit up, he ran

his tongue around his teeth. "Coffee. I'm begging you."

Because she shared the addiction, she was sympathetic enough to go into the kitchen and order him a double-sized mug, strong and black.

The cat was in his lap when she came back, kneading McNab's thighs and watching him as if daring the man to protest. McNab took the mug in both hands and downed half the contents.

"Okay, wow. I dreamed I was off planet on some resort island and making it with this incredibly built mutant with fur instead of skin." He eyed Galahad again and grinned. "Jesus."

"I don't want to know about your prurient fantasies. What have you got?"

"Right. I checked out all the high-end hotels in the city. No single man booked a room last night. I ran the midlevel ones, same results. I got personal data. Disc's on your desk, marked."

She went over to pick it up and slipped it into her bag. "Give me the highlights."

"Our man's forty-seven, born here in New York. Parents divorced when he was twelve. Mother was custodial parent." He yawned until his jaw cracked. "Sorry. She never remarried. Worked as an actress, mostly nickel-and-dime productions. She's got a history of mental illness. In and out of nut palaces — mostly depression. They didn't do the trick because she offed herself last year. Guess when?"

"Christmas."

"That's a bull's-eye. Simon, he got himself a good education, double majored. Theater and cosmetology. He's got a degree in both. Did some gigs as makeup producer. Took over the salon two years ago. He never married, shared living digs with his mama."

He paused to slurp down more coffee. "He isn't hurting for credits, but his mother's treatments took big bites out of his accounts. No criminal record. Nothing but standard exams and checkups on the physical end, and no mental work."

"Copy the personal data to Mira, then see what you can dig up on the father. Stick with the hotel checks. He's got to go somewhere."

"Can I get some breakfast?"

"You know where the kitchen is. I'll be in the field. Keep me updated."

"Sure. Uh, Dallas, you and Peabody okay?"

Eve lifted her brows. "Why shouldn't we be?"

"Just seemed like something was off with you."

"Keep me updated," she repeated, and left him drinking coffee, scratching the cat's ears, and puzzling.

Eve decided that her aide had either slept on a board or put extra starch in her uniform. Peabody was stiff and brittle as burned toast.

But she was prompt. Exchanging nods rather than words, they walked into the salon together. Yvette was already behind her console, busily plugging in the day's schedule.

"You're getting to be a regular," she said to Eve. "You ought to let me work in a manicure or something for you."

"Got an empty treatment room?"

"I've got a couple, but no free consultants until two o'clock."

"Take five, Yvette."

"Excuse me?"

"Clock off. I need to talk to you. We'll use one of those empty rooms."

"I'm really busy."

"Here or at Cop Central. Let's go."

"Oh, for God's sake." With an irritated huff, Yvette pushed off her stool. "Let me set up the backup droid. We don't like to use droids. They're not as personal."

She scooted around the corner and un-coded a tall cabinet. The droid inside was beautifully groomed and coiffed, outfitted in a smart pastel skinsuit that set off deep gold skin and fiery red hair. When Yvette initialized, the droid opened big, baby blue eyes, blinked thick, weighty lashes, and smiled.

"May I assist you?"

"Take over the reception counter."

"I'm happy to be of service. You're look-ing lovely today."

"Right." Obviously annoyed, Yvette turned away. "She'd say that if I had a face covered with warts. That's the problem with droids. I hope we can make this fast," she added, clicking her way toward the back. "Simon doesn't like us to leave our posts except on scheduled breaks."

"He's not going to be a problem." Eve stepped into the treatment room and wished it didn't remind her of an autopsy suite. "When did you last talk to Simon?"

"Yesterday." Since she was there, Yvette picked up a massage mitt, slipped it on, and engaged. It hummed low as she ran it over her neck and shoulders. "He had a breast plumper at four, finished up at six. If you need him, he'll be here any minute. Fact is, he was supposed to open up. Day before Christmas we're swamped with appointments."

"I wouldn't expect him today."

Yvette blinked and the massage mitt stuttered as her hand jerked. "Is something wrong with Simon? Did he have an accident?"

"Something's wrong with Simon, but no, he didn't have an accident. He attacked Piper Hoffman last night."

"Attacked? Simon?" Yvette bubbled out a laugh. "You're out of orbit big time, Lieutenant."

"He's killed four people, raped and murdered four people, and nearly did the same to Piper last night. He's gone under. Where would he go?"

"You're wrong." Yvette's hand shook as she ripped off the mitt. "You have to be wrong. Simon's gentle and sweet. He couldn't hurt anyone."

"How long have you known him?"

"I — A couple of years, ever since he took over the salon. You have to be wrong." Yvette held up her hands, then pressed them to her cheeks. "Piper? You said Piper was attacked? How badly is she hurt? Where is she?"

"She's in a coma, in the hospital. Simon

was interrupted before he'd finished with her, and he ran. He's been back to his apartment, but he's not there now. Where would he go?"

"I don't know. I can't believe this. You're sure?"

Eve kept her eyes level and cool. "I'm sure."

"But he adored Piper. He was her consultant, hers and Rudy's. He did all their work. He called them the Angel Twins."

"Who else is he close to? Who does he talk to about his personal life? His mother?"

"His mother? She died last year. He was devastated. She had an accident and she died."

"He told you she had an accident?"

"Yes, she fainted or something, in the bathtub. Drowned. It was awful. They were really close."

"He talked to you about her?"

"Yeah, we worked together, put in a lot of hours here. We're friends." Her eyes filled. "I can't believe what you're telling me."

"You'd better believe it, for your own safety. Where would he go, Yvette? If he's scared, if he can't go home. If he needs somewhere to hide."

"I don't know. His life was here. The salon, especially after he lost his mother. I don't think he has any other family. His father died when he was a kid. He didn't call me. I swear he didn't."

"If he does, I want you to contact me immediately. Don't play games with him. Don't meet him alone. Don't open the door if he comes to your place. I need to get into his locker, and interview the rest of the staff."

"Okay. I'll fix it. He hasn't been acting weird or anything." Yvette dashed a tear from her lashes as she rose. "He was all pumped up about Christmas. He's a real softie, you know. And last year, losing his mother put a cloud over the holidays for him."

"Yeah, well, he's making up for it this time around." Eve stepped into the staff room, and glanced briefly at a beefy consultant gulping down a mint-green nutri-drink.

"He's changed the combo," Yvette murmured. "He's got it blocked. I can't open this without his new code."

"Who's in charge around here with him gone?"

Yvette blew out a breath. "That would be me."

Eve drew her weapon, tilted her head. "This'll open it, but you have to give me assent for forced entry."

Yvette simply closed her eyes. "Go ahead."

"On record, Peabody?"

"Yes, sir."

Eve adjusted the setting, aimed, and fired at the lock. The gun gave a muffled blast, sparked. Then metal sheered away and crashed to the floor.

"Jesus, Yvette, what the hell?"

"It's cop business, Stevie." She waved a hand at the gaping consultant. "You got a nine thirty buffer. Go on and set up for it."

"Simon's going to be pissed," he said with a shake of his head as he left the room.

Stepping to the side so Peabody could get the right angle on record, Eve tapped a finger on the pull. "Shit." She winced and sucked her fingertip. "Too hot."

"Try this." Peabody handed her a neatly folded handkerchief from her pocket. Their eyes met briefly.

"Thanks." Using the cloth, Eve covered the pull and opened the locker door. "Santa was in a hurry," she murmured.

The red suit was balled up and shoved into the locker. High, shiny black boots stood on top of it. Reaching down, Eve pulled a can of Seal-It out of her bag, coated her hands. "Let's see what else we've got."

There were two cans of disinfectant, a half case of herbal soap, tubes of protective cream, an over-the-counter gadget that promised to destroy germs with high-frequency sound waves. She found another box of tattoo works along with templates for several complicated designs.

"This nails it." Eve took out a thin sheet with stylized letters:

## My True Love

"Bag everything, Peabody, and arrange for a pickup. I want it all in the lab within the hour. I'll be in that treatment room doing the interviews."

She didn't get anything more from the staff. Simon had been loved and appreciated by his people. Eve heard words like compassionate, generous, sympathetic.

And she thought of the horror and pain in Marianna Hawley's eyes.

The drive to the hospital to check on Piper was made in silence. Though the new vehicle's climate control pumped out pleasant heat, the air seemed very chilly.

Fine, Eve thought. That was just fine. If Peabody wanted to walk around with a stick up her ass that was her problem. It wouldn't affect the work.

"Bounce a call to McNab." Eve stepped into the elevator, stared straight ahead. "See if he's got any more on possible locations for Simon. Then see if Mira got the personal data."

"Yes, sir."

"You call me sir again in that snotty tone, I'm going to belt you." With this Eve marched off the elevator and left Peabody scowling after her.

"Status on Piper," Eve said and slapped her badge on the counter at the nurses' station.

"Patient Piper is sedated."

"What do you mean sedated? Did she come out of the coma?"

The nurse wore a colorful tunic crowded with spring flowers and a harried expression. "Patient Piper regained consciousness about twenty minutes ago."

"Why wasn't I contacted? Her chart was supposed to be flagged."

"It was, Lieutenant. But Patient Piper regained consciousness at the top of her lungs. She was incoherent, hysterical and violent. We were forced to restrain and sedate at the attending's recommendation and next of kin's approval."

"Where's the next of kin now?"

"He's in the room with her, where he's been all night."

"Page the attending. Get him up here."

Turning on her heel, Eve strode down the hall and into Piper's room.

She looked like a fairy sleeping. Pale and blond and pretty. Delicate shadows were under her eyes and a faint flush of pink from the medication traced her cheekbones.

A short distance from the bed, monitors hummed. The room itself was decked out like the parlor of a classy hotel suite. Patients who had the means could afford to heal in class and comfort.

Eve's first memory of medical treatment had been a horrid, narrow room lined with horrid, narrow beds where women and girls moaned in pain or misery. The walls were gray, the windows black, and the air thick with the stench of urine.

She'd been eight, broken and alone, without even the memory of her own name to comfort her.

But Piper wouldn't wake to such discomfort. Her brother sat beside the bed, holding her hand, gently, as if it would shatter like thin glass at the wrong pressure.

There were already sweeps and flows of flowers, in baskets, in bowls, in tall, spearing vases. Music, something soothing with strings, played quietly.

"She woke up screaming." He didn't look over, but kept his bruised eyes on his sister's face. "Screaming for me to help her. She made sounds that didn't even sound human."

He lifted that long, narrow hand and stroked it over his cheek. "But she didn't recognize me; she beat at me, at the nurses. She didn't know who I was, where she was. She thought she was still . . . She thought he was still with her."

"Did she say anything, Rudy? Did she say his name?"

"She shrieked it." His face seemed to have lost its texture as well as his color as he lifted his head. It was flat, waxy. "She said his name. 'Oh please God,' she said, 'Simon, don't. Don't, don't, don't.' Over and over and over again."

Pity, for both of them, squeezed her heart. "Rudy, I have to talk to her."

"She needs to sleep. She needs to forget." He lifted his other hand and stroked Piper's hair. "When she's better, when she's able, I'm going to take her away. Somewhere warm and sunny and full of flowers. She'll heal there, away from all this. I know what you think of me, of us. I don't care."

"It doesn't matter what I think of you. She's what matters." She moved closer, so that they could face each other on either side of the bed. "Won't she heal cleaner,

Rudy, knowing the man who did this to her is locked away? I need to talk to her."

"She can't be made to talk about it. You can't understand what she'll feel, what it's like for her."

"I can understand. I know what she's been through. I know exactly what she's been through," Eve said, pacing her words while Rudy studied her face. "I won't hurt her. I want to put this man away, Rudy, before he does what he did to her, and worse, to someone else."

"I have to be here," he said after a long moment. "She'll need me here — and the doctor. The doctor has to stay. If she's too upset, I want him to sedate her again."

"All right. But you have to let me do my job."

He nodded, and shifted his eyes back to Piper's face. "Will she . . . How long . . . If you know what it's like for her, how long will it take her to forget?"

Oh Jesus. "She'll never forget," Eve said flatly. "But she'll live with it."

# CHAPTER NINETEEN

"This will bring her out gradually." The doctor was young, with eyes that still held compassion and devotion to his art. He added the medication to the IV himself rather than ordering the pesky task to a nurse or physician's assistant. "I'm going to keep her down a couple of levels so that she won't be overly agitated."

"I need her coherent," Eve told him, and he flicked those soft brown eyes over her face.

"I know what you need, Lieutenant. Ordinarily I wouldn't agree to deactivate sedation on a woman in Patient Piper's condition. But I understand the necessity in this case. Now you understand, she needs to remain as calm as possible."

He gave his attention to the monitors while keeping his fingers on Piper's wrist. "She's steady," he said, then looked back at Eve. "Recovering, both physically and emotionally, from a trauma of this kind, is a difficult journey."

"You ever been to the rape wards down in Alphabet City?"

"There aren't any rape wards in that area."

"There were up until about five years ago, until they restructured the license requirements and standard fees for street LCs. They were mostly street whores in the wards, mostly young ones, too. Boys and girls fresh off the farm who didn't know how to handle a john pumped up on Zeus or Exotica. I worked that sector for six miserable months. I know what I'm doing here."

The doctor nodded, lifted his patient's eyelid. "She's coming around. Rudy, let her see you first. Talk to her, reassure her. Keep your voice quiet and calm."

"Piper." Rudy put on a hideous excuse for a smile as he leaned over the bed. "Darling, it's Rudy. You're okay. You're with me. You're absolutely safe. You're with me. Can you hear me?"

"Rudy?" She slurred the word, keeping her eyes closed but turning her face toward the sound of his voice. "Rudy, what happened? What happened? Where were you?"

"I'm right here now." A tear trickled down his cheek. "I'll be right here."

"Simon, he's hurting me. I can't move."

"He's gone. You're safe."

"Piper." Eve could read the panic under the sheen of medication in her eyes when she blinked them open. "Do you remember me?"

"The police. The lieutenant. You wanted me to say bad things about Rudy."

"No, I just want you to tell me the truth. Rudy's right here. He's going to stay right here while you talk to me. Tell me what happened to you. Tell me about Simon."

"Simon." The lights on the monitors scrambled. "Where is he?"

"He's not here. He can't hurt you now." Gently, Eve took the hand Piper waved as if to ward off a blow. "No one's going to hurt you. I'm going to keep him very far away from you, but you have to help me. You have to tell me what he did."

"He came to the door." Her eyes closed, and Eve could see the rapid movement behind the delicate lids. "Happy to see him. I had his Christmas gift, and he had a big silver box. A present. I thought, Simon's brought a present for me, and for Rudy. I said, Rudy's not here. He knew — *No, you're all alone, alone with me.* He smiled at me and he — he put his hand on my shoulder.

"Dizzy," she murmured. "I was so dizzy, and I couldn't see very well. Have to lie down, feel so strange. I hear him, hear him talking to me, but I don't understand. I can't move, can't open my eyes. I can't think."

"Can you remember anything he said then? Anything at all?"

"I was beautiful. He knew how to make me more beautiful. Something cool on my leg, tickling my thigh, and he's talking to me. He loves me, only me. True love, he wants me to be his true love. I wasn't the one, but I could be. The others don't matter. Only me. He keeps talking, but I can't answer. All the other loves are dead because they weren't true. Not pure, not innocent. No!" Abruptly she ripped her hand out of Eve's and tried to roll aside.

"It's all right. You're safe. I know he hurt you, Piper. I know how much it hurt you, and you were so afraid. But you don't have to be afraid now." Firmly now, Eve took her hand. "Look at me, talk to me. I won't let him hurt you again."

"He tied me up." Tears streamed down her face now. "He tied me up on the bed. He took my clothes. I begged him not to. He was my friend. He dressed up. Horrible. There was a camera and he posed and

440

smiled and told me I'd been a bad girl. His eyes, something was wrong with his eyes. I was screaming, but no one could hear me. Where's Rudy?"

"I'm here." He choked out the words, pressed his lips to her brow, her temple. "I'm here."

"He did things to me. He raped me, and it hurt so much. He said I was a whore. Most women were whores, actresses who pretended to be different but were just whores. And most men just used them then left them. I was a whore and he could do whatever he wanted. And he did, he kept hurting me. Rudy, I kept calling for you to make him stop. Make him stop!"

"Rudy came," Eve told her. "Rudy came and made him stop."

"Rudy came?"

"Yes, he heard you and he came and he took care of you."

"He stopped. Yes, he stopped." She closed her eyes again. "There was shouting and noise and someone's crying, very hard. Crying for his mother. I don't remember any more."

"Okay. You did fine."

"You're not going to let him come back?" Her fingers tightened on Eve's. "You won't let him find me?"

"No, I won't let him come back."

"He put stuff on me," Piper remembered. "He sprayed something all over me." She bit her lip. "Into me. His body, it's been waxed. It's hairless. He has a tattoo on his hip."

That was new, Eve mused. He'd had no tattoo in the videos she'd screened. "Do you remember what it looked like?"

"It said, 'My True Love.' He showed it to me, wanted me to look at it. He said it was new, permanent, not a temp. Because he was tired of being temporary to everyone he loved. And I was crying, telling him I'd never hurt him. Then he cried, too. He said he knew, he was sorry. He didn't know what else to do."

"Can you remember anything else?"

"He said I would always love him, because he'd be my last. And that he'd always remember me, because I'd been his friend." The glaze had cleared out of her eyes. Now they just seemed weary. "He was going to kill me. He wasn't Simon anymore, Lieutenant. The man who did this to me, I didn't know him. He became someone else in that room. And I think it frightened him almost as much as it frightened me."

"You don't have to be frightened now. I promise you." Stepping back, Eve looked over at Rudy. "Let's step outside a minute and let the doctor examine your sister."

"I'll be right back." He pressed his lips to Piper's knuckles. "I'm just outside the door. I don't want to leave her," he said to Eve as soon as the door closed behind them.

"She's going to need to talk to someone."

"She's talked enough. She told you everything, for God's sake —"

"She'll need counseling," Eve interrupted. "She'll need treatment. Taking her away isn't going to help her cope. I gave her a card a couple of days ago, one of mine with a name and number on the back. Contact Dr. Mira, Rudy. Let her help your sister."

He opened his mouth, then closed it again and seemed to make an effort to level himself. "You were very kind to her in there, Lieutenant. Very gentle. And hearing her describe what happened to her, I understand why you were neither kind nor gentle with me when you believed I was responsible for . . . what was done to the others. I'm grateful to you."

"You can be grateful when I've taken him down." She rocked back on her heels. "You know him pretty well, right?"

"I thought I did."

"Where would he go? Is there a place, a person?"

443

"I would have said he'd come to me or Piper. We spent a great deal of time in each other's company, professionally and personally." He closed his eyes. "Which explains how he was able to access the match lists. He wouldn't have been questioned by anyone in the organization. If I had told you that, if I had opened those doors to you freely rather than trying to protect myself and my business, I might have prevented this."

"Open them now. Tell me about him, his mother."

"She self-terminated. I don't know if anyone's aware of that but me." Absently, Rudy pinched the bridge of his nose. "He broke down one night and told me. She was a troubled woman, mentally unstable. He blamed his father. There was a divorce when Simon was a child and his mother never got over it. She was certain that her husband would come back one day."

"Her one true love?"

"Oh God." Now he covered his face. "Yes, yes, I suppose. She was an actress, not a particularly successful one, but Simon thought she was marvelous, stunning. He worshipped her. But he was often distressed by her behavior. She would slide into a depression and there were men. She used

444

men to bolster her moods. He was the most tolerant of men, but in this area, he was very close-minded. She was his mother and had no right to give herself sexually. He only spoke about it to me once, shortly after her death when he was lost in grief. She'd hanged herself. He found her Christmas morning."

"It's a perfect fit." Peabody sat rigidly in the passenger seat as Eve fought through traffic. "He has a mother complex, and he's replacing her, punishing her, loving her, every time he picks out a victim. The two males either represent his father, or his own dominant sexual preferences."

"Thanks for the bulletin," Eve said dryly, then rapped the wheel with the heel of her hand as she was jammed in once again on all sides. "This fucking Christmas shit! No wonder hospitals and mental clinics do booming business in December."

"It's Christmas Eve."

"I know what the hell day it is, goddamn it." She jammed the controls into straight vertical, veered sharply to the left, and zipped across the roofs of stopped cars.

"Uh, the maxibus."

"I got eyes." Eve skimmed past the bus with a stingy inch to spare.

"That Rapid Cab's going to —" Peabody braced and shut her eyes as the cab, obviously in the same mood as Eve, shot up out of the line of traffic.

Eve swore, swerved, skinned bumpers, and hit the siren full blast. "Set it down, you stupid son of a bitch." She tipped, squeezed over, and dumped her car so that it teetered half on the street, half on the sidewalk in front of a mass of irritated pedestrians.

She slammed out and stalked toward the cab. The driver slammed out and stalked toward her. Peabody could have told him if he wanted to go nose-to-nose with a cop, he'd picked the wrong one.

But, she thought, as she climbed out and elbowed through the crowd, maybe kicking a cabbie's ass would put Eve in a better mood.

"I signaled. I gotta right to a vertical lift same as you. You didn't have your lights or siren going, did ya? The city's gonna pay for that bumper, right? You cops don't own the road. I ain't taking the credit dip on the damage here, sister."

"Sister?"

Peabody actually shuddered at the jagged ice in Eve's tone. Behind Eve's back she shook her head with pity for the driver and took out her violation coder.

"Let me tell you something, *brother.* First thing you do is step back out of my face before I write you up for assault on an officer."

"Hey, I never laid hands on —"

"I said step back. Let's see how fast you can assume the position."

"Jesus, it's only a skinned bumper."

"You want resisting?"

"No." Muttering under his breath, he turned, splayed his legs and laid his hands on the roof of his cab. "Man, it's Christmas Eve. Let's cut each other a break here. Whaddaya say?"

"I'd say you'd better learn a little respect for cops."

"Lady, my cousin's a cop with the four-one."

Teeth set, Eve whipped out her badge and stuck it in his face. "See that. It says Lieutenant, not sister, not lady. You could ask your cousin the cop with the four-one."

"Brinkleman," he muttered. "Sergeant Brinkleman."

"You tell Sergeant Brinkleman with the four-one to contact Dallas, Homicide, Cop Central, and tell her why his cousin's an asshole. If he explains this factor to my satisfaction, I won't pull your license and report the fact that you cut an official vehicle off in air traffic. You got that?"

"Yeah, I got it. Lieutenant."

"Now, get the hell out of here."

Chastised, the driver slunk back into his vehicle, hunched down, and waited patiently for a break in traffic. Because her temper was still on the boil, Eve spun on her heel and jabbed a finger at Peabody. "And you, you want to ride with me any more today, you yank the stick out of your butt."

"Respectfully, Lieutenant, I was unaware of any foreign object in that region."

"Your attempt at humor isn't appreciated at this time, Officer Peabody. If you're dissatisfied in your position as my aide, you can request reassignment."

Peabody's heart clogged in her throat. "I don't want reassignment. Sir, I'm not dissatisfied in my position."

Barely muffling a scream, Eve pivoted away and plowed through the pedestrian traffic, earned a few bruises and rude comments, then plowed back. "You keep it up. You keep using that academy tone on me, we're going a few rounds."

"You just threatened to ditch me."

"I did not. I offered you the option of assignment elsewhere."

Peabody's voice wavered, so she clamped down. "I felt, and still feel, that you overstepped the boundaries last night in reference to my relationship with Charles Monroe."

"Yeah, you made that clear."

"It was inappropriate for my superior officer to criticize my choice of escort. It was a personal matter, and —"

"Goddamn right it was personal." Eve's eyes went dark, but not, Peabody noted with shock, in anger. There was hurt. "I wasn't speaking as your superior officer last night. I never considered myself addressing my aide. I thought I was talking to a friend."

Shame washed up from Peabody's toes to the top of her head. "Dallas —"

"A friend," she barreled on, "who was sloppy-eyed over an LC. An LC who was a suspect in an ongoing investigation."

"But Charles —"

"Low on the list," Eve snapped, "but still on it, as he'd been matched with one victim and with one of the attempts."

"You never believed Charles was the killer."

"No, I believed it was Rudy, and I was wrong. I could have been wrong about Charles Monroe, too." And the possibility clawed at her. "Take the vehicle back to Central. Update Captain Feeney and Commander Whitney on the latest data regarding our current case. Advise them that I remain in the field."

"But —"

"Take the fucking vehicle into Central," Eve snapped. "That's an order from a superior officer to her aide." She turned and pushed her way through the crowd. This time she didn't come back.

"Oh shit." Peabody slumped down on the hood of the car, ignoring the bad-tempered horns, the blast of insidious holiday music pouring out of the storefront on the other side of the packed sidewalk. "Peabody, you're an idiot."

She sniffed, reached into her pocket for her handkerchief, then remembered Eve hadn't given it back. Swiping the back of her hand under nose, she climbed into the car and prepared to follow orders.

By the time Eve reached the corner at Forty-first, she'd blown off enough steam to realize she wasn't going to walk another thirty blocks to the lab to pick on Dickie.

One glance at the jammed humanity crammed onto the overhead people glides convinced her she wasn't about to go that route, either.

A new wave of pedestrians caught her full in the back and swept her another half block before she could manage to dig in and shove her way clear. She choked on the steam of a glide-cart doing a brisk business on grilled soy dogs, blinked the resulting tears out of her eyes, and dug for her badge.

She clawed her way out to the curb, risked life and limb by stepping directly into the path of an oncoming cab, then slapped her badge on the windshield.

Climbing in, she tried to rub the stress of the last few minutes off her face, then dropped her hands into her lap and met the driver's miserable eyes in the mirror.

Recognizing Detective Brinkleman from the four-one's cousin, she let out one short bark of laughter. "It just figures, doesn't it?"

"It's been a crap day altogether," he muttered.

"I hate Christmas."

"I ain't too fond of it myself right at the moment."

"Get me down to Eighteenth. I'll take it from there."

"You could walk quicker."

She took another look at the teeming sidewalk. "Go over and punch it. You get tagged, I'll handle it with Traffic."

"You're the boss, Lieutenant."

He took off like a lightning bolt, and Eve closed her eyes, admitting that the headache scrambling in her temples wasn't going to vacate the premises without a chemical shove.

"You going to get grief over the bumper?" she asked him.

"The way these units get banged around? Nah." He angled over the corner at Eighteenth. "I shouldn't oughta've disrespected you, Lieutenant. This holiday traffic, it can turn you mean."

"Yeah." She dug out credits, slipped them through his pay slot. "We'll call it even."

"Appreciate it. Anyway, Merry freaking Christmas."

Her laugh was a little looser as she got out. "Same to you."

Pedestrian traffic was light in the sector that held crime labs and morgues and holding stations. Not a hell of a lot to buy, she mused as she jogged the half block over.

She turned into the ugly steel building that had been some idiot architect's vision of high-tech economy, crossed the soulless lobby, and went through the security arch.

The droid on duty nodded to her as she slapped her palm on the plate, recited her name, rank, code, and destination. Cleared, she took the glide down, and frowned when she saw the hallways and offices empty. Middle of the afternoon, middle of the week, she thought. Where the hell was everybody?

She cleared herself into the lab. And found a hell of a party going on.

Music blasted over wild laughter. Someone shoved a cup with a suspicious green fluid swimming inside it into her hand. A woman wearing nothing but a lab coat and microgoggles danced by. Eve managed to snag the sleeve of the coat and spin her back.

"Where's Dickie?"

"Oh, around and about. I gotta get me a refill."

"Here." Eve shoved the cup into her hand and worked her way through bodies and equipment. She spotted Dickie sitting on top of a sample table with his hand well up a drunk technician's skirt.

At least Eve assumed the tech was drunk. How else could she let those spidery fingers between her legs?

"Hey, Dallas, join the party. Not as classy as your little get-together, but we try."

"Where the hell are my reports? Where are my results? What the fuck's going on around here?"

"Hey, it's Christmas Eve. Lighten up."

Her hand snapped out, grabbed him by the shirtfront, and yanked him off the table.

"I've got four bodies and a woman in the hospital. Don't you fucking tell me to lighten up, you little cross-eyed son of a bitch. I want my test results."

"Lab closes two o'clock Christmas Eve." He tried to shove her hand away, but didn't budge it. "That's official. It's after three, hotshot."

"For Christ's sake, he's out there. Did you see what he did to those people? Do you want me to show you the goddamn videos he took while he was doing it? You want to wake up tomorrow morning and find out he did it again because you couldn't do the job? Can you swallow your Christmas goose over that?"

"Damn it, Dallas. I got next to nothing new anyway. Let go of me." With surprising dignity, he smoothed down his shirt when she released him. "We'll take a look in the side lab. No use spoiling everybody's good time."

He snaked through the crowd and unlocked the door of a side room. "Jesus, Feinstein, you can't go banging her in here. Take her into storage like everybody else."

Eve pressed her fingers to her eyes as a busily copulating couple unlinked, and sputtered as they grabbed discarded clothes. Was everybody insane this time of year? Eve

454

wondered as they darted by giggling like loons.

"We mixed a hell of a brew," Dickie explained. "All legal stuff, but it's a punch with real punch." He dropped down at the computer station and called up the file.

"We got his prints this time, but you already know that. No question on the ID. Same disinfectant traces on scene. The enhancements left behind match those used on the prior victims. The suit and shit you had sent down is consistent with the fibers already identified. You got your guy, Dallas. This goes to court, he's cooked."

"What about the sweep? I need something to find him, Dickie."

"Sweep of scene didn't turn up anything you wouldn't expect. The one of his digs? We didn't get much. This guy's a clean fanatic. Everything's been wiped and scrubbed and sucked. But there were fibers again — match the suit, a couple of stray hairs that are consistent with those from the last murder and the beard he left on scene last night. You get him, bring him down, I got plenty to help you lock the cage. That's all I can give you."

"Okay. I need you to shoot this to my unit at Central. Copy Feeney."

Since they both knew he should have

455

already done so, Dickie just jerked a shoulder.

"Sorry I took you away from the fun and games."

"City's going to close down in an hour or two anyway, Dallas. People need their holiday. They're entitled."

"Yeah. I've got a woman spending her Christmas in a hospital bed. She's entitled, too."

She went outside to let the cold air clear her head, wished she'd thought to ask Dickie for something potent enough to block the thudding behind her eyes. The light was already going, she realized. These were the long nights, the black month of December where the daylight barely bounced to earth before it bounced away again.

She pulled out her porta-'link and called home. "You're working," she said when Roarke picked up his private line and she saw the laser fax behind him spewing out paper.

"Just a bit longer."

"I've got a couple of more things to do. I don't think I'll be home for a couple of hours anyway."

He could see the headache in her eyes. "Where are you heading?"

"I want to do a follow-up on Simon's apartment. I never did a search-through personally. Maybe the team missed something. I need to look, Roarke."

"I know."

"Listen, I sent Peabody off with my vehicle. The apartment's closer to home. Can you send a car or something to that location?"

"Of course."

"Thanks. I'll call back when I'm done there, let you know when I'll make it home."

"Do what you need to do, but take a blocker for that headache, Eve."

She smiled a little. "I don't have one. Let's drink lots of wine after I get home, okay? And make love like animals."

"Well, I had planned on a quiet evening of trilevel chess, but if that's what you really want to do . . ."

It felt awfully good, Eve thought as she broke transmission, to really laugh.

So it shouldn't have surprised her to find not only the car but Roarke there when she got to Simon's building. "You could've sent it with a droid."

"Did you think I would?"

"No." She pushed a hand at her hair. "And I don't think you're going to agree to wait in the car until I'm done in there either."

"See how well we know each other." He reached in the pocket of his gorgeous topcoat, took out a small enameled box, and removed a tiny blue pill. "Open up."

When she frowned and firmed her lips into an uncooperative line, he only lifted an eyebrow. "It's a simple blocker, Eve. You'll think more clearly without the headache."

"No funny stuff?"

"None. Open." He took her chin when she opened her mouth, then used his hand to close it again after he'd dropped the pill on her tongue. "Swallow it, there's a good girl."

"Bite me."

"Darling, I've thought of nothing else all day. I brought your backup field kit."

"Well, one of us is thinking clearly. Thanks," she said when he got it out of the car. "I've got him cold," she added as they started into the building. "Physical evidence, eyewitness, motivation, opportunity, the works."

"You can add the fact that the enhancement case he left behind in Piper Hoffman's apartment is a one of a kind. He ordered it custom-made." Roarke ran a hand over the back of Eve's neck, rubbing lightly to help the blocker along. "My company offers that option to licensed cosmeticians."

"Great. Now all I have to do is find him."

"He hasn't checked into a hotel?" Roarke smiled at her. "McNab's been very busy. No hotel, and no private lodging — at least that he could access on a day where no one wants to work."

"Tell me about it. I walked into an orgy at the lab."

"And we weren't invited. That's insulting."

"I have a feeling an invite might have included the rare treat of seeing Dickhead naked." She took out her master and bypassed the police seal and block on the door of 35. "That's something I really don't want for Christmas. You gotta seal up if you're coming in."

Roarke glanced at the can with a hefty sigh. "Can't the department use something with a more pleasant odor?" But he coated his hands, his shoes, then waited for Eve to do the same.

"Record on. Dallas, Lieutenant Eve entering subject Simon's personal residence, December twenty-four, sixteen twelve. Investigating officer accompanied by Roarke, civilian, in capacity of temporary aide."

She entered, ordered lights, then simply stood and studied the room. It wasn't quite so neat now. The CS team had done its work and left a fine sheen on surfaces while checking for prints and trace evidence. The sweepers had shoved furniture out of place, upended cushions, removed art from the walls. The 'link had been disconnected and taken in.

"Since you're here," she said to Roarke, "poke around. Anything that strikes you, call me. I'm going to do the bedroom."

She'd barely started on the closet when Roarke came in, holding a disc between his thumb and forefinger. "This struck me, Lieutenant."

"Where the hell did you find that? They should have swept all the discs into evidence."

"Holiday help, what can you do? It was sealed inside a hologram frame — I assume the woman in the holo was his mother. It seemed the sentimental choice of hiding places."

"I've got nothing to run it on. They took all the electronics. I'll need to go in and . . ."

Her voice trailed off as Roarke took a slim black case out of his pocket, swiveled the lid, and opened it to reveal a small screen. "New toy," he said as she frowned at it. "We weren't able to get all the bugs out for the Christmas market. It'll be ready for the President's Day sales."

"Is it safe? I can't have that disc damaged."

"I reworked this unit personally. It's a little jewel." He slipped the disc into a slot, lifted a brow again. "Shall I?"

"Yeah, let's see what we've got."

# Chapter Twenty

It was a rambling and rather pitiful video journal. A year in a man's life when that life shatters into pieces and begins to fall away from the core.

Eve supposed Mira would have called it a cry for help.

He referred to his mother a dozen times or more. His true love, whom he canonized in one entry and vilified in the next.

She was a saint. She was a whore.

The one thing Eve was certain of at the end was that she had been a burden, one that Simon had never shirked, and never understood.

Every Christmas she had reboxed and rewrapped the gold cuff bracelet she had purchased for her husband, engraved with the words "My True Love," and placed it under the tree for the man who had left her and her young son. And every Christmas she had told her son that his father would be there on Christmas morning.

For a long time, he believed her.

For a longer time, he allowed her to believe.

Then on Christmas Eve the year before, sick of it, revolted by the men she let use her, he'd smashed the box and destroyed her illusion.

And she hanged herself with the pretty garland her son had strung around the tree.

"Not a cheerful seasonal tale," Roarke murmured. "Poor bastard."

"A lousy childhood's not an excuse to rape and murder."

"No, it's not. But it's a root. We grow our own way, Eve, one choice leading to another."

"And the choices we make we're responsible for." She dug out an evidence bag and held it open. After a moment, Roarke ejected the disc and dropped it inside.

Taking out her communicator, Eve called McNab.

"No luck on his hidey-hole, Dallas. I traced the father. He relocated to Nexus Station nearly thirty years ago. Got a second wife, two kids, grandchildren. I've got data if you want to contact."

"What's the point?" she murmured. "I've got a video diary from Simon's place. The crime scene techs and the sweepers missed it. I'll transmit to EDD. Go in and file it, will you, McNab? Then you're off duty. Relay that same status to Peabody. Both of you remain on call as long as subject is at large."

"That's affirmative. Hey, he's got to come out sometime, Dallas. Then we'll have him."

"Right. Go hang your stocking, McNab. Let's hope we all get what we want for Christmas. Dallas out."

Roarke watched her pocket the communicator. "You're too hard on yourself, Eve."

"He'll have to move tonight. He'll need to move. And he's the only one who knows where. And who." She turned back to the closet. "He's got his clothes organized — color, fabric. Even more obsessive about it than you."

"I see nothing obsessive with organizing your wardrobe."

"Yeah, especially if you own two hundred black silk shirts. Wouldn't want to pull out the wrong one and make a fashion faux pas."

"I take that to mean you didn't buy me a black silk shirt for Christmas."

She glanced over her shoulder, grimaced. "I kind of messed up on the shopping. I didn't understand the deal until Feeney pointed out you're supposed to buy in bulk for a spouse. I've just got this one thing."

He tucked his tongue in his cheek. "Do I get a hint?"

"No, you're too good at puzzles." She looked back in the closet. "So puzzle this. You've got shirts and trousers here, white to cream to whatever this color is."

"I'd say taupe."

"Fine. Then it goes into blues, greens. All of them hung in order. Now there's a gap, then we pick up browns, grays to black. What color do you suppose is missing?"

"Best guess is red."

"Right. No other red in here. Maybe he only wore red for special occasions. He had a backup suit, and he took it with him. Something else the sweepers didn't come up with. The rest of the tokens. Six geese whatever and so on. He's got them, too. He'll be ready for the show. But where has he stashed it all? Where's he keeping it, and himself?"

She circled the room. "There's no coming back here for him. He knows that. He risked coming back because he's got to finish, and he can't finish without his tools, his costume, his props. But he's too smart, he's too organized, too fucking anal not to have

465

had a place to go."

"His life was here, with his mother and the memories," Roarke pointed out. "And it was at his work."

She closed her eyes as it struck. "God, he went back to the building. He's in that building."

"Then let's find him."

Street traffic was vicious, the road skinned with thin icy patches, but the pedestrian jam had whittled down to a trickle. People rushed over the sidewalk, hurrying home to family, to friends. The few who were desperate for the eleventh-hour gift haunted the handful of shops and stores still open.

Streetlights blinked on and offered cold pools of light. Eve watched an animated billboard Santa fly in his sleigh and wish Merry Christmas to all.

And it began to rain ice.

Perfect.

When Roarke pulled to the curb, she got out quickly, slipped out her master code, then hesitated. After a brief internal debate, she bent over and unstrapped a weapon from her ankle holster. "Take my clutch piece. Just in case."

They stepped out of the cold and into the glow of security lights.

"There were people in and out of the salon, the shops, the health clubs all day. He'd need privacy. There's probably some empty offices, and we can run a check to save time, but my hunch is he'd use Piper's apartment. He'd know she's in the hospital and he'd know Rudy wouldn't leave her, not even to come back here. It would've been safe and quiet. No reason for the cops to go back in after the sweep was done."

She jabbed the control for the elevator, swore. "Shut down."

"Would you like me to activate them for you, Lieutenant?"

"Don't be a smart ass."

"I'll take that as a yes." He slipped the weapon away and took out a small tool kit. "Just take a moment." He removed the control plate, flicked a few keys on the mother board with his quick, clever fingers. There was a quiet hum, then the light over the glass doors blinked on.

"Slick work — for a businessman."

"Thank you." He gestured, then followed her into the car. "Hoffman apartment."

*I'm sorry. That floor is only accessible with a key code or clearance.*

Eve bared her teeth, and started to reach for her master again, but Roarke already had the controls unplated. "Just as quick this way," he said, and neatly overrode the block.

The elevator rose, smooth and fast and quiet. As it began to slow, Eve shifted, putting her body between Roarke's and the door.

He narrowed his eyes at her back, waited. When the doors slid open, he bumped her aside, pivoted out, and swept the foyer with his weapon.

"Don't you ever do that again." She hissed it at him, leaping out to cover his back.

"Don't you ever use yourself as a shield for me. I'd say we're clear here. Ready for the door?"

She was still vibrating with outrage. Something else to deal with later, she decided. "I go low," she murmured, bypassing the locks. "That's the way I like it."

"Fine. On three then. One, two." They hit the door, smooth as a training program.

Inside the lights blazed, and the recording system had been switched on to play bouncy Christmas tunes. Though the privacy screens had been pulled tight over the windows, the Christmas tree glowed in front of the glass.

She pointed toward the left. On the route to the bedroom she noticed small things. The smears and smudges the sweep would have left had been polished away. The air smelled of flowers and disinfectant.

There was a faint haze of steam over the spa. The water was still hot.

The bedroom was tidied, the bed made, the spills mopped up.

Eve tugged up the spread, swore under her breath. "He put on fresh sheets. The bastard slept in the bed where he raped her." With fury edging along her stomach, she yanked open the closet. There among the flowing styles Rudy and Piper preferred, several shirts and slacks were neatly hung.

"Making himself right at home." She crouched down and opened the trim black suitcase lying on the closet floor. "The rest of his props." Heart thudding, she nudged through the jewelry, muttering the numbers and lyrics. "All the way to twelve — this hair clip with a dozen guys drumming. They're all here except number five. He's got that with him." She rose. "He took himself a nice relaxing bath, dressed in his suit, packed up his tools, and went out. And he's planning on coming back."

"So, we wait."

She wanted to agree. More than she could stand to admit she wanted to be the one to take him down, to look in his face when she did. To know she'd beaten him, and that part of herself she faced in nightmares.

"I'm calling it in. We'll have a few slobs who'd've drawn duty tonight. I'll need some men on the building, some inside. It'll take an hour or so to set it up. Then we'll go home."

"You don't want to turn this over to someone else, Eve."

"No, I don't. Maybe that's why I need to. And . . ." She turned back to him, thinking of Mira's words. "I'm entitled to the life I've started to carve out for myself. With you."

"Then make the calls." He reached out to touch her cheek. "And let's go home."

Peabody filed the last of her paperwork, let out a long, self-pitying sigh, then caught sight of McNab in the doorway. "What?"

"Just passing by. I told you Dallas said you're off duty."

"I'm off when my reports are finished and filed."

He smiled blandly as her machine reported filing complete. "Then I guess you're off. Hot date with Mr. Slick?"

"You're really ignorant, McNab." Peabody pushed away from the desk. "You don't spend Christmas Eve with a guy you've only dated once." Besides, she thought, Charles had already been booked for the evening.

"Your family's not around here, are they?"

"No." Stalling, willing him to leave, she fussed around the desk.

"Couldn't get home for Christmas?"

"Not this year."

"Me either. This case has eaten away at my social life. I got no plans, either." He hooked his thumbs in his pockets. "What do you say, Peabody, want to call a truce, like a Christmas moratorium?"

"I'm not at war with you." She turned to get her uniform coat from a hook.

"You look a little down."

"It's been a long day."

"Well, if you're not going to spend Christmas Eve with Mr. Slick, why don't you spend it with a fellow cop? It's a bad night to be alone. I'll buy you a drink, some dinner."

She kept her head lowered as she buttoned her coat. Christmas Eve alone, or a couple of hours with McNab. Neither were very appealing, but she decided alone was worse. "I don't like you well enough for you to buy me dinner." She looked up, shrugged. "We split the check."

"Deal."

She didn't expect to enjoy herself, but after

a couple of St. Nick Specials, she decided she wasn't miserable. At least shoptalk was a way to kill a few hours.

She picked at the chicken nibbles she knew were going to go straight to her ass. Her diet could just go to hell. "How can you eat like that?" she asked McNab, watching with hate and envy as he plowed through a double-crust pizza with the works. "Why aren't you pig fat?"

"Metabolism," he said with his mouth full. "Mine's always on overdrive. Want some?"

She knew better. Fighting off the chunkies was a constant personal battle. But she took half a slice and reveled in it.

"You and Dallas straighten things out?"

Peabody swallowed hard and glared. "She talk to you about it?"

"Hey, I'm a detective. I notice shit."

The two drinks had loosened her tongue just enough. "She's really pissed at me."

"You screw up?"

"I guess. So did she," Peabody said, brow furrowing. "But I screwed up bigger. I don't know if I can make it right again."

"You got somebody who'd go to the wall for you and you screw it up, you fix it. In my family we yell, then we brood, then we apologize."

"This isn't family."

He laughed. "Hell it isn't." And he smiled at her. "You going to eat all those nibbles?"

She felt something loosen around her heart. The man might be a pain in the ass, she thought, but when he was right, he was right. "I'll trade you six nibbles for another slice of pizza."

Eve made an effort to put the surveillance operation out of her mind. She had good, experienced officers in place, electronic scans set up in a four-block radius. The minute Simon entered the perimeter, he'd be tagged.

She couldn't wonder, couldn't question, couldn't think of where he was, what he was doing. If someone else would die. It was out of her control.

Before the night was out, they'd have him. Her case was solid, and he'd go into a cage. Never come out. It had to be enough.

"You said something about wine."

"Yeah, I did." It was easier to smile than she'd expected. The simplest of matters to take the glass Roarke handed her.

"And making love like animals."

"I recall suggesting that."

It was simpler yet to put the wine aside and jump him.

■ ■ ■ ■

Peabody stayed out later than she'd intended, enjoyed herself more than she'd imagined. Of course, she thought, as she clomped up the stairs to her apartment, that was probably the result of the liquor and not the company.

Though, she could admit, McNab hadn't been as much of an asshole as usual.

Now that she was pleasantly oiled, she thought she'd like to bundle into her ratty robe, turn on her tree, and curl up in bed to watch some sappy Christmas special on screen. At midnight, she'd call her parents and they'd all get sloppy and sentimental.

It had turned out to be a halfway decent Christmas Eve after all.

She turned at the top of the stairs and, humming a bit, walked toward her door.

Santa Claus stepped around the corner with his big silver box in hand, and beamed at her out of mad eyes. "Hello, little girl! You're out late. I was afraid I'd miss giving you your Christmas present."

Oh, Peabody thought. Oh shit. She had a split second to make up her mind. Run or stand. Her stunner was strapped inside her coat, and her coat was buttoned. But the communicator was in the pocket, within reach.

She opted to stand. Straining for a smile, she slid her hand into her pocket, engaged the unit. "Wow, Santa Claus. I never expected to run into you right here in front of my apartment door. Bearing gifts, too. I don't even have a chimney."

He threw back his head and laughed.

Eve groaned, rolled over, and stretched. They'd never made it to the bed, but had torn into each other on the floor. She felt bruised, used, and fabulous.

"That was pretty good for starters."

Beside her Roarke chuckled and slid a fingertip down her warm, damp breast. "I was just thinking the same thing. But I want my Christmas present."

"Wasn't that it?" But she laughed, sat up, and rubbed her hands over her hair. "But next year —"

She broke off as she heard Peabody's voice coming out of a pile of discarded clothes.

*Wow. Santa Claus. I never expected to run into you right in front of my apartment door.*

"Oh my God. Oh God." She was already up, ripping at the clothes, dragging on trousers. "Call it in, call it in. Officer needs assistance. Oh Jesus, Roarke."

475

He was pulling on his pants one-handed and snatching his porta-'link with the other. "Let's move. Go. We'll call on the run."

"I've been waiting for you," Simon told her. "With something very special."

Stall, stall, stall. "Do I get a hint?"

"Something someone who loves you chose just for you." He started toward her, and she kept the smile in place as she frantically flipped open the buttons of her coat.

"Yeah? Who loves me?"

"Santa loves you, Delia. Pretty Delia."

She saw his hand come up, caught a glimpse of the pressure syringe palmed in it. Pivoting, she brought up her elbow to block, fighting to get past the stiff wool to her weapon.

"Naughty!" His breath wheezed out as he slapped her into the wall. She countered with a backhand punch, but it bounced off the box. And now her weapon hand was trapped between her body and the wall.

"Get off me, you son of a bitch." She swiveled, and kicked back to hook her foot around his ankle, cursing herself for indulging in that last drink. She felt the quick sting of the syringe against her neck even as he went down behind her.

"Damn, oh damn," she managed, as she

stumbled two steps away, then just slid bonelessly down the wall.

"Look what you've done. Just look." He scolded her as he opened her bag, searched through for her key card. "You might have broken something. I'm going to be very angry if you've broken any of my things. Now, you be a good girl and let's go inside."

He hauled her up first, steering her to the door, where he disengaged the locks, then simply let her drop.

She felt the jolt, but it was distant, as if her body were padded with foam. Her mind was screaming for her to move, the message so loud she imagined herself springing up, but she couldn't feel her legs.

Dimly, she heard him come in and close the door. "Now, let's get you into bed. We have a great deal to do. It's nearly Christmas, you know. There's my love," he murmured and carried her into the bedroom as if she were a doll.

"I don't give a flying fuck about skeleton crews and available units," Eve shouted into the 'link. "Officer Peabody is down! She's down, goddamn you."

*Profanity is unacceptable on this channel, Dallas, Lieutenant Eve. This offense will be on record. Units are being dispatched. ETA twelve minutes.*

"She doesn't have twelve minutes. If she's injured, you asshole, I'm personally going to come in and rip out every one of your circuits."

She pounded her fist into the 'link. "Droids, they put goddamn droids on Dispatch, on the desk, every place, because it's Christmas. Jesus, Roarke, can't you get this thing to go any faster?"

He was already up to a hundred and ten, screaming through the vicious curtain of icy rain. But he pushed it.

"Nearly there, Eve. We'll be in time."

She was suffering unspeakable agonies listening to Simon's voice through her communicator. She could picture it too clearly in her mind.

He was securing the restraints, carefully cutting away her clothes.

Eve's mouth went dry.

Spraying her, inside and out, so she would be clean and perfect.

She was out of the car before Roarke had fully screamed to a stop. Her boots skidded, slid, then she dug in and flew to the door. Because her hands weren't steady, it took her two tries to bypass the locks.

When she pounded up the steps, Roarke was beside her.

And now at last, in the distance, came the shriek of sirens.

Eve slipped the master through the slot and shoved the door open.

"Police!" Weapon out, she charged the bedroom.

Peabody's eyes were wide and dazed. Naked and bound, she shivered violently as the cold air rushed through the open window.

"He went out, down the fire escape. He ran. I'm okay."

Eve hesitated for a heartbeat then dived for the window. "Stay with her," she called to Roarke.

"No, no." Shaking her head frantically, Peabody strained against the restraints. "She'll kill him, Roarke. She means to kill him. Try to stop her."

"You hold on." He snatched the blanket off the floor, tossed it over her, then went out the window after his wife.

Her ankles sang as she leaped the last two feet to the ground, and her feet slid out from under her on the slick ground. She went down hard on one knee, then scrambled up. She could see him, heading east in a limping run, his bright red suit like a beacon.

"Police! Stop where you are." But she was already running after him, knowing she was wasting her breath with the order.

There were a thousand bees buzzing in her head, a thousand of them stinging on her skin. In her gut was a ball of hate so hard and bitter it burned. In a deliberate move, she jammed her weapon into the waist of her slacks. She wanted to take him down with her own hands.

She leaped on him like a tiger on the hunt, sent him skidding on his face and belly over the pavement.

She was clawing at him, pounding on him, but couldn't feel it. Cursing him between harsh, labored breaths, but couldn't hear it.

Then she was dragging him onto his back and her weapon was in her hand. At his throat.

"Eve." Roarke stood where he was, a foot away, and kept his voice quiet.

"I told you to stay with her. Stay out of this." She stared into the bleeding, weeping face under hers. And God help her, she could see her father.

Her weapon was on full stun — not fatal. Except when pressed directly to a pulse. She jammed it harder against his throat. And wanted to, craved.

"You've beaten him. You've stopped him."

Suffering with her, Roarke moved closer, crouched down, and looked into her eyes. "Taking that next step, it's not your way. It's not who you are."

Her finger trembled on the trigger. Little bullet points of ice hissed and cracked against the ground, pricked her skin. "It could be."

"No." He brushed a gentle hand over her hair. "Not anymore."

"No." She shuddered, shifted her weapon. "Not anymore."

While the man beneath her cried for his mother, she rose. On the pavement, Simon curled into a ball. Hot tears cut through the happy color he'd painted on his face.

And made him pitiful.

Beaten, Eve thought. Destroyed. Over.

"I need you to get a couple of uniforms back here," she said to Roarke. "I don't have my restraints."

"I have mine." Feeney crossed the pavement. "I still had my communicator tuned for her and McNab. The boy and I got here right behind you." He held her gaze for a moment. "Good job, Dallas. I'll take him in for you. You oughta go check on your aide."

"Yeah, okay." She wiped blood from her face, unsure if it was Simon's or her own. "Thanks, Feeney."

Roarke wrapped his arm around her shoulder. Neither of them had stopped for a coat. Her shirt was soaked through, and she was just starting to shiver. "Around or up?"

"Up." She glanced at the iron steps above her head. "It's quicker. Give me a boost and I'll pull you up after me."

He cupped his hands, and lifted when she set her boot in them, then watched as she vaulted agilely onto the platform. "I'll wait for you out front," he told her. "You'll want a little time with her."

"Yeah, I do." She stayed there, kneeling in the wind. Her nose was beginning to run, from the cold, from the storm of emotion still beating inside her. "I couldn't do it, Roarke. I wondered if I could. I was afraid I could. But when it came down to it, I couldn't."

"I know it. You've grown your own way, Eve." He reached up and squeezed the hand she held down to him. "Go inside, you're cold. I'll be in the car."

It had been easier, Eve realized, to go out of the window than to talk herself back in. She took a couple of bracing breaths, then pushed up the window and tossed her leg over the sill.

Peabody sat in bed, wrapped in a blanket

with a white-faced McNab's arm around her.

"She's okay," he said quickly. "He didn't . . . She's just shaken up. I told the uniforms to stay out there."

"That's good. We're under control here, McNab. Go on home, get some rest."

"I . . . I can bunk on the couch if you want," he said to Peabody.

"No. Thanks. Really. I'm okay."

"I'll just —" He didn't have a clue what to do or how to do it and rose awkwardly. "Should I report in the morning, to close this out?"

"Day after's soon enough. Take your Christmas. You earned it."

He managed a quick grin at Eve. "Yeah, guess we all did. I'll see you in a couple of days."

"He was really nice." Peabody let out a long breath when he left the room. "He kept everyone out, and got me loose and just let me sit. Closed the window because I was cold. So cold. God." She covered her face with her hands.

"Do you want me to take you to a health center?"

"No, I'm okay. A little woozy yet. Worse, I guess, 'cause I'd had a few drinks before I got home. You got him, didn't you?"

"Yeah, I got him."

Peabody dropped her hands. She fought to keep her face blank and calm, but her eyes were stark. "Is he alive?"

"Yes."

"Good. I thought . . ."

"So did I. I didn't."

Abruptly the tears welled up and overflowed. "Oh man. Shit. Here it comes."

"Okay, let it rip." Eve sat down, wrapped her arms around Peabody and held on while she cried it out.

"I was so scared, so scared. I didn't expect him to be that strong. I couldn't get to my weapon."

"You should have run."

"Would you have?" She drew in a shuddering breath, let it out. They both knew the answer. "I knew you'd come to back me up. But when I came out of it, and I was here and . . . I didn't think you'd be in time."

"You did good. You stalled and held him off just long enough." Eve wanted to hang on, to hold on to the sturdiness that was Peabody. Instead she rose. "You want a soother or something? You can take an inducer. He only used over-the-counters."

"No, I think I'd rather not. Alcohol and tranqs are a bad enough mix without topping it with a soother."

"I'm going to cut the uniforms loose. Do you want me to call someone to stay with you?"

"No." The distance was forming, Peabody noted. Inch by inch. "Dallas, I'm sorry. Last night."

"This isn't an appropriate time to discuss it."

Peabody set her jaw, then opened and closed the blanket. "I'm not in uniform, so I'm not speaking as aide to superior officer. That means I can say what the hell I want. I didn't like the things you said. I still don't. But I'm glad it mattered enough that you said them. I'm not sorry I jumped you for it, but I am sorry I didn't see it as a friend's concern."

Eve waited a beat. "Okay, but if you ever do hire twelve LCs to fuck you blind, I want details."

Peabody sniffed, and managed a watery grin. "It's just a little fantasy of mine. I don't actually make enough to afford twelve at once. But I did have another little fantasy come true tonight. Roarke saw me naked."

"Christ, Peabody." On a shaky laugh, Eve pulled her close again. This time, she held on. "We're okay."

She looked so steady, Roarke thought as he

watched her stride out of the building. So in charge and in control as she stood in the brisk wind in damp shirtsleeves and issued orders to the uniforms at the door.

There was blood on her hands. He doubted she knew it.

And the wave of love struck him like a fist as she shoved one of those smeared hands through her hair and started toward the car.

"Do you want to stay with her?"

Eve settled into the warmth of the car. "She's okay. Good cop."

"So are you." He tipped her face up, and laid his lips on hers in a soft, sweet, stirring kiss.

She blinked her eyes open, and laid a hand over his. "What time is it?"

"Just about midnight."

"Okay. Do that again." She fit her mouth to his, settled in, sighed. "There's a memory for the box — and a tradition. Merry Christmas."

The employees of Thorndike Press hope you have enjoyed this Large Print book. All our Thorndike and Wheeler Large Print titles are designed for easy reading, and all our books are made to last. Other Thorndike Press Large Print books are available at your library, through selected bookstores, or directly from us.

For information about titles, please call:
(800) 223-1244

or visit our Web site at:
www.gale.com/thorndike
www.gale.com/wheeler

To share your comments, please write:
Publisher
Thorndike Press
295 Kennedy Memorial Drive
Waterville, ME 04901

1\08

HOLMDEL PUBLIC LIBRARY
4 Crawfords Corner road
Holmdel, NJ 07733